Mary Renault

Mary Renault (1905–1983) was born Mary Challans. The pseudonym, Renault, she used from the time she became a professional writer. She grew up in London and in Bristol and went on to read English at St Hugh's College, Oxford.

From childhood she wished to become a writer and it was to gain a deeper understanding of life outside her own circle that she decided to train as a nurse. On the eve of the Second World War her first novel, *Purposes of Love* was published. *Kind are Her Answers* (1940) appeared the same week as work. Throughout the war Mary Renault worked as a nurse in hospitals in Bristol, London and Oxford. *The Friendly Young Ladies* (1944) was followed by *Return to Night* (1946). For this book she received the M.G.M. Award. The book was never filmed but Mary Renault was now financially independent and freed from war-work. The following year, together with her friend, Julie Mullard, also a nurse, she emigrated to South Africa. Living in Durban she wrote *North Face* (1948), and *The Charioteer* (1953). There followed the major part of her literary output, the historical novels for which she is most famous.

In 1959 Mary Renault was made a Fellow of the Royal Society of Literature. In 1982 she was elected Honorary Fellow of St Hugh's College, Oxford. Mary Renault died on 13 December 1983.

THE FRIENDLY YOUNG LADIES

Mary Renault

*With an Afterword
by the Author*

Virago

VIRAGO

First published in Great Britain in 1944 by Longmans, Green & Co.
Published by Virago Press Limited in 1984
Reprinted 1985, 1993, 1994
This edition published by Virago Press in December 2005

A CIP catalogue record for this book
is available from the British Library.

ISBN 1 84408 136 2

Typeset in Goudy by M Rules
Printed and bound in Great Britain
by Clays Ltd, St Ives plc

Virago Press
An imprint of
Time Warner Book Group UK
Brettenham House
Lancaster Place
London WC2E 7EN

www.virago.co.uk

CHAPTER ONE

Very quietly and carefully, hardly moving her thin young neck and round shoulders, Elsie looked round the room, first at the french windows into the garden, then at the door, measuring distances. Her calculations were instinctive, like those of a mouse; she had been making them since she could crawl. There was hardly any need to look this time; the way to the door lay flat across her father's line of vision. He was saying, 'I should have supposed it was obvious to the meanest intelligence almost anywhere, in fact, outside this household –'

Her parents' chairs were drawn up to the fire, for it was a chilly evening in March, and the Lane family always observed, punctiliously, the routine of domestic comfort. Elsie had begun her reputation for eccentricity at school by remarking suddenly, 'I do think radiators are nice.' She thought of radiators as she edged the pouffe on which she was sitting slowly backward, ready for a traverse behind her mother's chair to the french window.

As she moved, she remembered that her sister Leonora, in the dimly-remembered days when she lived at home, used to cross the room on occasions like this with three flying strides, slam the door, and be half-way down to the beach before there was time to say anything. Elsie had been, and still was, as incapable of following her example as she would have been of soaring through the air. She had always found herself left behind, to hear the comments and the retorts, while Leo had already joined Ted and Albert from the coastguard cottages, and would be looking for jetsam in the caves. Elsie had not envied her Ted and Albert – she agreed with her mother in thinking them very rough and unsuitable – and she rarely remembered now to envy her her technique, it was so long ago. She was free to use her own methods; and Leo, once so terrifyingly apt to heap a family fracas with fresh fuel, was never mentioned at all. Elsie herself hardly ever thought of her.

Her mother was saying, '. . . be spoken to like this in my own house.' It was now or never, before she noticed Elsie and added, 'in front of my own child,' after which it would be too late. Very softly and smoothly, with as much care as one might use to keep a lover's sleep unbroken, she closed her book, tucked it under her arm, and slid upright on her long schoolgirl's legs with their thick dragged stockings and sea-stained shoes. She was a dim, unobtrusive girl. One might conjecture that she had been afraid to grow up, lest the change should attract attention to her. She had acquired protective colouring which amounted almost to invisibility; almost, but not quite.

'Now,' said her mother indignantly, but also with the air of one who scores a point, 'see what you've done, Arthur, with your shouting and your bad temper. Driven poor little Elsie out of the house. And she's hardly better yet from that bad cold.'

Her father had been holding *The Times*, his observations lobbing over the top of it like mortar-canisters over a parapet. Now he suddenly dashed it down on his knee. Thick newsprint can make a dramatic noise. Elsie stood with her fingers contracted round the door-knob: her adolescent stoop exaggerated itself into an idiot slump; her vague, half-formed features grew dull and furtive. She could feel it happening, the familiar cycle. Guilt and shame made her stomach sink. She did not reject them, any more than the young African repudiates a tabu he has broken by accident in the dark. For a moment an etiolated shoot of personality stirred in her and wondered, 'What could I have done that would have been right?' but lacked vitality enough to attempt an answer. It had all happened a hundred times before. She cringed, and stared at the red Turkey carpet.

'This,' shouted her father, 'passes everything.' He raised his eyes, meeting those of a sepia Burne-Jones on the opposite wall, a very thin lady with a lily, whose evident misery seemed to Elsie a reflection of her own. 'Isn't it enough that my domestic life should be made a purgatory of nagging, without having these scenes of martyrdom staged for my benefit?' He flung *The Times* to the floor; Elsie gazed dully at a heading about something, or somebody, leaving the League, while a dangling thread of her mind wondered whether it referred to Geneva or football.

'Elsie,' said her father, 'come here.'

Letting go of the door-knob reluctantly, as if it were a source of protection, Elsie took a dragging step into the room.

'Next time your mother puts you up to something of this kind, just think it over for a minute. That's all your father asks of you. I don't think it's a great deal, do you? I don't think it's altogether unreasonable? Just ask yourself what would happen if your father, in spite of being treated like a pariah in his own home – a pariah,' he repeated (the word was a new acquisition) 'weren't willing in spite of everything to work for you and give you your food and your clothes and your pocket-money? Just think about that for a moment, and suggest to your mother that she does the same.'

Elsie had left school a year ago, after failing in the School Certificate Examination. The mistresses, one after another, had told her that her homework was thoughtless and showed no signs of concentration at all, and had pointed out what a disappointment this must be to her parents; a prophecy regularly fulfilled when her reports came through. All this accumulated guilt formed a steady reserve, ready to add itself to the guilt of any given moment. Where would she be, indeed? Hypnotized, she pictured herself trudging through the rain into the gates of a large, dark factory, wearing a man's cloth cap, or maybe a shawl.

The factory was drawn from imagination; her travels had been few.

'Well, Elsie?' said her father.

When things of this sort happened, if there was time to see them coming beforehand, Elsie was accustomed to pray, 'Please, God, don't let them ask me to *say* anything.' Her tongue seemed to be swelling inside her mouth. Perhaps, even now, if she waited a moment . . .

'Arthur,' cried her mother, 'how *can* you browbeat the poor child like this? It isn't my fault she can't bear to be in the same room with you. Never mind, darling; to-morrow morning when your father goes out we'll do something nice all by ourselves.'

Her mother's voice trembled. Elsie edged to the door-knob, and clutched it again. If only she had said something in time. She could not think what, but there must have been something. She had made her father angry, and now she had made her mother cry.

'This attitude,' said her father, 'is just what I expected. This is the kind of pernicious malice I see going on every day. Don't be surprised when it bears fruit. We already have one daughter outside the pale of decent society. If a second finds her way into the *demi-monde*, believe me, it won't astonish *me*.'

'*Arthur!*' Her mother's voice shrank to a kind of whispering scream. 'How can you be so wicked? Saying such a thing in front of a young girl.' She rose, clutching her knitting; several stitches dropped off the needle and began to run, which, to Elsie, seemed somehow to make everything more terrifying. She began to sob. 'If only one of my children had been a boy. He wouldn't have stood by to see his mother insulted in her own home.'

'If I'd had a son,' shouted her father, 'I shouldn't be subjected day by day to this petty conspiracy of women.'

A cold moistness was making Elsie's hand stick to the knob. Her memory had enhanced the horror of the moment with a recollection of the worst thing that had ever happened at home. It must have been quite nine years ago, but it seemed like yesterday.

Elsie herself, small enough then to hide sometimes, had crawled just in time under the table; but Leo had been standing in exactly the same spot where her sister stood now. She had been about Elsie's own age; but suddenly, as Elsie peeped, her familiar thin brown face and dark tumbled hair had looked different, and one had had the feeling that a third grown-up, more frightening than either of the others, had come into the room. With her feet apart, and her fists pushed down into her shabby tweed pockets, she had said, unbelievably, 'If I were a man I wouldn't be here. And I bloody well wish I were.' A silence had followed, beside which the preceding storm had seemed like child's play; and in the silence, Leo had walked out, without even slamming the door.

Merely to think of it made the present seem almost ordinary.

Then her father said, 'That will do, Elsie. You had better run away now,' in the voice of one wronged beyond the degree to which words can give relief; and, though it was a method of clos-ing discussions which he not infrequently employed, Elsie had a feeling that he remembered too. Since there was always a possi-bility that he might even yet follow it with 'But remember, before you go . . .' she went instantly, negotiating the door without grace, but with the most efficient silence and speed, and not for-getting to turn the handle firmly, because once she had been ordered back to do it, and, becoming on the strength of this a theme of renewed debate, had had to remain for another quarter of an hour.

Before she was half-way along the passage she could hear their voices rising again, and this decided her against going upstairs to get her coat. One day she had done this, to be met on her way down by her mother, who had left the room in the interval and was anxious to tell her why. Reflecting on this Elsie felt herself to be unnatural, heartless and wicked: but she was used to feeling inferior and inadequate and, indeed, expected it.

It was rather colder than she had thought; that year's spring had begun mildly even for Cornwall, the morning had been still and warm and the sea turquoise blue under a delicately faded sky. But the sun had gone in, and now it was after four. A damp heavy wind was blowing sluggishly from the sea, and swirls of mist, like clammy steam, hung on the brambles beside the lane. Already they looked soggy, and a film of moisture was covering the rough stone fences and darkening the earth that bound them together.

Elsie crossed her arms over her thin, immature bosom, partly for warmth, partly to protect the book she had brought away with her. Slowly and unwillingly she admitted to herself that it was too cold to sit and read. Perhaps if she hurried and kept warm, the sun would come out presently. She knew it would be setting in less than an hour, but continued to nourish the hope, obstinately, without examining the reason, which was that it happened to be, at the moment, the only hope she had.

A crimson stain began to cover the inside of her hands; it looked melodramatic, but was in fact a film of dye from the softening covers of *Beau Brocade*. She wiped her palms absently on the thighs of her stockings; the book had already lost all its glaze from previous applications of salt water and rain, and was one of half a dozen she kept for reading out of doors. Elsie was a great reader of romances. Her favourite work had been *The Idylls of the King*, until, learning that the plots were taken from Malory, she had saved up for weeks to buy him in the Everyman edition. This head-on encounter with the mediaeval mind had been a sad shock to her; its casual masculinity found her singularly ill-prepared. For the facts of life had recently been revealed to her behind a stand of mackintoshes in the school cloakroom. She had believed them, because they had been so much too frightful for even Gladys Hunter to invent; and the thought of her parents having, for a certainty, once been involved in them (since here was Elsie herself to prove it) had been so appalling that she had gone about like a hunted creature, weighed down by the horrible secret, till even her mother noticed it and asked her, one night at bedtime, if she had anything on her mind. A murderer, who sees someone dragging the pond where the body is, could not have surpassed the emotions with which Elsie scrambled together a lie about finding her arithmetic homework too difficult; and her mother (after a scene with her father) had written to the headmistress about it, so that she had to take mathematics with a lower form and a tangible reminder of all this inward sin was held up before her four times every week. And she had only been confirmed a month before! The little red book which the bishop had given her, its exhortations against impure thought suddenly and awfully explained, accused her every time she opened her dressing-table drawer. At last she hid it away under her party petticoat, for she already knew by heart the prayers it provided for such occasions. Sometimes she found it hard to believe that anyone in the world was as wicked as she.

But that was five years ago, and even so unpleasant a discovery had lost the force of its first impact. She had now reached the age when her mother could tacitly assume that she knew the purport of warnings about being spoken to by strange men. These she received frequently, and, sometimes, an even more impressive one about a wicked woman disguised as a hospital nurse, who went up to girls shopping alone, told them that their mother had met with an accident and been taken to hospital, and inveigling them into a taxi with the blinds pulled down, stuck a hypodermic needle into their arms. It never for a moment occurred to Elsie to reflect whether her pale melancholy face, her brown eyes like an anxious retriever's, her gawky sharp-kneed legs in their ribbed stockings, made up exactly the kind of quarry after which purveyors of vice might range. She lived under the threat of rape and seduction, and once, losing her mother in Truro, had wandered for nearly an hour sooner than ask anyone but a policeman the way.

The fact that she went nowhere, met nobody but her mother's friends, and lived in a world of her own imagination, had suspended her in the most awkward stage of adolescence for quite three superfluous years. At seventeen her mind was still like

Madame Tussaud's Exhibition, with Love, represented by kings and queens in velvet, on the upper floors, and Sex, like the Chamber of Horrors, tucked away underground. Usually she could forget about the basement in rapturous contemplation of the stately tableaux above. The deepening dye from *Beau Brocade* (the mist was condensing into a drizzle) comforted her now. A groom from the local riding school, exercising one of the horses, cantered by, silhouetted grey against the sky, and her imagination added to him a cloak and a black mask, silver pistols, a posse of blood-hungry redcoats behind, and a sweet distraught heroine weeping for his peril in a manor over the hill. If only the clouds would lift, and she could sit down and read, she knew that she would feel better at once. But the sad rain and sodden ground wrapped her unhappiness about her and, as always at such times, extended it into an eternal future. There seemed no reason why it should not all be the same ten, or even twenty years from now. Miss Matthews at the Vicarage was, she knew, over forty, and still lived with her parents at home.

A cold, heavy water-drop ran from her hair down the inside of her collar. She began to realize that she was really wet, and, in spite of walking as fast as she could, was beginning to feel oold. She knew that she ought to go home. But if she arrived dripping, she would be noticed, and questioned, and discussed. If the rain stopped soon, and she slipped in afterwards and changed quickly, it would seem much more ordinary.

In any case, she did not want to go in yet. This evening had been a bad one. Suddenly she remembered why. It was because of what her father had said about Leo. She had guessed, she supposed, for a long time; but it had seemed so incredible that, in the absence of anything but suggestive silences, it had been easy to convince herself that she must be mistaken. Perhaps, she had said to herself, Leo had simply cheeked Father so outrageously that he had ordered her out of the house; she remembered enough of her sister to feel that this was quite likely. But surely Mother would have mentioned her sometimes (and, she thought, reproached her father with it) unless there had been something more. There was only one thing too bad to talk about.

Even now that she knew it was true, it had the inconsequence of a bad dream. Such things never happened to anyone whom one knew, let alone to one's own family. But this had. When her mother took her to tea with the Matthews or the Garaways, people never asked, as they asked after other relations, if they had heard from Leo lately, or how was she getting on. Suddenly Elsie saw why. They all knew. Even if she conquered her wicked thoughts by prayer, even when she grew old enough to have a dress allowance, even if her mother let her have her hair waved, and she had an invitation to a dance, it was no use; she would never be like other people. Her parents quarrelled, quarrelled in front of visitors; and her sister was living in sin.

She tried to imagine what Leo would be like now. She would be twenty-six or seven, almost middle-aged. By now she must be walking the streets at night, speaking to strange men; for her mother had explained, deviously but often, that women who were led astray, or went with the hospital nurse in the car, always ended so. Probably she would have dyed her hair (Elsie's innocence never suspected hair of being tinted unless it was an alarming shade of orange or maroon, so it was thus that she pictured her sister's). It was all very difficult to link with Leo, for Elsie remembered her quite well, having been nine when she went away. She had spent her pocket-money, not on powder and rouge, but on telescopes, pocket compasses, knives fitted with screwdrivers and tools for attending to horses' feet, ordnance survey maps, and hacking at the stables down the lane. Even when promoted to a real dress allowance, twenty pounds a year, she had never laid out this envied privilege cleverly, as Elsie longed to do, on pretty lace collars and artificial silk stockings; she had been apt to spend half of it at once on a plain tweed suit, and even this she did not save for Sundays or going out to tea, but wore it for almost everything, bulging the pockets with apples and bits of string.

Elsie had always been a little frightened of her. They had never told one another their secrets. In the school holidays, Leo spent nearly all day over at St. Trewillian with Tom Fawcett and the crowd of boys he brought home to stay, coming back at night, dirty, and bearing trophies of rare eggs and crystal spar, with holes in her stockings, grazed knees, and once, Elsie recollected, with a black eye, which she had unconvincingly explained away. When she remembered Elsie's existence, she had been absently kind to her, and the old dolls-house in the attic was still full of furniture which Leo had made out of woven rushes and carved wood, all very neatly contrived. During her last year at home, after Tom had gone to sea with the Elephant Line, she had still gone off mysteriously, as far as Elsie knew alone. But Elsie, it seemed, knew nothing.

Leo's thin tanned face floated before her, with its look of being sloped up a little at all the edges – dark-brown eyebrows, light-brown eyes, high cheekbones, long mouth and narrow chin, all slanted at almost the same angle; an old silk shirt blowing apart at the throat. Straining after coherence, she imagined it topped with a frizzed mound of puce-coloured hair, raddled and powdered mauve. Suddenly, hopelessly, she began to cry. The light rain drizzled round her, matting her hair and mingling its salt spume with the tears on her cheeks so that they ran down together, coldly, into her mouth. Her vest began to stick to her back, wetly, like a bathing dress; the wind plastering it closer. She felt as if the rain were soaking past it into her body. Her teeth were chattering. Hugging the red, slimy cover of *Beau Brocade* with one hand, and groping with the other under her knicker elastic for her handkerchief, she stood still for a moment, desolate and ungainly, sharing the solitude with a rough red cow, cropping the verge beside the brambles; then turned back towards the house.

CHAPTER TWO

Elsie swallowed – it eased, for a moment, the soreness of her throat – fastened her coat a button higher, and stepped out beside her mother, doggedly, along the cliff-path to the farm. She was reflecting that her nose would not begin to run before to-morrow, and by then they might not remember to ask whether she had worn her mackintosh yesterday. The wind's fingers, searching between her lapels and up her sleeves, seemed to be tipped with ice; but her mother had just said that it was warmer, so she did not care to mention it lest it provoke questions.

The road to the village was more sheltered; she wished they had been buying the eggs there instead. She could not say so, for her mother had chosen the farm to please her. As a rule she preferred the cliffs to the village, which was, in certain ways, an extension of her home. More than half of it was of recent construction; it had become, in the last ten years, a kind of annexe to the large watering-place three miles away, and Mr. Lane was the local architect. He was responsible for about thirty per cent of the new building; the remainder was speculative makeshift, flung up by jobbers and let expensively for the summer months. The spare Cornish landscape, vulnerable as an impoverished grand seigneur, could do nothing to clothe or even to soften its squalor, it scarred the rough fields like leprosy, and, since its materials were of the kind that decay but do not mellow, time only made it worse. Every year a fresh eruption, slate-grey or yellow or red, broke out on some naked slope, and round it weeds seized on the scratched earth, and dumps of rusty food-tins appeared,

Mr. Lane's houses, on the other hand, belonged to the residents. Their stuff and structure were solid, their fittings fitted, and their gardens were kept by the same hands from year to year. This might have given them an air of assimilation and repose, had they not been the kind of houses which, like some women, reward care and attention merely by becoming smug. They were not built to disappear into the scenery, but for people who wished their dwellings, like their afternoon teas, to be a visible bastion between their own tier of the middle class and the one immediately below. This suited Mr. Lane, who was not himself a disappearing person; and he had devoted a good deal of gusto to making each one as conspicuous as possible and entirely different from those on either side. If 'St. Just' had been pebble-dashed, with a circular recess for the door and an enormous gable making the front a rhombus, 'St. Anthony' must be purple brick, with a portico supported on pillars like Tudor chimneys. They were not labour-saving; Mr. Lane had never done any housework himself, and it never occurred to him, at work or at home, to imagine the activities of those who did.

Elsie did not doubt – since even her mother never questioned it – that her father's houses were in the choicest taste. The grey Cornish farms she scarcely counted as houses at all, rather as extensions of the cliffs and exposed rocks. She liked them chiefly because she had never heard them discussed at meals. But to-day, when they reached Tregarrock's, she only noticed that in its warm kitchen the cold she had been feeling turned suddenly to waves of heat, which, curiously, made her dread the wind outside more than before. As they walked back over the cliffs it was straight in their faces, and she felt a sharp little pain in the top of her chest when she tried to breathe. It was not quite like the pain one got after running too hard; besides, they had not hurried. Her mother was chatting happily about people in the village, and pointing out signs of spring. Her round cheeks were glowing with exercise and recovered good spirits; presently she remarked that it was a shame to go in, and suggested a long detour.

Elsie agreed that it would be very nice. She could not even enjoy a feeling of unselfishness; in her heart she knew the truth, that she could not nerve herself for fuss and excitement of any sort, even the kindest. 'But, darling, why ever didn't you let me know first thing in the morning? Fancy coming out in a cold wind like this.' 'If you'd only *tell* me, dear, when anything's the matter . . .' It would all be so right and proper and natural that Elsie herself could not understand why she still went on, one foot after the other, in animal dumbness. Like a sick animal she felt guilty too. But it made no difference.

'You're very quiet, Elsie dear,' her mother said suddenly. 'You're not unhappy about anything, are you?'

'No, Mother dear, thank you, of course not. I say, look at those lovely new lambs.'

The moment, which Elsie knew well, tided over. Almost more than the scenes themselves, Elsie dreaded conversations with her mother about them afterwards. Each was too much involved to be of any assistance to the other, and the only result was to make jangled fibres, which might have straightened into silence, vibrate afresh. To this usual fear was added, to-day, a new one; that her mother might decide that this was the time to tell her what it was that Leo had really done. Once or twice before, during the warning about strange men, she had felt some special revelation trembling on the brink; now she knew, for a certainty, what it was, and the thought of knowing more added itself to the strange hot and cold and the pain in her chest, so that she shivered as if with ague.

Mrs. Lane allowed herself to be led away among the lambs; but she looked faintly disappointed. She always expected, in spite of all previous results, that talking things over would make her feel better. Elsie chattered away, about sheep, about birds, about the Tregarrocks, trembling all over with suppressed tension and with cold.

By the time they got in, it was almost lunchtime. Elsie parted reluctantly with her thick coat and scarf, feeling that she would have liked to keep them on for the rest of the day. She made up for it by putting on a short-sleeved jumper under her long-sleeved one. The extra bulk, clothing her thin curveless frame, made her look almost entirely amorphous, she surveyed the effect apathetically and went downstairs.

There was steak and onions for dinner. The smell greeted her in a rich golden-brown wave as she reached the dining-room; and without warning her stomach heaved. She sat down, wondering how much of her portion she could conceal as debris round her plate, or under her knife. She had reduced this to a fine art, for feeling sickish at mealtimes was no novelty to her; a sensational discussion had induced it several times. But it did not, as a rule, begin of its own accord.

Her father came in, complaining of the cold and of one or two people who had crossed him that morning. To Elsie's relief, her mother, still glowing from the walk, agreed sympathetically instead of urging him to see the best in them. Unluckily she added a short rider, for emphasis, which betrayed the fact that she had missed most of the point at issue. Mr. Lane indicated this, and went on to remark that the steak was overdone.

'Really, Arthur!' Mrs. Lane had just succeeded in persuading herself that the steak was very nice, so her annoyance was natural. 'There's no pleasing you. It's a lovely piece of steak, and only the least bit more cooked than last time, when you said it wasn't done enough. Elsie's enjoying it, aren't you,

Elsie picked up the forkful of meat which, in despair, she had just returned to her plate. She lifted it, slowly.

'Is she?' said her father. 'It looks like it. Don't force yourself, my dear. Stuff like this won't do you any good. I'm leaving mine.'

'Every day I wonder why I work and slave to keep this house going. Thinking and planning to make things nice, and my only return is that my child is urged to belittle and criticize everything I do.'

Mrs. Lane looked, with filling eyes, at Elsie. She shut her own, raised the piece of steak to her mouth, and put it inside. She did so with a short form of prayer, but it must have been unsupported by the necessary faith. For a moment she struggled, then jumped from the table and ran for the door, while her parents sat each with an apt rejoinder frozen on the lips. She had hoped to reach the bathroom in time, but was spectacularly sick on the stairs.

Suddenly, with that feeling of delighted surprise which comes when the body succeeds in short-circuiting the will, she found she could let go of everything. She might have thrown up all her dreads and resistances along with her dinner. When her mother withdrew the thermometer from her mouth and gazed at it in tardily disguised horror, she was unmoved. When asked, just as she had foreseen, why ever she hadn't said that she was ill, she replied easily and without shame that she hadn't realized anything was the matter. Passively, contentedly, she allowed herself to be put into a warm nightgown and a warmed bed, and lay watching the reflected light of the new fire flapping and furling on the ceiling. Her father came in, with an armful of books from his study; rather over-genial, so that she knew he was trying to make amends for what had happened at lunch. Ordinarily she would have felt embarrassed, but now she accepted the books with just the right amount of gratitude, and afterwards pretended to be sleepy, so that he went away.

She lay curled up, a rubber hot-water bottle in a snug velvet jacket pressed to her aching spine, wondering why she had been setting her face against this heaven-sent solution, this refuge from all tribulation. Strange perversity! How pleasant illness was; the freedom from responsibility, the willing dependence – for, her pleasures being almost all daydream and reverie, she would need nothing except the simple things her mother would bring her unasked – the magical smoothing-out of mental and physical strain. She hoped she would be ill for a long time. The firelight, and the odd twist which fever gives to the perceptions, made her little room look new and different. From where she lay she took a fresh inventory of her surrounding treasures; her shelf of novels, Baroness Orczy, Dornford Yates, Gene Stratton-Porter, in shiny red two-shilling editions, her pictures of the 'Piper of Dreams' and 'Peter Pan,' the blue china rabbits on the mantelpiece, and, over them, 'An If for Girls' framed and illuminated, which her mother had given her on her fifteenth birthday. Like the pink silk eiderdown, they lapped her safely in; the security of childhood spread welcoming arms, absolved from blame. She fell asleep, and, being restless, dreamed uncomfortably of haste and flight, and a river pursuing her upstairs.

She woke for a minute or two, some time in the afternoon, to hear her mother and father arguing, mildly it seemed and from habit rather than conviction, in the hall. Her mother was saying, 'Yes, Arthur, I daresay, but Dr. Sloane *understands* Elsie. Think how good he was when she had whooping-cough. It's so unfortunate it should have been just *this* month.' She could not hear what her father said; he was speaking from further away. It was all beautifully distant. She was glad that Dr. Sloane was on holiday, or wherever he was. He might have said she could go downstairs to-morrow. She slept again less heavily and with intervals of half-waking, so that her day-dreams continued through it with scarcely noticed lapses into absurdity. She was being rescued from renegade Arabs by Lawrence of Arabia on a milk-white horse. Culled from popular biographies and the yellow press, her portrait of this truth-driven hero was a sort of concentrate, in tabloid, of everything which had caused him in his lifetime to fly from one obliteration to the next. Happily indifferent to this, she was thanking him gracefully, and receiving his reserved expressions of admiration, when the bedroom door opened and woke her up. She turned on the pillow, to find a young man beside her bed.

He was a slight brown-haired young man, who demanded prompt attention with a pair of interested blue eyes, and looked quite used to receiving it. Elsie's consciousness, crawling forth from comfortable shadows, felt rather as people do who walk out of a cinema into direct sun – dishevelled, squinting, and embarrassingly revealed. She would have put her head under the clothes again, but was prevented by a sudden and compelling recollection that she was seventeen and a half years old. Instead she blinked, and allowed her eyes to go slightly out of focus.

Her mother, whom she noticed now for the first time, said 'Elsie, dear, here's Dr. Bracknell to see you. He's looking after Dr. Sloane's patients, you know, while he's away.' Her voice contained a well-bred, but inadequate, suppression of regret. The young man smiled at her as if she had paid him a charming compliment. She added, with flustered cordiality, 'So *good* of you to turn out again at the end of your round.'

'Of course not. I was grumbling this morning at not having enough to do.' His voice was like his eyes, brisk and alert. One had the feeling of something exploratory, a bright little ray, like the ray of a pocket-torch, flickering here and there. He turned it without warning on Elsie. She blinked, and sank down, imperceptibly she hoped, into the clothes. 'Well, young woman? You sound a bit wheezy. Been going out without your mackintosh?'

Elsie had, at once, the feeling that this was no more than she had expected. It did not occur to her to reply. Forgetting even to blink, she lay looking over the top of the sheet, waiting for whatever else he might decide to confront her with.

'Oh, *no*,' said her mother, shocked. 'Elsie's always *very* careful, ever since she had whooping-cough so badly.'

Elsie had hardly expected him not to notice her relief; but neither had she expected him to let her see that it amused him.

'There's a lot of 'flu in the towns,' he said. 'Breathing hurt you anywhere?'

'Only a bit at the top of my chest.' Her voice had grown very hoarse since the morning; she was thankful for this, suspecting that her nervousness would have made it sound odd in any case. She felt both bewildered and guilty about this. She took her own way of life very much for granted, and it did not occur to her as being out of the ordinary that, except for the curate and one or two assistants in shops, this was the first man between sixteen and forty that she had conversed with in years.

'How long ago was this whooping-cough?' he asked her mother, taking a thermometer out of its little metal tube and popping it under her tongue.

'Some time ago now. She was only ten. But Dr. Sloane made her wear a cotton-wool pneumonia-jacket, and since then we've been *very* careful.'

'Can I have the pulse a minute?' He sat down on the edge of the bed, so that she had to uncurl her knees to be out of his way, and took her wrist in a cool, firm hand. Then he produced a stethoscope, and slid it up under the jacket of her pyjamas. Elsie, feeling agonizingly shy, coughed and breathed and said ninety-nine when he told her; he was so close that she could hear his own breathing, even and easy as it was. She was relieved beyond words when he sat up and put the instrument away.

'This whooping-cough was about four years back, then?'

With what seemed to herself startling abruptness, Elsie croaked, 'I'm not fourteen. I'm seventeen and a half, nearly.'

'Well, well.' He went over and rinsed the thermometer in the washstand ewer. His voice, cheerful and impersonally friendly, made her feel for a moment quite at ease. As he wiped the thermometer on the towel, he glanced up at her. It gave her an odd, uncomfortable feeling, which only lasted a split second: he had had an almost proprietary look, as if he had collected a specimen of something, not beautiful but rare and curious, and were wondering how to set it up. Being both self-conscious and fanciful, and acutely aware of both, she dismissed the sensation with the shame of the adolescent, which comes so often that it is an annoyance, an irritation under the skin, rather than an emotion. He was looking down now at the thermometer as he put it away, and his profile, so detached and self-contained, underlined her foolishness.

Her mother was saying, with a pleased kind of casualness, 'People are often surprised when they hear Elsie's age. But I married almost out of the schoolroom, you see.'

It took Elsie nearly half a minute to define the vague unsatisfactoriness of this remark. Then she remembered her sister Leonora, who must now be twenty-seven. In the comfort of being ill, she had forgotten her. After Dr. Bracknell had given his clear exact instructions and gone away, she found herself wondering what he would say if he knew she had a sister like that.

The thought upset her so much that she put her head under the bedclothes, though there was no one in the room.

CHAPTER THREE

Mrs. Lane had reached the end of her tether. She told her husband so before she left the room, and repeated it to herself as she stood, wiping her eyes, in the hall. This declaration marked a certain high level in their temperature chart which they only reached once in a week or so; but she always believed at the time that it had some desperate kind of finality. In much the same way the white ewe-goat in the next field, brought up short by her length of chain, would suddenly look outraged, and go through motions of being about to pull the whole thing out of the ground. Presently she would forget, and begin to eat her way round in a circle again. With Mrs. Lane, the crisis lasted longer, and, though the outcome would be the same, she never entertained this thought for at least a few hours afterwards.

They no longer quarrelled, in any decisive sense of the word. In their first two years of marriage they had exhausted the materials for it. Even after the brief, remorseful, shamefaced attempt at turning a new leaf which had produced Elsie, the succeeding quarrel had been only a kind of pot-pourri of the first half-dozen. They had, now, no mortal shocks in store for one another, only reiterated exasperations. Arthur Lane knew that his trenchant criticisms of people and current affairs seemed to his wife an ill-natured picking of holes; and, resentful that so unjust an image of himself should be projected by one unable to meet him on equal intellectual ground, conformed to it more and more. Maude Lane could not understand, after two years or twenty-nine, why her husband should treat with contempt her wish to read cheerful books about nice people, rather than those she described as sordid, morbid, or gloomy; or why he should be irritated by her natural efforts to believe, on the minimum of evidence, that people and facts were as she wished them to be. The truth was that they had never loved one another, only images of their own devising, built up from books and the romantic conventions of their young day; no moment of pitiful, of humorous, of self-forgetting light had ever revealed either of them to the other, for the passion of mind, or even of body, was lacking which might have kindled the spark. So Maude did not mellow Arthur, but rather serrated his edges; and Arthur did not temper or sharpen Maude, but on the contrary led her to associate logical thinking with coldness and disillusion, sentimentality with kindness and faith. Having no trust in one another's fundamentals, it was hardly surprising that they felt no eagerness to concede in little things, such as the arrangement of rooms, or meals, or social engagements; their disagreements in these matters, like fragments of a cracked mirror, reflected in miniature their central dissatisfaction, but were too trivial and too hopeless to bring them back to it. Even Leonora had not shocked them into self-questioning: it had been too late. Each had seen in her an extension and condemnation of the other. Thus it was that they no longer had quarrels; only rows.

Each had effected a kind of semi-adjustment to this routine. Mrs. Lane's natural optimism was such that always, at the back of her mind, floated a cloudlike expectation of sudden, revolutionary good fortune or escape. Like Elsie, she daydreamed constantly, not of romantic encounters, but that some stranger to whom she had once done a kindness died and left her a comfortable income, or that she made the acquaintance of a charming family, well-to-do but not so smart as to be awkward, who invited her and Elsie for long country house visits, or on a world cruise. It was rarely that one or another of these visions was not present to tinge the background of her thoughts, and to give to the discomfort and unhappiness of her married life an illusion of transience. Thanks to their friendly company, she recovered from the family scenes in about half the time taken by Elsie after merely witnessing them, and rather more quickly than her husband, whose procedure was to exhaust their emotional possibilities and then bury himself in his work. After twenty-seven years of married life she looked, though they were much of an age, at least ten years the younger.

But now and again there came moments when, though she never really ceased to believe that something would turn up, she felt a kind of panic at the thought of having to wait for it. This was one of the moments. Only one consolation was in reach, to go upstairs and talk things over with Elsie. Dear little Elsie; one had been so careful, all this time she had been ill, to keep everything from her, though perhaps, being so sympathetic, she had guessed sometimes . . . But Dr. Bracknell had been so cheerful about her on his last visit, and seemed such a clever, experienced young man. Just a little chat, and then out to the village to blow the cobwebs away . . .

Within half a minute of slamming the dining-room door behind her, she was on her way upstairs. Within half an hour, she was walking up the lane towards the village, her face lightly powdered over, feeling better already. It was Gladys's half-day, but the grocer's man had been, and if anyone else called, Arthur would have for once to answer the bell.

Within twenty minutes more, after Mr. Lane, who did not concern himself with Gladys's free time, had driven off to visit a client, Peter Bracknell parked Dr. Sloane's coupé in the lane, and rapped smartly on the door.

When nothing happened, he assumed that everyone in the house was down with influenza, having already paid two visits that day where this had turned out to be the case. So, finding the door unlocked, he walked inside, not unduly anxious over the possibility that he might be mistaken, for, as he would have told anyone who was interested, convention never bothered him much. Having hung up his overcoat in the hall, he went upstairs, tapped perfunctorily at his patient's door, said 'Hullo. Can I come in?' and did so without waiting for an answer.

Elsie lifted a hot, blurred face from the pillow, and stared at him in horror, through eyes unbeautifully glazed with tears. She had been crying whole-heartedly for the best part of half an hour, and knew that this must be evident beyond any possible remedy. Dimly, however, she took refuge in the etiquette which had obtained at her school, and which laid down that if a person who had been crying, however obviously, decided to ignore the fact, those who might have to converse with her did so too. It was awful while it lasted, but somehow one got through.

'Good afternoon, Dr. Bracknell,' she said, indistinctly, but with as social a manner as she could manage. 'I'm so sorry Mother isn't at home.' With sudden inspiration she added, 'My cold seems to have got more runny again to-day.'

Peter walked over, and sat down on the edge of the bed. Mechanically she slid out a hot, moist hand to have her pulse taken. He took it between both of his, and squeezed it lightly

'That's too bad, isn't it?' he said softly; and directed a charming smile, full of the tenderest understanding, straight into her eyes.

Elsie's response had a beautiful inevitability, like the ring of colour that forms in a test-tube when the right reagent is dropped in. Her breath caught twice in her throat, and finished up in a violent sob. She turned over quickly on the pillow, so that Peter, who still had hold of her hand, found one of his own clasped somewhere under her collar-bone. Her shoulders shook with her efforts not to make an unbecoming noise. Peter bent over her and smoothed her hair, tangled into a mat from being lain on, with his free hand.

'I always knew,' he said, 'that some day or other you'd tell me all about it. I never hurry these things. They happen, in their own time.'

Elsie's sobbing ceased, and she lay still. There was a moment of silence; a perfect moment, mutually ideal, like that which exists between a good violinist and a very good audience, in the virtuoso passage of a sonata. Neither Peter nor Elsie, for different reasons, was precisely aware of its nature. A kind of after-vibration, more moving than the words themselves, seemed to hang in the air.

'You don't have to tell me, you know, if you'd rather not,' said Peter, with hair-trigger timing.

'I guessed you knew. Everyone who comes knows sooner or later. As a rule that's the worst thing. But I don't mind you. I thought I would. But in a sort of way it's a relief.'

'I was hoping you'd feel that.'

Elsie gave a damp smile. She took it for granted that no further explanations were needed. This might have created an impasse; but not for Peter, who took such assumptions about himself for granted, and hardly expected to start from anything less. He pitched his voice a tone lower. Warm, intimate, and disturbingly different from the most affectionate sounds made by her mother or her best friend at school, it sent a little shiver down Elsie's spine.

'Tell me about it just the same. I'd like it, and it will do you good. I want very much to help, you know.'

So, indeed, he did. His sincerity was evident to both of them, and a source of equal pleasure to each.

'There isn't really much to tell. It's just pretty terrible. I wonder if it often happens. One's people not getting on, I mean.'

'You poor dear.' Peter himself was scarcely aware of having received information; he shared immediately Elsie's conviction that he had known all along. 'Yes, I'm afraid it does happen pretty often, society being the daft thing it is. Only some people notice more and feel more, and you happen to be one of them.

Try not to be unhappy about it. It's better, you know, in spite of everything, to notice and feel.'

This was a point of view which had never occurred to Elsie. It shed over everything a magic and transforming light. Like a cat's first taste of fish, an actor's first publicity, a boy's first long trousers, is the first chance to be interesting that comes in the way of a girl in her 'teens. Peter saw the faint, astonished dawn of self-esteem in her dejected face, and was overjoyed. It was one of his most endearing traits never to elevate himself by lowering other people. He was a sociable creature, and liked company in the empyrean. Naturally his own head would always be a little the nearest to the sun, like that of the apex figure in a Raphael; but the rightness of this was so obvious to him that he never thought about it.

'I've noticed ever since I was a baby. But I've never told anyone but you.' She could not, if she had thought it out for a day, have thanked him more suitably. He squeezed her hand. With her heart in her mouth, she squeezed his back.

'Of course,' he said, 'it's obvious at a glance that things are badly wrong. What is it, exactly? Is one of them carrying on with someone else?'

Elsie gasped; she even let go of him. She was shocked to death. 'Oh, *no*. Nothing like that. I mean, they wouldn't.'

'M-m, no, of course not. Probably be a lot happier if they did.'

Elsie gazed at him, horror at this blasphemy mingled with a secret admiration. Her face registered both like a cinema screen.

'Well, after all,' said Peter, radiating the vast toleration of his twenty-eight years, 'they're just a part of universal human nature, you know, and subject to the same laws. What you want to do is to get it out of your head that you're the only person to whom this has ever happened. I'll tell you something if it'll make you feel better. My people got divorced when I was fifteen. I was at school when it came out in the papers. They had to take me away and send me somewhere else.'

'Oh. I *am* sorry.' Elsie felt as if years of experience had passed over her since this morning. Here she was, dealing with unthink-able situations, having them discussed with her as an equal. 'That must have been terrible for you.'

Peter smiled remotely. 'It was an upheaval at the time. Later on they both married other people, and now they're reasonably good friends. I get on quite well with all four of them.'

In Elsie's social circle, divorced persons were mentioned in almost the same breath as girls who spoke to strange men in the street. Her horizons were dissolving in every direction. The excitement of it was enormous. Her very blood seemed to be cir-culating at a different rate.

'My people don't believe in divorce,' she said.

Peter nodded. 'That's the tragedy. They imprison themselves, and you have to pay.'

'When it gets too bad I go for a long walk and try to forget about it.'

'That's how you picked up your bronchitis, I suppose?'

'It might have been. I did get rather wet.'

'God! You poor kid.'

He stroked his hand gently over her thin round shoulder. Should he kiss her? he was thinking. It seemed a shame not to; it would probably make her happy for the rest of the day. She was looking much less unattractive already. All she wanted was a tonic, the sort that didn't come out of a bottle. There were, how-ever, limits even to Peter's capacity for professional indiscretion; nor had he lost sight entirely of the fact, which had never crossed Elsie's mind, that when doctors visit young female patients, a chaperon is considered all to the good. He compromised by smoothing back the hair from her forehead. This seemed to do very well.

'From now on,' he said, 'you're going to feel different about everything. Aren't you?'

'Yes,' she whispered. 'I believe I am.'

'I know you are. I'll be here for another three weeks, you know. We'll go for a walk one day, and talk things over properly.

Shall we? Now I'll have to go. But I'll be thinking about you.'

The sun had come out. Elsie lay, after he had gone, and watched the golden square from the window move across the bedroom wall. A blackbird was singing. It was as though she had never heard one before.

Peter was bucketing the Ford along the rough road, whistling the 'Soldiers' Chorus' from *Faust*. The roof was open. He felt delightfully full of the sea air and of himself.

They had succeeded in making one another very happy.

CHAPTER FOUR

I t was shortly after this that Elsie began to keep a diary. It was her second. She had meant, after altering the dates at the top, to use up the unfinished third of the old one, which she had allowed to lapse when she left school, finding that few things happened except those she had no wish to record. With this idea in mind, or perhaps to postpone the pleasure of writing (since the words were already in her head) she beguiled a twilight interval between tea and supper by reading it through. Ritual meant much to her, and was beginning to mean more than ever, so she opened it, carefully, at to-day's date of two years ago. The entry was reticent; a row of five asterisks, with another row of five exclamation marks below. The pencil had broken off in the middle of one of them; this was the only incident she could remember of a day which she must evidently have supposed to be carved upon her heart. She tried again, a week later. This page was more informative. It began with a six-pointed star, drawn carefully in the margin with red ink.

'Did *Faerie Queene* in Eng. Lit. to-day. Got to the part about Britomart. It is lovely. I could just see her in her armour looking just like M. did that time she had us into the VI Form Room and put us on our honour about the cloakroom basins. I am going to call her Britomart to myself from to-day onwards. If Miss Taylor only knew!!!'

There were several more days with red stars. She read three or four of them, and presently remembered what the five asterisks had celebrated.

Her bedroom fire was still being kept up. She jumped out of bed, and, moving the fireguard, stood for a moment in her pink crochet bedjacket and winceyette pyjamas, holding a sombre Byronic pose with the book poised over the flames. When she had dropped it in, she watched it with an enigmatie smile, poked it well under, wiped her hands on the underside of her towel to get rid of the blacklead from the poker, and returned to bed.

This ceremony, satisfying in itself, left the new diary still unhoused; but she remembered her Latin Unseen book, of which only a page had been used. It began 'Then Horatius the gate-keeper, "Friends" he said,' and ended with a derogatory sentence in red ink. Removing this, she headed the clean new sheet:

IMPRESSIONS OF LIFE
ELSA LANE

and held it away from her to study the effect.

Through the left-hand wall she could hear a leisurely arhyth-mic sound, of moving and pausing footsteps and of light objects being shifted and set down again. She recognized it, without thought, as that of her mother dusting in the next room; it was a settled, soothing noise. Against its background, she bent her knees to support the limp covers of the book, chewed urgently at her pencil for a minute or two, and began to write.

'March 9th. I have been reading an old diary I wrote when I was a child at school. How long ago it seems! Now I am older I realize how foolish it is to imagine that something worth writing down would happen to one every day (at least to an *ordinary* person, particularly a girl), so I shall not use this book to put down going for walks or what I had for dinner, but only thoughts that I may wish to remember in later years. Recently I have been thinking a good deal, owing to my illness and to a new influence that has come into my life.

'For instance: when one is young one is always worrying about whether one's parents understand one. As one grows up, one realizes that this is a mistake to expect, as old people are less adaptable and the important thing is that one should get to understand *them*.

'At school one gets crushes on people and later one thinks one has been silly. But when one is more mature one knows that it is Nature and that one's feelings have only been practising, ready for something real and beautiful.'

This completed a page. She had, in any case, meant to begin the next paragraph on a fresh one.

'There is something very touching to the heart about a Doctor who is *young*. One thinks of the years before him, with his eyes bent on sad and sordid things, doing good all around him, but missing romance in his own life, like Sir Galahad.' She re-read the last two words doubtfully, altered them to 'St. Francis,' crossed it out, and decided to end the sentence with 'life' after all. 'He would need to marry someone with a great love of Beauty to keep him from becoming lonely and disillusioned in middle age. Someone younger than himself would probably be best for this.'

She re-read this paragraph several times, elaborating the capitals and adding shape to the down-strokes; and was going over it for the fourth time when footsteps, and the rattle of crockery on a tray, sounded on the stairs. She thrust the book quickly down the neck of her pyjamas, and tied the pink ribbon bow of her bedjacket firmly over it.

It happened that, at much the same time on the same day, Peter was writing too. He had just finished making up the books for the evening; there was a good fire in Dr. Sloane's consulting-room, and a comfortable patient's chair; writing materials lay around him, and it required less energy to start a letter – which would, in any case, have to be written sooner or later – than to resettle himself in the sitting-room with a novel. He poised his pen, full of that virtue peculiar to the bad correspondent who writes a letter in any circumstances at all.

'Darling, – Blessings on you for yours of the other day' (it could hardly be more than three weeks, after all) 'which was full of delights, as always.' (He had lost the letter, or, if not, it was somewhere upstairs.) 'This is a far cry from St. Jerome's, and it requires a definite effort of the imagination to picture you, at this moment, mentioning the deficient swab to Tonky, while a queue of caesars and ruptured fallopians forms in the anaesthetic room.' (This was putting the day back some hours; 'washing instruments,' he felt, lacked style.) 'But I don't doubt your humanizing and humourizing influence has the usual Orpheus touch in the jungle of temperaments.' (He wondered, passingly, whether she would know who Orpheus was; but, if not, she would certainly look it up.) 'Queer to think that my leaving-party and all that went with it – and still does, praise be – was a year ago last Christmas. What a night that was; and queer, too, to remember how it surprised us. Yes, you're right' (he remembered this part) 'of course it's time I struck roots somewhere. But I still think I'll strike firmer ones as a result of nosing around first and doing a bit of spotting. It's no use sinking one's exiguous capital irrevocably in a practice, only to find that the surrounding scenery saddens your guts, and the natives worship a divine aspidistra on Sundays. I wouldn't bury that shining wit of yours in the thick brown wool of an industrial suburb.'

He read this over with approval, and looked out of the window in search of further ideas. The wind was getting up, and a bleak handful of rain rattled the glass, mixed with the sound of a rising sea. 'How, I wonder,' he continued, suddenly inspired, 'would you like to settle around here? It lacks some of the trimmings, of course – nearest cinema and shopping centre three miles along the sands when exposed, or six by bus when running; water supply pumped by hand from the bottom of the garden, and cooking mostly by oil. But it has a kind of acid charm. Cliffs made of hard edgy volcanic rock, holding in a beautiful but rather evil sea – like a fire-opal with a bad history set in blackened silver – and, perched on top of it all, a surrealist arrangement of bungaloids, made mostly of cast concrete blocks which the local architect, who must have an individual sense of humour, has titivated with stone rabbits, witch-balls, and dear little gnomes.' He considered this with his head on one side, recalling Norah's penchant for Regent's Park and the Circus at Bath.

'By the way, I am treating the daughter of this artist for a mild broncho-pneumonia. An interesting case, psychologically I mean, and rather a pitiful one. The child is nearly eighteen, but what with the stone rabbits and the Atlantic and the fact that her parents live like cat and dog and she knows the whole village knows it, she has taken refuge between the covers of a Girls' Annual and, unless someone snaps the poor little brat out of it, is in a fair way to going through her adult life in a sort of fifth-form daydream. Which would be a pity, as she obviously has the makings of emotion and intelligence, combined with the kind of painful plainness which in a year or two, with sexual animation, might suddenly become attractive, and without it will get more dismal from year to year. I think subconsciously, under a ton or two of inhibition, she dimly realizes this; which makes a fascinating problem of an otherwise humdrum case. It's a pity you're not here; you would do her a world of good. Failing you' (he could not help thinking, quite consciously, that this was rather handsome), 'I'm doing what I can with her. There is some local story about a disowned elder sister who eloped with I forget who, no doubt a woman of character, of whom she has been taught to be ashamed. I am hoping to draw her out, discreetly, on this as a starting-point. Meanwhile I have got her receptive, which of course is tricky going, but I think I have succeeded in hitting the right note.'

At this point the clock surprised him by striking eight. He had written the last paragraph chiefly for his own amusement, and hastily ran over the letter from the beginning to see if it would do. It was a satisfaction to him (he lit a final cigarette on it) to decide that there was nothing in it which could possibly hurt Norah's feelings. His dislike of hurting anyone was entirely genuine, as traits which people use for effect often are; and from this it followed that if anyone insisted on being hurt by him, he found the injury hard to forgive.

A smell of frying mushrooms warned him that his supper must be almost ready. Concluding the letter with a prettily phrased but censorable valediction, he slapped the writing-pad shut over his still-wet signature, and went upstairs to wash his hands.

CHAPTER FIVE

'So you see,' said Peter, 'there it is.' He gave a conclusive little smile at the cobalt-blue limits of the sea.

'Yes,' said Elsie. If the waters of the bay had been turned to blood, she would not have known, or, probably, cared. She leaned against her supporting rock, stroking with absent fingers a rosette of yellow lichen, and looked at Peter. So might a twelfth-century mystic have looked at an archangel, manifested on a sunny day out of blue cliff-top air.

'Trust yourself, first and all the time. It's your life. Hang on to it. Nobody else, however much they care about you, can do it for you.'

'Yes,' said Elsie, 'I will.' It was not a declaration, it was a response in a litany. However much they care about you. It came back to her in waves of light from the clouds and grass and the long white lines of the rollers ruled across the beach.

'You're losing your muffler.' He caught at its blowing end, and, leaning forward where he sat, tucked it snugly in for her. She sat quite still; only her spirit seemed to tremble and shiver at his touch, like an image refracted in the heat of the sun. 'Don't let them throttle you up in woollies for the rest of the year, though. Start getting some light and air into you as soon as it gets warm.'

'Oh, I will.' She wondered how it would be possible to hold

more of either than at this moment. It seemed to her that she could have floated from the cliff-edge and balanced, like the gulls, on the upward eddies of the wind.

'You've had a tough break. I know, if anyone does, what it means to hang on alone.' His eyes seemed to be sharing a secret with the horizon. He was remembering, not without satisfaction, certain stimulating encounters with more rigid and less enlightened minds. To Elsie, this transient vista of a splendid loneliness was almost too much for her heart to hold. She could not speak. It was not, in any case, required of her. Peter returned to earth, and propped himself more comfortably on his elbow against the sea-pinks and the rough grass. 'It's too bad,' he said, looking at her thoughtfully, 'that you're an only child.'

Elsie dug her fingers into the flake of lichen, with such force that it came away in her fingers.

'I'm glad you said that.' She felt so breathless that it seemed strange to hear the words coming, while her lungs were empty. 'It's what I was going to tell you. It's the other thing that I said there was. You see . . .' He reached out his hand and put it over hers. With a little rushing gasp she finished, 'You see – I'm not.'

'What aren't you?' He moved his fingers gently over the back of her hand.

'An only child. I had an elder sister, you see.'

'Poor little Elsie.' He turned her hand palm upwards, and stroked it again. 'How long has she been dead? '

'She isn't dead. She – went away. No one talks about her.'

'Don't they?' said Peter softly. 'Don't they, indeed? Well, it seems about time you and I did, doesn't it?'

'I wanted to. I thought it would seem – less awful, if we did.'

'I think so too.' He smiled at her; but she was looking down at his hand covering hers. This was already miracle enough. 'And they never told you what it was, this awful thing that no one talks about?'

'No. At least, not . . .'

'But you think you know, don't you?'

Elsie looked down at the broken flake of lichen. 'Yes,' she said.

She knew that he was looking at her. She raised her eyes, quickly, ready to look away again. He held them with his own.

'Everything has a name, my dear. And some things have several. Don't you think, knowing your parents as you do, that perhaps the reason they don't talk about her is that they haven't got a word for love?'

Elsie said nothing. She did not think of speaking; one does not answer the morning star. The word had never been spoken, until his voice clothed it. She thought that she would hear it every moment, now, for the rest of her life.

Peter saw her face, like a face stilled by incantation. It did not much perturb him. The word transference floated, with the comfortable assurance of text-book and experiment, across his mind. Rather more briskly, since time was getting short, he said,

'Do you remember your sister well?'

'Yes. Quite well.' Elsie's face stirred, as if the sound of her own voice had waked it. 'I was nine when she went away. She wasn't really – at all like that, I thought.'

Peter smiled at her benignly. 'My dear, you're not nine now. Everyone's like that. You are. I am.'

Elsie's heart stopped dead, and then raced so that it seemed to be shaking her body.

The sun was growing warmer, an outcrop of rock sheltered them from the wind. Peter stretched himself pleasantly on the grass. It was going well, he thought.

'There are people who refuse life, and people who accept it. That's all. Your sister would understand what I mean. So will you when the time comes, unless you run away from it. Don't do that; you're much too nice a person.' His eyes, bluer from the reflection of the sky, smiled into hers.

Elsie took a breath, trying to speak. She wanted to say that she would not run away, though terror and beauty should destroy her; but only a little breath came back again from between her lips.

'You trust me, don't you.' It was an encouraging statement, not a question; he did not waste time by exacting a reply. 'You don't think I'm something that ought to be shoved into the cupboard under the stairs and never mentioned? Well . . . I'm twenty-eight, you know: and I haven't spent the last ten years in a monastery. And I'm not ashamed of it. Like your sister. Does that make you wish you hadn't come here to talk to me?'

Elsie spoke at last. 'No,' she said, in a voice that cracked into a whisper.

'You see. I look just like anyone else. And I am just like anyone else. I've enjoyed life more than your parents, perhaps, because I believe in life, that's all. Your sister believed in life too. If you were to meet her, you'd feel that in her just as you feel it in me. You *should* meet her. Where is she now?'

'I don't know,' said Elsie, speaking as people do in their sleep.

'Haven't you ever tried to find out?'

'Not properly.' She looked down at the grass.

'But your people know, don't they?'

'I don't know.' She hung her head. Her fears and avoidances burned her, as if they had been of him. From among them, memories shaped themselves together. 'Sometimes,' she said, 'I've thought that Mother knows.'

'Well, it's up to you. Find her.' That, he thought, would be a good note to finish on. It would leave her with something to think about; it was time, after all, to carry the process of transference on to the next stage. 'And whatever you find, don't run away.'

'I'll try.' She looked down into the peacock-green sea two hundred feet below, as if he had bidden her climb down and search there, and she were measuring the depth.

'Good. And write and tell me all about it.' For good measure, he talked for ten minutes more, decorating and underlining, quoting (and toning down with some tact to her level) Bertrand Russell and Havelock Ellis, and illustrating them with little stories about the more amusing of his friends, reduced delicately to implications, for she must not be startled or over-hurried yet. He went on longer than he had meant, loth to cease his labours in so promising a soil, where even as one watched, the good corn struck root and the green shoots appeared. He had had one or two disappointments in the last few months; a case like this, he felt, made up for them all. He was a little sad within himself, because he would not be there to observe results. One so seldom was. But he felt that an otherwise trite and trivial month had been justified. He did his best, as he talked, to keep the main headings of the discourse in mind, because Norah would be interested to hear about it. Norah was always interested, bless her.

'I'll have to go in a minute,' he said at length. 'I've got a lot of straightening-up to do.' He had let the panel cards get behind-hand, and Sloane had had a pernickety regard for them. 'You won't forget me, will you?'

'No.' Since it pleased him to ask questions without a meaning, she gave with a dreaming smile the meaningless answer.

'Because I shan't forget you. You're the only worthwhile thing that's happened to me down here. We'll meet again, you know. Hang on to yourself, and remember all we've said. And don't run away.'

He got to his feet. She followed; not pursuing any purpose, but as water follows the moon. He took her hands in his, looking down at her rapt face with affection and a certain pardonable pride. 'Good-bye, Elsie dear.' He drew her forward gently, and kissed her on the brow.

She was still standing like a tree, rooted, blind and trembling, when he vanished round the dip of the cliff. She heard him, in the receding distance, whistling 'Bobby Shaftoe' as he went.

That day and the morning after she got through the mechanics of living with the somnambulist's luck. In the afternoon she went on the cliffs again, not in the hope of meeting him, for he had said that he was busy; only to re-create more clearly, against every detail of stone and flower and grass, each moment they had spent. Hope had no place in a heart too full to give it lodging. Some time, she supposed – perhaps not for years, as he had seemed to imply, what did it matter? – she and Peter would be married. It was like a sun still below the level of the horizon, whose brightness one does not fear because it will come softly, after the long cool stillness of dawn. She did not think much about it; the guilty curiosity of the schoolroom had disintegrated; instead, misting the outlines of things, there was only a cloud of shyness, like mild vapour touched with light.

It was the following morning when, walking a little further than she had been allowed till now, she saw, outside the village post-office, the familiar car. She retreated immediately, for she had never met him in the presence of strangers and the prospect confused her. But, even while she turned, the bell on the shop door tinkled, the door opened and slammed. It was Dr. Sloane, with his old-fashioned black bag, his stethoscope peeping out of his overcoat pocket. Smiling his plump rosy smile, he raised his hat to her, and asked her if she were taking good care of herself.

She answered something; dazed, while she spoke, only by the sudden shock of having expected to meet Peter unprepared. It was only after he had driven off that she stood still in the white dust of the village street, knowing what it meant.

Perhaps she had missed him by coming here, perhaps he was searching the cliffs for her at this moment. She was nearly through the village when she remembered the stamps she had come to buy for her mother. If she returned without them, she would be asked why. It would not be easy to lie well, after saying good-bye to Peter. The few minutes could make no difference; on the cliffs she would see him for a long way off. She turned back, tinkled the little bell, and stood among the jars of boiled sweets, the picture postcards and cards of combs and headache powders, looking through the little brass grill.

'Half a dozen three-ha'penny stamps, please, Mrs. Coppock.' She added, because not to do so would have been unthinkable, an enquiry for Mr. Coppock, who was convalescing from a gastric ulcer.

'He's nicely, Miss Lane, nicely, thank you. Dr. Sloane said to-day it wouldn't do no harm to try a little meat. Getting about a bit now, George is. I won't have him in the shop on account of the standing, but he does a bit of driving. That young doctor that took Dr. Sloane's place, he had the car to take him to the station, but he wouldn't let George lift none of the luggage and that. Said it might strain the stomach. Very clever he seemed, and talked very interesting. But Dr. Sloane's more homely, if you under-stand what I mean.'

Elsie assented, to what she did not know. She walked out into the sun, along the gritty rutted road, between the old granite cot-tages and the new concrete bungalows, surveying the emptiness of people and things, the ebbing of life from the earth and its creatures, the hostile desolation of the sea.

After the first dead minutes, thought came to her rescue, hur-rying, as beavers hurry to repair a broken dam. Something, an emergency call perhaps, had prevented him from meeting her on the cliffs, from leaving a note, from doing whatever he had planned. Or they had missed one another somehow. Or he had minded leaving her too much to say good-bye. Not one of them but convinced and solaced while it lasted. But there were too many of them. They fed the mouth, but left the belly empty. Peter had left this morning; perhaps even yesterday. Whatever sort of covering one found to throw over it, the shape of the fact underneath remained the same.

Before she slept, however, she had found the answer. Peter would write. Everything would be solved then, everything con-firmed. That would be the real beginning. Meanwhile (since Peter was busy, and she had all time) she would write to him.

Within three days, the third copy was ready to be sent. She knew every word by heart, and used to rehearse the phrases to herself at mealtimes, or in the sitting-room after tea, becoming so detached from her surroundings that her parents, too, sometimes forgot that she was there. She had been too shy to speak of the future, or to ask what plans he had made for them to meet again. Peter would know how such things were done. She knew where to send it, for he had told her that, when he went away, it would be to his old hospital, to take a house appointment there. She had not known what it meant, and it had seemed very remote and far away. But she had remembered the name. She knew that letters from Cornwall were often two days on the way; so it was half a week before she began seriously to watch the post.

She rarely received letters, and in these her mother took a kindly interest, saying, as she handed them over, 'Look, here's one for you, Elsie, isn't that nice? Isn't it from Pamela? How is she getting on with her elocution now?' Marjorie was the elocutionist, and Pamela was at a secretarial college; but Elsie had good reason to know that Peter's hand was alarmingly different from either; she wore, pinned to her liberty bodice by day and the inside of her pyjamas by night, a prescription for ferrous sulphate tablets, which she had found in the wastepaper basket.

Her day pivoted, now, round her casual-seeming shifts to intercept the mail, or, for variety, the postman. By the second week she had developed a good deal of skill in both. In the third week, she ceased to encounter the postman personally, feeling ashamed to do so; in the fourth, she pretended even to herself that she happened to be in the hall only by chance. In the fifth week, the phrases of her own letter hid in the back of her mind, and came out at odd, sudden moments, running out and across like darting mice when she was in church or sitting at tea, and making her tighten her fingers, or twist her leg painfully round the leg of her chair.

In the sixth week, in the middle of a scene at breakfast, while she was staring about her in vacant, almost unseeing misery, she saw it lying on the table a foot away from her, at the top of the morning pile. Because the scene had started before the letters came in, she was able to pick it up and put it in her pocket.

She took it to the only safe place she knew of; the outdoor

lavatory half-way down the garden. It had walls whitewashed over raw stone, with cobwebs in the corners; last year's parish calendar, fixed in the mortar with rusty nails, showed a Christmas crib with very clean shepherds, and angels who looked as if they had all been to the same public school. A number of earwigs lived behind this. The place had been an old potting shed, and was big enough to hold, besides the wide, scrubbed wooden seat, the garden roller, mower and hose, and a wooden box full of dead-looking bulbs. Through the open window a wild fuchsia dripped with crimson and imperial purple, the small firm flowers and shiny dark-red stems shining half transparently between her and the light of a bright-grey morning sky. Elsie sat down on the dirty garden roller; it would have been sacrilegious to use the edge of the seat, and its presence shamed her. She wished there had been somewhere else to go; but it would be time, in a few minutes, to help her mother make the beds. She did not open the letter at once, though there was so little time. Perhaps it was the residual wretchedness from breakfast, or the cold, cloudy light, or those barren posts and slowly cooling expectations, that made her pause with her finger hooked in the envelope, feeling chilly and damp in the palms. But she interpreted her dread as the turmoil of ecstasy, and, ripping the fold, took out the letter, two sides of one sheet and one and a half of the next.

Dear Little Elsie,

It was good to hear from you and to know that you still think kindly of me and that our talks together helped, maybe, to give you a fresh slant on things and make life seem less on top of you. I am glad that I was there, though no doubt if I hadn't been someone else would; you were due for a new impetus of some sort, and the *Zeitgeist* has a way of producing such things at the appropriate moment from one source or another. It has been my luck to assist at such moments once or twice in my life and each time it has made me very happy, as happy as when I delivered my first solo baby, which I did in a back kitchen assisted by a girl of fifteen and four canaries in a cage over the bed, who shouted encouragement at suitable intervals. I wondered then what the baby would make of its job of living, as I wonder now about you; it's an awesome business launching people off and watching them make towards the horizon out of your ken. But something tells me you will get there and come back with the Golden Fleece, for I saw a Jasonish look in your eye. Sometime we will meet and you shall tell me travellers' tales.

I have been very busy of late . . .

Elsie ranged through it, as a hungry bird will range through straw, seeking a stray ear of corn. A novel Peter had read and thought well of; a hospital dance about which he hinted, without actually specifying, doings both broad and deep; and the fact that Peter must now be on his way to the wards, as he had a bunch of case-histories to get for his chief.

Think of me sometimes [it finished] for I shall often think of you and wonder how you're making out.
    Love from
    Peter.
P.S. Give my respects to your sister when you see her.

She turned the letter over; perhaps this was not, after all, the last page, people sometimes skipped one and then came back. But no, there was nothing more. She put it down in her lap, and looked at the small square of the window. Years afterwards she remembered the cracked green paint showing the wood, a chrysalis, brown and glossy, gummed to one corner, and the little hanging flowers like clear drops of blood.

It was her sense of inferiority, the arrested child in her, that saved her faith. It kept from the death of her dreams the sense of outrage; so that it differed not in kind, but only in degree, from the times when she had had to come back from reading *Beau Brocade* on the cliffs at sunset, to a quarrelsome supper of tepid cocoa and cold brawn. It was cruel indeed, but natural and explicable; striking the present from under her, it did not destroy the future, only made it recede to the old and familiar distances. The style of the letter, set against those of aunts and school friends whose eloquence was the point of exclamation and the word twice underlined, dazzled her so much that its substance became, after all, inevitable, and even its patronage a compliment. When, having shed a few tears, she tucked the envelope inside her knicker-elastic and got up to go, a new mirage was taking shape already in the haze of her horizon.

'Give my respects to your sister when you see her.' It broke the emptiness, giving imagination a point to rest on. It was not a new idea, it had only increased its urgency. Second only to Peter, Leonora had become a symbol. During the weeks of post-watching, Elsie had often found vicarious compensation in thinking about her and picturing, in the light of Peter's instruction, what she had become. The rouge and the maroon hair were long forgotten. Intense sombre eyes, and a heavy dark knot worn low on the nape, took their place; for Elsie had decided that it could only have been an artist with whom Leonora had accepted life. Artists were the only romantic strangers with whose appearance she was familiar; she often passed them, at a shy distance, on the cliffs or in the more presentable parts of the village, tanned, absorbed and interestingly shabby, and had longed to edge up, like the children, for a nearer look at the canvases which transmuted the daily scene into something rich and strange. One or two of them had been quite young, and by agglomerating the most attractive features and clothing of these, she had arrived at a satisfying image of Leonora's. That, of course, would have been eight years ago; by this time he would be famous, probably an R.A. (it happened that Peter had never given her the benefit of his views on art), and Leonora, dressed in a Chinese shawl or (for one must not run away) naked on silk cushions, posed for him, arranged fruit and flowers in his studio, and entertained his gifted friends. *Trilby*, which had rather shocked her at the time of reading, came in very usefully now. She had read somewhere of the Café Royal, and saw it in her mind's eye buzzing with excitement as Leonora (she had dropped Leo, which did not go) floated in on the arm of her lover, who, since his rise to eminence, wore a cloak and a pointed beard. The lesser artists would point them out to one another: 'Yes,' they would say, 'he met her in a little village in the wilds of Cornwall, and ran away with her. It caused a terrible scandal, and her family have quite cast her off. But he worships the ground she treads on, so I don't suppose she cares.' Or perhaps she was in her own right a celebrated model, living beautifully and passionately, not with just one R.A. but with two or three.

She must, of course, have changed a good deal. Recalling the ample nudes in the Senior School library book on Modern French Art, and comparing them with her dimming memories of Leo, thin and brown and dressed in the out-at-elbows ruin of good tweeds, Elsie could not help feeling that this was very likely. But that would only make their meeting more touching and dramatic.

As she lay in bed that night, she got out the letter again. She had read somewhere, she remembered now, that people often put the most important thing in the postcript. Perhaps it had all been leading up to that. Perhaps it was a test. 'When you see her'; not 'if.' She sat up in bed, her brain too restless to let her body be still, and, going to the window, stood staring at the strip of moonlit sea which showed beyond the tamarisks and firs.

CHAPTER SIX

Elsie stood at the door of her mother's bedroom, with her hand on the knob. Before she turned it, she looked again at her watch. It was half an hour since Mrs. Lane had started; long enough to be fairly sure that she would not come back for something she had forgotten, which happened two or three times every week. There could hardly be less than a couple of clear hours. Gladys was ironing, and her father did not count, for, though he would have been affronted if a paper-weight on his own desk had been displaced, he took for granted that the women of the house lived on top of one another in a conspiratorial huddle. She opened the door.

With the door still open, she stood still inside the fresh, neat, cologne-scented room, with its Edwardian display of silver-topped glass and photographs in fancy frames. She had done nothing yet. She might be here for anything; to see if it had been dusted, or if the flowers on the table wanted fresh water. She could look and see, and go away again.

Perhaps, if she committed this wickedness, it would be for nothing. There might be several reasons, if one could think, for putting a birthday present, unopened, quickly away among the wrappings of the rest, and saying nothing about it. Perhaps her mother had had a girlhood sweetheart, who had remained faithful for thirty years. Perhaps . . . But after every theory was exhausted, Elsie was still sure. She simply knew.

She went over to the little glass vase of primroses. The water was quite clear, but one of the flowers was drooping. She lifted it out, then put it guiltily back again. Perhaps she had been mistaken about the whole thing, after four months. She ran her mind over it, seeing it all as clearly as yesterday; her father saying 'Many happy returns, Maude' with the ceremony that belongs to a military armistice, and handing the invariable envelope with the cheque; the dry ritual kiss thankfully got over; her mother turning to the presents, opening Elsie's first, as she always did. She always had, ever since Elsie knew what birthdays were, when she and Leo had both been children. Elsie remembered reflecting once that before she was born, Leo's must have been first; but, as her mother used to say sometimes, Elsie was the baby now. Leo had always got on with her breakfast, and seemed not to notice. Elsie's present had always been 'just *exactly* what I was wanting,' and Leo's 'How *very* nice.' It had seemed to Elsie that Leo spent a lot of money on odd, plain-looking things. She had felt rather superior about it. It was queer to think of this to-day.

Last year's birthday had been just like all the others back to the beginning of time. Leo's absence had never showed very much. There had only been the small unopened parcel, and the fact that when she had been about to say, 'Look, Mother, you've forgotten one,' something or other had prevented her.

Elsie went over to the window, and looked out. Leo had suddenly become confusingly vivid, an intruding presence before which Leonora began to grow somewhat cloudy and to dislimn in her mind's eye. She pushed the memories away. It was Leonora who would prove her to Peter, whom she had promised him to find. Until she had found her, she would be ashamed to write to him again. Decision stiffened her. She walked straight back across the room to the dressing-table, and opened the china box with the Morris rose pattern on the lid. From among the gilt safety-pins and dress-clips inside it she took the little key, bright with much handling, of her mother's locked, left-hand drawer.

The worn lock opened smoothly. The drawer exhaled its familiar smell, the same since her earliest years, of mystery and romance; a mixture of violet, sandalwood, feathers, eau-de-cologne, and paper, mixed with an indefinable smell that was simply the smell of time. In front of it were the things she had always seen quickly as it opened and shut; the blue leather jewel-case and the two velvet jewellers' boxes, an oval one for a necklace, an oblong one for a brooch; behind them a tissue parcel, with a torn place in it through which a cluster of pink silk rosebuds showed. Beside this was a fan of flat pink ostrich feathers with mother-of-pearl sticks and, here and there amid the soft down, little scattered silver sequins. Elsie could not resist opening it and watching it wave and glitter; this at any rate could not be very wrong, for she had been allowed to take it out sometimes for a treat. The fan and the rosebuds had always been tangible proof of the glamour with which Mrs. Lane invested the nostalgic stories of her girlhood; the very sight of it evoked kid gloves above the elbow, programmes with gilt edges and tiny silk-tasselled pencils, ruched flounces swaying to the 'Merry Widow' waltz.

Underneath it was another tissue parcel. This, Elsie knew, contained the real lace from her mother's wedding dress. Just beside it lay the wedding prayer book, ivory with a gold cross. It did not seem strange to her to find these objects cherished. Her mother loved weddings, and had often described her own with undimmed delight, as a thing in itself, detached from causes and consequences, like presentation at court. However bitterly she might be lamenting her lot at the time, she never pronounced the words 'old maid' without pity and patronage. Elsie thought all this quite natural; she had for years planned her own wedding in minute detail, down to the bridesmaids' gifts.

She pulled the drawer open a little wider, and saw that the whole back third of it was filled with papers. Her heart quailed. Every one of these dozens of envelopes must contain something very private – or why keep them here? – and to go through them all would not only be a dreadful and shocking thing to do; it would take the rest of the day. The thought of it made her look at her watch in panic, to find that only five minutes had gone since she entered the room. She stared, helplessly, at the neat piles. At least she could rule out the ones on the right. She had often been shown them; they were her mother's shares. They brought in about fifteen pounds a year, but once they had brought in twenty, and her mother had bought her a silver brush set. She could hardly bear to think of this now. When she had begun to have a career, she decided, she would give her mother a diamond watch.

The next bundle was immensely thick, and tied with pink satin ribbon. The writing at the top looked somehow familiar, like a neater and more flowing version of one she knew. Suddenly she realized that it was her father's. A prickling sensation, like fear but not quite like, came at the back of her neck. She had sometimes meditated, in a vague bewilderment, that the ivory prayer book and the Maltese lace must have been preceded by some relationship rather different from the one which had conditioned her life since she could remember; but to see, within reach of her hand, this wad of concrete evidence was different. The tidy packet was like a door leading into darkness which both drew and repelled her. The topmost envelope, she saw, had been slit along the edge; it would be possible to peep inside without doing more than slide the ribbon. Even while the thought appalled her, she found herself with the packet in her hand, separating the edges. In the fair, elegant script which, she remembered, her father still used on his professional drawings, she could just see the words, 'My own little darling.'

She pushed the packet back into its place, as if it had scorched her. Without being clearly aware of any thought or emotion, she felt tears rushing into her eyes. Scarcely knowing what she did, she straightened the ribbon, wanting nothing in the world but to get the drawer shut, the key back in its box and herself away. She had already begun to slide the drawer inward when, with eyes almost too blurred to see it, she noticed a little packet, loosely wrapped in brown paper, which had slipped down between the pink silk rosebuds and the shares. She knew with instant certainty that it was what she had come for. Now she had it, she only cared for it as a kind of partial justification.

The packet contained a silk-covered box which came open as she unwrapped it, revealing a little carved button of white and green jade made into a brooch. She would certainly have noticed that if her mother had ever worn it, it was so unlike all her other things. But where was the letter? Perhaps it had been destroyed; perhaps, even, there had never been one. Then she saw that it had come away with the wrapper, like a white lining.

It was quite short, only a sentence. She could have read it in one glance, but, keeping the promise she had made to herself, folded it so that it showed only the signature and the heading. The writing was not as she had imagined it, flowing and delicate, but awkward and firm, with the carelessness that comes of having held a pen too long to treat it tenderly. With a sudden contraction of fear, she knew that her dreams had changed into something real. Over a date which was that of the day before her mother's birthday, she read, at last, the strange unexpected address.

CHAPTER SEVEN

Sitting, as she had been taught, in a corner with her back to the engine, Elsie watched the big rounded trees and smooth hills of the Home Counties hump and swell and recede, listening to the wheels of the train playing the 'Soldiers' Chorus' from *Faust*. 'Ta ra-ta-ta-ta, ta ra-ta-ta-*ta*, ta *ra* ta-ta-ta.' Her watch told her that she was within half an hour of her station. She told herself, firmly and frequently, that she was eager to arrive.

She had kept the address for a week, telling herself that she had decided, but doing nothing, while resolution cooled. Then she had said to herself, in excuse, that she was waiting for a sign, while, within her, two conflicting consciences applauded and accused. On the tenth night, the sign had come. She had been in bed, and already growing sleepy, when her mother had come to her room. There had been, of course, a scene downstairs. It had all been, externally, like a dozen other nights; her own leaden, inarticulate efforts to be adequate, the very phrases of her mother's complaint: but beneath it had been different, a secret taking of the auspices. Every phrase had swung her, forward and back, till almost the last. Her mother had said – and it had seemed new, because it was months since she had last heard it, before anything had begun – 'If I hadn't had to make a home for my children, my life would have been very different.' Elsie had known that it was the sign.

It was she, after all, who had imprisoned her parents, the last chain after Leo had gone. She had the power, not only to seize her destiny, but to set them free. She could almost hear Peter's voice, pronouncing the words. It did not tell her precisely what use her mother, at close on fifty, would make of her unforeseen liberation; but then, Elsie was equally unsure what she would make of her own. She had a dim vision of some comfortable and charming lady, encountered in a manner not precisely defined, inviting Mrs. Lane to share her home; where, after a few adventurous and successful years ending in marriage, Elsie would join her to be forgiven and thanked, even bringing, perhaps, Leonora and her R.A. for a grand reconciliation scene. As for her father, the freedom from domestic strife might set loose his talents for who knew what creative energy. He might end by designing a cathedral. In the sleepless excitement of that night's planning, dream had succeeded dream with opium-eating vividness; and the escape had seemed dreamlike and effortless too, the suitcase smuggled out of the house before anyone was astir, and hidden in the bushes up the lane, the lie about spending the day with Phyllis and shopping in Newquay, the letter, containing high sentiments but no clues, handed to the porter at Exeter to post. Then the day-long journey, the longest of her life, with the lovely detachment of all journeys, the sense of suspension between the world before and the world behind, the magical certainty that from the hour marked 'depart' to the hour marked 'arrive' nothing would be demanded of one, nothing would happen except the smooth scene-shifting of the line.

Now, in half an hour, it would be over. The sun was dipping below the moving horizon. When she got there, it would be almost dark. At the thought of it her dreams grew formless and thin, and a chilly twilight spread over them too. She pulled her coat closer round her, and thought of Peter. Him, at least, she had not imagined.

Above her head on the rack was her large suitcase, beside her on the seat a small one with things for the night; tightly clutched in her lap, her handbag, containing more money than she had ever carried before, nearly five pounds left from her money-box after paying her fare, and the three pounds which, she had found, was all the Post Office had been prepared to part with at short notice. Besides this formidable sum, most of it in notes, was her savings-book entitling her, after due warning, to fourteen pounds ten shillings more. She thought with envy of the canvas belts with which seasoned travellers were said to secure their valuables next to the skin.

Opposite her sat a stout man in a navy suit and bowler, smoking a miniature cigar. He had given her the only bad moment of the trip by boarding the carriage at a panting run, just as they left Reading. Her mother had warned her most carefully against men who employed this technique. They did it, after having marked down a woman sitting alone, in order to make sure that it would be too late for her to change her compartment. It was a local train too, with no rescuing corridor. Clammy with panic, and pretending to look fixedly out of the window, she watched him out of the tail of her eye open an attaché case and take out typewritten matter, which he proceeded to mark heavily in pencil. The lid of the case was raised towards her, so that anything might have been inside it still; chloroform, for instance, on a handkerchief, a weapon which played a most important part in her mother's cautionary tales.

Five minutes later, her worst suspicions were confirmed. They were passing the blank wall of an embankment, and, reflected in the window, she could see that he was looking at her fixedly, and groping in the case at the same time. She shot a lightning glance at the communication cord above her head. Once he had seized her, she would not be able to reach it. But what if she pulled it in time, and when the guard came he pretended to be perfectly innocent? She would have to pay five pounds for its improper use: which would leave her with only half the price of a second pull.

'Excuse me,' said the man.

Elsie turned, with the rigid compulsion of a bird fascinated by a serpent. He was bringing his hand out of the case, and in it was something wrapped in a white cloth. She did not even look at the communication cord. It was too late now; it would only accelerate his spring.

'You'll pardon a liberty, I hope, miss. But being there's no tea-car on this train, it crossed my mind if you'd care to help me out with these sandwiches.' He unfolded the wrapping and displayed them, a thick, juicy pile, the top half filled with sardine and the bottom half with egg. Could one drug sardines, and if drugged, did they smell so good? 'My better half puts them up for me,' he added apologetically. 'Can't bear to think of me missing my tea. Fact is, if I get a good filling meal at midday, like what I had at Oxford to-day, they spoil my appetite for my supper, and that upsets her. But she'll have me on the carpet just the same, if she finds any left.'

'Thank you,' said Elsie, 'very much.'

The sandwiches were moist and delicious, most comforting to a stomach frugally sustained since morning with odd cups of tea and buns in railway refreshment rooms. The man lent her the *Daily Mail*, and she responded with *John o' London*, which she had bought because she had felt it would be a cultured object to have with her on arrival. Her spirits mounted. Here she was, mature and sophisticated, emerging triumphant from a situation fraught with danger, conversing with a strange man on a train, and honour intact. She felt ready to cope with anything, even her destination. Her travelling companion eyed her paternally, between respectful glances at a potted life of George Sand. She reminded him of his own girl at the local high school, but it would have been a bit of a liberty to tell her so.

'Well,' he said, glancing at his watch, 'mine's the next station.' He folded *John o' London* with a certain alacrity. 'Much obliged for the loan of your magazine. Very interesting. I see you're like my daughter. She'd appreciate a good intellectual paper like this. I must draw her attention to it.'

'Do please take her this one, if she'd like it. I've quite finished it, really.'

'Well, that's very kind, I'm sure. This'll keep our Doris quiet for the rest of the evening. Doris is the brains of our family. Even in her holiday time she can't keep away from her books. You'll be on holiday yourself, I shouldn't be surprised? '

'Well, yes, I am in a way. As a matter of fact, I'm going to stay with my sister.' This verbal statement seemed to give the thing a new solidity. To prolong its comforting effect she added, 'She lives at Mawley – on the river. Do you know it? I haven't been there before.'

'Really, now? Why, yes, I know Mawley, in a manner of speaking. Not to get down there, but I've passed it in the steamer many a time, taking our Doris for a trip. Very nice and enjoyable at this time of the year, I should reckon for those that like a quiet spot. The steamer doesn't pull up thereabouts. A place always appears more interesting, I've noticed, when one's carried past it.'

'I wonder if you could tell me . . . You see, my sister isn't expecting me by this particular train. She lives in a houseboat, on the river. Would there be a rowing-boat, or something, I could get to take me out to it?'

Something in her face made the man look paternal again. 'Ah, you've no call to worry, miss; you won't experience any difficulty like that. These so-called houseboats, they're not what you might call afloat. More house than boat really, see what I mean. You pass them quite close on the steamer, and you can see they hitch right on to the bank, and there's a little bridge runs up to them as easy as a garden path. Would your sister's be on the south bank or the north, if I might ask?'

'I'm afraid I don't know.' Feeling that this sounded very queer, she added, blushing, 'I think my sister did tell me, but I've forgotten.'

'Why I was asking, the station will be on the north side, if I remember. But these places where both banks are lived on they all have a ferry. Let me see, the post office will be shut but it's a small place, anyone will be bound to tell you which side to go.' He gathered his case and mackintosh together; with regret and the sense of impending loneliness, she noticed that the beat of the train was slowing. 'Well, miss, this is where I get down, and Mawley's the next stop. Pleased to have made your acquaintance. Our little talk's passed the time very enjoyably, if I may take the liberty to say so. I trust you'll have seasonable weather for your holiday.'

He jumped out, scanning the platform right and left till he was lost in the crowd. Doris, she supposed, would be at the station to meet him. His better half would be laying the supper by now. Liver and bacon, or a nice chop; with the other end of the table cleared for Doris's books. She looked out of the window. The evening light was growing grey and mournful; sliding past into shadow, and broken now by hoardings and bunches of new villas, was the alien corn. The kind and fruitful landscape, in which she had no place, filled her with solitude more desolate than the solitude of the barren cliffs at home. The ruses of escape which had seemed so adventurous in the morning, exhilarated no longer, they were so many boats burned fatally behind her. Why had she not left herself a line of retreat? She might have invented a visit to a school friend, from which, at need, she could have returned in a few days and no one the wiser. She need not have posted the letter yet.

Misgivings which had never occurred to her before began to rise like the evening mists, as the train, and the hands of her watch, converged on the significant hour. Suppose Leo's artist were a struggling genius, as yet unrecognized, and they had no spare room? What was the inside of a houseboat like? Did everyone sleep in bunks, one over the other? Intruding on an unmarried couple would be so much worse than on a married one. If she had only brought a hammock with her!

She perceived that the train was slowing down.

Yellow lights flared; a voice, thin and hoarse in the dusk called 'Maw-ley! Maw-ley!' Her heart seemed to be sliding down into a dark corner inside her.

It was quite a small station. The handful of people who alighted with her, hurried off with the speed of familiarity, leaving her, hampered by her baggage, aimless and forlorn. It came to her for the first time that she could have written to Leo, or even wired, to say that she was coming.

A porter came at last, to take her ticket and put her heavier bag in the cloakroom. 'I'll keep the small one.' Her voice sounded thin and apologetic in her own ears. 'Could you tell me, please' – perhaps it would not do to ask for Miss Lane, perhaps she was calling herself something else, why did one only think of these things at the last moment? – 'I'm going to one of the houseboats here. The *Lily Belle*. Could you tell, me, please, which side of the river it is?'

'Ah, the *Lily Belle*.' A smile became visible under the porter's ragged moustache. She felt the trembling incredulity of the desert wanderer who sees at last, on the skyline, a fringe of palms. 'You'll need to take the ferry over to that. Straight down to the water, and then it's twenty yards or so to your left. If you see the boat and no one there, you try the Green Lion, a little way along, and ask for Mr. Hicks.'

'Thank you,' said Elsie, in a tone which she hoped would not reveal too obviously that she had never entered a public-house in her life. Gripping her little night-case and her handbag, she went out into the street, shivering a little in the cool air, and tasting its unfamiliar tang; smells of weed, water, live mud and rotting wood, with a whiff now and again of fresh paint, shavings, and varnish, for a little boat-building yard ended the street at the water's edge.

The evening sky was luminous and unclouded, and the ruffled Thames reflected it; broad shivering gleams came and went over the water, as if a huge invisible wing had swooped and passed. A straight row of poplars grew on the further shore. Before she had noticed the houseboats below them, her eye was caught by the reflected lights lying along the water, and wriggling like little snakes as the gusts went by.

There were several of them strung out at irregular intervals, but it was growing too dark to see detail so far away. Some of them had no lights at all. Her heart sank as a conviction grew in her that it was to one of these that she would be ferried in vain. What would the boatman think? There was his boat, deserted too. A family of swans glided past it, father and mother with all sail set magnificently to the breeze, their grey woolly cygnets like bumboats round a couple of crack clippers.

Elsie looked unhappily to right and left. Her eye was caught almost at once by the frosted windows, lavishly lit, of the Green Lion. She approached them with dragging steps. Pubs are few in North Cornwall, and local residents of any social standing, if they drink at all, do so in hotels. Drawing upon literature, Elsie envisaged beer-soaked sawdust, on which she would stand, the butt of tipsy revellers, like the Quaker lady in *The Everlasting Mercy*. She stood still for a moment, thought about Peter, and pushed open the swing door.

Thick waves of tobacco-smoke met her, and a loud, deep burr of conversation. The place, as she had feared, was full of men: middle-aged men leaning against the bar, in earnest confabulation; old men sitting in a row against the wall looking solemnly at the mugs in front of them; younger men round a dart-board, encouraging one another in mysterious terms. The noise continued, indifferently, around her. She had half-expected it to break off, while everyone turned to stare at her in insolent curiosity; but this was nearly as bad. She would have to go up to the bar, and the barman would think she had come to ask for beer. Practically anyone in the room might, as far as appearances went, have been Mr. Hicks.

The group round the dart-board was re-shaping. She noticed with surprise, but little reassurance, a pretty fair-haired girl in the middle of it. She was trimly dressed and looked respectable; but in a place like this, with five men, Elsie knew better than that.

Gripping her case like a defensive weapon, she went up to the bar. The barman, listening sympathetically to a little man who was saying, 'You wouldn't never know you was a 'uman being, according to them,' took no notice of her at all.

The fair girl took a dart, poised it easily, and threw. There were noises of approbation; exaggerated, Elsie thought, seeing she had only hit the very outside ring of the target; but she was popular, no doubt. A slim, dark-haired youth in a fisherman's jersey came up and thumped her on the back, before going over to the bar to order drinks. The barman attended to him at once. Elsie waited, resentfully, while six half-pints were drawn, and the players, whose game was apparently over, went into a huddle around them. Now someone else was coming up with a mug. Nerved by desperation, she leaned over the bar and said, tremulously, 'Please, is Mr. Hicks here?'

The barman gave her a half-glance over his shoulder, remarked into the thick of the dart-players, 'Eh, Foxy, lady for you,' and turned to the next customer. Elsie watched, crimson with shame, a rufous little man detach himself from the group and approach her. To her relief, he ignored the barman's equivocal introduction and said immediately, 'Wanting the ferry, miss?'

'Oh, yes, please. I hope – I mean, I'm sorry to disturb you.'

Mr. Hicks made a deprecatory noise and, reaching for his glass, emptied it down without taking breath. She added, to cover the interval, 'I want to go to one of the houseboats on the other side. The *Lily Belle*, it's called.'

Mr. Hicks scratched his head. As the glass came down, she saw the dreaded answer shaping itself on his lips. When he had wiped them and his moustache, it came.

'I can take you, miss. But you won't find no one on board of her, not now.'

The accumulated weight of the day's alarms and excursion seemed to descend on Elsie in one sickening heap. She was at the end of her journey, desolate and benighted, surrounded by drunk-ards in a public bar.

Hopelessly, she forced out the words, 'Are they away?'

With an air of solid patience, Mr. Hicks replaced on the mahogany his prematurely vacant glass.

'They're 'ere,' he said.

Elsie's mind seemed to stop. It had come to the end of what it could deal with. Nerveless and blank, she watched Mr. Hicks edge his way along the bar and tap the fair girl on the shoulder.

'Young lady along 'ere, Miss Vaughan. Asking for *Lily Belle*.'

The fair girl turned round. She had a clear, pale skin, dark-grey eyes, and the air of one permanently interested but rarely surprised. She was not, Elsie noticed, made up as crudely as her milieu had led one to expect. Following the line of Mr. Hicks's thumb, she looked at Elsie with kindly vagueness, looked again, and touched the arm of the dark-haired boy in the fisherman's jersey; whose back view, the only one Elsie had so far seen, revealed little but a pleasant carriage and the fact that he wore his hair rather effeminately long.

'Look a minute. I think this must be someone for you.'

The boy turned round: and in one moment there fell from Elsie not only the events of the day, but those of the last eight years also. For a glance was enough to show her that Leo had hardly changed at all.

CHAPTER EIGHT

She stood with an elbow propped on the bar, drawing her brows together in the way Elsie remembered she had always had when puzzled or in doubt. Nothing was strange about her except to discover that she was not, as Elsie had always pictured her from the remembered angle of childhood, very tall; not even as tall as Elsie herself. All that had happened was that she had got, now, the trousers she had wanted at home and never been allowed to wear (it had been almost the only thing on which her parents had invariably agreed). Her skin was the same clear brown; the upward slant of brows and cheekbones was, perhaps, a little more noticeable than before; her eyes looked, as always, more ready to discover than to reveal, only one felt that now they had discovered rather more, and revealed rather less. A quiet-toned lipstick defined, but did not alter, the long curve of her mouth; her hair was tidier, it looked cared for, competently if intermittently; but, as always, a loose strand was finding its way down across her left temple. As Elsie looked, she pushed it back again with exactly the old flick of the hand.

She had not seen Elsie yet, for her eyes, though once they had seemed to pass over her, were still searching the room, in every direction, now, except the right one. After a moment or two she said, over her shoulder, 'Keep an eye on my beer for me, Joe,' and strolled forward; the conversation continuing behind her, without the change of key which is usually observable when the last of the female element leaves.

'Where are they?' she asked the fair girl. 'Waiting outside?'

'No. There. Over by Foxy.' The fair girl's voice was gentle, with the discretion that suggests kindness rather than the conventions; Elsie only heard it because the surrounding noises happened to sink.

Leo looked again. Surely, Elsie thought, she must see her now. She felt the remembered, faint uneasiness at the leisured approach of the light-brown eyes; eyes just the colour of Italian vermouth, though this was not a comparison which Elsie was qualified to make. They met Elsie's squarely; but still nothing happened. She only looked back again, enquiringly, at the fair girl, who shook her head. Leo paused for a moment, then walked up, one hand in her trouser pocket, a cigarette in the other.

'Hullo,' she said, and smiled.

Elsie remembered only her laugh, The smile seemed to shut her off, like a wall of glass. It reminded one, at last, that she was a grown-up person. There seemed nothing at all to say.

Presently she added, in the same pleasant boyish voice, 'Helen said you were looking for me.'

It was like being a ghost, tapping with insubstantial fingers at a window-pane; like a ghost, one wanted to speak and nothing came. At last she said, as if she too had been talking to a stranger:

'Don't you know who I am?'

'Why, yes.' She was still smiling, friendly, indifferent, at ease. Elsie felt, rather than saw, her attention stray for a moment to the talk in the group behind her. 'I mean, of course, I remember meeting you quite well. In London, wasn't it? I'm terribly sorry to be so dim, but just for the moment I can't lay hold of your name.'

Like a ghost who, achieving speech, finds words strange and rusty on the tongue, Elsie listened to her own thin voice saying, 'I'm Elsie. Elsie Lane. Your sister. Don't you remember me?'

Leo stood still. Even her smile, for a moment, did not alter.

Her slim firm body seemed to grow compact and set. At last she said, slowly, 'My God.'

The fair girl, Helen, had come up beside her. All her movements were slight and evenly poised; Elsie had not seen her approach, only found that she was there, quiet and unsurprised, looking not at her but at Leo, with a watchfulness that might have been critical if it had not contained also something protective.

Leo appeared to rouse herself. Speaking like someone whose words are moving a beat or two behind her thoughts, she said, 'You're Elsie. I can't take it in. You were just a little nipper when I went away.'

'I'm nearly eighteen now.' She did not feel it. She was back again in the room which was still the nursery, watching Leo from the hearthrug, wondering what she was thinking about, and being afraid to ask.

'Who sent you here?' Her eyes and voice had the same sudden wariness that Elsie remembered when she had been guarding her queer unexpected privacies at home. Why hadn't one known, Elsie thought, that it would be like this? All her expectations were like dreams which startle by their futility when one wakes in the morning. This had always been the inevitable thing. Her mouth felt suddenly dry.

'Nobody. I just came.'

'Is Mother ill?'

'No. I –'

The fair girl put out a cool-looking hand, and touched Leo's arm.

'There's a table in the corner. Let's go and sit there.' She gave Elsie a gentle unrevealing smile and added, 'I expect you're tired.'

'That's old Bloxon's place. He'll be outraged.' Leo's voice was suddenly light and easy again. 'Oh, well, we can move if he comes.' They went over to a round marble-topped table with two empty pint mugs and an ash-tray advertising whisky. Leo said, 'I may as well bring our drinks along. What'll you have, Elsie?'

'I don't think I –'

'You can have a soft one, you know, if you like. Ginger-beer?'

'Lemonade, please.' Leo went back towards the bar. As she reached it, Elsie heard someone in the group of dart-players say, 'Just going to throw sides for another, Miss Lane,' and Leo answer, 'Sorry, I'm afraid we're out for to-night. Don't wait for me, Joe, it doesn't look as if I'd make it.' A new voice, not of the kind Elsie would have associated with the company, said, 'Too bad. O.K.'

'Have you travelled far to-day?' Elsie found Helen's grey, reflective eyes on her face.

'I have, rather. I took a bus to Newquay and went on from there.'

'But my dear, that's the width of England. You must be worn out. You're putting up for the night with us, of course.' Elsie swallowed, but the moment was deferred. 'Leo's often told me about you.' She said it kindly and charmingly; it was something quite unconscious in her voice which made Elsie feel like an old school chum being made welcome into someone else's family.

She said, trying to make bright and natural conversation, 'You and Leo have known each other a long time, I expect.'

'About seven years. We've lived together for the last five.' One might have supposed that accounting to people for the way that their nearest relatives had spent the last five years were the most natural thing in the world. To Elsie, used to the violently oscillating emotional barometer at home, her composure was almost frightening. She was quite plainly dressed, in a dull leaf-green that set off the pale gold of her silky hair, not a very new frock, but, covert glances discovered, beautifully made, and fitting perfectly the pretty rounded figure under it. Elsie's own brown Sunday marocain, which she had worn to make an impression, felt suddenly shiny, loose and tight in the wrong places, and the lace collar somehow redundant. But Helen herself seemed quite unaware of comparisons. One felt that she rarely disapproved; and that her approval was a trophy almost beyond ambition. Already, shyly and secretly, Elsie longed for it.

'As a matter of fact,' she began, feeling her heart getting in the way of her breathing. But her voice trailed off, because Helen had looked away from her, smiling. Leo had come back.

She set down her tin tray of glasses, pulled up a chair, and crossed her arms on the marble edge of the table. She was smiling too; only her long brown hands, clasping her elbows, had a separate tension of their own. Helen took the glasses from the tray, and distributed them round the table.

'Well,' said Leo, 'cheers.' She looked at Elsie, and then at Helen, over the top of her glass; the look was less like a greeting than a fencer's salute.

It had not seemed to Elsie in any way remarkable that her sister had not offered her a kiss of welcome. The Chinese-shawled Leonora in the dream-studio had done so indeed, but from Leo in the flesh it would have been an embarrassing surprise. Elsie could not remember having ever seen her kiss anyone, except the ritual good night to their mother at bed-time. She took a quick deep drink, and set her glass down.

'Now,' she said, 'where do you want to begin?'

Her face and her attitude, leaning forward a little over the table between them, the groups of men behind, reminded Elsie of something, in a film or a play. Her romantic mind was always apt at such comparisons. Presently she thought of it; it was like a young captain, an adventurer in a rebel force sitting in his head-quarters and receiving an envoy with an ultimatum. It was a moment of which Elsie felt the dramatic possibilities; but she felt them like an onlooker. It was so different from all that she had planned; she had written herself no script for this. Baldly and flatly, looking down at the glass of lemonade in front of her, she said, 'Well, you see, I was wondering – I mean, if you've got room – if I could stay with you for a little while. I've done like you did, I've run away from home.'

Leo drew a long breath. Her hands relaxed; she sat back in her chair. A little line smoothed itself out from between her brows.

'Good Lord; why ever didn't you say so. Is that all? I thought you'd come to ask me to go back there.'

Everything seemed, to Elsie, to have come to a standstill. She had come two hundred miles; she was here; and she was very tired. That was all.

'No,' she said. 'I just ran away.'

Helen had been sitting still, watching both of them out of her level grey eyes.

'Does anyone know you're here?' she asked quietly.

'No. I said I was just going to Newquay.'

Helen too seemed to relax; though it was so impalpable a motion that it was only as if the quality of her repose had changed. She said, her soft voice suddenly warm and kind, 'Leo, she's travelled all the way from Newquay to-day.'

'Since this morning?' Everything felt different. Leo's smile was friendly and concerned. Her eyes had lost their wariness. She put a thin brown hand on Elsie's and gave it a quick pressure, awkward, like a shy boy's. 'You must be half dead. Come straight back with us now and get a hot meal inside you. You can talk about it in the morning. Is that all the stuff you've brought?'

'No, I've got a case at the station.' Elsie remembered her lemonade, and drank it. She had not realized till then how thirsty she was.

'Leave it till to-morrow. Drink up, Helen; here's old Bloxon, taking umbrage.' A tiny little old man with a satchel of newspapers was, Elsie saw, eyeing their table with disfavour and suspicion. Helen raised her glass, and lowered the rest of the contents with what seemed to Elsie incredible smoothness and grace. They went out, into a cool, blue twilight, Leo lifting a hand in greeting, or good-bye, to someone by the bar as they left.

The little ruffles of wind from the water passed, coolly and sweetly, across her face. A stray gull flew overhead and balanced for a moment, with a thin evening cry which seemed different from the strong voices of the gulls at home. She became conscious of her hat, because the wind tugged at it, because the train had given her the beginning of a headache, and because the heads of the others were bare. But she clung to the brim; it would have seemed odd to remove it now. Leo and Helen walked on either side of her towards the ferry. She supposed that Mr. Hicks would have started another drink, but it was so pleasant here that she did not care.

'This is ours,' said Leo. A small dinghy, very tubby and old, was tied near the ferry-boat. Leo took a neat cat-like jump from the high stone quay, landing squarely in the middle. 'It's all right, just get in anyhow, you couldn't upset her.' She steadied the boat with a hand on the mooring-ring, and handed Elsie down with the other.

They set off across the wide, darkening stream, Helen steering in the stern, her fair hair blowing back from her face, looking, as she had looked in the bar, incongruously right. The thick stubby oars dipped smoothly, seeming light to Leo's measured pull. There was nothing incongruous about her; the boat and the river seemed like extensions of herself. She looked simple, happy, and, thought Elsie with a half-resenting wistfulness, like the younger sister of the two. It still seemed unnatural to find herself the taller. She tried to think of conversation, but could not feel that it was important, and was content to answer the others when they asked about her journey and the way she had come. She took off her hat, because after all, this seemed not to matter either, and enjoyed the cool hands of the wind stroking her forehead. The lights of the bank they had left began to recede, honey and amber against the deepening blue. Two or three hundred yards down the river was a little island, full of willow-trees, with a low wooden building at the nearer end. She thought what a picturesque, but inconvenient, place it would be to live in, and wondered who did.

A shadow fell across the water; the gunwale of the dinghy bumped against a matting fender. She saw, above her, a long wooden railing with flaking white paint, and a gap in the middle of it to which the boat had come. Helen jumped out, and helped

Elsie after her on to a platform which gave a little to the water under their feet. They had arrived; it was one of the boats whose unlit windows had misgiven her on the way to the Green Lion. There was still light enough to see its outline; a hull curved bow and stern, like a Noah's Ark, a buxom figurehead breasting up-river; a long low structure full of windows, with a shorter, newer-looking tier above, and, running round the flat roof, a turned railing which might have belonged to the older part before. It was all white paint, rather blistered and shabby; but the shabbiness had a look of affection rather than neglect, like that of much-used toys. Between the lower windows was some sort of crest or device painted over like the rest.

'I'll just take the boat round,' said Leo. 'Go in and get off your things.'

There were two glass doors in the middle, which had stood open so widely that they had only seemed like a gap in the wall. Helen went in ahead of her, and switched on a light. It was, after all, very like a room on land, except for its shape, long and narrow, the windows either side, and the lockers that ran all round so that the lower three feet of the walls was all cupboard-room. Elsie was vaguely surprised to find the furniture quite solid and comfortable; deep armchairs and a wide couch, covered in a soft faded red which matched the curtains and looked warm against the maize-coloured walls and ceiling; a firm-looking table, and, she noticed gratefully when Helen switched it on, a big electric fire (she had thought everything would be done with paraffin). Even the usual offices, to which Helen considerately led her at once, were quite remarkably usual. Through a half-open sliding door, she glimpsed a tiny, compact kitchen-galley, with shelves of butter-coloured china, a sink, and an electric stove. She said, wonderingly, when they got back to the living-room again, 'It's just like a house.'

'Well, I suppose it is one. They only move once in a lifetime or so. Things are only different on ships because of the way they pitch about. Did you think there'd be bunks, and portholes, and everything screwed to the floor? You get that on a launch, of course. They go to sea. We're going to buy a launch one day, when our ship comes in.' She went to one of the lockers, and took out cutlery and a yellow and white cloth.

Elsie, her scramble to help waved aside, sat down on the couch and picked up a couple of magazines which were lying there. One was *The Aeroplane*, and the other was *Vogue*. Hastily rejecting the first, she stared at the quelling elegancies of the second, while half her mind watched Helen moving about the table, and the other, freed for a moment from the jostle of new impressions, was delivered over to a chaos of speculation. It had seemed so impossible, when she saw Leo at last, that she could have been other than she was, that only now Elsie began to remember how little it squared with what she had known before. Perhaps, she thought, their parents had made a terrible mistake. Perhaps they had accused Leo falsely, driving her by the injustice to run away. Or perhaps Leo had pretended as an excuse to go; but Leo had never, she remembered, pretended things very much, only, when it suited her, refused to talk about them. She wondered whether Leo would ever tell her, and knew that she would never have the courage to ask.

The place looked, above all things, permanent, settled, a home, not prosperous perhaps but secure. One couldn't live here, thought Elsie, and work all day in, for instance, an office. Leo had never had any money of her own; she had never even saved, except by fits and starts which ended in a burst of spending. She couldn't have left home with much more than twenty pounds. Was it possible – could it be that she was being Kept by a Man after all? The thought of it, suddenly terrifying because it did not go with a beautiful stranger in a Chinese shawl, but with Leo who was here, brought her back full circle to Peter. She shut her eyes, trying to see him. She remembered that she was within a few miles of him; perhaps another hour, perhaps less, in the train. She had even forgotten that.

A warm, delicious smell began to creep in from the galley.

Scrambled eggs; her stomach seemed to reach out and embrace it. Just then, Leo put her head in through the door; Elsie realized that she must have been in the galley some minutes, having come in by another way. She gave Elsie a quick, cheerful grin, just as she might have done years ago when things were going quietly at home.

'Food in a minute. I should think you could do with it.'

'I do feel hungry. It smells wonderful.'

Leo disappeared; and Elsie thought again about Peter. For the first time, it came to her that she had never told him what Leo was like, how she looked or dressed or behaved; only the one thing which seemed as dreadful as ever now that Leo was the same. It had been filling her mind for weeks; for years it, or the silences in place of it, had been all of Leo that there was to know. She wished that she had told him more. If she had, he would have had a place, now, in all this. He wouldn't have seemed farther away at this moment than he had in Cornwall, after the long base of England had slid between them. There would not have been this groping, forlorn moment when, with her memory stretching and straining, even his face and his voice seemed to blur away. She wanted him here; to tell her that she had done well, that the future was taking shape ahead of her; to reconcile, in his wisdom, the present with her (and his) anticipations. It wasn't his fault. She had never properly told him. She only wanted him here. She tried to imagine him, sitting beside her, telling her that it was all quite simple and what, obviously, would be; that even if Leo – her sister, who had just grinned at her as she did when she brought apples out of her pocket in the school-room – were the mistress of some unknown man who might suddenly appear, making everything different and horrible; still it was all natural and beautiful and mildly funny, and she mustn't mind.

'Here we are,' said Leo in the doorway. She had a tray with three plates on it, mounded with egg which just matched their colour; a juicy crest of fried tomato on top. It looked so good that

Elsie ceased, on its appearance, to be anything more complicated than a hungry schoolgirl. She scarcely ever had such an
appetite at home, even after bathing or the longest walk. Leo and
Helen talked, in the loose disjointed way that arises between
people each of whom knows that the other will have picked up
the meaning before the sentence is half finished. The very fact
that she could not follow half they said was curiously soothing;
no explanations hammered home, no patient re-statements, no
trembling verge of exasperation; only a kind of lazy shorthand.
She felt herself growing warm and sleepy, lulled by the rare
luxury of being able to concentrate entirely upon her food.

'Did *you* cook this?' she asked Leo, half-way through it.

'Yes, why? Does it taste peculiar?'

'No, it's awfully good. But Mother used to say you'd never
give your mind to it.' Many things of this kind were coming back
to her.

'I taught her,' said Helen. She exchanged with Leo the kind of
look which embraces many jokes too old to bear further repeti-
tion.

Leo picked up a crust of bread, and shamelessly polished her
plate with it. 'I suppose,' she said, 'I ought to be asking after everyone. But I gather they're much the same, only rather more so.'

'Yes.' It seemed, indeed, to exhaust the subject. She was a
little shocked by the crudeness of the summary, but even more
relieved by its brevity. Because Helen was there, she added
rapidly, 'Great Aunt Gertrude's dead. She died of cancer. And
Harriet – Aunt Eveline's Harriet, you know – she's married and
has a baby. The place is a lot bigger since you went.'

'Has Father built it all?'

'Most of it. And some are bungalows.'

'It must look like the New Jerusalem.' Leo passed the crust
again, critically, over her plate. Without looking up she said,
'Are the Fawcetts still there?'

'No, Mr. Fawcett died and they moved to Bristol. Tom's still at
sea. He's a first mate now.'

Leo ate her crust, and said when she had finished it, 'I shall
soon be owing him five bob. We had a bet he wouldn't get a
master's ticket before he was thirty-five.'

Elsie was beginning to feel chatty, as she did at the rare times
when she met an old school friend. 'I always thought Tom was a
very nice boy. I expect you missed him when he went to sea.'

Leo looked up from her plate. She seemed to Elsie to have lost
the thread of the conversation, so she repeated her last remark to
make it clearer. 'Oh, yes,' said Leo. 'Yes, Tom was a very good
sort.'

Elsie was saddened by so slight a dismissal of so old a friend. It
brought back again, now that her hunger had been disposed of,
the doubts she had had before. Outside the uncurtained windows, which were now quite dark, vague dispersed creaks and
splashes seemed to her like the sound of approaching oars.
Presently even Leo noticed her strained attention.

'The river's full of noises. Like *The Tempest*, you know. You'll
have earache if you listen to all of them.'

Shielded by the tablecloth, Elsie twisted her hand round and
under her knee. Gripping a fold of stocking, she said, 'I was wondering if you were expecting any visitors. I mean, if you are, I
could do my unpacking. You mustn't ever let me be in the way.'

'*Visitors?*' Leo stared at her, with that blankness which is the
least easily simulated form of surprise. 'At this time of night? It's
nearly eleven. This isn't St. John's Wood, my dear. Even Joe
doesn't often blow in as late as this.' She walked over to the
window, looked out, and added, as if in comment on something
she saw, 'Besides, he's working.'

She turned back into the room and gazed at Elsie, whose
expressive face was full of half-hesitant relief. Suddenly she threw
back her head and laughed. It was a clear, amused laugh, as open
as a schoolboy's; yet, Elsie thought, perhaps after all she had not
remembered it quite right. 'I see,' she said. 'Of course, I should
have thought. I was beginning to wonder what it was they *had*
told you.' Elsie's crimson face made her laugh, quietly, again.

'Don't worry. You've seen the household. All of it. No one belongs here except Helen and me.'

'Oh.' Elsie let out a long breath. 'I'm so . . . I mean, of course –'

'We'll tell each other the story of our lives in the morning.' Leo sat down across one of the chair-arms, and brought out a packet of cigarettes. 'Do you?' she asked, holding it out.

'Well . . . not really, very much.'

'Quite right, they're bad for your wind. I get into it when I'm working.' Helen, Elsie perceived for the first time, was no longer there; she had been vaguely aware of her absence without seeing her go. She had the power of putting herself, as it were, into soft-focus.

Leo struck a match. Across its spurt she said, slowly, 'I suppose this is all pretty different from what you expected.'

'Well, I suppose in a way . . .'

Leo smiled. The lamp was behind her; the flame of the match threw into relief, like the selection of a brilliant caricaturist, the odd slanting lines of her face. She looked, for a moment, different and subtly inhuman, like a mocking Oberon surveying one of the simpler attendants of his Queen. Then the match went out; she pulled at her cigarette, and Elsie saw that her smile was, after all, quite a kindly one.

'You look dog-tired,' she said. 'Helen's fixing up her room for you. You'll be able to turn in in a minute.'

'Oh, no!' Elsie had forgotten this minor fear, preoccupied with the major one. 'No, truly, I shouldn't think of it. Please don't let her. I'll sleep here on the sofa. Really, I sleep awfully well.'

'That's all right. We call it Helen's room. She keeps some of her things in it. We always put people up there.'

These, Elsie knew, were the specious protests of hospitality and sisterly kindness; but she was too sleepy to argue any more. Secretly she had been nervous of being invited to share with Leo. Leo's room at home had always been a kind of fastness, and the thought of invading it unnerved her even now.

'I'm sure it will be lovely,' she said.

It was Helen who took her up. Her room, Elsie decided, was very like her, quiet in its buff and green, neat without fussiness, giving the illusion of space in small compass. It was also entirely free from her personal trifles; even the cupboards and drawers were empty. Elsie admired the tact with which she had eliminated so completely all reminders of the fact that she had been turned out.

'I've put two bottles in the bed,' she said, turning down the green silk eiderdown. 'I do hope it won't be damp. It happens here so quickly.'

'I'm sure it won't be.' Elsie looked, contentedly, round the room again. Her eye was caught by a charcoal sketch, pinned up unframed on the wooden panels of the opposite wall. 'Why, it's Leo,' she exclaimed.

'Yes. Do you think it's like her?'

'Oh, yes,' said Elsie politely. Indeed, it was very like her at the moment when, just now, the light of the match had produced so disconcerting an effect. It was a head and shoulders, the face half-turned, the shoulders bare; the eyes had a look of keeping something amusing to themselves. The technique was spare, hard and bold, and had an odd effect of deliberate ruthlessness.

'It's very clever.' Elsie had learned from her mother to shelve, with this adjective, unsettling ideas. 'Who did it?'

'I did,' said Helen in her gentle indifferent voice. 'I do hope you'll sleep well. I've put you a tin of biscuits in case you get hungry in the night.'

'Are you an artist?' Elsie stared at her in awe and curiosity, mingled with satisfaction at having placed one of them, at least, against a practicable background.

'Goodness, no,' said Helen briskly. 'There are too many artists; and not enough good ones. It's just an amusement. I'm a technical illustrator.'

'Really? What do you illustrate?'

'This sort of thing.' She took a portfolio out of a rack against the wall.

Elsie opened it, phrases of admiration forming ready upon her lips. She stared at one diagram, then turned the page hastily and stared at another, wondering if she had got it the right way up. She had expected designs for jewellery, or evening gowns; not this meaningless, but somehow repugnant, arrangement resembling a nexus of interwoven worms, framed in what looked like folds of cloth. She gave up the effort to be suitable. 'Whatever is it?' she asked.

'A tumour in the frontal lobe of somebody's brain,' said Helen casually. 'Just before they got it out.' She turned on to the next diagram. 'This is a cross-section of an eye. Of course, that had been removed already.'

'Oh.' Fascinated horror kept Elsie's eyes glued to the page. Close behind her shoulder, Helen smelt faintly of some light scent, fresh and warm and silky. Elsie had a feeling that if one more incomprehensible thing happened she would burst into tears.

'Where did you draw them?'

'In the operating theatre,' said Helen, 'of course.'

'But don't you mind?'

'No. Why should I?'

'I'm sure it must be – very interestinsg.' Elsie's mental picture of an operating theatre comprised chiefly a welter of blood and sawn-off limbs. She looked at Helen in a kind of daze. 'But don't you find it rather terrible?'

'A lot less terrible than commercial advertising. It's honest anyway. Besides, I'm a trained nurse, you know.'

'Are you?'

'Yes. Don't I look like one?'

'Not at all,' said Elsie, with heartfelt truth.

'That's fine,' Helen closed the folder and put it away. 'Well, I won't keep you up any longer. I expect you're dropping on your feet. If there's anything you want, knock on the wall. Leo and I will be next door, you know. Good night, and sleep well.'

Elsie undressed mechanically, and, when she was ready,

switched off the bedside lamp. Going over to the window, she put her head out into the moist, murmuring night. The leaves of a willow-tree made a nickering whisper; water slapped stealthily below her; people were singing, to the strum of a ukulele, somewhere in the distance; an owl hooted and a gull cried. Down in the midst of the boat were voices, soft and intermittent, which did not argue or contend, like the voices at home, but went on, evenly and mysteriously, and ceased, and began again. A long way off, it seemed in the midst of the river itself, a solitary light burned. She remembered the island, with its low wooden house; it was too dark now to see its outline, but the light must be there. It winked sometimes, and twinkled like a star, as a branch of the tree close by swung across it in the light wind.

She began to think, as she always thought last thing before she slept, of Peter. She would write to him soon; not yet, but when the jumble in her mind had straightened. She thought how pleased with her daring he would be, how astonished to find that she was so near. The thought of his approval made her feel solid and real, and almost confident in the midst of so much that was lonely and strange. She would see him again! There was that; and there was Leo, who, though one might sometimes be afraid of her, though she still seemed like a creature of another race, had still about her some of the unwritten certainties of childhood; she had never broken a promise, or told tales, or, if she knew where one was hiding, given one away. For to-night, that was enough. She slipped into bed; felt, with her extended toes, beyond the warmth of the bottles, a faint dampness in a fold of the sheet; and, almost in the moment of feeling it, fell asleep.

CHAPTER NINE

She woke to a green light of sun in leaves, and a sensation, curiously unterrifying, that the ground was shaking under her. The movement went on, a gentle rocking and bumping, and died gradually away. She remembered where she was, jumped out of bed, and looked out of the window. The river glittered in a clean, cool, early light. Two great, low barges, linked together, were passing down-stream; it was their wash which had shaken the houseboat. They were almost abreast of the little island, on which no life seemed to be stirring. She dressed quickly. At home she was a lazy riser; only the vague tenacious hopefulness of youth, mixed with the need to avoid trouble, had launched her sluggishly on each returning, motiveless day. She had no idea what time it was, having forgotten to wind her watch last night. It might well be several hours till breakfast, but she did not care. It was good to have this shining, empty world of leaves and water to herself. She curled her toes against the rough matting on the floor; happiness seemed to burst up within her and float out of her, like bubbles, into the surrounding air. It was to Peter, she thought, that she owed all this.

The little wooden door of her room gave out on to a matting-covered balcony, part of the original roof on to which the upper rooms had been built; ladders led from it, up and down. She climbed to the flat top, and stood there in the wind; her hair and clothes blew the same way as the willow-leaves and the waves on the water; she felt like a flag on a mast, floating in blue air above the world.

Someone was moving on the boat; she heard quick, light feet, falling softly, and a creak and click which seemed to belong, not here, but at home. She remembered why; it was like the noise of the pump which, almost every day of her life till now, she had heard drawing up the sparse Cornish well-water to its high cistern. A familiar clear alto began singing quietly to the rhythm.

Says I to the pretty girl, How do you do?
    To me way-oh, blow the man down.
Says she, None the better for seeing of you-oh . . .

Elsie ran down the ladders to the after deck. The pump was real, and just like the one at home. Leo was swinging the upright wooden handle, her faded blue silk pyjamas blown close to her body by the morning breeze. Her bare feet were as brown as her hands. She looked slight, taut and effortlessly happy.

Elsie felt suddenly too neat, too tightly buttoned-up in too many clothes of not quite the right kind. At home, Leo had been the odd one; Elsie's things, a kind of preparatory version of her mother's and those of her mother's friends, had always been in the picture. She hesitated, shyly, on the ladder.

'Hullo.' Leo stopped singing to smile at her. 'You've made a pretty quick comeback. I was going to bring you your breakfast in bed.'

'No, really. I don't feel tired at all. May I do some pumping?'

'If you like. Then I can get the breakfast. I want a swim first, though. I'll wait if you'd like to come in too.'

Elsie eyed the coldly gleaming river. 'Will it be out of my depth?'

'All but a couple of feet by the bank. You can swim, though. Damn it, I taught you.'

Elsie had, till this moment, forgotten it. She had never gone beyond knee-depth, after Leo went. No one else had succeeded (or, for that matter, tried to succeed) in coaxing her out among the Atlantic rollers. It had been Leo who had taught her to dodge their fall, and to launch a surf-board on the white, tumbling rush when they had broken. She had been too small, then, for all but the little ones. Afterwards there had been no one to go with, and the terror of finding one above her, piling itself up by stealth and hanging at its height, had overcome her when she was alone. For a moment she thought of mentioning her bronchitis; but Leo had had a way of looking at one when one made excuses, and, thought Elsie, probably had it still. 'I'd rather pump,' she said. Leo received this untrimmed fact quite cheerfully; she always had.

'All right. Thanks. About fifty turns it wants now.' She stepped out of her pyjamas on the open deck, with an indifference which shocked Elsie though no one was about, pulled on an old swim-suit which had been lying there, and dived, capless, over the side. Elsie swung the pump-handle, watching her dark, wet head and the neat knife-cut of her overarm stroke. She was back just as the pumping was finished, hoisted herself on to the flat floating deck, and went in. Through the open door, Elsie could see her in the galley, naked, putting on a saucepan with one hand and drying herself with the other. Her body was straight, firm and confident; it moved as though clothes were an accident about which it had no particular feeling, for or against. Her skin was creamy-brown all over, except for a belt of white round the loins, across one side of which ran a deep, puckered scar. It looked old, but Elsie felt sure she hadn't had it when she went away. She did not like to ask Leo how she had got it.

'How are you getting on?' Leo came out into the cabin, rubbing her hair. 'You must have done enough by now.'

'I've just finished.' Elsie came in too, and looked out of the window. She was embarrassed, not for Leo but for herself. There was a kind of arrogance in that slender, fluent shape with its small, high breasts, straight shoulders and narrow hips which made her feel as if it were she who had been stripped, and found to be pale and flabby and self-conscious in the light. Lest Leo should notice, she said, brightly, 'I suppose all that water has to be boiled?'

'*Boiled*?' Leo stared, and burst out laughing. 'Lord almighty, you didn't think we were pumping up the Thames to drink? That's the bilge. It seeps in a bit every day; you have to keep shifting it, to prevent the whole joint from sinking. We're on Company's mains. If you look on the land side, you can see the pipes running through the water, along with the electric cables. All the houseboats have it. Not Joe, of course; he has to ferry his drinking-water in every day, and use the river for everything else. Nobody lived there before he did. But he doesn't notice that sort of thing.'

'Who's Joe?' asked Elsie, rather nervously. She felt she had heard the name before, but without its registering. Leo looked at her in vague surprise, as if she had pointed to some object in common use, a chair or a jug, and asked what it was.

'Joe? He lives on the island. He's just the chap next door, as you might say. You'll be seeing him, he's always around.' She unhooked a striped towelling bath-robe from behind the galley door, hitched it round her, and began setting the table. 'You can watch the coffee, if you like.'

'Who lives on the other two houseboats?' Elsie asked. 'The ones on either side?'

'The one down-river belongs to a couple called Jennings. They're only here at week ends. They bought it because it was the only place where Pop Jennings' mother couldn't stay with them; she's rheumatic. They do their best to pretend they're living in comfort at Golders Green, and play bridge every evening to pass the time. You don't play bridge, do you?'

'No, I'm afraid not.'

'Stick to that if you meet them, you won't regret it. Otherwise they're rather sweet. Then the *Anitra* on the other side, the big place with the yellow awnings, that belongs to a technician from Elstree. He isn't here much, but when he is you'll know it. He's quite intelligent when you get him alone, but to keep up with his crowd you need twelve evening frocks and a head like old teak, so we just grin at each other in passing. I'm afraid you won't find much more social life here than you did at home. The bacon's ready; come on and eat.'

'Where's Helen?' asked Elsie, missing the third place.

'Left for town an hour ago. The man she works for to-day starts his list at eight-thirty. Probably she'll be hanging about till after eleven, but she has to be there. She'll be back for tea, I expect.'

'I like Helen,' said Elsie, 'very much.'

'Everyone does.' Leo spoke like one who states a common-place fact.

'She's rather a *deep* character, isn't she? I mean, she makes you feel there must be more in her than meets the eye.'

'Do have some mustard.'

Elsie did not pursue the subject. Conversation with Leo, she remembered, had always been liable to dead ends. In the old days one had come to them with a jolt; but now it no longer seemed to matter, one merely continued with something else. When the meal was over, and cleared away, Leo said, 'Come up to my room and talk to me while I dress. You haven't seen it yet.'

There was a second ladder, in the bow end of the boat. It led straight into Leo's room, a big light one with windows on three sides. Through the ones at the end showed the back of the carved figure-head, a stout nymph whose bosom must have been bared for many years to the breeze, for it was cracked here and there, and weather had blunted her nose; though patches of gilt still clung to her serpentine tresses. The room itself was more like a living-room than a bedroom, and, in places, even more like the garden shed at home where Leo had kept her things. It had become tidier in the interval (Helen would see to that, Elsie thought), the big divan bed had a blue silk cover, the wall-cupboards housed clothes that looked decently kept, and there were many new books; but there was still a corner full of fishing tackle, another corner contained two old canoe paddles and one new one, and a shelf of the book-case was given over to tools.

Elsie wandered round, while Leo brushed her hair and rummaged for clothes. Only two pictures, and in such a big room. Elsie liked them three or four to a wall. One was a photograph of Helen, with all the light coming from one corner and the rest dark; the other a pen-and-ink drawing of a cowboy 'fanning' a bucking horse with his Stetson. She went to the book-case; not very hopefully, for Leo's books had always been disappointing. Time, she found, had brought no improvement. Fishing, sailing, climbing; a beginner's textbook on flying; a huge volume called *Gray's Anatomy* – that would be Helen's, she supposed – Shakespeare, Hakluyt's *Voyages*, a good deal of poetry and some flat, yellow, paper-covered books in French. Perhaps the novels were somewhere else. Over the big roll-top desk there was a shelf that looked more promising; the nine or ten books in it had the red shiny covers with which Elsie felt more at home. She explored them, but with diminishing zest. *Silver Guns*, by Tex O'Hara. *The Mexican Spur*, by Tex O'Hara. *Quick on the Draw, Yippee-ih! Lone Star Trail*, by Tex O'Hara. One might have known; Leo had never possessed what Elsie, following Mrs. Lane, called nice books. She took down *Lone Star Trail*, whose title had some faint suggestion of romance, and sat down with it on the hard chair at the desk,

'I don't suppose,' said Leo without looking round, 'horse-operas are much in your line, are they?'

'This one looks very nice.' Elsie spoke politely; Leo must think highly of Tex O'Hara to have collected what might well be his complete works; perhaps one ought to have heard of him. She dipped into the middle, as her custom was, looking for a love-scene, but encountered, as she had feared, only strife and masculine pronouns.

Leo was dressed, in fawn corduroys and a cream wool sweater. Elsie put down the book without reluctance.

'Do let me help you make the bed.'

'Don't bother, it doesn't take a minute.'

'What a pretty nightgown. Do you wear them for a change sometimes?'

'Good Lord, no, that's Helen's.' Leo folded it, neatly for her, and put it under the pillow. 'She's gone and left all the lids off her powder and stuff again. They won't have any smell. Must have been late getting up – I was too sleepy to notice.' There was a little walnut chest of drawers near the bed, with an eighteenth-century swing glass on top; when Elsie, eager to be helpful, began putting the jars and boxes to rights, the faint scent that came from them seemed to make Helen present in the room. So, Elsie thought, she had turned out with a vengeance, taking all her things, and camped with Leo. It was very good indeed of both of them to put up with it so cheerfully. She would have liked to say so, but felt, for some reason, too shy.

'Well,' said Leo, 'in a minute we'll go out in the canoe and get some food.' She pulled a lipstick out of her pocket, lined in her mouth with a few brisk strokes, lit a cigarette, and sat down with it, cross-kneed on a corner of the bed.

'Look here,' she said. 'About this running away. If you don't feel like talking about it, don't. These things are bad enough when they happen, without digging them up afterwards. On the other hand, if it makes you feel better, go ahead. It does, sometimes; it depends what it was, I suppose.'

Elsie looked at her shoes. She would have been happy, indeed, to talk about Peter: but not now. Everything prevented her; the room, the books, the memory of Leo, brown and stripped and confident, standing in the morning sun and drying her hair.

'Nothing happened really. Except the usual things. It just came to me that I had to get away.'

'You mean,' said Leo, 'that you don't want to go into the final row. Well, I don't blame you. I didn't myself, for a year or two afterwards. It seems odd, though, to think of you bursting out. Didn't Mother mind a good bit when you said you were going? You and she always seemed to belong, somehow.' Her face had a look which, for the second it lasted, took Elsie a long way back. 'I suppose it was Mother who told you where to find me You know, don't you, whatever she said at the time, sooner or later she'll be here to bring you home?'

'She won't,' said Elsie. 'Nobody will.' She stared, again, at the floor between her feet. Suddenly Leo seemed too sharply out-lined, too direct and clear, to be looked at without flinching. 'There wasn't any row. No special one, I mean. Mother doesn't know I know where you are, or anything about you. I – I looked in her drawer when she was out, and found the address.'

'Oh,' said Leo slowly. 'I see.' She pulled at her cigarette. Elsie moved her shoe a little, watching a crack across the toe. 'I think, if you don't mind, you'd better just tell me this. Are you going to have a baby?'

'Why, no!' Elsie was so shocked that she looked up. Leo was gazing at her, thoughtfully, with her light-brown eyes; her brows were contracted a little, as if she were trying to understand some-thing difficult. 'Of course not, Leo. I mean, I've never . . .' She knew no way of saying it, and stopped.

'All right,' said Leo. 'Sorry. I only asked because I couldn't think of any other reason to do it . . . Mother was so fond of you. You and she did everything together. You dress like her, even now.'

'It wasn't anything – anything sordid. I just wanted to live a life of my own.'

Leo looked at her cigarette smoke. A faint smile, half bitter and half amused, moved the corners of her long mouth.

'You mean,' she said, 'you got sick of it. Don't you think per-haps you'd better just scribble a note to Mother to let her know you haven't been knocked on the head and put in a brothel? She probably thinks you have. Helen can post it for you, in town.'

She had spoken quite coolly; but the sense of injury and injustice prickled under Elsie's skin. She did not, as she would have done at home, put it into words; but Leo answered it.

'I never pretended. I never wanted them to pretend. If they ever faced a single plain fact in their lives, they must always have known that I'd go away. Even before I told them so . . . I'm sorry. I've no right to talk like this. I got out eight years ago. The fact is, I suppose, I always excused myself by thinking they had you.'

Elsie looked away, trying to think of Peter; Peter who had made her feel exalted, emancipated, brave and in the right. She had kept faith with his revelation; but he was not here to tell her so. Only Leo was here, lighting absently another cigarette, perplexed, uncompromising, cruelly real. Elsie snatched her handkerchief up from the hem of her stocking, and burst into tears.

'I can't help it,' she sobbed. Confused thoughts, which she had never shaped consciously even to herself, broke from her in words, to which she listened as if someone else were speaking. 'I'm not like you. I can't live like that, standing by myself and fighting everyone. I haven't wanted to be deceitful. I wanted to be good to both of them, and for everyone to be happy. It's easy for you to talk, you've never tried. You don't know what it's like to think up something that will please one of them, and know if you do it the other will behave as if you'd done it to hurt them. And in the end you just never do anything, you're afraid even to *be* anything, you just go on one day after another, making yourself smaller, and flatter, and duller; you daren't say yes or no because it's sure to be taking sides, you feel mean and wicked if you go out of a room and mean and wicked if you stay. You've forgotten what it's like to try extra hard to be good and find you're more in the wrong than ever . . . I know I've been underhand, going to Mother's drawer and saying I was spending the day in Newquay. It makes you underhand. And now you say I'm wrong, too. I may as well go back. I'll never know how to live properly. I'll make a mess of everything I do.'

Leo had blown out her match before it touched the tobacco. Slowly she put the unlit cigarette back in the box, and got to her feet. She came round behind Elsie and put a hand on her shoulder. Her touch was diffident and Elsie, shut in her own misery, did not feel it.

'Elsie. Elsie, stop a minute. Don't. There's nothing to cry about.'

But Elsie, deaf and blind, wept on.

'Shut up!' shouted Leo in her ear. 'Stop it! I want to speak to you.' A sharp twinge of pain shot through her shoulder, as Leo's strong fingers dug into it. She winced, gulped, and opened her eyes.

'What is it?'

'Well, when you've got a minute to listen, I just wanted to say I'm sorry. I've been a fool. I often am. What do you want to do?'

'I don't know. I thought I'd train at something. I've got fourteen pounds.'

'We'll think later. Don't worry; you can stay here as long as you like. No, I mean it, we'd love to have you.'

Elsie was silent; only her eyes ran over again. She wondered, as she mopped them, why sudden kindness should produce this effect; there seemed no sense in it.

'I'll be a nuisance to you,' she sniffed.

'Of course you won't. You'll probably be a great help. Look how you did the pumping.' She retrieved her cigarette and lit it. 'Helen and I spend a lot of time working. I hope you won't be bored.'

A momentary concern arrested Elsie's tears. 'You'll get into trouble, staying away because of me.'

'That's all right.' Leo looked a little amused. 'I take a morning off now and again. I'll do some in the afternoon. Come on, let's get out the canoe.'

'I'll just get my hat.'

'Hat? Don't be crazy. What you want to do is powder your nose. Use some of mine.'

The canoe was beached, in the garden. To find a garden was such a surprise that Elsie forgot the aching sensation of recent tears. It ran the length of the houseboat, reached by a little plank bridge, and ran about a dozen yards deep along the bank; it was fenced with a white wooden rail overgrown with ramblers, which, as thick as a hedge, overflowed the top of it and dripped down again into the long grass of the lawn. There was a rickety arch, covered with roses too – some of them had the beginning of buds already – and, in the tangled grass, an apple-tree in flower. The willow she had seen from her window grew there too, at the water's edge.

'It's in rather a mess,' said Leo unregretfully. 'We just do it when we feel like it, you know. You'll have to watch out in the canoe, if you're not used to them. It's just a question of sitting tight.' It was a Canadian canoe, not at all new, but light, slender and well made. Leo, holding it steady, showed her how to drop her weight all at once into the middle. It seemed, at first, terrifiyingly unstable; but, as with a bicycle, the sense of balance came in time. They glided out into mid-river; Leo, perched in the stern, dipped the single paddle with long firm strokes, almost soundless, which thrust them forward with effortless speed. 'There's Joe,' she said suddenly, and lifted the paddle over her head with a carelessness which rocked them dangerously, so that Elsie, clutching the sides, was too frightened to look at the island and see who replied, and next moment they had turned away. She watched Leo instead. Her face was quiet, open and impersonally happy. She looked, Elsie thought, like a nice boy but less alarming. It seemed, at this moment, strange ever to have been afraid of her; stranger still to have taken seriously the things that were said at home. Elsie wondered, all over again, what reckless scrape could have created the misunderstanding.

'A penny for them,' Leo said.

Elsie blushed; but here in the sunlight, with the fresh wind in her face and the open water ahead, there seemed no undertones, no mystery, no danger except the decreasing one of upsetting the canoe. She smiled and said, 'Nothing, really.'

'What did you expect me to be like?'

'Well – I suppose I expected you to have changed a lot.' Suddenly and to her own surprise, a gust of confidence carried her on. 'I mean, I see now there must have been a mistake. Or perhaps they meant something else, and I missed the point. They sort of – said things, you know, without saying them. And nobody talked about you, as if there was something queer. And then my being away at Aunt Lottie's when it happened, and everyone refusing to say where you were and that I'd know when I was older . . . you don't ever like to ask, when people say that.'

Leo trailed the paddle; the canoe glided onward with its accumulated speed.

'Well, if you feel old enough now, why didn't you ask me?'

'I was going to. But I didn't know if you'd like it.'

'Compared with watching you deliberate about it,' said Leo, 'it's a holiday.' Her voice was light and careless; but to know that after all these years it was coming now so simply, gave Elsie the sensation that everything around them was standing still to listen. 'It's a long time ago. Eight years. I can't think how you managed not to find out. But I suppose you didn't want to very much. One wouldn't. Did you get the general impression that I ran away with a man?'

Elsie put her hand over the side, and fished up from the cold pull of the water a strand of weed. Examining it closely, she said, 'Well, yes, I suppose.'

'Don't look so nervous. You're not having breakfast at home now. Of course I did.'

'Oh,' said Elsie. She pulled off some of the weed and dropped it back into the water.

'Well, you must have known that.' Leo dipped the paddle again; a movement as easy and unconscious as walking. 'How astonishingly tactful ordinary people are. You've lived all these years in the village and nobody ever told you who it was?'

'I didn't think it would be anyone I knew.'

'How could it be anyone you didn't? It was Tom Fawcett.'

'Tom *Fawcett*?' Her imagination stopped of its own accord, unassisted. She remembered only an overgrown, light-haired schoolboy who made elementary jokes with the unpredictable effects of a half-broken voice, and had a reputation for foolhardiness on the cliffs.

'I don't think you met him,' said Leo, 'after he went to sea.'

'I hardly met him at all. I didn't know he was back, or there when it happened. Nobody said.'

'Social amenities are a wonderful thing.' The smoothness of Leo's stroke disguised its increasing force and speed. Her face looked bright and hard. She seemed, Elsie thought, very cheerful about it all. 'It's a silly story. You may as well have the whole thing and get rid of it, mayn't you? There's nothing to it, anyway.'

With sudden inspiration, Elsie said, 'So *that's* why we stopped calling on the Fawcetts any more.'

'Yes, that would be why.'

'I used to think,' Elsie's voice was tinged with faint regret, 'that it was an artist.'

'Well, no.' Leo's mouth curled at the corners, making her look a little like Helen's portrait of her. 'No, not exactly. Look out, keep her steady while this launch goes by.'

The canoe bobbed and plunged on the triangular wash; but Elsie was too preoccupied to think about drowning. When the water was smooth again, Leo said, 'He'd just finished his first year as an apprentice. He had an extra spell of leave, as it happened, because his ship had fouled a lighter and sprung some plates. He came straight home from Avonmouth to please his people, instead of going up to town on a binge with the others, and of course he got a bit restless and bored. We saw a good deal of each other. I envied him like hell, naturally, and wanted to hear all about it; and we had a look round some of our old climbs. And one morning one of us, I forget which, said, 'What about that thing we always said we'd do, climbing the Green Man and staying there till the next low tide?' You know the Green Man.'

Elsie nodded. It was a great tooth broken off from the point of the headland, with a grass cap on its flattened top, and sides like those of a tower.

'*Can* one climb the Green Man?'

'Oh, Lord, yes, we'd done it before. So we thought we would. We got up it all right, and the tide came in according to plan, and surrounded us – it runs to about fifty feet out there – and it was all rather fun. We still had plenty to talk about, or rather Tom had, and it was quite amusing when the sea was right up and the spray breaking round. But it was a long time going out, and we finally got to the end of our conversation. So after a while Tom told me what a nice girl I'd grown into, and started kissing me. It was a bit of a novelty – to me, at any rate – and it seemed to pass the time as well as anything, so we kept it up for a bit. It's a place that gives you the feeling of being very remote from everywhere; all the houses, and so on, on shore look rather like toys. I suppose it can't have occurred to us that a couple of people on the Green Man, at high tide, are rather more noticeable from the other way on. Anyway, Father got the field-glasses out, and before long, he and Mother were snatching them from hand to hand. At least, that's what I gathered when I got back.

'Well, I suppose I expected some sort of dressing-down, for the climb. But Father had hardly started before Mother wanted to know when the engagement was going to be announced. The sort of thing one can laugh off if one's had time to think of it oneself beforehand. Silly to get annoyed, anyway. Father, of course, immediately took the opposite line, and said no one was likely to have me after making a public show of myself. And they started on each other, fixing the blame for my upbringing. You can guess. I suppose I was feeling a bit on edge, what with one thing and another. Anyhow, I said they could settle my future between them any way they liked, because I wouldn't be there; and left rather quickly. I went blinding along, the way one does, and ran slap into Tom, who'd been down to the village. He knew what it was like at home of course, who doesn't, so I didn't need to explain much; I just said I was going away and not coming back. I don't suppose I really meant it. But Tom said 'Damned good show, let's go together somewhere.' After that I didn't like to back down; I never had with Tom about anything before.

'So we just doubled back and collected a few things. When I got in I could hear them still at it. I went upstairs and packed a rucksack without disturbing them. Tom told his people some story about having run into an old pal who'd asked him down for the week-end, and we met up at the station, with our luggage, under the eyes of the vicar's wife, who was there meeting some-one's train. We thought that was the funniest thing yet. We decided we'd go as far as Exeter and then think where to go next. So we did that.'

'And where did you go next?' asked Elsie after an expectant pause. Leo seemed to have forgotten to finish; she was exchang-ing salutes with a weathered-looking man in a new, pencil-thin sculler.

'That's Bill Brooks,' she told Elsie, as if this were more inter-esting and important. 'He builds boats.'

'Does he? You were going to tell me where you went to, after you got to Exeter.'

'Where we went? Oh, nowhere. At least, nowhere together. Soon after we got to Exeter, we decided it wasn't such a good idea, after all.'

Elsie loosed a deep sigh of relief. She had known, she said to herself, that it had only been something like this. But how good it was to have it said, clear and tidied away; no more doubts, no dark corners. The sunny morning, unshadowed now, expanded her heart.

'What a *good* thing,' she said earnestly, 'that you realized in time.'

'Yes.' Leo looked at the twist of her paddle in the water. 'Wasn't it?'

'But then what happened?' Elsie prompted; her sister's attention showed, again, an irritating tendency to wander. 'What did you do next? How did you get here?'

'Oh, the next part's even sillier. I thought after that I'd go up to London.'

'But why didn't you come home? I mean, if you hadn't . . .'

'Well, there was the vicar's wife. And besides, I didn't feel like it . . . Tom was a bit worried about what was going to happen to me. You might say, I suppose, that he could have thought of that sooner; but we were both only nineteen, and he'd had a year of taking life pretty much as it came. I didn't want him fussing. I cooked him a tale about someone in town who'd promised to get me into journalism any time I liked, so that cheered him up, and we went our various ways. He was too scared to go back home himself; I don't altogether blame him, old Fawcett was Anglo-Indian and frightfully pukka, if you remember. However he was all right, because he was due to sail in a few days anyway so he didn't have long to lie low. I expect his people had simmered down by the time he got home again.'

'I do think,' said Elsie, giving the judgment due weight, 'that after he'd compromised you, he ought to have looked after you better than that.'

'Oh, rubbish. I ran my head into it. He did try to give me what money he had, poor kid, and I wasn't very nice to him about it . . . There's nothing I blame Tom for. Nothing at all.'

She had spoken the last words as if they had been a summary and a conclusion. Once again, Elsie had to urge her on.

'And what did you do in London?'

'I took some rather peculiar digs near Paddington Station. I'd never been in town before. Then I bought a lot of papers such as the *Telegraph*, that have advertisements for jobs. If I'd had a shilling for every time they used the words 'experience essential,' I wouldn't have needed a job at all. I got a secondhand typewriter for five pounds and spent my spare time – well, it was all spare really, of course – teaching myself to type. When I could do it nearly as quickly as writing, I tried some of those little articles that look so easy, and sent them in to various periodicals; need-less to say, they all came back. I earned thirty bob one week addressing envelopes, and another ten the next selling silk stock-ings, but I didn't like that so I stopped. I always typed hard in the evenings, because a tart lived in the room next door, and the sounds that came through were rather off-putting if you didn't make some sort of noise. As the journalism seemed to be getting nowhere, I dug out some old exercise books I used to scribble in at home, and typed them out instead. In the morning, of course, I looked for jobs But all the simple ones, like holding horses out-side theatres, seemed to have gone out. I tried the Labour Exchange, and they offered to send me to a hostel and train me for domestic service. They said it wouldn't cost me a penny, but I put it off for a bit; after all, fish and chips are pretty cheap. But whether the fish was bad one evening, or what it was, I don't know; I started having pains in my stomach, and one night I woke up feeling so odd that I had to knock up the tart – who was pretty decent about it, luckily the last customer had gone by then – and get her to go for a doctor. It was rather embarrassing, as I hadn't enough money to pay him; but luckily that didn't arise, because he promptly whistled up an ambulance and had me delivered to the hospital. They had me in the theatre about half an hour later. I'm never sure how much of that night I remember or whether I dreamed some of it. The only thing I'm really sure about is being sick afterwards into a rather chipped enamel pot.

'I got quite used to being there later, because the appendix had gone bad in some way and didn't heal, and I had rubber tubes stuck through the seam and it was all rather sordid. In fact, I didn't see much prospect in it all. I noticed the doctor used to take the sister carefully out of earshot before discussing me, and I knew what that meant; but it gets not to matter. I used to be a little dimmer every day, and go off into long dozes and forget where I was.

'Then, one night, I woke up while the night-nurse was stand-ing by my bed, and I noticed something white on the locker and said 'What's that?' 'It's a letter,' she said. 'It must have been there all day, don't you want to read it?' She was a nurse I hadn't seen before and I thought she looked rather nice, so I said, 'You read it, do you mind, and tell me what's in it.' I suppose I must have been feeling pretty vague not to have thought of its being probably a demand for the rent. Anyway she opened it and said, 'It's to say that a story of yours is going to be published in September, and will thirty pounds' advance royalty do? I didn't know you were a writer.' 'Nor did I,' I said. 'What's the story called, do they say?' Even after she read out the title I couldn't for the life of me remember posting it off. She called it amnesia, which made it sound rather grand, and said it was nothing to worry about, and could I remember the plot? The funny thing was, I did, and told her. We talked for ten minutes – I realized later it was the first time I'd conversed with anyone for about a week – and then I slept for four hours, which is a lot in hospital, and woke feeling fine. By the way, we're just about to land. Don't try to get out before I do; I'll hold the canoe for you.'

Elsie scrambled ashore. It was fortunate that Leo made this operation foolproof, for she was concentrating on it very little. She was anxious to continue the conversation, but Leo's rapid and decisive progress from shop to shop (she hated household marketing) made this impossible. It was not until the cargo was stowed and they were paddling home that she found opportunity to say, tentatively; 'Do you still write books?'

'Yes, of course. About two a year. That's what I live on.'

'Would you mind awfully if I read one of them?'

'You've got one there, you ass.'

From home-acquired habit rather than purpose, Elsie had brought *Lone Star Trail* along with her. Leo kicked at it with a shabby brown sandal.

'Oh.' Elsie's voice went sharply upwards, not so much from surprise as because Leo had made the canoe wobble. 'But it says Tex O'Hara.'

'Be your age, girl. Who do you suppose is going to buy a

Western signed Leonora Lane? I shouldn't waste your time on that one. It's full of howlers. I did it before I knew Joe.'

Elsie gazed at her sister with slowly-widening eyes. Almost her bright Bohemian visions were ready to re-form.

'Then really you're a famous author all the time.'

Leo looked at her helplessly, began to say something, and thought better of it. After a controlled pause, she asked, 'Would the expression "a competent hack" convey anything to you? Even the top-line Western practitioners aren't what you might call literary giants, you know.' Her irritation dissolved suddenly in a laugh. 'All the same, it's pretty good fun.'

The fact that she seemed to mean this made Elsie feel deflated. Indeed, what she had read of the story had sadly borne it out; it had looked the sort of thing a lively but unintellectual young man might write for boys.

'But after all your experiences . . .'

'When I write,' said Leo, 'I like to enjoy myself.'

'But don't you sometimes long to write a *great* book?'

Leo grinned. 'The book you got that one out of wasn't great, anyway,' she said. 'If you knew any frustrated geniuses, you'd be damned glad not to be staying with one. A couple of cocktails is enough, take it from me . . . Personally I always think people are rather sickening who make out they could write better than they do. It's like losing a game and then saying you didn't try. I do what I like doing, and do it as well as I can, and make a living at it; and you can't ask much more of life than that, can you?'

Elsie said, 'No, I suppose you can't.' Privately, she was unable to imagine how anyone could ask much less. Was it possible, she wondered, that Leo was concealing something from her? After so full and evidently truthful a recital, there seemed little room for it. It had never been easy, at any time she could remember, to know beforehand what would content Leo. She gave it up. By way of saying something, so that conversation should not languish, she enquired, 'And how did you and Helen get to know each other?'

Leo looked at her in surprise.

'But I told you that. Surely. She was the night-nurse at the hospital. You can't have been listening. That was really the whole point of the story.'

CHAPTER TEN

L eo bit the end of her pen, and stared out of the window beyond her desk. Late afternoon sun caught the gilded hair of the *Lily Belle*'s figurehead like a fiery halo; she blinked, and returned to the writing pad in front of her.

'Sitting astride the shattered window-frame,' she wrote, 'his Colt balanced on his knee, the unknown rider laughed. It was a quiet laugh, but Cavallo stiffened where he stood; he had heard it once before. He knew: even before the mask was lifted from the lean, coldly smiling face, he saw the ungloved hand that held the gun, and on it his old brand, the Bar-Q; the brand he had blotted everywhere that he had made it. Everywhere but here.

'"Montana Mick!" His voice rattled in his throat.'

Leo, who was beginning to feel that this would be enough for to-day, paused to light a cigarette. With the matches in her pocket were a couple of letters, which she had omitted to read when the post came in, and she opened them.

The first was long, personal, and offended, beginning, 'My dear Leo – Your behaviour at our last meeting came as something of a shock, and in view of a certain evening last week, I think I have some excuse for feeling bewildered. You gave me, as far as I remember, no cause to imagine . . .' and so on, for several pages.

Leo skimmed the first and last of them, tore all four quickly in half, and dropped the pieces into the basket. The second was a shorter and more formal affair: 'Dear Mr. O'Hara, I have read all your books and am writeing to ask you if you can send me the adress of a ranch that is taking beginners,' ending correctly, 'I hope you are well, yours respectfully, Ernest William Smith.' She read this one carefully through, and put it into a pigeon-hole marked 'Urgent.'

Stimulated, she turned to the beginning of the chapter she had been working on, made one or two corrections, and settled down to writing again. As concentration deepened, her face grew expressionless, shut-in and plain, and a loose strand of hair slipped down over her forehead. Her fountain-pen scratched on. She did not hear Helen coming till she was inside the room.

'Hullo, darling,' she said absently.

'Don't stop, I'm early. I'll get the tea.'

'I have stopped, really; but I had a fan-letter and it started me off again. What did you do?'

'Oh, a ridiculous afternoon. Scuttling backwards and forwards between two theatres, from a cerebellar astrocytoma to a bone-graft on a maxilla. Of course the crucial moments were almost simultaneous. However, Harvey took me to the Savoy Grill at the end of it.'

'Becoming expensive, aren't you?' Leo tilted her cigarette and one eyebrow.

'Oh, it didn't matter. David can't afford it and Lewis would regard it as an investment, but Harvey can and doesn't, so he's all right. You've done a lot. What's happening, is Mick still going around in that mask? It seems a pity when he's so good-looking.'

'He's just taken it off to shoot up the half-breed.'

'Let's look . . . You know, I don't think you ought to say "with a vile oath" so often. It will lead the reader to suspect that you don't really know any.'

'Well, I don't, in Spanish, do you? I made him say "Caramba!"

a paragraph ago, and I doubt if it's all that vile, anyway. What's the Spanish for bastard?'

'You ought to buy a dictionary.'

'It's sure to be something awfully colloquial. Joe may know some. But his are generally too vile to pass the publisher's reader.'

'I met Joe on the station. He said he was looking in.'

'Oh, did he? If I'd known he was going up to town I'd have asked him to see if those galleys were in. Did you tell him about Elsie?'

'Only that she was staying here. However, he's eager to meet her. He asked me whether she was like you. I said the family resemblance wasn't very striking.'

Leo put down her cigarette. 'There's only one thing,' she said slowly, 'that could make me more worried about keeping Elsie than I am already.'

'What's that?'

'A feeling I have that you don't much like her, and that in spite of everything you said last night, you don't want her here.'

'I did mean it. I should never have forgiven you if you'd turned her away. She's like someone coming up for the third time, isn't she? Suppose she were my sister instead of yours.'

'The fact remains that she isn't your sister, and this is your home.'

'It isn't that.' Helen took one of Leo's cigarettes and lit it abstractedly. Her dark, trim town suit, with its glimpse of crisp white collar between the revers, looked out of place against Leo and the room. 'I don't dislike her – what has she got that one could dislike? – and I don't mind having her about. After five years we'd be rather maudlin if we couldn't bear not to live tête-à-tête for a week or two. And we can manage the money, of course, if we're careful. But – well, yes, I suppose I do resent her. Not because of herself, because of you.'

'Me? How?'

'Isn't it obvious?' Helen's softness and gentleness were suddenly absent; even her physical contours seemed to have hardened a little. 'It's all being made so easy for her. You didn't see yourself in that ward all those nights. You forget, I suppose; but I don't, not in eight years or eighteen. And now she comes along, the good little girl, who's never been short of a square meal, or had anything worse to put up with than a little family bickering; she takes it perfectly for granted that you'll wrap her up in cotton-wool and absorb all the shocks, and thinks she's been through a heroic ordeal because she's crossed England in the train without her mother putting her in charge of the guard. Why should she fall on her feet? What about you?'

'I fell on my feet too,' said Leo with her dark slanting smile. 'Didn't I?'

'That's an evasion.'

'There's nothing to evade. You're being ridiculous.'

'I know. But I can't help feeling it.'

'Give her credit for the pluck she has. She couldn't be sure she'd find anyone here.'

'She had her return fare, and she'd have used it.'

'You don't mean half you say. If she came in now you'd be nicer to her than I would.'

'She's so helpless. I do it in spite of myself.'

'Well, after all this, here she still is. We'll have to think. Maybe we can find her a job.'

'Can she do anything?'

'Of course not. What about that tea?'

'Wait while I change.' Helen unbuttoned her jacket and tossed her blouse, which looked as fresh as a narcissus, into the linen-basket. 'I met Roger Brent to-day,' she said presently. 'He gave me a cocktail.' She looked up from folding her skirt to watch Leo's face.

'Oh,' said Leo, putting her papers together. 'How's he keeping?'

'He kept me for three-quarters of an hour, not counting the time he took coming to the point. As far as he ever did come to it. I guessed what had happened, from his taking notice of me at all.'

'I'm sorry. I ought to have told you. I would have done if I'd remembered you might run into him. Was he embarrassing?'

'He has his pride, I suppose, like anyone else. He just looked unhappy, and asked me casual-seeming questions about your psychology.'

'How awful. I'm sorry. He suddenly got boring about a week ago. I did mean to tell you. I suppose I was feeling too sick about it, at the time. What did you say?'

'Some form of mild euthanasia. That you were liable to moods and it was better to let you alone till they passed off even if it took some time. He knew what that meant, he isn't a fool . . . Why ever did you let it happen? You must have seen it coming on; even I did.'

'Oh, I know. I hoped I was wrong, I suppose. He's fun to be with, you know, full of good talk. And then, when it began, it seemed all right, for half an hour . . . If you want his side of the story, it's in the waste-paper basket. I think I only tore it in half.'

'Damn it, Leo. You can be a cad.'

'That's what Roger found.'

'But why? You wouldn't hear a breath against him. He's the same person.'

'He was a friend of mine.'

'Well, you might be fair to him now.'

'I know,' said Leo wearily. 'Do you think I don't realize? I liked Roger, we got on together. Nothing's fair.'

'Did he set about it badly?'

'Rather well, I think. I hardly remember, now . . . Yes, it was my fault, of course. Don't ask me why I do it, because I don't know. It's like going on a blind, only the damage is more lasting. I hoped I'd grown out of it.'

'But, my dear, what of it? Why not take it as it comes? Roger isn't heavy in hand. He even has a sense of humour, within reason. You could have amused yourself while you felt like it, and no bones broken.'

'I thought that too.' Leo looked out of the window, at the

fading sun on the figurehead's gilt hair. 'I always do, till it's too late.'

'But what happened? From what I could gather between the lines, you must have fairly sliced him up.'

'Nothing happened.' Leo got up and stood, with her hands in her pockets, looking down the river. 'He was no more good to me, that's all. Nor I to him. So I cut it out.'

From the folds of the frock she was pulling over her head, Helen said, 'I thought perhaps this time . . . You seemed to like him so much.'

Without looking round, Leo said, 'It's always someone I like. That's the hell of it. That's how it all began.'

'My dear, I know. For a year or two, perhaps. But all this while . . . A boy of nineteen. Who told you baldly that the two previous women in his life were prostitutes in – where was it? – Cairo and Shanghai?'

'He didn't tell me that to be beastly. He was trying to apologize.'

'Well, if you can see all that –'

'Oh, God, I can see it. I saw it at the time. I can remember. I thought how straight and decent he really was; I knew that. I'd known him for years. I'd knock anyone else down, I thought, who spoke to him like this. And if I'd had anything to do it with quickly, before I'd had time to think, I believe I'd have killed him . . . How do I know it was his fault at all? Perhaps I'd have treated anyone like that. Roger, perhaps. That's what I thought, when it came to the point.'

'Roger's an adult, civilized man. You know that. You know it wouldn't be the same.'

'But I might be. How do I know? I liked him too much. I couldn't risk it. It was for his sake, really; because we'd been friends. But it has to be someone you like. You see, there's no answer. It's time I gave up looking for one.' She turned back from the window, into the room. 'After all, what does it matter? My life's good enough as it is. I'd only spoil it. The only thing I really mind is – well, just knowing there's something one hasn't got the guts to face. But at least one needn't take it out on other people. I never will again. For heaven's sake let's do something about this tea. I'm empty.'

Helen put her puff and lipstick away with her gentle, precise movements. Like one who continues a conversation, she said 'Elsie ought to have got the tea, while you were working. She'd be some use if I could train her to look after you when I'm not there. She can start by helping with the washing-up.'

CHAPTER ELEVEN

It was not her book – a promising one from the twopenny library, entitled *Stargleam* – or the sleepy afternoon sun on the deck, which had carried Elsie, oblivious, past tea-time, and the first stirrings of a healthy appetite. She had been writing, and with a concentration more earnest than Leo's. She was composing a letter to Peter.

In a sheltered spot in the stern, she had assembled a pile of cushions and settled with her writing-block on her knee, glad of the silence that had settled on the boat since lunch-time. She wrote slowly, filling in the lengthy intervals between the sentences by watching the passing river traffic, and enjoying to the full the waves of melancholy, yearning, adoration, and hope which her occupation engendered. The thought of Peter filled her, as water fills a cup. It also invaded her literary style.

'It is wonderful to be free,' (she wrote) 'and living among untrammelled' (how many l's? Perhaps unshackled would be safer) 'unshackled people. Life here is all and more than I hoped for, and I feel that for me a new phase has begun.' She paused here for some time; the moment had evidently come for description, and this, she found, was where the difficult part began. 'My sister lives a very Bohemian life,' she continued triumphantly, 'on a houseboat where she has lived since she became successful.

She has told me all about her love affair but I feel that perhaps I ought to treat that in confidence.' (She liked very much the grown-up look of this.) 'Her life was tragic for a time but she has surmounted it.' Leo, she thought, couldn't possibly mind that.

She raised her eyes, in search of further inspiration. They met those of a youngish man in a punt, which he was poling expertly and straight towards her. For a moment, indeed, she thought he was about to ram the *Lily Belle*; but a last-minute leverage on the pole brought him up alongside. He was square-built but lean, wearing dirty grey flannel slacks and a thick leather belt of great age. Above the waist he was bare and very brown. He was probably in the early thirties. He eyed Elsie with interest, but had the air of one who takes his own presence for granted. His eyes were screwed up against the sun; he had coarse, curly hair, dry with weather, and an intelligent, contented face.

'Hullo,' he said. 'Is Leo working, do you know?'

'I – I think she is, said Elsie, in a flutter. She had never seen so much of a man at such close quarters, and was anxious to conceal the fact that it disconcerted her. He had crisp bleached hair on his forearms, a shade lighter than his tanned skin; long tough muscles showed when he moved. His forehead was wet along the hairline, and he breathed audibly; he had been punting fast. Elsie found him rather overwhelming. 'I'll go up,' she said, scrambling to her feet, 'and let her know you're here.'

'No, don't do that. I was only going to give her a shout to say I'd be along later. But you can tell her. How are you liking it here?'

'Very much, thank you. I'm having a lovely time. Are you sure you wouldn't like me to fetch Leo down?'

'No, it'll interrupt her. I was only passing. So long; see you later, I expect.' He leaned hard on the punt-pole, and, crouching till his hands were almost in the water, glided away with gathering speed. Elsie, who had not had nearly time to get used to the fact of his being there, and only now remembered that in order to announce him to Leo it would be necessary to know his name, gazed after him with her mouth slightly open. It was some time before the letter got under way again.

'She is a very independent person. She does not seem to take much notice of the men who come round to see her, but they keep on calling. It is difficult to know what she thinks about it as she is very reserved really I think.' A sudden emergence of female instinct caused her to add, to her own surprise, 'I have just been meeting one of them; he seems very nice and I am expecting to meet him again this evening.' She gazed at this sentence for some time, and was on the point of crossing it out, but, getting more used to it on a second reading, liked it and decided not to. After all, she thought, none of it was untrue.

'She has a great friend, called Helen Vaughan, who also lives on the boat. She is very artistic, and has a very interesting job in town, drawing pictures of operations. I think she leads a rather exciting life though she does not talk much about it. She is very pretty and wears lovely clothes, but has a very sweet nature.

'I forgot to mention what my sister does. She is a novelist.' She re-read this several times, feeling quite impressed by it herself. Surely Peter would think her worth knowing now! 'She writes . . .' The pen hung in mid-air, and wavered. Elsie went over the letter again, from the beginning. It only made her more acutely aware of an approaching drop in the intellectual temperature. She found herself wishing that Leo had written even one book with a title like, say, *The Problem of Sex*, or *Whither Womanhood?* which might tempt Peter, with a promise of intellectual equality, to come and call. 'She writes . . .' Leo's most recent work, she had found on a re-examination of the shelf in some such hope, was called *Rustlers' Roundup*. A gull, leaning for a moment flat-winged on the air before her, gave a derisive mew. Its unwinking eye must, however, have conveyed some message, for Elsie's pen came down with sudden decision. 'She writes under a *nom de plume*, which she keeps a secret, but actually her books are very well known.'

Her sigh of relief was interrupted by voices, and the sound of a closing door; Helen must have come back while her attention was elsewhere. She folded the writing-pad; there would be time to think of a final paragraph after tea.

'Would you like to come out into the kitchen with me?' asked Helen, with gentle decision, when they had greeted one another. 'I expect you'd like to know all the workings.'

'Thanks ever so,' said Elsie, much flattered at having her company sought. At the galley door she paused, remembering something.

'Oh, Leo. A man came and said he was coming to see you, and I'm awfully sorry, but I forgot to ask him his name.'

'What sort of man?' said Leo quickly. Her face looked as it had when she had first recognized Elsie in the Green Lion.

'Well – not any special sort. I mean –'

'Did he come by the ferry?' Leo pulled a spoon, which she happened to be holding, through her fingers.

'No, he came in a punt. I think,' she added bashfully, 'he must live in the neighborhood, because he only had a pair of trousers on.'

Outside in the galley, Helen began to laugh quietly.

'Oh, Lord, she means Joe.' Leo was laughing too; as if, thought Elsie with faint annoyance, it were she who had made some amusing error. 'Thank God for that. I was forgetting you hadn't met him. Come on, let's get tea started.'

Puzzled and a little ruffled, Elsie joined Helen and trailed behind her devotedly, bringing in the wrong things and changing them with eager obedience, so that the meal was ready only a few minutes later than it would have been if the others had got it unaided. They were just settling down to their second cups when the bump and scrape of a boat sounded outside. Leo put out a long leg and hitched an outlying chair up to the table; Helen lifted the lid of the teapot and appraised the contents; but the entrance of the young man from the punt seemed, to Elsie's secret disappointment, to disturb them no more than if it had been one of themselves. He was dressed as before except for the addition of a sweater rather cleaner than his slacks, and made himself more confusing than ever by kissing Helen casually, and smiling across at Leo as he did so.

'I'm sorry, I'm a bit early,' he said, sitting straight down at the table. 'I thought you'd have finished tea.'

'We ought to have.' Leo hacked off a thick wedge from the cake. 'Would you rather have beer?'

'No, tea, thanks, if there's any left. I've had it, but I always think one's second tea tastes better than one's first, don't you? What a nice squelchy cake.' He smiled at Elsie over the top of it, remarking, when his mouth was empty, 'Your sister and I have met already,' as an afterthought. Elsie noticed that Helen, without asking him how he took his tea, pushed over to him a brew like a labourer's, dark brown and with three lumps of sugar.

'If it isn't strong enough I'll make some more.'

'Just right, bless you. Oh, Leo, I was passing Hassal's this morning, so I thought I'd look in and see if your galleys were ready, and they were, so I brought them.' He pointed to a thick package he had dumped on a chair.

'Oh, good; that ought to be the final lot. How soon do they want them?'

'Two days if possible. I did about half for you in the train, I thought you wouldn't mind.'

'How right you were. I don't know how you do them in the train, though, I always need the floor. Did you see anything that ought to come out?'

'Only a couple of quite short bits. I'll show you in a minute. It's rather a good one, I think. I like the part where he rides that horse into the saloon.'

'You are a fool, Joe. You always like the most incredible parts.'

'I believed every word of it while it lasted. It was a pleasure, I assure you, no trouble at all. Mason says he doesn't really approve of your eliminating the love-interest completely.'

'I did put a girl in. I'm sure I did. Her name was Susie, or Sadie or something. And I mentioned her again at the end.'

'Maybe he bit too far, or not far enough, like the boy with the sausage roll.'

'I always think it would save such a lot of trouble if you could just indicate it with a row of crosses, or BERT LOVES MABEL, or something quick, and get on with the story.

'Well, you practically do. Mind you, it suits me all right.'

'I'll put more in the next if they make a fuss. The more intelligent section of my public thinks girls are soppy, anyway.'

Elsie was beginning to feel a little at sea in this conversation, and to suspect that Joe – of whom calling manners were, apparently, not expected – had forgotten she was there. What was the use, she asked herself, of having a sister who was an authoress, and being left out of all the literary talk? A momentary pause gave her the chance to remedy this.

'I am reading a very nice love story,' she stated, 'at the moment.'

'Really?' said Joe, turning on her at once a grave but friendly attention. 'Who by?'

Elsie had no idea. She chose most books by their titles, supplemented by a peep inside; she hardly knew what it was in Joe's kindly voice which suddenly made her suspect that this might turn out not to be good form. She went pink.

'Lucille Something-or-other. I – I can't quite remember the rest of it.'

'What's it about?' Joe asked, with a companionable smile. They all waited for her to tell them. Elsie's blush deepened. All at once she was acutely aware that she was out of key, that they were being kind to her, that she had arrested a conversation that interested them and that they were concealing the fact from her as best they could. Now she must go on, and she wished the floor would open and let her quietly down into the Thames.

'It's quite a simple story really,' she said rapidly. 'I mean it isn't deep at all. It's about a girl who's a mannequin, and she's very beautiful, and everybody admires her except the chief dress designer who's very handsome, but he only cares about his work and doesn't seem interested in women.'

'I met a dress designer once,' said Helen reminiscently, 'at a cocktail party.'

'Fancy your never telling me,' said Leo. 'Was he handsome and keen on his work?'

'Yes, very. I remember he had his nails varnished a sort of dull mauve. He wasn't interested in women, either.'

'Do go on, Elsie,' said Leo hastily. 'What happened then?'

Once again it seemed to Elsie that the conversation had changed gears for her benefit. Acutely miserable, she floundered on.

'Well, this girl, Star, has a bet with one of the other girls that she'll get him to take her out, and she does, and they fall in love; and then this other mannequin, who's jealous, tells him about the bet and he thinks she doesn't really love him and instead of designing a dress specially for her, as he was going to, he designs one for the other mannequin instead. That's as far as I've got.'

There was a pause. Presently Joe said 'Hot stuff!' His voice reminded her, somehow, of patting a strange dog. For a very little she would have wept.

Then Leo smiled at her. It reminded her of something; an occasion at home, when she was six years old. She had been standing in the corner, and Leo had grinned at her, very much like this, and given her a sweet when no one was looking.

'Elsie ought to be a connoisseur of romance,' she said cheerfully. 'She lives in a whirl of it. We didn't tell you, did we, Joe? She's just run away from home. Leaving a note on the pincushion, and everything.'

'No?' said Joe. 'Not really?' He gazed at Elsie with new interest. Her spirits mounted. She was, after all, as original and important as anyone else.

'It was rather a step,' she said modestly. 'But I felt it had to be.'

'Well, you managed better than I did,' Joe told her. His straight hazel eyes had the least embarrassing stare she had met. 'I ran away once, too. I was eight, or maybe nine. I had the idea of seeing the sea; I couldn't seem to form an impression of it

from the things people told me; maybe it was because they hadn't
seen it either. Anyway I didn't make a very good job of it; in fact,
I only got about thirty miles to the next place, because the man
who owned it knew my father and brought me back on a buckboard. My father was rather tickled, I think, though he gave me
a strapping of course; but my mother took on a bit, so I didn't try
it again.'

Elsie found this anecdote a little confusing. Before she had
time to ask him what a buckboard was, Helen said, 'I'll clear
now, then you two can use the table. You'll help me, won't you,
Elsie?'

Elsie rose reluctantly. She was just beginning to enjoy herself,
and felt that Helen could have left it till a little later. Through
the open door, as they washed up, she could see Joe and Leo
with their heads together over odd-looking strips of print a yard
long.

'You'll have to slip a bit in here,' she heard him say once, 'and
give a pretty good reason why he didn't look at his cinches. It
comes second nature, let alone riding a killer like that. You'd
better say he did, and have the Mexican get at them afterwards.'

'I'll fix that.' Leo pencilled a margin. 'I ought to have thought
of it. What have you marked wrong here, about the corral?'

After supper, when he had gone, Elsie's curiosity nerved her to
say, 'Does Joe often help you with your books like that?'

'He gives me a lot of very sound dope for them,' said Leo. 'He
doesn't help with the writing, naturally.'

Elsie thought this natural indeed; Joe struck her as the least
literary-looking person she had ever met. Leo was smiling to herself at some private amusement.

'If he did,' she added, 'the effect would be pretty peculiar. Like
a deal table with walnut inlaid promiscuously here and there.'

'How do you mean?' asked Elsie, puzzled.

'Well, I mean that about a mile beyond where I leave off, you
come to the things Joe takes for granted before he begins.'

'Begins what?'

'Writing, of course. Surely we must have told you who he is.'

'I don't suppose you did,' said Helen. 'You take Joe for granted as if he were the morning's milk.'

'Oh, well, he's like that. It's difficult not to. Actually, he's J. O. Flint.' Elsie's blank face caused her to add, 'Perhaps you don't read him?'

'I don't think I have, really. Does he write about cowboys, like you?'

'Good Lord above, no. Joe really writes.'

'Well, he seems to know a lot about them.'

'He was born in Arizona that's why.'

'But he doesn't talk at all like an American!' People had no business, she was beginning to feel, to be so systematically mis-leading.

'He left when he was twelve. His mother was English. Went to a rodeo, and married a rancher she sat next to. When his father died (he was shot, by the way, occasional things like that were still happening then) she brought him back home She'd had enough, I suppose. I think he was rather sore about it at the time, but he settled down; he would, of course. His real name is one of those vague American ones that isn't a Christian name at all, Jackson or Jefferson or something. No one can remember it, and he's never been heard to divulge what the O. stands for, so everyone calls him Joe. Partly because he looks like it, I dare say. He's an American citizen still, I believe.' She added, carelessly, 'He had a very happy sort of childhood; he rather enjoys remi-niscing about it, I think, once you get him going. Useful for me.'

'What are his books like? Are they nice?'

Helen gave one of her quiet private smiles; but Leo replied quite seriously, even with a certain effort of concentration.

'He's got one of those very plain styles – like bread, you know – that you forget is good because it disappears into what he's saying. And he has a way of making you see people against their background without putting the background in, rather the way Ruth Draper can on the stage. What people generally enthuse about is his structure, of course; he's got a lovely sense of form. His books always seem just to have happened in one piece. It's quite difficult to imagine him sitting and chipping away at them, unless you've actually seen him doing it.'

'But what are they *about*?' asked Elsie, bewildered by this mass of inessential detail. 'Are they adventure stories, or love stories, or sort of psychological?'

Leo lit a cigarette at some length. 'Sort of psychological,' she said gently. 'But you don't notice it.'

'Oh,' said Elsie, discouraged. 'Do they have sad endings?'

'Three of them have, rather. He's only written four.'

'That doesn't seem very many, does it,' said Elsie, keeping up as best she could a show of polite interest, 'at his age?'

Helen laughed. Addressing Leo rather than Elsie, she said, 'He's bone lazy.'

'Joe's a ruminant animal,' said Leo, with the calm of one who is not to be drawn. 'He likes to digest an idea for a year or two and then chew it again, before he spits it out.'

'It sounds insanitary,' said Helen to Elsie. 'doesn't it?'

Elsie smiled back dubiously. She had a feeling that they were sparring an inch or two above her eye-level; but, with Leo and Helen, this never seemed to matter.

'Why does he do that?' she asked Leo, so as to be quite impartial; it still came by instinct.

'I really don't know. Unless it's because he feels too strongly about things at the time to get them fair.'

Elsie, who had always taken for granted that white-hot emotion was a first requirement of the inspired state, was finally convinced that Joe's work must contain every essential of unreadability. She abandoned the discussion to Helen, who for her part had been looking at Leo in some surprise.

'Well,' she said, 'the sight of Joe feeling strongly about anything would be news. Man Bites Dog. Don't tell me you've ever seen it.'

'Only once. Let's clear supper and go out and have a drink.'

'What was it about?' asked Helen, leaning back in her chair.

Leo met Elsie's eyes fixed on her in expectant interest. She sounded, for the first time, a little irritated.

'Nothing in particular. We were having tea in town and a rather dim sort of couple were quarrelling at the next table. Finally the woman – rather a fool of a woman, really – started to cry. I missed most of it, I hadn't been properly attending.'

'What did Joe do?' asked Elsie helpfully

'Well, nothing, naturally. He just said 'Let's go,' without noticing I hadn't finished my cigarette – he has very nice manners when he's out, as a rule – and walked me the length of Bond Street at a breakneck speed and in dead silence. Then he went on talking again as if nothing had happened.'

Helen said, in her placid voice, 'Probably it hadn't. It doesn't sound much like Joe. I expect he just had indigestion or something.'

'Maybe,' said Leo coolly. 'If he had it was probably the first time in his life, so it would attract his attention a bit.'

'Did you ask him afterwards what he thought about it?'

'Good God, no. Nor would you have done, if you'd been there.'

Elsie, who had been feeling it time that she added something more dynamic to the conversation, said, 'I should have thought he'd get rather out of practice, not writing for so long at a time.'

'He practises living in the intervals. And reviews books now and again. It seems to work out all right.'

'Then I suppose he must have money of his own?' He had scarcely looked like it; but Elsie had ceased to regard his externals as reliable.

'He's only got what he earns. When he's finished a book and got in some of the royalties, he buys a few things he wants and puts the rest in the bank, ready to live on when he starts another. Then he takes a job for a year or so, till he gets an idea.'

'What does he work at?'

'Brewing.'

'Oh,' said Elsie, other words failing her.

'Of course, it isn't a job you can take up and put down as a rule. But he's got an uncle who's a director or something and likes him in spite of his peculiarities. He's not difficult to fit in somewhere; he doesn't mind what he does, you see. Once one of the firm's licensees died suddenly, and there was no one they could put in straight away, so Joe took the pub over for a month. He did quite well at it, too, and they said he could keep it on if he liked; but while he was there some of the people in the bar had given him an idea, I suppose, and he knocked off again. He says he'd like to do a spell driving one of the horse-drays, but so far the uncle's stuck in his heels.'

'Well,' said Elsie helplessly, 'he must have had a very interesting life.'

'He's had a very interested life, anyway. You'll see plenty of him, I expect; he's working on a book now.'

'A fat lot he's done to-day,' said Helen, affecting tartness.

'Oh, he'll be at it all night, probably. He likes keeping peculiar hours; he says he gets enough of clocks when he's brewing. He ought to be here for another six months, at least.' She looked pleased. Elsie eyed her sidelong, reviving, only to abandon again with regret, an interesting theory. Perhaps it was Helen; after all, it was Helen he had kissed. With Helen it was always impossible to tell. A train of thought like this was bound to bring her, sooner or later, to Peter.

She looked at Helen, who was buttering a biscuit, quiet, collected, absolutely self-assured. It was admiration and envy, as much as anything, which caused her to say, with rather breathless nonchalance, 'I know a very interesting man too. He lives in London.'

'What's he do?' asked Leo, whose mouth was rather full.

'He's a doctor.'

'Is he at a hospital?' asked Helen, with genuine interest. 'I might know him.'

'He works at St. Jerome's. His name's Bracknell. Peter

Bracknell.' Her heart was thumping so that it nearly choked her.

'No, I haven't a surgeon there. Ask him along sometime, why don't you?'

'Yes, do, of course,' said Leo. 'Any time.' She spoke a little absently; her mind having wandered back to the galley-slips, she was working out an interpolation about cinches.

'Thank you very much.' The effort at casualness made Elsie's voice nearly crack. Supposing she dared to ask him, and they knew she had asked him, and he did not come. 'Perhaps I will sometime if I feel like it. He's frightfully busy always, though.'

'Oh, well, of course.' Evidently this had convinced Helen at least. 'Just ask him to drop along any time he can. If we're tied up you can look after him, which will be all the better won't it?'

Elsie blushed.

She posted her letter next morning. It ended, 'P.S. I told my sister about you, and she says do come down here any time, if you feel like a breath of fresh air.'

CHAPTER TWELVE

Peter strayed desultorily into the housemen's common-room, found it empty, and looked about it with dislike. It was a reasonably comfortable but dingy place, had the air of having been treated with indifference by many generations, and faced a blank wall. Tea, of which only the used crockery remained, had been served there an hour before. He sat down in an out-at-elbows armchair, beside an overflowing ashtray on a burnt tablecloth, and picked up a copy of the *Statesman and Nation*, which turned out to be last week's and one he had read before. Peter pushed it irritably into the waste-paper basket, and turned the radio on. A light orchestra rewarded him, playing one of those light orchestral works of which one ought, but feels no inclination, to remember the name.

It was supposed to be his free afternoon; but an emergency, coming in after his relief was already occupied with another, had kept him till half-past five. It had been one of those depressing cases which spin out an infinitesimal chance of life until every expedient has been exhausted, and then die leaving an unde-served sense of failure behind. Peter felt discouraged in proportion to his efforts, which had been wholehearted. He now remembered that he had intended taking one of the nurses out to tea – a first-year probationer, wide-eyed and pretty and rather promising – and that her off-duty time was already over. Norah was in charge of a diabetic bishop in Regent's Park, and would not be free till nine. Peter picked up a copy of *Razzle* (May of the previous year) and studied without amusement a joke about a blonde leaving part of her underwear in a taxi.

Miss Perkins had been discharged that morning; perhaps, he thought, this had contributed to his disillusioned mood. He had put a good deal into Miss Perkins – two blood transfusions, liver extract, Vitamin B, and (he felt) his immortal soul. As for her anaemia, it had improved; but a student could have seen to that. For a case in his own line, she had been bitterly unrewarding. Miss Perkins was a schoolteacher of thirty-nine, with a thin sad face, straight hair, and spectacles. The deficiency of her red cells, as his experience had recognized at once, had only been symptomatic of a lack more fundamental. It was palpably obvious that the only men to whom the poor creature ever spoke were the Vicar and the Board of Education inspector. He had gone out of his way to remedy this. He had lent her books, progressively advanced; sat with her much longer than the taking of her simple history demanded; sympathized with her; talked about himself; and, when she became confidential, held her hand. At first she had responded beautifully, and become, now and then, animated and almost pretty. She had left her glasses off, and put rachel powder on. The ward sister reported that her appetite had improved. Encouraged, he had visited her again, talking more and further; about human relationships, about God, about his views on marriage, about the way in which he and Norah intended to put these into practice at some still unspecified date. And then, suddenly, she had relapsed, gone back into herself, ceased to respond. One might almost say that she had frozen up on him. She had gone out, in the end, as plain and apathetic as when she had arrived. Peter simply could not see any reason for it. And, when he had related the case history to Norah, she had actually laughed.

Sometimes he found himself on the verge of thinking that

Norah had not been entirely rewarding either. Her departure to Mrs. Craven's Nursing Co-operation had seemed to him odd and unnecessary; and her explanation, that she thought they had been seeing too much of one another lately, still had him completely baffled.

Except for this unaccountable remark, and a somewhat escapist enthusiasm for eighteenth-century prints, there had been only one respect in which she had failed to model herself on his precepts; and this, one day, he had pointed out to her with the truthfulness on which they prided themselves. He didn't want her to think he looked upon her possessively, he had explained, or that he wished to keep her in a rut; if she felt like a diversion or experiment elsewhere now and again, he promised to extend to this event all the toleration which in like case, he would expect for himself. She had received this with a lack of comment which was a little unlike her; merely thanking him and saying she would bear it in mind; but she had appeared to be pondering the matter – or, at any rate, to be pondering – and it seemed strange that so soon afterwards she should have betaken herself to private nursing, where leisure was so limited and the opportunities for social contact were so few. He had not, of course, so far forsaken his principles as to question the step, still less to argue it; but sometimes he wondered. He was wondering this evening, when the disregarded wireless gave its signal for the news.

It was one of those happy seasons when no urgent world events were pending, so he continued with his thoughts, and it must have been his subconscious mind which, listening on its own, arrested them.

'Missing from her home,' said the well-bred impersonal instrument, 'since Monday last, Elsa Lane, aged seventeen and a half; height five feet five inches, dark bobbed hair, pale complexion, brown eyes; when last seen was wearing a brown hat and coat, dark brown marocain dress with lace collar, brown stockings and shoes, small gold cross and chain. This girl has been ill recently and it is thought that she may be suffering from loss of memory. She is known to have taken a ticket to Bristol and it is possible that she may have obtained employment there. Will any person having information as to her whereabouts please communicate . . .'

'Good Lord!' said Peter aloud, and dived for his jacket pocket. He had only just remembered the letter he had received that morning; a letter of, he had felt, rather daunting thickness, which he had put aside to read when occasion served. His first thought, as he began slitting it open, was that it had been unexpectly smart of her to rebook at Bristol, where she was sure to pass unnoticed in the crowds; his second, that she might arrive at the hospital at any moment. Such was the effect of this on a hand normally steady, that he found he had torn the envelope almost in half.

The first sentences were such a relief that for a few minutes his eye ran on with little co-operation from his brain. A striking phrase or two, however, recalled his attention, and when he had finished he turned back and read the letter a second time. It was then that the postcript, which was overleaf, first attracted his notice. He gazed at it, in thought, for a moment or two; finally he tore off the address, and put it in his pocket-book, before throwing the rest on the fire.

CHAPTER THIRTEEN

'Don't you feel like writing to-day?' asked Elsie. Leo had got up late that morning and, breakfast cleared away, was reading the magazine pages of the newspaper in the manner of one who may as well do that as anything else.

'Not much.' Leo put the paper down, and stretched apathetically. 'Well, one can't do nothing all morning, I suppose. I think I'll get through some of Helen's mending. She's done a lot of mine.'

Moved partly by lack of occupation, and partly by curiosity – the picture of Leo sewing was difficult to form, though one supposed she must have done it sometimes at home – Elsie went upstairs half an hour later to look. Leo had spread a dust-sheet or something similar on the floor; a heap of satin and *crêpe de Chine* lay on one side of her, on the other the necessary implements, arranged in rows like tools on a bench. Sitting on a cushion in the middle, Leo was stitching with dogged, but workmanlike application; in her serge slacks and fisherman's jersey, she put Elsie in mind of a sailor doing something to a sail. The result looked, however, on closer inspection, quite competent.

'Got something to amuse yourself with?' asked Leo, looking up. Her face looked, Elsie thought, a shade lighter-brown than usual; but she seemed cheerful enough.

'Yes, thank you. I've got lots to do.' Leo did not look in need of help; indeed she never did. Elsie, who had been used to her mother's more leisurely and diffuse household methods always found herself a beat or two behind, and had got out of the way of offering; Leo had never seemed to miss it. This morning she had her diary to write up; for two different and, it seemed to her, very significant thoughts about life had occurred to her last night in bed, and she had memorized them carefully. She took the volume (it was already a third full) into the living-room, and flattened it on the table; re-read the last entry, and chewed her pen with lingering anticipation. There had been nothing for her in the morning post; but it was only three days since she had written, and there would be another post in the afternoon.

She had got to the second thought when a voice outside shouted 'Le – o!' from the water. Elsie, who had recognized it, withdrew herself reluctantly from composition, and went out on the floating deck. She found, however, that Leo had forestalled her by appearing on the balcony half-way up. She had hitched a knee on the rail and looked, in contrast with her earlier lethargy, quite brisk.

'Wotcher, Joe,' she called, with a vulgarity for which Elsie remembered their mother reproving her. 'Come in and help yourself. How's life?'

Joe eased in his punt, which contained a large enamel water-can, towards the deck.

'Hullo,' he said, smiling up at her. 'Shame to rouse you out. I could have asked Elsie, I didn't see her. Morning, Elsie.' To Leo he added, 'Get on, don't mind me, you look busy.'

'I'm only charing round.' Leo balanced on the rail. 'I'm dead from the neck up. I thought you were in London.'

'I've just got up,' said Joe, with what appeared to be complete satisfaction. It was then a quarter to twelve.

'You needn't be so filthily smug about it.' They grinned at one another, downward and upward, with vague morning cheerfulness, posed like a heavy burlesque of *Romeo and Juliet*. 'What time did you go to bed?'

'About eleven. Then I woke up and worked till four. It went rather well.'

'Have you had breakfast, or lunch or anything?'

'Both, thanks. If you're really not busy, can I ask you about something?'

'I don't see why not.' Leo came down, and sat on the rail of the floating deck. It did not occur to Elsie, as it might have done with other people, to disappear; Leo and Joe never had the least appearance of having anything private to say to one another.

'Well' – Joe anchored himself and the punt to the rail with one arm – 'You know Alcox's page in *The Centaur*, and all those significant little thumbnail what-have-you's they scatter about the columns? Can't call them illustrations exactly, sort of relevant notions. Frenchman called Brunier did them. He's going to Russia, indefinitely. They'll certainly want to keep the layout if they can find someone else. I'm seeing Alcox this afternoon, and it struck me some of those doodles of Helen's might fetch him. It's nominally up to the art editor, but anything Alcox says will go. I don't know, of course. Anyway I could try. Is she around?'

'No, she's in town for the day. But Joe, not really? It's awfully good of you. It's just the sort of thing she's always wanted to get her foot into. I'm glad she's out, let's not tell her until it comes off. Look, I'll get you her stuff and you can go over it and pick out what you think. Shan't be a minute.'

She disappeared. Joe, who seemed full this morning of surplus energy and animal spirits, stepped from his punt into the canoe, which was moored ready for use at the rail, undid its painter, and, standing, began to manoeuvre it along with the punt-pole.

'Well, I'm damned,' said Leo in the doorway. She put down Helen's portfolio on the table, and came out. 'What have you been holding out on me, Joe? You never told me you could pole a canoe.'

'Undergraduate stuff,' said Joe, rocking precariously. 'Looks flash and serves no useful purpose whatever. Haven't tried in ten

years. The sight of this barge has the most unwholesome psychological effect on me.' He reeled and recovered, remarking to
Elsie, disjointedly, 'My college barge, this was. They scrapped it
after it sank one year. Leo and I met that way. Had to come over
and see who was using it. Top floor's built on, of course.'

Leo remarked, 'If you sink that canoe, you can go down after
it and get it up again.'

Spurred by this, Joe gave his undivided attention to the matter
in hand. He swung the pole; travelled, with great dash and efficiency, for twenty yards; turned half-round to wave to Leo, and
went spectacularly into the river. The canoe itself he saved, at
the penultimate instant, by performing a kind of vault out of it
on the pole. Elsie, much alarmed, was reassured by the sight of
Leo standing with her hands in her pockets and laughing whole-
heartedly.

Joe came to the surface with unruffled cheerfulness; his short
wiry hair, as he shook the water out of it, looked like a wet
retriever's. He appeared to be enjoying himself. Having shoved
the canoe and pole in the direction of the deck, where Leo collected them, he heaved himself up and, squatting on the planks,
wrung water from the surplus parts of his trousers. Elsie now
found their normal state easier to understand. His upper half
gave him no trouble, being, fortunately, unclad.

'O.K., try it yourself,' he said to Leo, who was still laughing. 'I
bet you a pint you don't get it any further than I did. Elsie can see
fair.'

'Done,' said Leo immediately. 'You stand there, Elsie. And
don't move till I get there. Where did you start off?'

'About here. No, I'll give you the benefit, call it here. Done it
before?'

'You'll see.'

'Why not change into a swim-suit first; I would.'

'Oh, you would, would you?' Leo stepped neatly into the
centre of the canoe, balanced, and picked up the pole.

Elsie thought, suddenly and embarrassingly, of her letter to

Peter. She had thought much about the moment of his arrival, and prayed inwardly that his first impressions might be good. Last evening, the technician from Elstree had dropped in and talked about montage, and Leo had been expert-sounding and intelligent. That would have been an excellent moment. But it was depressingly likely that it would be this kind of thing which would be going on. Only once, so far, had she heard Leo and Joe engaged in anything like a serious intellectual discussion, and that had been in the galley, where she had surprised them one morning peeling potatoes into the sink and arguing about Prince Henry's treatment of Falstaff as if these characters had been personal acquaintances and it had all happened yesterday. Elsie almost wished that she hadn't said Leo wrote at all. Lost in gloomy forebodings, she moved away from her station, lengthening Leo's course by several yards.

Leo was off. She made a good start; but even Elsie's inexpert eye noticed the difference made by three stone less of stabilizing weight. The canoe, several inches higher in the water, frisked like a dancer. Her sureness of foot would have made up deficiencies, if it had not been for the heaviness of Joe's pole, which was stout and, as poles must be in that part of the river, very long. Even so, she got ten or twelve yards before the inevitable happened. She came up laughing, and towed in the canoe; she was too light for her fall to overturn it. Joe leaned out from where he sat, and reached a hand to haul her in.

'Well,' he said,' if that was your first try, as I suspect, it was far the best effort I've ever seen. Masterly.' He slapped her waist, making a loud wet noise. 'I remember distinctly I didn't as much as get the thing moving till my second shot. I consider I owe you a pint, on that.'

'You win, all right. I'll have to practise. Take you on again in a week or so. Come on in and have the stakes.'

Joe collected the pole, which had drifted in of its own accord. 'Go and get changed first. You look a bit blue. Water's cold today.'

'Is it? Well, maybe. What about you, like a bath-wrap or some-thing till you go?'

'No, thanks; they're so disgustingly clammy when you put them on again. I'll remember not to sit on the upholstery. I can go over Helen's stuff while you're gone.'

'Give him a towel, Elsie, or he'll drip over everything.' Elsie went up after her to get it, and heard her teeth chattering from several feet away. She came down, however, five minutes later, changed and smiling, though with rather more make-up than she generally wore, and poured out the drinks, keeping up with Joe one of those desultory and cryptic conversations, broken by terse and allusive jokes, to which Elsie had become accustomed and only listened, now, with half an ear. After fifteen minutes or so she remarked, casually, 'Well, take whatever you like of those things. She'll never notice they're gone. I think I'll get back to work now; I feel suddenly inspired. Must be the beer.'

She went upstairs, leaving Joe with the sketch-books and port-folio. Elsie thought it a little abrupt, but Joe seemed to take it as a matter of course. They behaved like this, Elsie supposed; and thought how comically inept her first speculations had been. Imagine herself strolling away in the midst of a conversation with Peter. Life must be very simple Elsie thought (with the secret feeling of superiority which this reflection always engen-ders) for people so easy-going and tough.

Joe provided himself with a kitchen chair, dried his hands carefully, and settled down to the drawings, going steadily through them and putting his selections in a pile. He had evi-dently forgotten Elsie's existence, and she got out her diary again, almost forgetting his, for he was a person in whose presence this came easily. One or twice, in search of an idea, she happened to glance up, and it occurred to her for a moment that he looked rather different without his usual half-smile of indolent good-humour; coolly critical, decisive, and surprisingly shrewd. But the diary soon engrossed her thoughts again. When he had fin-ished he filed what he had chosen, filled his enamel can at the sink, and went away humming. Elsie, remembering what Leo had said about being inspired, carefully refrained from disturbing her until lunch-time had passed by three-quarters of an hour.

It was just after four when Helen came in, earlier than she had expected. Elsie was, by this time, more than usually pleased to see her.

'I'm in time for tea after all,' she said. 'Where's Leo? Lying down?'

'Yes, she is.' Elsie stared, in amazement at Helen s prescience. 'I don't think she's quite herself this afternoon. She didn't eat any dinner; she just drinks tea all the time. She doesn't *look* very well.'

'Bother.' Helen spoke with concern, but no surprise. 'She hasn't had a go like that for ages. She was in quite good shape this morning, too. Has she been doing anything silly?'

'She did fall in the river this morning. I hope it hasn't given her a chill.'

'*Fall* in the river?' Helen's voice mingled astonishment and outrage. 'However did she manage to do that?'

'The canoe upset.' Seeing that Helen now looked frankly incredulous, she added in explanation, 'She was standing up in it. Joe bet her she couldn't punt it with a pole.'

'Oh, *damn* Joe,' said Helen heartily, and went upstairs.

From her curled-up position on the bed, huddled under a thick winter coat, Leo looked round with a pale guilty grin. Her face had the tinge of greenish vellum, and her eyes were underlined, as if with streaks of kohl.

'I'm going to get up in a minute,' she said. 'I feel fine now.'

Helen sat down on the edge of the bed. 'Elsie told me. Whatever on earth possessed you? You were bad enough that time you just got wet in the rain.'

'It wasn't anything. It just cropped up, the way things do.'

'Cropped up. Don't talk to me. This hot-water bottle's stone cold. Have you had some A.P.C.?'

'About twenty grains . . . He fell in and I laughed at him; I couldn't back out myself after that, could I?'

'After which you went and swallowed a pint of cold bitter, I suppose.'

'Well, naturally, seeing I lost.'

'But why on earth? Why didn't you tell him you had an off day, like anyone else would?'

'Maybe they would, in one of your filthy hospitals.'

'Oh, nonsense. It isn't 1890.'

Leo's mouth shut in a straight obstinate line. After a while she said, awkwardly, 'It makes you feel a fool.'

'I just don't get it. Joe of all people, too. I don't know what you've noticed in his books, or his conversation either, to make you think his mother didn't instruct him in the facts of life.'

'There are times,' said Leo, 'when the facts of life strike me as so damned silly I stop believing in them. Have you got any cigarettes? Mine were in my pocket when I went in. A smoke's all I want, and I'll be fine.'

'Of course. Couldn't Elsie have gone out and got you some? What's she been up to, hasn't she done anything about you at all?'

'She flaps about. I told her to read a nice book or something. Asking what's the matter. One feels such a fool . . . This is better. Don't bother with that bottle, I'm coming down now.'

Elsie, who liked to please, had taken Leo's injunction literally. Her diary had been brought up to the minute, and there had been nothing else to do. Partly from a sense of social duty, partly because Leo's library contained nothing more alluring, she had settled herself with the thinnest of four volumes severely bound in dark blue, which she had found in the downstairs book-case where the more presentable books were kept. *Remission*. J. O. Flint. She need only read enough to be able to converse intelligently about it. Recalling Leo's remark about fairness, she had formed beforehand a very good idea of the kind of book it would be; the kind, no doubt, which had been recommended to them at school to broaden their minds on social problems. They had read them up in the holidays and had informal discussions about them

in class. Each side of each problem had been represented by one
good character and one bad, and the debating points shared out
between them in equal numbers, like counters in a board-game.
She had been quite expert in picking out the argument without
reading every word. Sooner or later, the subject of Joe's books was
bound to come up when he was present; and she was anxious not
to hurt his feelings by making it evident that she had not read
even one of them. So far, no opening had occurred; he had discussed with Leo, at various times, the sales, binding, advertising,
printing and general negotiation of books, but had not referred at
all to the process of writing them; and once, in the belief that she
was listening to another of such conversations, she had been
some time in realizing that it was beer he was talking about
instead. It was all very odd and unlike what one had imagined.
None the less, she was determined to be ready with something
appropriate and polite to say about *Remission*, even if it were all
as dull as the title. She opened it in the middle, the first chapters,
explaining everything, generally by long conversations between
distinguished men in clubs, were always the worst.

She read a paragraph, a page, three pages, with growing sen-
sations of discomfort and surprise. No politics, no economics, no
pro and con; instead a clear and meticulous description of a dead
baby, which its mother was washing on her lap and dressing in
the clothes it was to be buried in. Elsie had never seen a baby, or,
for that matter, anyone else dead. After reading a hundred words,
she felt that she had, and that her previous ideas on the subject
had been inaccurate. It would have been excusable, she felt with
an obscure sense of injury, if it had made one cry in a pathetic,
comfortable way. One ought to be told what to feel, eased into a
nest of emotion which had been warmed up for one beforehand,
not left to feel on one's own responsibility, to ask questions that
disturbed and frightened one, to be made, somehow, ashamed of
not wanting to ask them. The worst of it was that there was
nothing to take hold of, nothing to argue with except what one
felt oneself. Without a word of generalization, only a picture

built up with a detail here and a detail there, one was left not simply with a dead baby, but with death itself. For no reason on which one could put one's finger, it made death seem a thing with which one had to come to terms while one was living, even a kind of door in oneself through which it was necessary to pass in order to live. It was all very quiet, terrifyingly quiet and cool. It offered no escape and no promises. It simply put the thing before one, and left one alone with it.

Elsie would have known what to say about a book like this if it had come out of the library in the ordinary way. There was enough suffering and sordidness in real life; a good book should make one happy; one asked the library assistant for the next one on the list. This was her mother's method and Elsie had always followed it out; for she too disliked depressing books and demanded suffering, if any, in the grand manner. She had never imagined the possibility of being confronted with this kind of thing by a personal acquaintance. It was too awkward for words. She turned over a number of pages rapidly. A phrase met her eye which she had not thought possible outside the Old Testament. She looked again, to make sure. Yes, it was true, and so was the preceding paragraph. What was more, not three hours ago she had been sitting, all unaware, in the same room as the man who had written it. She shut the book, blushing to the roots of her hair, looked over her shoulder to see if anyone was watching, and put it back on the shelf, offering up a prayer of thankfulness that she had not told Leo she was going to read it. It was unfair of Leo. She ought to have warned her. Of what, Elsie was not sure, but she found herself resenting Leo more than the book itself; for taking everything as a matter of course, for being always unembarrassed, for being able to discuss books like this in terms of royalties and serial rights in the same voice as if they were bottled beer; for the whole armour of masculine impersonality which Elsie had sensed without knowing what it was that she had felt and resented; for an unsettling suspicion that one was living on a brittle surface, and that underneath it things might be other than what they seemed. She thought of this morning's horseplay, so childish that she herself had felt, by comparison, quite mature. It caused one to wonder, at what seemed the safest and most ordinary moments, where one was, where everyone was. It engendered thoughts which, Elsie felt, it would not be possible to communicate even to Peter.

Her mind, following methods of its own, set about tidying up this uncomfortable mess. It did so partly by a process of forgetting; partly by the use of disinfectant adjectives such as 'clever' and 'difficult', partly by going into Mawley to exchange *Stargleam* for *Mirabelle's Man*. Like the aspirin, phenacetin and caffeine which Leo had been swallowing upstairs, these remedies might have been inadequate separately; but taken all together, they worked in time.

She had dreaded Joe's next appearance; but, when it happened, the cure was already almost complete, and his presence finished it. She was washing up the tea-things, and looked up from the rattle in the bowl to find him at her elbow, drying them. 'Leo not in yet?' he said, in the manner of one who has already ascertained the answer; and turned to replace the crockery in its correct places on the dresser, with which he seemed rather more familiar than Elsie herself. It was, immediately, as if he had been in the place all day. As he moved about the galley he told her about trouble he had had in the morning with the corpse of a dog which had fetched up against the island and, when dislodged, persistently returned. 'Finally I roped it, and towed it down river. I never roped a floating body at home; nothing much for bodies to float in. Too bad Leo wasn't there.' He drifted into the living-room, and settled down with a book. It would have been as difficult to be disturbed by the comings and goings of the post-man.

He had come, as it turned out when the others got back from the village, to tell Helen that Alcox liked her drawings and wished to see what she could do with an article. This he had brought, together with an invitation to lunch with Alcox at

the Ivy. Helen said 'Joe, *darling*!' and cast herself into his arms.
But Elsie's excitement and confusion were only momentary. It
was as if a nice, spontaneous child had been offered a visit to the
circus by a reliable uncle. Joe returned the demonstration in a
comfortable, matter-of-fact way, remarking 'Wear your fleecy-
lined bloomers, ducky; he's a licentious old goat.' In a last
anticipation of drama, somewhere between hope and dread,
Elsie stole a glance at Leo. She was sitting with a cigarette on
the edge of the table, looking at least as pleased as either of the
other two.

When Joe left, Elsie went with him. To fill in, as he remarked,
the interval till opening time, he had offered to give her a punting lesson. She went. She had forgotten every word of *Remission*.

'What a pity it seems,' Leo said when they had gone, 'that she
didn't know somebody like Joe ten years ago.'

Helen looked up for a moment. Leo had spoken absently,
without emphasis; the thought seemed, somehow, an old one,
older by a good deal than Elsie's coming.

Helen only said, 'And after all that, I never asked him to my
party. Or did I?'

'Yes, you did. Or perhaps it was me. He's coming, anyway.'

'I hope it won't bore him, all hospital people.'

'Not him. He likes trade jargons. He'd listen fascinated to a
party of undertakers, I feel sure. Bearing in mind your previous
hospital parties, it's Elsie's reactions that bother me, if you want
to know.'

'But I'm having it partly for her benefit. She wants to meet
people, doesn't she? It's going to be quite simple and ordinary.'

'Oh, well,' said Leo reflectively, 'I dare say it will do her good.'
She lapsed into meditation, from which she emerged presently to
say, 'I wish I were more used to family responsibilities. We're no
nearer deciding what to do with her than we were the day she
arrived. Are we abducting her, do you think? I mean in the legal
rather than the moral sense. I suppose you can abduct your sister.
Or not? I only thought of that this morning.'

'Ask Joe. He knows most things. I should hardly think so. We didn't entice her to come.'

'No, indeed. If we could only afford to train her at anything . . . How about nursing? That's free, isn't it?'

'She's a year too young for any decent hospital. As she's your sister, I won't go into the other reasons.'

'Don't be hard on her. Everyone's got something they can't take.'

A look had crossed her face which checked Helen's neat rejoinder. She said, gently, 'There's a young man somewhere, isn't there? Some sort of dim medical student, or something. If he comes, we'd better take a look at him. He might be quite worthy and respectable. If we could only get her engaged, she could go home quite comfortably and wait till he was qualified.'

'Well, that would comfort Mother, I suppose. She always hoped indefatigably that one of us would get married. She'd even have got over Tom, I think, if he'd made an honest woman of me and she could have carried a sheaf of chrysanthemums and cried in the vestry. People are odd. It never seemed to occur to her that anything that went on at home could possibly have put me off . . . We could have asked this lad of hers to the party, if we'd thought of it.'

'We'll have another, and ask him to that.'

Elsie got back an hour later, wind-blown, and with a band of early sunburn across the bridge of her nose, to eat a substantial supper, her mind lulled in the peaceful vacancy of a healthy physical fatigue. As she proudly mastered the craft of disengaging the pole from sticky mud without leaving the punt herself, she had been unconscious of her own contentment, the simple product of an hour spent in preoccupations which were, for once, entirely real. Joe had treated her with the friendly detached interest he was equally ready to spend on men, machines, children, places, and most of the women he met. (Helen, near the beginning of her acquaintance with him, had remarked to Leo that he had a mind like a grazing horse; she had been feeling a little annoyed at the time.) The result, in Elsie's case, had been to give the uneasy growing-pains of adolescence an interval of happy anaesthesia. She came back feeling good, and even looking it. Leo's bald announcement of next day's party, however, threw her at once into a violent flutter.

'It's only some of Helen's rowdies,' Leo assured her, 'coming to make a noise. Half of them won't ever know you're there. Oh, by the way, I've bought you a frock. Just a cotton thing. No one will dress up, so you could wear that if you like.'

The dress was a bright, simple thing of Viennese inspiration, with a red top, full blue skirt, and bands of bright formal embroidery. It dazzled Elsie; she repressed with difficulty, from her confused thanks, the words artistic and bohemian, having detected in Leo, and still more in Helen, a curious lack of enthusiasm when they were uttered. But she thought them the more. If Leo had told her the price – approximately what she had saved for repairing the wireless, which had wanted valves for the last few months – Elsie would not have believed it. For the rest of that day, and most of the next, the thought of wearing it to meet Peter absorbed her mind to the exclusion of nearly everything else; and she put it on three hours before the party was due to begin. Neither Leo nor Helen had the heart to suggest that she took it off again to tackle the cleaning and tidying necessary for the event. They left her to experiment with the inoffensive and subdued lipstick which Leo had thrown in with it, and set about the sweeping and polishing by themselves.

Elsie, in spite of her growing trepidation, was at pains to be down early. It seemed, however, that one of the guests had been even earlier than she. A slim young woman in a plain, but excellently cut scarlet frock, her back turned, was lighting a cigarette, and taking what seemed to Elsie a rather ill-bred interest in the arrangement of the drinks. Overcome by nervousness at the thought of being left alone to make conversation, she was about to vanish again, when the stranger turned round. It was Leo. She had on lipstick that matched her dress; silvery clips curled upward along her ears, emphasizing subtly the slant of her brows; there was an almost imperceptible green shadow along her eyelids, and she had done something different with her hair. Elsie stared at her, frankly open-mouthed.

'What's the matter? You look alarmed.' Leo flicked her cigarette in its ivory holder. 'Have I got something showing?' She glanced down at her long silk legs and *suède* shoes.

'No, really. But you look so different, I didn't see for a moment it was you.'

'It's me,' said Leo, 'up to a point. Let's have a sherry before they come.'

Almost immediately after Helen had joined them, looking like porcelain in black with a cream lace yoke, the party began. They heard it coming, for it arrived *en bloc*, squeezed into two transits of the ferry-boat, each load announcing itself loudly on the way. When the preliminary turmoil was over, it added up to six young men dressed in varying stages between town suiting and corduroys, and four young women, two pretty, one smart, and one dowdy but quite unconcerned about it. Several of them devoted the first five minutes to explaining the trouble they had had in getting away, with confusing effect, as all the obstacles, simultaneously described, were quite different.

'. . . tried to get me back just as I was leaving to pass two more, but I told him how good it would be for the students to do it . . .' '. . . and believe it or not, this very morning Sister was on the verge of changing my off-duty, but I managed . . .' '. . . can't bear to stitch up without taking something no matter what, so he finished by anastomosing the soundest bit of gut I ever hope to see; I thought we'd be there till morning.'

Helen, and even Leo, seemed not only to understand but to be interested in these events, related as far as Elsie was concerned in a foreign tongue. The introductions at least were less of an ordeal than she had feared; they were brief, sweeping, full of goodwill and succeeded at once by the same din as before, under cover of which Joe added himself to the gathering almost imperceptibly, like a quiet regular entering a pub. He came to rest, apparently by chance, in the relatively quiet corner where Elsie was trying to hide, and settled himself on the floor beside her. Within two minutes, however, he had struck acquaintance with a young man on his other side; their conversation, which they conducted as peacefully as if they had the room to themselves, worked through beer and ballet to the latest developments in plastic surgery. Elsie noticed that Joe was an excellent listener.

The sherry and sandwiches were gone in what seemed to her a matter of moments, and everyone settled down to the more serious business of drinking beer. Joe got up unobtrusively, fixed Elsie a shandy, and continued his discussion where he had left it off. The shandy was nearly all ginger-beer, and she drank it gratefully, taking care not to empty her glass lest someone else should refill it.

The company, nearly all of which was on the floor for lack of chairs, began to settle itself more easily. Each man collected a neighbouring girl and propped her comfortably against his person with a supporting arm. Elsie shrank further into her corner, partly from shyness, partly from the motive which leads wallflowers at dances to linger in the cloakroom. A long arm reached for her and hauled her back again. She found herself settled against Joe's shoulder with the kind of firm reassuring grip one uses on a child when telling it to keep still and be good. His body felt hard and stable, and as quiet as a resting animal or a tree. There was a simplicity in Joe which defied even Elsie's powers of misconstruction. She stayed where she was.

It was during a fortuitous lull in the half-dozen conversations that Helen remarked, in her clear gentle voice, 'I think we ought to sing.'

The suggestion was evidently so usual as to be practically routine. Elsie was pleased by it, for she enjoyed singing, and, indeed, did it passably and with a good ear. When the chosen ditty had triumphed over two others which had started up at the same time, she was disappointed to find that she did not know it, but listened carefully in the hope of picking it up.

The first verse struck her as rather jolly. The second winded her like a punch in the midriff. At the third, she was unable to believe her ears. She stared, frozen like Lot's wife on viewing the cities of the plain, at face after cheerful face. It was impossible to credit that these people, looking happy and unselfconscious as scouts and guides at a jamboree, could really be uttering these words; not uttering them merely, but bawling them aloud, in mixed company, meeting one another's eyes as candidly as children meanwhile. Worse – if anything could be worse – she could feel against her back the regular rise and fall of Joe's chest and the interior vibration of a deep pleasant baritone joining in the chant.

It seemed to last for hours. Whatever must Helen be thinking, who had so innocently suggested a song? She turned to see. Helen, looking frail and delicate, tucked into the arm of a large athletic young man, was leaning back her head and carolling prettily, as if she were in church.

Horror and shame, combined with sherry and ginger-beer, caused the room to swim before Elsie's eyes. Dimly she perceived Leo beating time on the shoulder of her neighbour, an intellectual-looking person who had removed his horn-rimmed spectacles and was waving them to the rhythm. Between two especially outrageous verses he remarked, suddenly, 'You know, that's very interesting,' and explained why in terms of the latest psychological research. Everyone agreed that it was, very; and at once fell to with the same zest as before.

Elsie scarcely knew when one song ended and another began. This time it was the ancient classic about the rich man getting the pleasure and the poor getting the blame. They had, naturally, improved it a little. It seemed to Elsie scarcely less appalling than the first. Several people had pet verses of their own, and contributed them solo. During one of these she realized that Joe's arm was still round her waist, and felt herself grow cold all over. She was wondering how to get away when, in the most natural way in the world, he withdrew his arm to light a cigarette, and did not put it back again.

See 'is heir in silken cradle,
   With attendants by the score,
While she lays a nameless barstard
   Down beside Barnardo's door.

'Getting a bit hot in here, isn't it?' said Joe in her ear.

Elsie turned on him the eyes of a hunted hare.

'It is,' she whispered, 'a bit.' She was surprised to find that she could still speak.

See him at the billiard-table,
   Potting cannons off the red,
While the victim of his passion . . .

'Like to come out on deck for a bit, and have a blow?'

'Yes,' said Elsie, 'please.'

No one seemed to notice them go. Outside the air was cool and sweet, and in the light from the windows behind them, the water rippled like black satin. Joe sat down on the low rail, straddled a leg over it, and took a deep breath, smelling the night. He looked as if he were alone; and Elsie, too, felt peaceful, unmolested and free. Even the song, drifting through the window, seemed musical and remote.

'A lovely night,' said Joe, breaking a silence of nearly a minute. 'Isn'tit?'

'Yes . . . It *was* a bit hot indoors.'

As if he were pursuing the same subject, Joe said, 'You don't want to pay any attention to that. It does them good, you know.'

'Oh,' said Elsie. She picked up the end of a splinter from the rail, and became absorbed in pulling it off.

'Not that I've had much truck with hospitals myself: but it stands to reason. No one who does what these people do, and sees what they see, could go on taking the human body seriously all their spare time. If they did, they'd go loco – I mean it would get them down.'

'Oh,' said Elsie. 'I see.'

'The women particularly. On top of their own troubles, they've got several generations of hush-hush and brooding in corners, and then all that nervous frank-and-fearless stuff in the twenties, to get off their chests. Personally, it makes me feel good to see them. Healthy as your mother sweeping house.'

Elsie felt a little offended by this simile; her mother had never been without a good general and help with rough, and she would have liked to indicate this; but suddenly it seemed less important than she had thought. She looked at Joe's silhouette, square and angular, planted firmly on the rail, and thought, she did not know why, of the man with the sandwiches on the train. He had given her a feeling that was rather the same, like a glimpse from shipboard of a safe and happy land. Indoors, the voices rose to a fortissimo for the final chorus.

It's the same the 'ole world over –
    It's the poor wot gets the blame,
It's the rich wot gets the pleasure;
    Ain't it all a bleedin' shame?

'I'm all right really,' she said.

'Of course you are.'

She moved her hand over the rough wood of the rail. Its grain and texture, the flaking paint under her fingers, were new and delightful, as if she were feeling them for the first time. Her senses seemed to clear and quicken, making her aware of smells and sounds unregarded before; the plop of a jumping fish, a whiff of Turkish tobacco mixed with the dankness of water-weed, the whistle of a distant train. Joe's cigarette glowed against the pale translucence of the reflected sky. His even voice ran on, without insistence, indifferent to reply.

'You know, this reminds me of something. When I was a kid, if I'd behaved myself for a week or two beforehand, they used to let me tag along with the remuda now and again. I'd help with the bedding-rolls and give a hand on the chuck-wagon, easy jobs like that. The nights were the best. We slept in the open, mostly, in blankets round the fire; there was a smell of wood-smoke and coffee and old leather and grass, and you could hear the wrangler – that's the fellow who keeps an eye on the horses – singing somewhere to pass the time and keep himself awake, just bits of things, you know, as they came into his head. Some of them were as sentimental as a valentine, and some – well, they'd make to-night's repertoire sound like nursery rhymes. I remember one beautiful night, rather like this – clearer, of course – waking a bit before dawn and being slightly astonished by what I heard, and thinking to myself, 'Oh, well, it's only Slim, so it must be all right,' and turning over and going to sleep again. Queer how one forgets things for years, and suddenly they come back. Do you smoke, by the way?'

'I've tried,' said Elsie with an honesty that surprised herself, 'but I couldn't get on with it.' She looked down at the water, unembarrassed by the silence that had fallen again. She felt foolish and trivial, and yet, somehow, the feeling was good. At length she said, 'Have you ever been back there?' not for the sake of conversation, but because she wanted to know.

'No. I've never been back ... You see, all these people were friends of mine. They'd been bringing me up, ever since I could walk, to be one of themselves, and I'd taken it for granted too that I would be. I should have had my father's ranch when I was twenty-one. But I was up at Oxford by then and I knew I didn't belong any more. My uncle had been running it so I turned it over to him. He's often asked me to go over, but – well, I couldn't take to the idea of dropping in and gawping at them all like a tourist. Now I'm older and not so scared of being laughed at, and there'll be hardly anyone left who remembers me, perhaps I might some day.' He paused, as if he were thinking it over. His voice had been quite matter-of-fact, without self-pity or discontent. Presently he glanced round at her and said, 'You're not dressed very warmly for out here. Have my jacket. Or would you like to go in now?'

'Yes,' said Elsie. 'I think I would.' With sudden decision she added, 'I think it's a very nice party.'

'Sensible girl.' He opened the door for her, as if she had been grown up. 'Go ahead and have a good time. You're doing fine.'

Elsie settled herself back into the circle. To her surprise she found that everyone seemed, mysteriously, more friendly and interested. The guests, knowing nothing of her and very little of Joe, and observing that she looked the better for whatever had taken place, had drawn the obvious conclusion; but this fact did not occur to her, and Joe, who had counted on it to further his endeavours, observed the effect with an enjoyment which he kept, like much else, to himself.

The young man on her other side actually engaged her in conversation. He had spent a holiday in Cornwall some years before and was interested in caves. The caves had interested Elsie also, with the vividness of acute fear; warmed, however, by the glow of success, she discussed them with an enthusiasm in which even she herself believed. The young man said it was too bad that while she was there they hadn't met. When Joe drifted away to sit beside Leo, she never missed him.

The shandy and the advancing night began to make her a little sleepy. She watched the party, comfortably, taking part in it less and less, but no longer feeling left out. When it finally broke up, the young man bade her an individual goodbye, and said that when next he was down that way they must certainly get up an expedition. 'Always happy to meet a cave-woman,' he said, and they both laughed. It was the greatest social triumph she had ever achieved. She was still lit up with it when the noise of Joe's last punt-load – the ferry had long since gone to bed – was fading across the water.

'Do you think it went off all right?' said Helen, rubbing off beer-stains with a duster from the furniture and floor.

'I thought it was tremendous fun.' Elsie spoke from the heart; she was busily collecting the empty glasses with a confused idea of remaining by this means still in the swim.

'I thought you seemed to be getting along with Barry very well.'

Elsie blushed with pride. 'We were just talking about caves.'

'Well, take my advice and don't go too far down one with Barry.'

'Oh, *Helen*, what nonsense.' Elsie's cup of happiness was full.

Outside, on deck, Leo was shaking the table-cloth and the rug. Through the open door, Elsie heard the flurry of wavelets under the flat prow of a punt, and the drip of water from the pole.

'Just looked back,' said Joe's voice, 'to let you know that nobody fell in.'

'Come in and have another before you go.'

'No thanks, I've just reached my optimum. It was a darned good party. I like your people.'

'They're Helen's, really.'

'Oh, well, it's the same thing, isn't it. What's the name of the ginger lad I talked to, by the way?'

'Boyd-Smith. He's at Guy's.'

'He said I could come and look at the post-mortem room if I liked. I think I will; you never know when a thing like that will come in useful.' There was a little bump from the punt or the pole as he drew alongside. 'You know, it's quite some time since I last saw you in a female manifestation. Very nice, if I may say so. That frock's a good red.'

'It's all right for a minute. I soon get bored with it.'

'What a night, isn't it? It seems a shame to go indoors. Why don't you get in the punt, and we'll go up river for a bit. It's a good finish to a party, I always think.'

'Not to-night. Thanks all the same, Joe. I can't leave Helen to do all the clearing up; she had to get up early this morning. To-morrow sometime.'

'O.K. I'll go on my own, I think.' The pole scraped again He lifted his voice. 'Good night, Helen. Thanks for the party. 'Night, Elsie.' The sound of the ripples quickened, like crisp stuff tearing, and died away. Leo came back into the room.

'Lord, I'm sleepy,' she said. 'Let's leave everything till the morning.'

They went up to bed.

Elsie, when at last her stimulated imagination settled to the edge of sleep, was wakened again by the flapping and rattling of the casement. When she crept, reluctantly, from her warm bed to close it, she felt rain on her hand. Presently it was driving down in sheets, drumming on the flat roof, flicking willow branches, like whips, against the windows. But in the meantime, Elsie, worn out with mental effort and new experience, had fallen asleep.

'What a lovely noise,' said Helen. She stretched herself, soft and catlike. 'Particularly when it's Sunday in the morning.'

'It would be lovely' – Leo's voice was suddenly wakeful – 'if I hadn't left the pumping this morning. Do you know what? I think this might quite easily sink us, if I don't go out and do some now.'

'What, in this, and one in the morning? What a ghastly idea. We left it nearly three days once.'

'Yes, but it was dead fine. It's no good, I'll have to and that's all about it.'

'I'll come and help.'

'Of course you won't, it was my morning to do it.' She slid out of bed.

'Well, take your pyjamas off, or the legs will get soaked under your mac.'

'I shan't bother with a mac either. One's skin dries so much more easily than anything else. It's quite warm and there's no one about for miles and the moon's gone in.'

'You'll catch pneumonia.'

'Nonsense. It hardens you.'

She stepped out into the downpour and returned ten minutes later laughing, naked and wet as a fish, reaching for the towel she had hung ready on the knob of the door. Helen had switched the fire on, and the room was bright with a coral glow.

'That was marvellous. I can't think why I never did it before.'
A light steam rose from her in the warmth of the fire.

'Get your pyjamas on, for heaven's sake, and drink this while
it's hot.'

'This is good. What have you put in it? '

'Arsenic. Get into bed.'

'Perhaps you ought to have married a sailor. We don't know
any sailors, do we. I'm beautifully warm. The fish were jumping
like mad, and a swan took off from practically under my feet, like
a sort of white explosion, and went away honking. I can't come
for a minute, my hair's still wet. I could stay up all night, now. I
wish there were something amazing to do.'

'You ought to have gone with Joe when he asked you. I
wonder if he got back before the rain.'

'He won't mind if he didn't. It's a good job we got that hole in
his roof mended. I helped him do it on Thursday. We made quite
a good job of it, with tarred felt and beaver-boarding.'

'That crazy shack of his will blow down some night, if you ask
me.'

'Not it. He built it himself, and he knows how. It's perfectly
solid really; I've slept there on a worse night than this and it
didn't budge.'

'You never told me you'd slept at Joe's.'

'Oh, I must have. That time one of the piles gave way, when
you were in town.'

'What happened?'

'I told you what happened. Some fool crashed a launch into it.
Tight, I suppose. I'd have had to sleep on the roof if Joe hadn't
put me up.'

'You know that's not what I meant. What happened at Joe's?'

'Nothing, of course. Except Joe tried to teach me to play the
mouth-organ. What a fool thing to ask.'

'There's no need to be cross. I suppose it was. But why? That's
what I can't understand.'

'Why what?'

'Why is it a fool thing to ask? You like him five times as much as any of these people you've picked up and dropped. And I should think you could have had him years ago if you'd done the first thing about it. I started wondering again tonight when you wouldn't go on the river with him. I didn't mean to say anything, I knew you wouldn't like it. But then again, why? I've wondered for years, I suppose, on and off. At first I thought I'd mind, but then I knew I wouldn't; he'd have been so right.'

'So right? Joe?' The quick movement of her head tossed a handful of drops, with fierce little hisses, against the glowing bars. 'What's come over you, Helen? You must have had too much to drink.'

'You see, it makes you angry. Why?'

'Why? Well, naturally. It's – it's indecent. I just feel it is. I don't know why.'

'Hasn't he ever tried?'

'He did once when he was mildly plastered after one of Emma's parties. I forgot to warn him about her cocktails, and he had four. We laughed about it all the rest of the way home. That must be more than a year ago.'

'Well – didn't you care about it?'

'I didn't stop to see, I twisted his ears.'

'And yet you let Roger Brent . . . Sometimes I can't make you out.'

'Roger Brent? Good God, what does he matter? Here, I'm coming to bed. This is the most idiotic conversation I ever took part in.'

She reached for her pyjamas, tugged them on, and switched off the fire. The golden rods faded to crimson, to dusky red, and went out. But with a perversity born of the hour rather than her nature, Helen persisted. 'Wouldn't you be jealous if you knew he had another woman?'

'What do you mean, another woman? He has a woman, of course. I've always known that.'

'You didn't tell me.' Helen's voice was suddenly subdued.

'What of it, anyway? That's his business. It's got nothing to do with me.'

'Who is she? What's she like?'

'How on earth should I know who she is? You don't suppose he'd talk about her. And if you want to know what she's like, you can read I suppose. He didn't get his stuff for *The Pillar of Cloud* by listening to the conversation over the bar.'

'I suppose not. It didn't strike me.'

'It probably didn't strike him either. It's a pretty good novel. But one would know, I should think, if he'd never written a line. It takes a healthy digestion and a sound sex life to produce a temperament like Joe's.'

'Why don't they get married, then?'

'Ask him, why don't you? It could be that he picked a woman who isn't half witted. Maybe she can read too. What'd he do, take a nice settled job and write for an hour or two in the evenings? Or write for a living? He's not very inventive, you know; it has to be something he's felt about. Five years' hack-work and he'd be finished. Shooting would be too good for a woman who'd domesticate Joe.'

'All right, don't wake Elsie. You don't have to shoot anyone now.'

'Sorry. What are we talking about? I don't know, do you?'

'No, darling. It's only that sometimes I wish I did.'

'Let's go to sleep. Anything looks vague and complicated at two in the morning. Particularly the simplest things.'

'Sometimes I think I ought to approach you more scientifically. My knowledge of you is all so empirical.'

'I shouldn't worry,' said Leo sleepily. 'It works all right.'

CHAPTER FOURTEEN

Sunday was memorable, in the first place, for being the first really hot day of the year. The white mists of morning were gilded with sunlight which, before ten o'clock, had drunk them all, and by noon was beating on the water as on a polished mirror, throwing up ripples of light against the sides of the houseboat. Elsie, who had got up for the early service, felt a promise of summer in the air. The trouble she had felt in church dispelled before it. Finding on her return the others still asleep, she ran to the pump in her church-going clothes (the ones catalogued so faithfully by the B.B.C.) and pumped for twenty minutes. This completed the cure. Everything was still fresh from last night's rain; the green willows danced; overhead a lark was singing like a bubble of sparkling air. The handle she pulled on moved very easily; she wondered why it had never occurred to her to do this before. Her hat, which she had forgotten to remove, slipped to the back of her head, and her hymn-book lay on the hardly dry boards of the deck at her feet. So happy was she that it even occurred to her that too much of her time was spent in anticipation of the future; it seemed, at this moment, to be a waste. Presently she smelled coffee and went in, full of virtue, to find that Leo and Helen had breakfast ready.

'I've done all the pumping for to-day,' she announced proudly. 'It wasn't a bit hard work.'

Leo and Helen exchanged glances.

'Thank you,' said Leo at length. 'That was very nice of you. Was the sermon good?'

'You don't have a sermon at early service,' said Elsie with gentle reproof.

'We'll just get the place straight,' Helen said, 'and then have a really lazy day. No work and no people. How lovely.'

Elsie, who felt that her day's good deed was well and truly done, went upstairs to take off her tidy clothes while they did the accumulated washing-up.

In the afternoon the sun was dazzling, with just enough breeze along the water to temper it. Helen brought out from its winter wrappings a bright flowered sun-suit which made her look at first glance like a pretty and intelligent child; Leo wore a two-piece bathing costume which covered, all in, about an eighth of her length; and to Elsie, whose packing had not provided for such occasions, they lent a sports shirt and some linen shorts which were a little small for Helen, and reached a third of the way down her thighs. She felt self-conscious in them at first, but the delightful play of sun and air on her skin soon made her forget it. They took all the cushions in the place on to the flat roof and sprawled there; swam in the river (it was so hot by now that even Elsie needed no coaxing); ate a scrap lunch and sprawled again. Leo went over the page-proofs of her new book, complete with the title (*Outlaw Marshal*) and the chapter headings (such as 'Lefty Rides Alone'); she plodded through it till the heat made her fountain-pen leak, when, losing interest, she wiped off the surplus ink on the seat of her bathing costume, produced from somewhere a penny whistle, and began to play. Helen retrieved the proof and read it idly, beginning in the middle. Elsie lay on her back with her arm across her eyes, getting hotter and hotter as it drew to mid-afternoon. Her skin felt shiny and tingling, but she bore it with confidence because Leo's and Helen's had already the smooth creamy look which precedes a tan.

Her head ached a little; stars of green and red light, printed by the sun's bright reflection, swam under her eyelids. She wondered when Peter would answer her letter, and what he would say. The little jiggy tune that Leo was playing (it was *Auprès de ma Blonde*) ran through her head like a beating pulse and mixed itself with her thoughts. She was almost asleep. Helen, with her smooth cheek on the description of a lynching-bee and her silky hair entangled with Lefty's smoking guns, slumbered outright, relaxed like a cat in a sunny shop window. Leo, propped with her back against the flagpole, played verse after verse of *Auprès de ma Blonde*, accompanying the words as they ran through her mind; it was an easy tune and she lacked the energy to change it. She was the only one of the three suflficiently awake to have heard the door-bell tinkle below, and the sound of her own piping masked it in her careless ear.

Elsie's reverie was disintegrating into dream. She was standing on the lower deck, hot and flushed from the party; the people in the room behind were whistling a song, whistling on her account because she had not liked the words; it embarrassed her and made her feel hotter than ever. Suddenly the music stopped, in the middle of a phrase. The reality of the silence woke her. She turned, trying to focus her sun-dazzled eyes. Leo still sat against the flagpole, her long bare legs curled under her, a lock of dark hair curling damply on her forehead, her penny whistle suspended half-way to her mouth. The sun had given her arms and shoulders a polish like bronze. Her long throat, and her slanting brows, were lifted in a kind of detached enquiry. Elsie, collecting herself, looked in the same direction. Standing at the head of the ladder, in the act of mounting its final rung, was Peter. He too had stopped, and was meeting Leo's eyes with a boyish, charming, tentative smile.

In the first few seconds, Elsie experienced practically no emotion at all. Similiarly, people feel very little in the early stages of being knocked down by a car.

'I do hope you don't mind my coming upstairs. You sent me a sort of invitation to call.' He transferred his smile, briefly, to Elsie; she blinked dazedly, feeling, as she struggled to respond, a blush stinging her face like fire where the sun had caught it. It did not occur to her that he was waiting for her to introduce him. When nothing happened, he added, quite unperturbed, 'My name's Peter Bracknell.'

Helen's eyes opened. The sound of a young, male, attractive voice reacted on her slumber like morning sun on a daisy's. She awoke charmingly, like the unfolding of rosy petals, and smiled like the golden eye of a flower. The exchange of approval that followed was as pretty as a pastoral. Leo watched it for a moment amusedly, then, as she remembered, her eyes slid round to Elsie. Good heavens, she thought, poor little wretch. I must get her in quickly, while there's time.

'How do you do?' she said aloud. 'I guessed who you were. So glad you were able to get over. You're just in time for tea.'

'I guessed who you were, too.' It would have been difflcult to charge a short sentence more highly with subtle and flattering implication. He followed it with a long, speculative, intimate look; the kind of look appropriate between people who, in a wilderness of mediocrity, are going to understand one another. Then, 'Hullo, Elsie,' he said. 'Lord, you do look fit.'

'I'm awfully well, now,' said Elsie, blushing again. If only, she thought, the sun had not given her this dazed, blurred feeling, which made everything seem a little unreal. She sat up on her cushion, trying to arrange herself becomingly; the movement sent a throb of pain across her forehead. She felt, suddenly, sticky and dirty, and was aware of the smallness of her shorts. While Peter was settling himself on a spare cushion which Helen threw him, she tried inconspicuously to pull them lower, and, this fail-ing, to copy the composure of the others. Leo, after all, was practically naked, but betrayed no consciousness of it at all. What a terrible thing it was, thought Elsie, to be in love; what a hopeless, insurmountable disadvantage.

It would be helpful, Leo was thinking, to know just what Elsie has been telling this man about me. There seems no conceivable reason why he should look at me as if he were putting my latch-key in his pocket, prettily as he does it. It isn't so much what he suggests, as what he takes for granted. He can't even light one a cigarette without somehow implying that you and he have just got out of bed together. (It was a fact that she felt even a little shy, a sensation which she always resented and generally avenged.) Where did the unfortunate child manage to catch this tartar? '—Yes, we live here in the winter as well; we're used to it, I suppose.' I wonder if she's ever seen him with other people before.

Elsie never had. She sat silent on her cushion, taking no part in the exchange of amenities, and wishing for none. She would have enjoyed an equal, perhaps a greater rapture during these moments if she had been invisible. There he sat, the truth, the reality which had been fading, the image which had worn almost threadbare in the constant trafficking of dreams. 'In the flesh' – it was an ugly phrase, suggesting parts of the Bible which one wished afterwards one had not read. There ought to be other words for the miracle of substance. She stored it as a desert plant stores rain, seizing on small details which would help afterwards to re-create it, for it must bear the weight of reverie again; a smooth concavity in the temple, an irregularity in the line of the eyebrow, the dark worn strap of his wrist-watch and the figures on the dial. On the back of his right hand was a little scar, a very old one; it must have been there since he was a boy. Some day perhaps she would ask him how it happened, and he would tell her that he had fallen off a bicycle, or slipped climbing a tree. But now for a little while, until one was acclimatized to felicity, it was better to watch silently, to see him for the first time with sophis-ticated, critical people, as brilliantly self-assured as he had been with her alone, and making the impression which anywhere in the world, thought Elsie, he would be bound to make. To know him, to have brought him here, was in itself success beyond triumph. Presently the others would go to get the tea, and they would be left alone. Her hands grew cold at the thought, her heart beat till it shook her diaphragrn, her legs felt like lead. She remembered the kiss he had given her on the cliffs; and put away the thought because, though he was talking to Helen, it seemed that he would know.

Helen was thinking very little. It was not her habit to think about new people at first, particularly about new men. She allowed them, passively, to seep into her subconscious, making in the meantime such responses as called for the minimum of effort. People were apt to be misled by the outward part of this process, and to receive surprises when, at a suitable moment, the silent commission within presented its findings. Peter offered little disturbance to this routine; to be gazed at like chocolate cake in a tuckshop window was for her a social commonplace, interesting only in its slight variations, like the custom of shaking hands. She absorbed it along with the sunshine, making as little effort over the one as the other; a course which had always answered so well that she had never had occasion to examine it.

Leo threw her cigarette over into the river, and stood up.

'We'll give you a call,' she said, 'when tea's ready. Come on, Elsie.'

'I cut beautiful bread and butter,' said Peter winningly. 'I'm very domesticated.'

'It's cut already. You stay and talk to Helen. We shan't be long.'

Elsie got to her feet, turning on Leo eyes of incredulous reproach. She knew that tea had not been started yet. Leo's lack of perception almost stunned her. As she went indoors, the shade seemed darkness after the sun's glare. She felt her throat grow hot with angry tears and a burning in her eyes. She hardly noticed that she was being propelled, not into the kitchen, but into Leo's room, until she found herself pushed down on the stool before the little walnut dressing-chest.

'Here,' said Leo. She thrust under Elsie's nose a pad of cotton-wool, soaked with something cool and scented. 'Do your face over with that. Don't wash it, whateveryou do. Then put some of this cream on, and I'll come back in a minute and do the top layer for you. Don't worry. I'll fix you up all right.'

She was gone. Elsie sat, with the pad of lotion in her hand, confronted by the small oval mirror which always made so perfect a frame for Helen's fair-head. Perhaps it had grown spoiled and hard to please. It showed her a pink, boiled face, glazed with fresh sunburn; a mouth which, without make-up looked almost the same colour as the surrounding skin; a beef-red V, shaped to the opening of her shirt, between her collar-bones; tousled hair, from which every trace of gloss had been baked away. The eyes, round and tragic with realization, turned the total effect from comedy to grotesque. Memory presented her suddenly with the image of Helen, smiling and golden, leaning on a dark-blue cushion in her fresh flowered print. She put her hand up to her eyes; the touch hurt her forehead as if it were raw, and she saw that her nails were grubby round the edges.

A chink of crockery sounded downstairs. Leo despatched domestic jobs very quickly, because they bored her. In a moment she would be back again. Desperately, without hope but only to escape more trouble, Elsie drew the wet pad over her face. It was cool and soothing; after wiping her hands too, she reached for the cream and smoothed it on. She felt more comfortable, but looked no better than before. At least, she thought forlornly, Leo would be changing; she looked, when she took the trouble, quite interesting and distinguished, a relative to do one credit and show that one amounted to something after all. An author too. Perhaps Peter wouldn't ask, just this first time, what it was she wrote.

The quick pad of bare feet sounded on the steps.

I've brought you your frock. Good Lord, haven't you done your hair yet? Here's a pair of silk stockings you can wear if you like; it'll save having to do your legs, anyway. Now keep still and I'll see to you.' She pulled open one of the drawers, and rummaged in the back of it. 'I'm sure we kept it. Yes, here it is.' The powder in the box was a delicate shade of green. Elsie stared at it in horror, but dared no protest while Leo patted it on. She expected to look like a corpse, but only found, when she screwed up her courage to see, the pink polish miraculously toned down. Leo dusted it with a soft brush like a baby's, and covered it with powder of a more normal shade. 'Now grin, and hold it while I do your mouth. No idiot, not a face like that. Oh, hell – smile! That'll do. Now stop wriggling and shut up.'

The lipstick – a kindly, non-committal shade – went on; the shirt came off; Leo brushed brilliantine into her hair, and stroked a film of liquid powder thinly over her arms and chest. She held out the Viennese dress. Elsie beheld a miracle. There was no painted look, only fresh smoothness and vitality. She murmured incoherent thanks, and drank it in, turning this way and that, till she remembered that Leo would be needing the mirror too.

'What are you changing into?' she asked, eager to please by showing interest. She still found it hard to tear her eyes from the new face in the oval frame.

'I've changed,' said Leo briefly.

Elsie turned round. Leo's handful of bathing-suit lay tossed in a corner. She had on her old fawn corduroy slacks and a faded blue cotton shirt. As she spoke, she gave the waist a perfunctory twitch and, picking up a comb, ran it without looking through her hair. A packet of cigarettes must have been in the pocket already; she lit one, and, pulling at it, glanced over her shoulder.

'Right,' she said. 'Let's get going.'

Elsie did not move. She sat on the dressing-stool, gazing at the slim shabby boy whose appearance in the last few weeks she had grown to take for granted; but not to-day. Disappointment choked her. Descriptive phrases from the letter she had written to Peter rose up, tauntingly, mixed with memories of Leo at the party in the scarlet dress. Now, when it mattered so much more, surely she could have taken the trouble! Elsie felt that she was being made, deliberately, to look ridiculous.

'Come on,' said Leo. 'You look all right now. I'm going to make the tea.'

'That isn't what you're really going to wear,' said Elsie at last, 'is it?'

'Yes, of course. Do get a move on.'

'Aren't you going to wear your red dress?'

'What, in the middle of the afternoon? Don't be daft.'

'You've got lots of others. You showed me.'

'I can't be bothered; it's too hot.'

'I think you might.' Elsie stared at her toe, which she was digging into a rough place in the matting. 'I told Peter about you. He was looking forward to meeting you. It wouldn't be much bother.'

Leo stood back on her flat heels, staring at her sister. She opened her mouth to say something, and drew at her cigarette instead. At length she said, with unexpected gentleness, 'What does it matter? It's you, isn't it, he's come to see?'

Elsie looked at the floor. Even to herself her feelings were obscure. Mixed with the indignation whose cause she knew were hostilities more universal; the enmity of enforced humility for pride; of those whom convention comforts, for those who threaten it; strongest of all perhaps, and suspected least, of the unmixed female for the unfair, unaccountable sitter-on-the-fence.

'I think it's a bit mean of you,' she said in a shaking voice. 'When you had people coming I took ever so much trouble to look nice.'

'You almighty little fool.'

Elsie looked up. It was a voice she had never heard Leo use before, and it frightened her. It was like being roughly handled by someone whose strength one had not guessed. Leo stood with her hands deep in her trouser pockets, her cigarette in the corner of her mouth, looking down at her; her dark narrowed eyes, for an unguarded moment, loaded with the whole withering retort of the other side. Elsie did not recognize the answer which her

vague, ill-digested resentment had called forth; she did not
understand it; but what it contained of angry, half-compassion-
ate, hopeless disdain crumpled her flat. The headache shot across
her eyes, mixed with the pricking of tears. Leo saw, and, collecting herself quickly, laughed and put an arm round her shoulders,
roughly, like the boy she looked. 'Don't you fuss,' she said. 'It'll be
all right. I'm looking after you the best way I can.'

This bewildering transition was too much for Elsie's shaken
emotional balance. She made a gulping noise.

Leo withdrew her arm and said, crisply, 'If you cry all over that
face I've done you, I'll wring your silly neck.'

'I wasn't . . . I've got a bit of a headache from the sun.'

'Well, why on earth didn't you say so? Here, have some of this.
It's a sort of cocktail they use in hospital. Helen brought it back.'

She poured some whitish stuff from a bottle into a glass; it
tasted of aspirin with some extra bitterness added. 'It'll work in
about ten minutes. Now come on, and pull your socks up . . .
Helen hasn't had a chance to change; I must be a bit unsmart to
keep her company, mustn't I? Don't worry, we'll see it goes off all
right. Ready now?'

'Yes,' said Elsie. 'I'm sorry, Leo.'

'Oh shucks.' She put her head out of the doorway. 'Hey! Tea's
just ready.'

They went down.

Peter, with Helen, reached the dining-room a couple of minutes later. It had been very pleasant on the roof; he was feeling,
already, more than pleased that he had taken the trouble to
come. His eyes still a little dazzled from the sun, he returned
with puzzled cordiality the smile of the lad in the blue shirt and
corduroys.

'I've put you here,' said Leo, 'between Helen and Elsie. It's
rather a squash, I'm afraid.'

Peter blinked, stared and blinked again. But by the time he
had accepted from Helen his cup of tea, a new brightness had
come into his eyes. Inconspicuously he looked from the dark

head on the other side of the table to the fair one bent over the tea-tray, and about him at the room with its mixture of possessions, so clearly individualized, the accumulation evidently of years. He was delighted. It was all going to be even more original and interesting than he had supposed. They were both so untypical, so different from the conventional idea. All kinds of possibilities opened . . . Something was being waved in front of him. It was a plate of cress sandwiches, held in an unsteady wavering hand. He turned, with his most engaging smile, and took one.

'Why, Elsie,' he said, 'what a marvellous frock you've been getting since I saw you last.'

CHAPTER FIFTEEN

The ferry-boat receded. Leo and Helen waved, amiably, until it was half-way across. They turned, caught one another's eyes, went indoors, and sat down.

'Well!' said Helen.

Leo lit a cigarette and said, 'Well?'

'Don't look at me. I could have. But I didn't.'

'I should hope not. What, on the roof? You were only up there fifteen minutes.'

'It seemed longer . . . Elsie. I can't fathom it. Can you?'

'I'm not sure. I think I can, as a matter of fact. Poor little swine.'

Helen locked her hand behind her head, and stared mistily at the ceiling. Leo lit her a cigarette, and passed it over. She smoked it for a minute or two before remarking; 'Your gentlemanly behaviour impressed me very much.'

'Well. That was obvious, I should think.'

'It was only too obvious to me. At that stage of an encounter, it struck me as the worst possible sign.'

Leo laughed, and said nothing.

'You know, don't you, you told him the train time half an hour early.'

'Of course. She'll have that with him, even if it is in a draught in the waiting-room.'

'You're generally so vague about these things. I thought it might be an accident . . . You're a fool. We're both fools. The kindest thing we could have done would have been to play him along, and let her see in time.'

'I'm not particularly good at doing kindnesses like that to other women. It would make me feel sick, rather. In time for what, anyway? She's up to her neck now.'

'Couldn't you talk to her, or something?'

'Don't be silly.'

There was another silence. Helen said, at length, 'You could always send her home.'

'I know. How good do you think you'd be at amputating someone's leg without an anaesthetic?'

'Not very, I suppose. There must be *something*.'

'One thing, it'll fall of its own weight, inevitably, before very long.'

'Perhaps we could find her someone else.'

'Darling, you dazzle me. Perhaps we could turn a keen Evangelical into a Buddhist. Or perhaps not.'

Helen said, after another pause of fruitless thought, 'If it were anyone but Elsie. You know, taken with a pinch of salt, he's rather sweet.'

'And vice versa. I don't know, but I have a feeling it's someone like Elsie rather often.'

'I wonder what they're talking about now.'

'Us,' said Leo, 'I expect.' She blew a puff of smoke up into the air.

'What?'

'With, on his part, such exquisite tact that she won't have the remotest idea what he's driving at. I saw it in his eye.'

'Do you realize,' said Helen, 'that he'll probably come here again?'

'I realized that within two minutes, thanks.'

'So what?'

'Your answer's as good as mine.'

'I don't know . . . Ask Joe what he'd do.'

'For God's sake. What do you imagine Joe and I talk about? He'd say 'All you can give her is rope,' I expect. He believes in using rope very extensively.'

'That must save him a lot of trouble.'

'It doesn't, because he minds rather what's going on at the other end. He pretends not to, but . . . What on earth are we wandering off about Joe for? Where were we?'

'Deciding what line to take next time Peter called.'

'We can always be out, I suppose.'

Helen considered this. Her conclusion was to remark, thoughtfully, 'Has something rather unusual struck you about us?'

'Not for several years. Why?'

'Only that I can't remember an occasion when we've ever reacted to the same man.'

'It's a providence,' said Leo lazily, 'that watches over us.'

'My feeling is that it's taken an afternoon off.'

'You're crazy.'

'Sure?'

'No. Well, at least . . . It's all so damned ridiculous.'

'I thought so . . . Elsie's our providence this time, I suppose. But honestly. If she weren't there?'

'Well, I think . . . No, it's absurd.'

'Taking that for granted, what?'

'His temptation, as far as I'm concerned,' said Leo slowly 'would be his complete invulnerability. He's pure gutta-percha. He'd come back from anything. When you've – hurt people who don't deserve it, it's rather inviting.'

'I think it's rather unkind.'

'Oh, he's not like that all through. In his job, for instance, it wouldn't surprise me to find him deeply perceptive and a hundred per cent sincere. I could work with him and like it. But in a personal relationship, you'd never puncture that beautiful understanding . . . However, don't worry. I'm not proposing to try. Are you?'

'Not while Elsie's here, anyhow. You're right; one couldn't. It's a form of selfishness, I suppose.'

'Very likely. I wish we could get her out of it some other way.'

'We'll have to think. We make that remark rather a lot lately, don't we . . . We've never thought, have we, what we'd do if we both did react the same way, really, some time.'

'Just act natural, I suppose, and let it evolve. What else could one do?'

'Nothing, of course. It wouldn't be important, anyway.'

'Well, this has all done Elsie a lot of good, hasn't it? What a long time we've been getting nowhere. Let's clear the tea. She won't feel like anything as sordid as washing-up when she comes in.'

With the sinking sun throwing her long shadow stealthily before her, Elsie crept down the ladder from her room, hugging under her arm the little bundle she had made. There was no one in sight. She crossed the plank bridge into the garden, and, taking from the border a large stone, thrust it carefully into the centre of the package. The water below the bridge looked deep; but it would be deeper, no doubt, on the other side. She went down to the floating deck, and, leaning far over, dropped the bundle in.

'Whatever on earth,' said Leo behind her, 'do you think you're doing?'

Elsie gave one of those internal jumps which are so slight to look at, so horrible to feel. She spun round, gasped, and said, 'Nothing, really. It's quite all right.'

'Sorry,' said Leo. 'I didn't mean to startle you. But people do look odd, dropping their clothes into the river. I mean, it seems a bit drastic. If you'd had the lace collar off and put on a plain one, and taken in some darts here and there, that frock would have been quite wearable, you know. Maybe with the hat it *was* the only thing. Well, it's your business, of course.'

'It wasn't that. I – I thought I'd better.'

I suppose, Leo reflected, he has expressed a dislike of nigger brown. I must have spoiled the flavour of a *beau geste*. One shouldn't do that. It leaves her, as far as I remember, with one jumper and skirt and a cotton frock. I wonder how it feels to immolate the third part of one's wardrobe to love. Very beautiful, I shouldn't wonder.

'Never mind,' she said. 'I've got a green one you can have instead, if you like. I hardly ever wear it. It'll only want the hem letting down. Come up and I'll show it you.'

Elsie dropped her eyes. 'You are good to me, Leo,' she said to the planking.

'Oh, rubbish. You probably won't like it. Come and try it on.'

'I ought to have told you. It was awful of me not to, when I'm staying with you and everything. I meant to tell you really. You see – I'm Wanted.'

'Oh,' said Leo. There was a short pause, while she took counsel of herself. At last she said, diffidently, 'Don't think me terribly interfering. But just what way does he want you, if you don't mind my putting it like that? He's very nice, of course. Great fun and all that. But you haven't known him awfully long, have you?'

'I didn't mean that.' Elsie's stress of mind was such that she did not even blush. 'I mean I'm wanted by the police.'

'By *who*? Are you feeling all right?'

'Really. Peter told me. I've been broadcast for by the B.B.C., Scotland Yard. My hat, and my frock, and the gold cross and everything. I've hidden the cross in a crack in the floor, I didn't like to throw it away . . . Suppose they had a clue, they could come here and search, couldn't they? Only this morning I wore everything to church.'

Leo sat down on the wooden rail. She looked down at the water, then up at Elsie with straight troubled eyes.

'The family must have been pretty well wrought up,' she said, 'to do that.'

'Perhaps the police did it on their own. Can they?'

'No. I don't think so . . . Mother always used to talk about having one's name in the papers as if it were the last infamy. It won't do Father any good in his job, either, unless local society's changed a good bit since my time.'

'If they find me, can they send me to prison?'

'Oh, pull yourself together. Of course not . . . They must have been going through hell. And each blaming the other, I suppose. Don't you ever think about it at all?'

Elsie's conscience had worked overtime that day already. She put her hand up to her head; it seemed to her that something would break there, that one should be able to call out 'Enough,' and make it stop. The sun had melted Leo's make-up on her face, and the sticky remains of it made her sunburn feel worse than before. The skin burned on her arms and forehead; she felt as if she had fever. She was beyond tears.

'Of course I think about it. I wake up in the middle of the night, and can't go to sleep again for hours. Sometimes I feel as if I were the wickedest person in the world.' The words trickled away from her, without pressure, like the overflow from something that can hold no more. 'When I was at church this morning I couldn't go up to Communion, I felt too bad. I kept thinking perhaps I'd go to hell if I didn't go home, and then that I'd go to hell if I did. I feel wicked at home too, you see, nearly every day. And then it was such a lovely morning I felt better; and in the afternoon . . .' She looked down at the water, and shut her eyes. 'And now it's worse than ever.' She faced round to Leo and said with slow, dull horror, 'You think I ought to go back. I know you do.'

'Don't,' said Leo. 'Please.'

Elsie looked up. The shell of her egoism was pierced by the voice. Leo had spoken as if to a grown-up person. She too was unhappy, and, more remarkable, was allowing it to be seen. Elsie had not guessed before; but Peter had known. Peter knew everything. He had shaken his head and said 'Poor Leo!' as if he expected her to know what he meant, so that she had not liked to confess her ignorance by asking. Perhaps Leo was going to tell her now. Curiosity, and the thought of Peter's omniscience, eased a little the tension in her head. She waited.

'How can I think you ought to do anything? My God, just how smug do you think I am? Surely you realize that a good half of any guilt you're feeling really belongs to me?'

'I don't see that.' To have had her emotion taken seriously by Leo was giving her, already, a dim feeling of importance. 'Just because you let me be here . . . You didn't ask me to come. I did it of my own free will.'

'And what did I do? I went off with my own life and left you holding the baby. There wasn't any way out of it, and I couldn't take you with me. Still, the fact remains. You could have afforded to go away, couldn't you, with a good elder sister living at home. Never mind, I used to say to myself they've always got Elsie. Why shouldn't you have been able to say, Never mind, they've always got Leo? Guilt isn't just sin. That would be simple. Guilt is being responsible for the consequences. Orestes found that out. You're my Eumenides, I suppose.'

Elsie had not read of Orestes, and did not know what Eumenides were, but the ringing mysterious words gave a kind of grandeur to her trouble, and she registered it for future use. Her brain relaxed, she was even interested.

'It isn't either of our faults' (she had often revolved this problem at home) 'that they married each other, is it? I've often wondered why they did.'

'We were born because of it. And whether we like it or not they gave us the power to make them suffer.'

'We didn't ask them to. We didn't even ask to be born.'

'Well. Here we are.'

Elsie shook her head. 'I don't know. I seem to have been wondering all my life.'

'There's no answer,' Leo said. She sat down, as Joe had sat once, on the broad painted rail, and there came into her face and the set of her body a certainty different from his which yet somehow recalled it. She looked ahead of her, and seemed to be speaking chiefly to herself. 'Innocent or guilty one can't get away from having caused someone to suffer. It's a thing which is. One pays for it, somehow, in the end. We shall both pay, I suppose. We have to face that.' Her face had an inward look, as if much more than the present had gone into its decision. 'Never make it inevitable for someone to hurt you. It's a terrible wrong to do another person. Or if it happens, and you can't prevent it, never let them know.'

Elsie found this doctrine strange and unpalatable. Suffering was, in her imagination, a noble condition, a pageant of the spirit, an Elizabethan progress of black velvet and plumes; the necessary panoply of a distinguished emotional life. Such actual suffering as she had experienced at home she would have defined as 'being miserable,' a different thing in a class with acute toothache or mumps, but worse. The thought of associating such a state with Love would have horrified her, if her mind had been capable of grasping it. The pride and splendour of adolescent dream-sorrow invested her with a kind of dignity as she answered, 'If one can't feel the great things of life without suffering, one must be prepared to suffer.'

Twenty-seven looked at seventeen, across a gulf as unbridgeable as interstellar space.

'Oh, well,' said Leo, 'never mind.'

Elsie stared down at her hands. She held something in them which she was turning over and over, secretly, as one might a charm. Averting her face, she said, 'I know I ought to be looking out for a job, or something. I ought to start on a career. I want to do something important with my life, and be a credit to – to you and Helen. But if you wouldn't frightfully mind having me, Leo, I would like to go on staying here, just for a bit. Well, for about two weeks, anyway. It's – it's rather important.'

'Of course you can stay. You know that. Why are the next two weeks so special – something about the boy-friend?' Leo spoke with exaggerated flippancy, as people do in uncertainty of mind.

Elsie winced, but it was too late now, and the matter too urgent, not to continue.

'It is about Peter, actually.' Desperately she tried to make her voice sound light, matter-of-fact and sophisticated, like the voices of Helen's friends. It was impossible to make anyone understand. 'He was telling me at the station, while we were waiting for the train. He has this post for a year, so you see he gets a fortnight's holiday. He's taking half of it this month. He's thinking of putting up at a hotel near here; it's a good centre, he says, and we could see a bit more of each other. It would be rather fun. I mean, now he's made these plans, it would seem rather rude and unkind to leave, wouldn't it?' Leo's face, she saw, had not changed at all. She was looking ahead of her, hard, shut in, incalculable. How was it possible, Elsie thought, that one could feel so much, and someone a couple of yards away be so untouched by it? Eagerly, like one who offers a bribe of inestimable value, she added, 'He likes you and Helen very much. He told me so He thinks you're two very complex and unusual people. He wants to see more of you as well.'

'That's very nice of him.' Leo got down from the rail, and threw her cigarette down into the water, where it went out with a little hiss. 'We wouldn't turn you out anyhow, I told you that. I think we shall have to rely on you, though, to do most of the entertaining. Helen has a lot of jobs on in town, and I'm getting well into the new book now.'

'Oh, thank you,' said Elsie. 'Thank you ever so.' She went away, to be alone with her happiness. Leo was kind – very kind for someone who had, by her own confession, never properly been in love. Elsie pardoned her incomprehension with a charity which, after the walk to the station by the evening Thames, she felt she could well afford; besides, she felt that Peter would approve it. But it was better to be alone. She opened her hands, hot and sticky with emotion and the sun, and looked at the trophy they contained. It was a cardboard packet which had held ten Gold Flake; Peter had thrown it aside on the way to the train, and on the way back she had gathered it up. In the safety of her room she raised it reverently to her lips, before slipping it under her pillow.

CHAPTER SIXTEEN

'Are you sure,' asked Helen, pausing in final doubt in front of the Corner House, 'that you'll really be all right?'

'Of course I will. Really.' Elsie spoke with convincing stoutness; if her plans for the rest of the afternoon had involved a traverse of Snowdon instead of central London she would have been hardly more terrified, but equally determined. Through the broad canyon of Oxford Street, London surged past her, full of its mysterious preoccupations, its compound smells fresh in her unaccustomed nose; dust and petrol, passing perfumes of women, green leaves in a drift of wind vanishing swiftly into the sickliness of warm gear-oil and overclothed humanity, a waft of beer from a crawling dray. Helen, her pencil-case and drawing-block under her arm, seemed already in anticipation to have vanished into it, merging as easily into this strange jungle as a bird into its tree, one more neat female figure among the dozens hurrying past.

'The District Railway back,' Helen reminded her, 'from Charing Cross to King's Cross. I'll meet you under the clock at five. And don't worry about getting lost. If you do in London, it can't mean anything more than wasting half an hour. Any bobby will put you right. Or almost anyone else, for the matter. I'll have to take this bus. See you at five.' She vanished, in what seemed the clap of an eye, into a hot red monster which a traffic jam had slowed down beside them. Elsie was alone, with three hours, London, and the four pounds in her handbag, all to spend. She looked about her. Down the side-street on her left were large, quiet, rich houses, and a humble-looking barrow piled astonishingly with peaches and grapes and roses. Beside her, a shop window was full of complicated corsets, at which a fat woman was wistfully staring. A man in a purple suit and brown boots collided with her as she swayed indeterminately in mid-stream, said 'Pardon me,' and was swallowed up almost before she knew he had been there. A perambulator was bearing down on her. Like a swimmer caught in a current, she began to move along.

Had Peter, she wondered, ever passed over this pavement where her own feet fell? Almost anyone who lived in London must, she supposed, have done so at some time. She tried to imagine him, a yard or two ahead of her, outside this sweetshop window, for instance, where the mechanical chromium arms manipulated an endless rope of nougat. Perhaps he might, in reality, suddenly appear, emerging without warning like the man in the purple suit, and saying 'Hullo, Elsie,' while she was confused and all unready; in a hurry, full, like all these other confident people, of concerns about which she knew nothing. The thought made her feel more than ever bewildered and lonely – Peter, herself, her love, her very consciousness, minute as light-motes in the endless powder of the Galaxy. She walked on, trying to look busy and purposeful and like other people, growing more desolate at every step.

Like a beacon promising harbour, she saw in the middle of the street the reassuring mass of a policeman on point duty. He was directing someone, with the inexhaustable patient courtesy of his kind, and the apparent ease of a juggler who, keeping three balls in the air already, casually adds a fourth. She was already making towards him when she remembered. That rock of changeless security was for others, not for her. Probably her description was copied neatly into his notebook, along with the distinguishing marks of burglars and those whom Scotland Yard was anxious to interrogate. She was outside the law. Receding quickly into the crowd again, she walked on, eyeing the passing faces with nervous distrust, her mother's stories recurring to her one after another. A comfortable-looking woman with three children in tow seemed, at last, a reasonable risk.

'Excuse me. But can you tell me, please, how I could get to St. Jerome's Hospital?'

The woman could; her eldest boy, she explained, had had his tonsils out there. Elsie boarded the bus she had recommended, and, almost at once it seemed, was being carried away from the crowd and glitter into narrow, dingy streets. The wide polished shops, with windows like glasshouses of rare flowers, gave place to small tobacconists, fried fish emporia, and second-hand clothes dealers; the word 'Noted' occurred with increasing frequency on their signs. The bus threaded a street-market, swarming and raucous; inside it grew hotter and hotter, and the close air began to make her feel sick. Another turning, and they ran between huge, black, sinister warehouses; round again and there were tenements, great houses foundered and rotting, where grey washing hung from the windows and dirty children played last across the road. She began to grow anxious; had she taken the wrong bus after all? But no, she had asked the conductor, when she got on. Perhaps she ought to have changed; in a moment or two she would ask again.

The conductor put his head inside.

'St. Jerome's Orspital,' he shouted, looking straight at her.

The bus slowed down; she got dizzily to her feet. In another moment she was alone, among the piping, scuffling children, seeing the shrine of her pilgrimage straight ahead.

She stood on the pavement, her handbag clutched in her hands, staring up at its tall black front, at the iron balconies with their red-blanketed beds, the great dim windows, the covered ways roofed with sooty glass connecting block with block, at the vast hoarding, peeled in places with wind and weather, which cried aloud for money in astronomical sums. At a side-door, marked OUT-PATIENTS, a slow, sullen stream of humanity, derelict, dirty, crutched, plastered and bandaged, was trickling in, without purpose it seemed and without hope. Within, somewhere, a child screamed. A collarless man brushed past her; she saw, with horror, that half his face was painted over in patches of purple. As if the devil were after her, she ran to the other side of the street, narrowly missing a van, and stood panting, her stomach sinking inside her, to look again.

From here she could read the hoarding, which before had been just over her head. It told her, with two-foot emphasis, that St. Jerome's Hospital was fifty thousand pounds in debt.

She squeezed her bag in her hand, trying to deny her misery. This was where Peter spent his nights and days. Where was the austere, aseptic whiteness she had seen in hospital films, the polished metal, the crystal glass, the great wide silent spaces, the background she imagined every night before she went to sleep? The dirt, the squalor, the suffering were like a physical weight, a stifling blanket pressing on her spirit. At this very moment he must be somewhere within, in the dark of this evil labyrinth, where her mind must now forever stop short, afraid to follow him; in which he too must surely suffer some unknown, assimilating change. Heat and wretchedness, and the prevailing smells, made an oppression inside her so that she did not know whether she wanted to faint, or weep, or be sick. Suppose she were really to faint, and they should rush upon her and carry her inside, and call Peter to attend to her? The shockingness of this notion revived her like sal volatile. She perceived one consolation; the place, as the hoarding assured her, was on the verge of having to close down. Perhaps it would.

She had no sooner formed the thought than shame overwhelmed her. Peter's heroism was proven now, if she had never believed in it before. Here was his life-work, at its last gasp for money, and she had actually been glad! Her soul expanded under the light of adoration. She crossed the road, and, groping in her bag, pushed a ten-shilling note into the big wooden box under the hoarding. Comforted and uplifted, she walked back to the stopping-place for her returning bus.

She reached King's Cross ten minutes early, and Helen was ten minutes late; but she waited happily. The thought of her ten shillings warmed her through. Presently it would be taken out of the box and with it, perhaps, an instrument would be bought, or some expensive drug which the hospital with its load of debt could not afford; and in some critical emergency, Peter himself would use it and, it might be, save someone's life, and would never know it had come from her.

'Hullo.' Helen appeared out of the hot crowd, fresh and clean as if she had stepped out of her own bedroom. 'I'm sorry I'm late. How did you get on?'

'Awfully well, thank you. I didn't get lost at all.'

'And you bought a frock?' Helen stole a glance full of kindly interest and hidden misgiving at the nameless bag.

'Yes. It was rather a bargain. They reduced the price specially for me, wasn't it nice of them? It's sort of jade green with a gold collar. An afternoon frock, you know. Would you like just to peep at it, or shall we wait till we get in the train?' Her fingers were busy already with the string.

Helen looked, and paused appalled, weighing the possibility of getting the thing changed. Not a chance, she reflected, at the kind of place where that had come from. She gave her warm gentle smile, and fixed the string back into its holes again.

'It's sweet,' she said. 'You must let me see you in it tonight.'

The rushes that half filled the little backwater stood up all round the punt, cutting off their field of vision from everything but the sky. Sounds from the main river came muted by distance and the afternoon heat. The air was still.

They were both working, with the length of the punt between them; Joe with his elbow and writing-pad propped on the flat

end, Leo on her stomach at the other. They had been at it for
more than two hours; the shadows had shifted, leaving them in
the sun, and its warmth was beginning to make them lazy.
Neither had announced the fact, for fear of disturbing the other.
Their pauses for thought became more frequent, longer and less
intense. Joe crooked his arm under his head, and half shut his
eyes. Leo found a young frog in the rushes, sat it in her palm to
admire its dapper bronze, and let it flop back in the river again.
Encouraged by this sign of levity, Joe heaved himself up and
swore at his manuscript, quietly, in the manner which invites
comment without insisting on it.

'Stuck?' asked Leo, with concealed hope.

'Uh-huh. Carry on, I can go to sleep.'

'It's too hot. I've been bogged half an hour. Want to go in?'

'If you like. Might fish.'

'I brought some cheese along. Do for chub or something.' She
looked vaguely about for it, rolled over and relaxed again, her
arms behind her head. Joe knocked out his pipe, made a half-
hearted movement towards his tackle, picked up the writing-pad
instead and stretched himself beside her. To Leo, who knew him
well, the fact that he had not dumped the manuscript somewhere out of sight indicated a willingness to talk about it. She
said, 'Sorry you've seized up. I thought you seemed to be going
rather strong.'

'I was. It's all right. It's only that I've got through the amusing
part and come to connective tissue. The prospect of work's all my
trouble. I'll get down to it to-night. Damn Milton, and his father
before him.'

'What did his father do?'

'Most of the damage, probably. Gave him a classical education
and brought him up respectable. God, to think what he might
have produced if he'd knocked around like Shakespeare did,
instead of sitting indoors ruining his eyesight and thinking up
filthy words like connubial and affable and congratulant. I suppose when they were fresh, all the writers in the country must

have gulped them down like unspoiiled savages getting their first taste of gin. Now we're sodden with 'em, and all the rest of his fancy diseases. *He* can afford them; he's never less than archangel ruined, blast him. But he's left the English tongue like Satan left Adam and Eve – fig-leaved and self-conscious. If I ever get to heaven I'll tell him what I think of him.'

'How he'd love having you thrown out for obscene language, wouldn't he? Go back home and read Berners' *Froissart.*'

'What's the good. He crawls in like original sin. Simplicity can never be innocent any more; only penitential, like a whore parading in bare feet and a shift.'

'It'll probably read better in the morning.'

'I'll try some on you in a minute. Not this last part; it stinks. I'll have to do it over. How's yours?'

'Oh, slogging along. Rather boring, really, because I've written the next three chapters in my head and now it's just clerical work; I could almost do it straight on the typewriter . . . I don't like Milton either, but it's probably a bias due to a suspicion I have that he wouldn't like me.'

'Well, maybe you've got something there.' He grinned at her with the sun in his eyes, and sprawled down more comfortably. 'I suppose the first, spontaneous flavour of those Adam and Eve passages is one of life's incommunicable things, like the taste of cod liver oil.' He expanded his chest and began to declaim with sonorous relish, directing his piece at the sky or, possibly, at the author.

Leo, lying with her eyes closed against the deepening light, listened and lost half the sense of the words. She wondered why it had never occurred to her before that *Paradise Lost* was primarily a composition for a male voice.

'God is thy law, thou mine; to know no more
Is woman's happiest knowledge and her praise –

Revolting, isn't it?'

'Horrible,' said Leo, rousing herself. 'Do you know any more?'

'Yards. It fascinates me. "Nor turned, I ween, Adam from his fair spouse, nor Eve the rites mysterious of connubial love refused." The first love-scene in creation, and that's what he does with it.'

'Don't you know any decent bits?'

Good-natured as always, Joe obliged with a dozen lines about Hell.

'That's better,' remarked Leo when he had run himself to a standstill. 'Thanks.'

They lapsed into drowsy silence, their minds drifting back, through the receding Miltonic echo, to their labours of the afternoon.

'Do you ever worry,' said Leo sleepily, 'about the situation you leave your characters in when you stop writing? I mean, they've got to stay put like that till one starts again.'

Joe opened his eyes to laugh. 'Why, no. Do you?'

'Well, you notice it more in the sort of thing I do. When you've left a man bound and gagged in an upright position in a ruined shack with night coming on, and coyotes, and he's had nothing to eat since breakfast, it makes you think a bit.'

'You silly ass,' said Joe with affection. 'Well, anyway, my people can't complain. I left them in bed. First time, too. They should be O.K.'

'Oh, have you got that far? Milton apart, how's it going?'

'Not too badly, as a matter of fact. Funny thing, I often like the stuff best that I've turned out working with you. Other people around put me off.'

'You can feel people's minds fidgeting if they're not as busy as you are. I'm working too, so I'm as good as not there, that's all it is.'

'Maybe it's that.'

'When do you reckon to finish?'

'Oh, not for months yet. This is a side-line, the real subject's only just getting under way. I aim to get it out next spring, if possible. So far, it shapes better than the last.' He added, thoughtfully, 'I hope so, anyway. Because before very long I fore-see an interruption to one's experiments lasting several years.'

She knew what he meant. They had discussed the thing before from the political angle, and did not reopen it now. She only said, 'Why interrupt them? I don't suppose one sane war book would come amiss.'

'Four or five years after it's over – just about the time when the reading public's sick of the subject – I shall probably decide the conditions are ideal for trying to write one.'

'Yes,' said Leo with an irony that had no cutting edge. 'When it's too late to cash in on the action or the reaction, I'm sure you will.'

'Good books will be written, mind you. There's no virtue in being unable to handle your stuff till it's cooled. It's just a matter of knowing your limitations. But if you do work cold it imposes certain obligations, I think.'

'Which might conflict with certain others?'

'Which would, inevitably. If it's done with your eyes open it doesn't take much to damn your soul. Just leave out a little some-thing, and shift the high-lights somewhere else, and change a bit that would never do for something that will do at a pinch. Well, it's all right if you can take to it, I suppose. I'd sooner go to bed with a woman for money.'

'So what?'

He shrugged his shoulders.

'I suppose I shall use my intervals of leisure, if any, noticing what traces of ordinarily conditioned human behaviour, if any, remain on view, and doing what I think about them. Too bad.'

'And when you're at the front, up to the knees in muck and stink, you'll get a wad of clippings from London telling you what an escapist you are.'

'Shouldn't wonder,' said Joe, unmoved. 'Though without – as yet – any personal experience, I imagine war is about the most potent escape from the problems of its own solitude that the human ego has ever thought up.'

'Yes,' said Leo, half to herself. 'I think that's possible And at the end of it, one's problems would be just what they were before. Or rather worse.'

Joe asked for no elaboration of this. They were both people who could rely on one another to say, with or without persuasion, exactly as much as they wished.

'Your books will boom, anyway,' was all he said. 'They'll appeal to the nostalgia of the mechanized cavalry.'

'There was a rumour earlier on,' she reminded him, 'that you were going to read me some of yours. Or have you gone off the idea?'

'No. You had it coming. I'd be glad to know what you think, as a matter of fact.'

'Good,' said Leo lightly, 'go ahead.' She settled herself, her head turned a little away from him, to listen.

He fished the manuscript out of its folder, settled himself on one elbow, and began to read. Being confident of his work and his audience, he read very well, without the monotony or over-stress which self-consciousness produces; his pleasant, even voice intruding itself as little as a page of well-spaced print.

It was a dialogue between a man and a woman, dropped in, after a manner Joe had, with a delusive air of sudden irrelevance and with practically nothing in the way of preliminaries. The effect of these passages was apt to be curious, ranging from the Elizabethan intrusion of a lyric to a general impression on the reader that a hitherto sober and solid fabric had been struck by lightning. This extract was of the second sort. Joe read it like the work of someone else, to which he was anxious to be fair.

How can he? thought Leo, as she had thought once or twice before at such times. He was actually writing this an hour ago. Hasn't it left anything behind at all? She felt her own breathing quicken a little, and, ashamed both of this and of a failure in crit-ical detachment, devoted all her strength of will to imagining herself alone. The chapter came to an end before she had suc-ceeded; and Joe put it away as coolly as he had got it out. He made no comment and asked for none; but she knew he was waiting, he was human enough for that.

'Well,' she remarked, 'I see your difficulty in getting down to sea-level again from there. It must be about as good as anything you've done.'

Her voice was boyish and hard. The emotion it suppressed appealed to Joe as a compliment both subtle and sincere. His mind warmed to her; he thought, as he often did, what reliable company she was and how free from difficulties. He smiled down at her, leaning on his elbow as he had propped himself to read. The wind had blown the powder off her smooth skin, but her mouth was a clear scarlet in her cream-brown face. Her silk shirt, limp with the heat, had moulded itself to her small high breasts. She met his smile and looked past him into the sky, her eyes following the flight of a passing bird. Joe stayed as he was, and looked at her. He had not, in spite of the appearance which seemed to him good form, been wholly unmoved by what he had been reading.

A lace-wing fly, pale and helpless as a Victorian lady, fluttered over the side of the punt, and settled in Leo's hair. Its delicate green pleased him against the glossy darkness; he watched it till it began to be entangled and to wave, in feeble fright, its transparent wings.

'Keep still a minute,' he said. 'There's a creature losing its way in your hair.' He rescued the lace-wing, and put it over into the rushes; but the dark hair was warm and vital and sweet-smelling. He stroked it lightly, and slid his hand under its weight. Leo felt his touch; she supposed him to be still seeking the mayfly or whatever it might be. Partly to help, partly in a drowsy impulse of contentment, she turned a little, it brought her head into the palm of his hand.

The sun was hot, the air languid and still; a light haze hung over the river, promising greater heat to come. A pleasant lazy ache, too gentle yet to be called desire, crept over Joe and filled him with a vague and aimless tenderness. It came as naturally as breathing to smooth the warm silk with his free hand, gently and confidingly, till it came to rest over the light upward curve. A tiny movement, a breath perhaps, lifted it; the slightest of responses, but making his senses aware of themselves. To kiss her became obvious and necessary. He bent to do it, and met her eyes. She was looking at him as if she had surprised him with a knife levelled at her heart.

Softly and very carefully, with the tact he would have used equally to a frightened animal or child, Joe withdrew, blaming himself for a fool. An unprejudiced and considerate person, he made the deduction which was reasonable on such facts as he knew. It's true, then, he thought, though I wouldn't believe it when that woman told me. Well, she makes a damned good job of keeping it to herself. She thought I was safe, and so I ought to have been. What a lout I am, to have played her up like this.

He trailed off his caress into a friendly nothing, as if he had intended it. One ought to be able to tell, he thought; it seemed for a moment . . . oh, well, one imagines things. She remained unnaturally still. He said aloud – it was almost the same voice he had used to scared colts when he was a boy – 'Sorry. I must be getting absent-minded.' As she gave no sign of having heard, he added, 'Just formless emotion; bred, like your crocodile, from the operation of the sun'; and smiled at her, watching her fixed face relax.

'I know,' she said. 'Don't worry. I was half asleep, and you woke me up. I suppose it startled me.' There was a brittle quality in the naturalness of her voice. His hand was still under her head; he took it away, giving her hair a jocular little tug. She smiled and sat up.

'What about trying that cheese on the chub?' he said.

'Yes,' said Leo. 'Let's.'

Neither of them got a bite. Leo sat staring at her float on the water. She had braced the end of her rod against the punt, to hide the unsteadiness of her hands. It will pass off, she thought, in another minute. Please God, let it go away and don't let me think about it any more. She fixed her eyes on the cool water that went slowly past, as if it would carry away with it, out of sight and mind, what she wanted to lose; the moment when his closed mouth, stooped over hers, had been beautiful and inevitable, making a heaviness in her throat, the shiver of regret that had shocked her when he had turned away. The water flowed on slowly, too slowly; the willow-leaf by which she had first reckoned its progress had hardly travelled a yard. She heard him move, and the scrape of a match as he lit his pipe again; presently the spent stick added itself to the willow-leaf in the slow procession downstream. Worst of all had been when he had spoken to her, and she had not been able to answer; she had wanted to strike at his gentleness and his friendly toleration, to hurt him, even physically, to punish, yes, but also to rouse him. She had sought escape as one seeks in a dream where there is no escape except by waking; and, when he had smiled at her, she had wakened in time. But the memory, the fact, remained, shaking and refracting the peaceful sunshine, rocking the settled happiness which, half an hour ago, had been too stable to know its own existence. She found herself dreading the moment when he would turn or speak, lest his face or voice should show that something remained with him also.

She wanted only to forget about it, not to shape it into thought; but like an image on water into which one has thrown a stone, thought re-formed, making its clear pattern on the surface of her mind; showing her the preciousness of what was threatened, a contentment which the very perception of it endangered. So easily, so casually and so long this friendly gate had swung ajar, till she scarcely remembered that it could be locked against her, or that there was, for her, no other passage through which the life of her instincts and imagination could enter the real world. Whether it was his gift of sympathy which naturally inclined him to take people as they wished to be taken; whether it was a sense of personality in him so strong that it made him, often, indifferent to sex where the personality interested him more; or whether it was simply some fortuitous miracle between them, she had neither known nor cared. With him, and through him only, she had the company of her kind; freely and simply, without the destructive bias of sexual attraction or rejection, he let her be what her mind had made her and her body refused. For the rest, her way of life had always seemed to her natural and uncomplex, an obvious one, since there were too many women, for the more fortunate of the surplus to arrange themselves; to invest it with drama or pathos would have been in her mind a sentimentality and a kind of cowardice. Because of this confidence she had got what she needed from women easily, and without the sacrifice of pride. But no one, except Joe, had given her what she had wanted from men since she had swum and climbed with the boys of her Cornish home; a need as deep and as fundamental, to be a man with his friend, emotion-free, objective, concerned not with relationships but with work and things, sharing ideas without personal implication to spoil them, easily, like bread or a pint of beer in a bar. She had accepted this gift from the first almost without thought, not analysing its goodness, only feeling it to be good; it had been so elementary and wholesome a part of life that she had never questioned it till now when it was threatened.

It should never be questioned, she saw, never be handled or dissected; the structure was too fragile, too much a matter of environment and chance, it might disintegrate with a moment's clumsy jarring. Beneath the surface of her mind all these conclusions must have been shaping for years, they came together so readily and swiftly now; Joe's matchstick, the yellow leaf, were still in sight, only a little way astern. His pipe, since she became aware of them, was scarcely alight; she could hear him pulling at it to make it draw. She remembered that sometimes thoughts had passed between them before either had put them into words, and tried again to shake her mind free, lest it should be happening now.

If, perhaps, she thought about someone else, someone harmless

and amusing, involving one's emotions a little, but lightly and
without consequence; interesting enough to provoke speculation, but whom one might, or might not, ever see again . . . She
had gone quite a long way into these generalities before she perceived the concrete image behind them; it brought her mind up
all standing, and without warning she found herself full of the
sense of absurdity, and laughed.

At once it was as if a thread of tension had been snipped in
half. Everything settled; the leaf and the matchstick, caught
in a sudden eddy, gave a twirl and vanished. Joe hauled in his
line, found a minnow on the end of it, and laughed too. He
swung round to look at her, his face open and untroubled. The
lark was singing again, or perhaps she had only been ceasing to
hear.

'I keep meaning to ask you,' he said; 'there's a lot of boat-var-
nish over from those gadgets we were knocking up at my place.
Couldn't the canoe do with a lick? If so I'll bring the stuff along
sometime and we'll have a go at it.'

'Really? I was telling Helen we'd have to get down to it sometime soon. It's getting the old stuff off that's going to be the job.'

'Oh, it won't be more than a morning's work between us. I
should sink it overnight first, to fill out the seams. A fine day, but
not too hot, we'll want for the new coat. We could start the
other any time.'

'Good. Not to-morrow, I've got to go to town. Any time after
that. What about getting along? We don't look like catching
anything here, and it'll soon be getting cool.'

Joe reeled up his line, and stretched himself. 'We-ell, right
now it's not so darned cool I couldn't use a pint of bitter. C'mon
and get it.' For a few startling seconds, his leisurely unmannered
voice held clearly the echo of a Western drawl. It happened once
perhaps in a month or so; Leo found it perennially fresh and
fantastic, like the appearance in a familiar landscape of some
rare migrant bird. 'What's the matter?' he enquired. 'Signed the
pledge, or did I say something?'

She laughed. 'Sorry. Just professional interest. You were talking Arizona. Didn't you know?'

'People tell me sometimes. I can never hear it myself.'

'Do it again.'

'On your way, hombre, let's hit the saloon.'

'That's bogus Hollywood, you fool.'

'It goes if you think about it. Ten to six. Where'll we get this drink?'

'The Bell will be the nearest. I wonder if they've fixed the skittle-alley yet. It's too fine for darts to-day.'

'Suits me. I've lost too many pints playing darts with you.'

'Mind if I punt now? I'm getting out of practice.'

'O.K. Thanks. Maybe if I go over this stuff again now I shall see what's wrong '

Leo swung the punt out into the main stream, her mind and her muscles given over to acquiring the style which so far had eluded her competence. The trick of it came easily to-day. Joe sat frowning at the manuscript on his knees; presently he got out his pen and began eliminating sentence after sentence with long hard strokes. He was as distant from her as if he were at home. In his withdrawn presence there was a kind of freedom which was better than solitude. Her mind sought its own thoughts, and the wind blew through her hair.

Happiness crept near again, like sleep, like a shy wild animal that approaches when no one heeds its coming.

CHAPTER SEVENTEEN

Leo was bored. She had missed her train home, and had thirty-five minutes to wait for the next; the terminus was hot, dirty and noisy; she was wearing London clothes; and she had just seen the cover-design for her new book, which showed the hero, with the wrong kind of face and a musical-comedy costume, soulfully kissing the supernumerary blonde, as if the plot depended on it. She had brought nothing to read. Running an indifferent eye over the bookstall, she bought *The Aeroplane* and sat down with it on a seat.

A smell of liquorice and of very young, very warm humanity invaded her neighbourhood in gathering strength, as a small boy, who had been kicking his heels half-way along the bench, edged nearer to look over her shoulder. Presently, feeling no doubt that their common interest was already an introduction, he stabbed a black-rimmed finger at the page.

'Is that undercarriage re – the sort you can pull up?'

'Retractable. Sure to be, they all are now.' Leo, to whom such encounters were nothing out of the way, glanced up without surprise. 'Yes, look. Here it is in the air.'

'How's it work?'

Leo fished a pencil and an old envelope out of her pocket. 'Well, roughly, like this.' They bent over the diagram, their heads together.

'Suppose,' he enquired, having mastered the principle in two or three minutes, 'it was to stick when you were flying?'

'You'd just have to keep on flying till you could get it down again, if the petrol lasted; if it didn't, you'd look for a good place to crash-land.'

'Coo. You might have to bale out, then. What do they have them for?'

Leo explained, adding, as an afterthought, 'Is someone waiting for you anywhere, by the way?'

'No, I've got a platform-ticket.' He displayed its remains. 'They're only a penny. Can I see some more?'

The conversation became increasingly technical. Leo's look of boredom disappeared. Luggage was dumped round them and gathered up again; the other end of the seat was occupied by two women who, secure in the presence of such absorption, discussed a family quarrel as if they were alone. Pictures of a racing Supermarine led to matters of slipstream and wind-resistance. He looked up, his scrubby mouse-coloured hair tickling her face.

'You don't half know a lot. Can you fly?'

'A bit. I've taken over now and again with a dual control. You can't call it flying, of course, till you've gone solo and made a landing.'

'When are you going to?'

'I don't know. I've stopped doing it now.'

'What did you stop for?' His hot firm little body leaned eagerly nearer. 'Were you in a crash?'

'Oh, no. I got on all right. It's easy.' The simple brag in this statement, boy to boy, seemed perfectly natural to both of them.

'You ought to of got your licence, then, didn't you?'

'I didn't have time.'

'Why not?'

'Well, I knew a man with a plane who used to take me up, but I haven't seen him lately.'

'Why?'

'No special reason. Just one thing and another.' She looked

away, remembering several things, among them the station clock. Her glance travelled towards it, but was intercepted. Peter, looking pleased, interested and reflective, was standing a few yards away from her. He had evidently been watching her with enjoyment for several minutes. Allowing her just time enough to appreciate this fact, but not enough to resent it, he made towards her, with a smile full of intimate, perceptive appreciation.

'Oh,' said Leo abruptly. 'Hullo.'

'I thought I'd wait a minute,' he said, 'till you weren't so busy.' His voice and his eyes added, Charming, charming.

The grubby, confiding warmth at Leo's side drew away. Her new friend was not without perceptions of his own. He had an elder sister, and knew the approach of soppiness when he saw it. It was a disappointment, when one had seemed to be in the company of an intelligent human being; but there it was, women were all the same, and one might as well be getting along. In any case, the Scotch express was almost due. He moved off without formality, as he had arrived.

'You can keep this if you like.' Leo held out *The Aeroplane*.

'Thank you,' he said, accepting it with distant courtesy, and clumped away. A faint smell of healthy dirt and liquorice lingered behind him.

Peter settled himself in the vacant space, bringing a sharply-contrasted aura of tweed, antiseptics, tobacco and soap.

'I'm sorry if I interrupted anything,' he said charmingly.

Leo found this irritating. His smile, however, was impossible to ignore without active rudeness, and she returned it.

'Are you travelling by train,' he asked, 'or meeting one?' Into this simple question he conveyed, without effort, the assumption that her private life would naturally be interesting and discreet, together with a delicate tact founded on like experience.

'I'm only on my way home.' She felt for her bag; she only carried one when she was in town, and was liable to forget it. 'Forgive my getting up just as you arrive, but the train's almost due.'

'It won't be in for ten minutes. We've plenty of time.'

Leo accepted the correction. Unlike Helen, she visited London seldom, and with a reluctance which did not make for efficiency about it. As she groped in her pocket for her ticket (a handbag was for non-essentials) the plural pronoun arrested her. She looked up.

'It's my train too,' he explained. 'I'm on holiday, you know.'

Leo had, in fact, forgotten completely; her mind had been taken up, lately, with other things.

Her cordiality, a purely social reflex to cover her lapse of memory, seemed to please him.

'I was frightfully disappointed,' he said at once, 'at not being able to look you all up yesterday evening. As a matter of fact, I had a rather special case on hand and I thought I'd see it through the night, anyway, before I started off.'

The eyes of Leo's memory were opened. She recalled Elsie's painstaking toilette, her restlessness, her unusual interest in what they were going to have for supper, her glances at the clock; her deepening silence as night drew on and the headache with which, refusing Helen's offered remedies, she had finally gone to bed. An exasperated sense of the absurdity of women, from the cradle to the grave, caused Leo for a moment to relinquish the thread of the conversation.

'. . . about eight years old,' Peter was saying, 'from one of these waif and stray places. He came in with an acute intussusception, and . . .'

Leo found herself listening after all. She could attend indefinitely, at any time, to someone talking about a job in which he was expert. She attended now. Indifferent to the flattering effect of her concentration, she devoted to Peter's recital much the same single-mindedness as her late companion had lent to the study of retractable undercarriages. Under its stimulus, Peter gave increasingly of his best. With a sense of style which was all the happier for being mainly unconscious, he began to touch in the dramatic high-lights and shadows, to re-create the tension and comradeship, pathos and danger, the split-second triumph in the moment of defeat, the tired, commonplace satisfaction at the end of it all. He was even sometimes a little sentimental, as people who deal with realities can afford to be; it came off very well, and suited him.

Leo's attention held. Both the woman and the boy in her were aware of a certain willingness to impress, and each, in its different way, was secretly entertained. But at the bottom of it all was a genuineness which disarmed amusement, and made it impossible not to like him. He capitalized his quite real assets so openly that it became somehow endearing. Even while she wanted to smile, she saw round his eyes the honest evidence of strain and a sleepless night, and was at pains to say the right thing at the right moment instead. It was Peter who remarked in the end: 'Well, I suppose we ought to go and do something about this train.'

He supposed truly, but five minutes too late. Leo's theory about its time of departure had, in fact, been the correct one. It was the last of the rush-hour series; the next was not due for nearly two hours.

Peter apologized, but not excessively. With the air of one who would have thought it cheap to contrive such an effect, but found it pleasing as a gift of circumstance, he suggested that they should go back to his place and have a drink to pass the time.

'Is it far?' Leo's brows drew together; the boyish note roughened her voice a little. 'I don't want to miss the next one.'

'Eight minutes by tube,' said Peter briskly.

'Hadn't you better use the time getting some sleep, if you were up all last night?'

'I got in four or five hours this morning. Plenty for me.'

'All right. If you like, then.'

The tube was full, and conversation in it impossible. Peter led her out at a station whose name she did not trouble to peer after; she emerged, quite disorientated, into a main road of cheap shops, and the rattle and shriek of trams. It was the peak shopping period of such quarters, just after working hours. Peter threaded his way with the ease of habit; the effort not to become separated from him in the crowds left her with little attention to spare. She supposed that they would turn some corner to find, by one of London's sudden transitions, a street in which someone might conceivably live. He took her by the elbow, checking her in a stride hardly shorter than his own.

'This way in,' he said.

She had scarcely noticed the hospital, except as something characteristic of the street, like the trams. He gave her a gentle push through the great iron gates of the main entrance, into an asphalt courtyard edged with borders of seedy, soot-choked flowers. She stopped to stare at him.

'What are we going in here for?'

'I live here.' Her vagueness amused him, and gave him a kindly sense of patronage. 'I'm a resident, didn't you know?'

'Oh, yes,' said Leo. 'Of course.'

They went into the entrance hall, with the porter's desk and telephone exchange, and up a huge dark stone stairway. Leo looked about her with an interest which Peter accepted as the wide-eyed wonder of the explorer, being unaware of the fact that Helen had continued to work as a nurse for more than a year after Leo had known her.

'Isn't this the Sisters' corridor?' she asked suddenly.

'Yes,' said Peter soothingly, 'but it's all right.'

· They climbed again, to the next floor; at the foot of the stairs a Sister, capless and apronless pottering about in felt slippers during a restful but eventless period of off-duty, gazed after them in unformed resentment.

'Nearly there,' Peter said.

They were at the top of the central, oldest block of the hospital, in a corridor tall, bleak and grim like all public utilities of the Victorian era, but, because of its height, relieved here by light and air. Otherwise it was nearly identical with the floor below, except for the differences, trivial but enormous, which

marked the transit from a feminine to a masculine world. Down
there the doors had had a guarded look, an air of preserving,
watchfully, small face-savings and shifts from a prying eye; here
they were slammed for quiet or stood carelessly open, revealing
the method, or litter, or unabashed chaos within. Leo remembered the probationers' rooms she had seen on her visits to
Helen, their cowed symmetry and tidiness, clamant of daily
inspections and of rules. She felt no resentment at the contrast,
only a sense of naturalness where she was; apart from Helen
herself, the other had been always like a foreign region, quaint
in its strangeness, an existence of which, by no effort of the
fancy, she could have imagined herself a part. Through a couple
of doors which faced one another along the passage, two young
men were shouting across to one another and rummaging about.
She listened, half-unconsciously, to what they said. One of them
came out, pushing his shirt absently into his trousers, saw Leo,
and went in again, looking annoyed. It made her feel irrationally
foolish and hurt.

'Here we are,' said Peter, and threw open a door.

They gazed at the room: Peter, indeed, with more interest
than Leo, for she had seen it more or less in replica several times
on the way, while he was enjoying a pleasure which seldom palls,
that of viewing an extension of one's own personality through
the fresh medium of someone else. The room took on new values
and perspectives under his eyes. Its utilitarian bareness – it
looked what it was, a place for the hasty changing of raiment and
for sleep – assumed a brave but somehow pathetic austerity; the
awkward overflow of books from the single shelf to the table and
chair was full of intriguing intellectual clues; the crayon carica-
ture pinned to the wall (of a friend he had lost touch with for
years) looked casually popular and witty; the black iron bed-
stead, its mattress flattened at the edge from being sat on, and
sagging in the middle under its washed-out counterpane, ceased
to be merely an object that took up half the available space, it
was a reagent, a tactful and tacit question-mark, an experimental

catalyst. Murmuring conventionally deprecating platitudes, he smiled at her, bright-eyed and observant.

'Well,' remarked Leo, 'if one must live in London, it's something to live on top of it.' She strolled over to the window, looking out over the recession of roofs and chimneys and the haze of smoke gilded with late sun.

Peter had a psychological theory about this procedure: he had given one or two previous visitors the benefit of it at later and suitable moments, with interesting effect. With reluctance and regret, he abandoned it this time. The back view, thus idly presented, was as free from conscious curves as his fag's at school.

'It's a unique view,' he told her. 'You can't see the Crystal Palace, even on a clear day. Cigarette?'

'Thanks.' She looked vaguely at the two chairs, the hard cane and the unsteady basket, and sat down on the edge of the bed. Peter settled himself beside her, a little more centrally. To set the ball rolling, he turned on her a gentle, quizzical, well-here-we-are-what-now smile.

Leo looked at him reflectively, speculatively, and, as far as he was concerned, enigmatically. London always made her thirsty, and something, surely, had been said about a drink.

Fortunately Peter arrived almost at once at the same concept, though by a rather different mental train. He produced the heel-end of a bottle of whisky, souvenir of a recent celebration, and two not very clean glasses. Leo, who did not care for spirits and would have preferred the soda unembellished, accepted from politeness and because she was dry.

'To our better acquaintance,' said Peter, with light delicate significance.

'Cheers,' Leo said.

They drank. Leo thought, I wish I could tell good whisky from bad; it's uninformed. The stuff only makes you thirstier, and beer's no good after it. I'll get back to the station in time for a lemonade or something. Outside the door a houseman passed, in conversation with a porter; he had been called to an urgent casualty, and was getting details as he went. Interested by the odd phrases she caught, she turned her head for a moment to listen. This must be a good life, she thought; hard, but good. Working at something you know beyond doubt to be useful, under a boss who's only your boss because he's a better man. Nothing about you concerning anyone, except whether or not you deliver the goods. She turned to look at Peter, the only representative in view.

'Well?' he said. His voice was tentative, personal and softly challenging. Oh, blast him, thought Leo; and took a long impatient drink.

Peter considered her, well content with the sense of his own originality and enterprise. How few of his friends and acquaintances, he reflected, would have bothered with this girl. She had no physical provocation; a cruder and simpler taste would have rejected her at sight. But to the more highly trained intelligence, there was a deliberateness about this lack of sexual window-dressing, which intrigued and asked to be explored; nothing like the well-meant flounderings of the younger sister. A less expert investigator would, he realized, have had the diagnosis pat. Peter wasn't so sure. It was well worth looking into. She was sitting with her drink balanced on one knee, leaned back a little against a propping hand; a boyish, angular, lounging pose; there was about her a kind of obstinate rawness. Someone, definitely, ought to take her in hand. She had, he remembered, a dreadful family background (it was helpful to begin knowing this) but it was probably not too late. A little adjustment now might alter her whole destiny, and she would remember it, very likely, with gratitude all her life. He hoped her immediate response to the treatment would not be too embarrassing; but with a worthwhile case one must take such risks.

'What do you do?' asked Leo, looking round from a cursory inspection of the books on the shelf. 'General surgery, or medicine, or something specialized?'

Peter told her, in detail. He prided himself on never rushing things.

'I wondered, when you told me you were a resident. Because I rather got the impression, from the way Elsie talked, that you were a psychologist.'

This came unexpectedly near the knuckle. Peter took refuge in a modest indulgent smile. 'Not officially. But it's indispensable, of course, in any branch. Unfortunately far too few people can be got to realize that.'

This sounded to Leo like good sense. She wished to know more.

'Have you ever,' she asked, 'found psychological treatment really decisive in curing a patient?'

Peter could have asked nothing better than this. He was off. In skilfully linked succession he recounted three instances of cases (they were, by some coincidence, all female cases) where he personally had restored the will to live at what had seemed, to less imaginative colleagues, the eleventh hour.

Leo listened, gratifyingly. There was information to be had; and, besides, she found the narrative style rather charming. At the end of the third history, however, she interrupted the flow; cutting, somewhat unfairly, into a pause whose intention had been purely dramatic.

'But,' she asked, 'what happened afterwards, when they found out?'

Peter looked at her gravely. Her trick of gaucherie, he reflected, was effective up to a point; it was a pity she overdid it.

'They went out, I think,' he said, 'happier and less lonely people than they came in. It isn't much one can do. The rest one just has to hope for.'

He means this, said Leo to herself; he really means it. This is fascinating; I'm glad I came.

'I'm sorry,' she said aloud, 'but I still don't quite get this. In the end, what did they make of it? I mean, they must either have thought you were really taken with them, which would lead to a certain amount of disappointment when you didn't follow it up; or else they'd gather at some stage that you'd just been doing them good, in which case one would rather expect them to hand you a clip on the ear. Still,' she concluded reasonably, 'I suppose the great thing at the time was to save their lives. Like jabbing a boathook into someone who's drowning.'

Peter received this with a complex series of emotions. In the first moment sincerely hurt and offended, he found, in the second, the assault – if it was an assault – subtly promising. It showed a personal interest, perhaps a personal application . . . Boathook. Drowning. He knew his Freud. A highly significant choice of symbols and, obviously, unconscious. The first thing was to crack this defensive shell, and then the possibilities were really fruitful. A forgiving, understanding warmth irradiated him.

'I don't think they would feel that way about it. Why should they? One's affection is perfectly real, and one's desire to help. They'll have had that, you know. It does mean something to people who haven't had much of either in their lives.'

Fundamentally, Leo thought, he's a far better human being than I am. If I were half as nice, I'd be telling him now how wonderful he is. I wish I were.

'The only drawback is,' she said, 'that women' (she used the noun with objective detachment, as one might say 'horses') 'don't really enjoy being helped and done good to. Not emotionally, anyway. They'd much rather think that against your conscience and better judgment you were jeopardizing their souls. It gives them more self-respect. At least, that's been my experience.'

There was a serene matter-of-factness in the way this last remark was delivered which seemed to Peter somehow misplaced. It took him a few dubious seconds to reach the idea of picking it up by the other end. But surely, he thought, damn it all . . . She was returning his gaze with perfect sangfroid.

'Take Byron,' she pursued. 'Mad, bad and dangerous to know. He swept Europe with that line; and they still fall for it, believe me. And then look at Shelley. He did good like blazes to every woman he took up with, and what happened? They got madder than hornets, or threw themselves in ponds. None of Byron's women ever committed suicide, that I can remember offhand.'

'You're an amazing woman,' said Peter, who felt the need of gaining a little time. Leo accepted it as a form of puncutuation, which it was.

'That's where you're wrong,' she said. 'The others just don't tell you.'

'Have another drink.'

'Better not. I'm offensive enough on one, aren't I?'

'There's only a drop left. Shame to waste it. There isn't likely to be any by the time I get back.'

He refilled their glasses. It afforded another interval for constructive thought. The impulse towards lame dogs and stiles had, he found, curiously evaporated. However, he reaffirmed it to himself, for he was a lover of good reasons. There was something, it seemed to him, impalpably changed in her voice and physical poise, rather less of the lad in petticoats. She seemed, oddly, to have become more feminine as she grew more malicious. A defence mechanism, he said to himself; very interesting ... He had not found the allusions to Byron and Shelley altogether distasteful, their effect, though a subconscious one, having been to make him feel endowed with the diablerie of the one and the tragic weird of the other.

'Your mistake, I think,' he said, 'is expecting other people to have your own rather exacting standards. You, I imagine' – he looked searchingly and sympathetically into her eyes – 'are a person who's taken some hard knocks from life, and said very little about them. In that, anyhow, you and I are rather alike.' He paused to gauge the effect of this; Leo merely waited, with cool attention, for him to continue. 'You're conscious in yourself of things which – separate you from the herd, and you'd rather die than seek any concession from people whose stupidity and lack of imagination you despise. Isn't that true?'

'Good Lord, no,' said Leo. 'Of course it isn't.' She looked simply surprised; indeed, the wish to remove this misconception had ousted, for the moment, all other impulses. 'For one thing, stupidity about people like me is all to the good and makes life much more comfortable all round. This sort of thing is all right once in a way, but if everyone I met started exercising their imagination on me, it would embarrass me to death. For another thing, I don't feel separate from the herd, if by the herd you mean ordinary people and not public mobs, as I suppose you do. I like them. Why should they pamper oddities, anyway? It's they who are in charge of evolution. They think it's better not to be odd, as far as they bother to think at all, and they're quite right. There are shoals of women made up pretty much like me, but a lot haven't noticed and most of the rest prefer to look the other way, and it's probably very sensible of them. If you do happen to have had your attention drawn to it, the thing to do is to like and be liked by as many ordinary people as possible, to make yourself as good a life as you can in your own frame, and to keep your oddities for the few people who are likely to be interested.'

'I'm interested,' said Peter. 'I've been wanting to tell you that for a long.time.' Removing the glass gently from her hand and setting it down, he put his arm round her shoulders.

Leo did nothing. Her face had a faint, almost impersonal smile. She looked a little like someone in a theatre, who is waiting for the curtain to go up.

Peter kissed her; lightly and experimentally at first, then with enthusiasm. A certain cautious instinct had caused him to keep his right hand free for emergencies; but, this proving not to be necessary, he put it firmly round her, and tilted her into a more convenient position. She looked up at him with a smile in which irony and encouragement were curiously mingled. He kissed her again.

'I've been wondering about this,' he murmured, 'but I was afraid you might mind.'

'You underrate your talents,' said Leo politely.

During the short exchange that followed, Peter revised several preconceptions. The implied compliment, however, was equally satisfactory. Presently he paused, by way of a few bars' rest before changing the tempo; she was gazing up at him with level, half-open eyes.

'Don't look at me,' he said, 'as if you had a knife in your garter.'

This amused her, and she laughed.

'I don't wear garters.'

'Nor you do. What lovely long stockings.'

'Do you know, Peter, I think I really like you.'

Peter scented more defence mechanism in this, to him, need-lessly guarded statement. Pursuing his mission, he gathered her in compellingly and whispered. 'Darling, I love you,' with all the expressiveness at his command, which was a good deal. It was true by his reckoning; his capacities for love were varied and extensive, a fact of which he was pleasantly aware.

Leo made some soft-sounding reply to which, since her recep-tion of the accompaniments was so suitable, he paid little attention. It was, in fact, 'Don't be such a bloody liar.' He took it as a form of pleasantry, in so far as he took it in at all. In this he reckoned without his guest. Leo disliked verbal inaccuracies. Possibly this trait had been fostered by working with Joe, who, though not an elaborate stylist, had a fondness for the exact use of words, like that of a cabinet-maker for close dovetailing. Unlike Joe, however, she carried it to unreasonable lengths. Peter had, by her standards, cancelled the rules, and had received a formal notification of the fact. Happily and, on the whole, excus-ably unaware of this, Peter was following equally logical procedure on a different set of data.

There is something unmistakable about the movement, how-ever slight, of one's companion consulting a wrist-watch over the back of one's neck. Peter noticed it, but thought, after all, that he must have been mistaken. He continued to follow logic. There was no particular sign of a fallacy until a much later stage of the discussion, at which Leo simply remarked, 'No, really, thanks. I shall miss my train.'

Anyone hearing her voice alone would have supposed that he
had offered her a cigarette. It shook, for a moment, even Peter's
equilibrium; during the interval, Leo sat up briskly, fished in her
pocket for a comb, and began straightening her hair.

Good losers are of two sorts, the modest and the invincibly
confident. Peter was a very good loser indeed. It would have
taken, in fact, a good deal more than this to persuade him that he
had lost at all. He had, besides, beautiful manners, even at excep-
tional times. Before she had proceeded from her hair to her face
he had recovered his poise and had even handed her his shaving-
mirror, with a slight flourish whose sarcasm was barely
discernible. It had, after all, been extremely interesting, and
would probably become even more so later on. Annoyance, he
felt, would have ruined the effect, both outwardly and in inward
retrospect. Meanwhile experience had been increased, some original notes added to the file, and an evening filled in without
boredom; he was twenty-eight, there was plenty of life and any
amount of time. All the same . . .

'Thanks for the drink,' said Leo, rising. (She had given the
mirror a polish on her sleeve; she was particular about borrowed
things.) 'Well, we'll be seeing you sometime. Don't bother to
come down with me. No, really, I remember the way quite well.'

Evidently she meant this, so he let her go. It was not till he
was half-way through a cigarette that he remembered her train as
having been his own also. The next one would probably be tire-
somely late; but it would be too ridiculous if they were to meet on
the platform. He ascertained that the Home Sister had not yet
had the sheets removed from his bed. He could just as well go
down to-morrow. It occurred to him that a telephone call now to
Norah would catch her in plenty of time before she left her
patient. It would be a little surprise for her to find him still in
town; and an analysis of the case, in general terms, would probably interest her. He strolled down towards the telephone
exchange.

CHAPTER EIGHTEEN

'Of course it's absurd,' said Leo, kicking off her slippers. 'But for some reason that makes it all the worse.'

Helen, who was in bed already, looked up from polishing her almond-pink nails.

'If he had turned up she'd probably be far more miserable than she is now.'

'Tell me I'm an egoist. I know. The sort who'll eat a chicken but won't be the one to wring its neck.'

'Quite a lot of people are funny like that.'

'I just didn't think, I suppose. He was so restful, you know.'

'Did you say restful, or wasn't I listening?'

'Yes, of course. He never left one in the slightest doubt, for a single instant, that he didn't give a damn. He was so kind and understanding and off the point. I've never felt so safe with anyone. I simply forgot. Till I got back here and found her all dolled up and waiting, poor little wretch. I felt as if I'd snatched a penny out of a blind man's tin. It was horrible.'

'Except that the penny was never really there.'

'And Santa Claus was never really there, but you don't tell them before they can take it.'

'Santa Claus will attend to that, if you don't.'

'Oh yes. As soon as it occurs to him that any misunderstanding

needs clearing up. The sooner the better, I suppose. It will be bad
enough to be there when it happens, without being involved in it.'

'Well, I should think you've provided against that. If I'd been
him I'd have blackened your eye; someone will, you know, one of
these days.'

'Perhaps it's the one thing I've been waiting for, who knows. A
gentleman friend of mine did it when I was thirteen. But that was
a decent scrap, and all in order . . . I wish I understood more
about young girls. It's a handicap never to have been one. How
do they feel, what do they really want? I wish I knew.'

'Bless you, I've been one. They feel what they've read in
books, mostly, and they want what doesn't exist. You can't do
anything about it. Why should you? It has its moments, you
know.'

'Has it? You're always so comforting . . . Joe said something
once, or wrote it, I forget. Something to the effect that it's good
for youth to be hurt once or twice, provided it's done with a
sharp instrument.' Her face had changed as she spoke; its restless
vitality was quieted, she looked, for a moment, peaceful and
grave. Helen looked away, feeling, while it lasted, the breath of
loneliness that passes for jealousy in generous souls.

'Joe isn't always very original, is he?' she said smiling.

'I suppose not. I never thought about it. I expect he doesn't
need to be.'

'It was about this time last year you went climbing with him.
Do you think you'll go again?'

'Not this season. He wouldn't break off in the middle of a
book.'

She fell silent, and absently put out her cigarette.

'It rained a good deal,' she added at length.

It had rained three days out of the seven, while they sat in
horsehair chairs in the little climbers' pub, spreading maps on the
mahogany table, marking routes in pencil, eating, attending to
their boots, reading, and saying nothing unless they had something
to say. On the other four days they had climbed, scientifically,

silently in the main, roped together once or twice when it was advisable, taking the legitimate risks. She had never had to ask him for any help beyond what is accepted from the leader to the second climber, and he had never had to offer it. He had taught her a good deal, as he would have taught a boy who was shaping well, and with as little patronage. In the evening they had drunk their pint and chewed over the day; when she went up to bed, and heard the two men in the room next door kicking off their boots side by side and talking about cracks and finger-holds till they fell asleep, it had seemed to her silly, but unimportant, that convention prevented Joe and herself from doing the same. She had been the only woman among the six or seven people there, but no one had been curious about their relationship. Everyone was there to climb, and took this and one another for granted, gathering together at the day's end to compare routes and methods and gear with the impersonality of their kind, and keeping their secrets of exaltation, or fear, or fulfilment to themselves. She had been accepted among them precisely as Joe was accepted; she had worn, without attracting attention, almost precisely the same clothes. 'Difference of sex no more we knew than our guardian angels do': not an ecstasy, but three thousand feet of rock, taken steadily in nailed boots, remained Leo's idea of the ascent to the state of the blessed. Once, striking rotten rock, they had both been in real danger, and had got out of it, and had sat on the ledge of their endeavour getting back their breath, with no comment beyond a raised eyebrow and a grin. Joe had not felt called upon to apologize because they had nearly died together. He had not asked her if she felt all right to go on. They had shared bread and cheese and chocolate with their feet in space, and it had tasted better than any food in the world. 'It rained,' she would say to people afterwards, 'three days out of seven.' She had said little more than this even to Helen. She kept it whole with silence; it had been the greatest happiness of her life.

'Lord, I'm sleepy,' she said. 'Well, sufficient unto the day.'

*

Elsie too was awake. Curled up in bed, with the amber-shaded lamp beside her, she was reading the sonnets of William Shakespeare. Earlier in the day she had noticed the book on one of Leo's shelves, and had secreted it away; for she had never read them all, only, at school, the ones quoted in the standard anthologies. 'Let me not to the marriage of true minds,' and 'When in disgrace with Fortune' – she had had no difficulty with these, they were clear and absolute, like something in the Bible; she knew them, of course, by heart. The others, after their metrical and rhythmic virtues had been explained to her, she still found a little confusing; not, somehow, complete in themselves, but like part of a story whose plot one did not know. Half-way through the long evening – for quite early she had been sure that Peter would not come – she had decided that to-night she would read them all. She had experienced so much in the meantime; she would, she thought, understand them now.

As she undressed, she had been a little surprised to find herself less miserable to-night than the night before. Sorrow, this second day of disappointment, ought surely to have accumulated, not softened into this dreamlike melancholy, a purple twilight lit with sad stars. It was, she thought, because her love was of the spirit, a marriage of true minds, not needing the material communication of words and eyes. It did not occur to her – indeed, if anyone had told her she would indignantly have denied it – that real contact with Peter entailed prodigious strain, of several kinds; the effort to appear grown up, to understand everything he said, to make answers that would not sound silly; the effort to assimilate an actual personality into a mind full of cherished, fixed ideas, an effort full of subconscious fear; the effort to tidy up afterwards, to take stock, to accept, to suppress, to rearrange. To-night there were no new impressions, and those which were already there were settled in, homely, tinged with the kindly colours of the imagination. She had coped with and contained them; there they were, like a bit of wedding-cake in its white and silver box, ready to put under the pillow and dream on. Love alters not (she thought) with his brief hours and weeks, but bears it out even to the edge of doom. She sighed happily, and opened the book.

Knowing it to be Great Poetry, she was slow to admit to herself that she found it disappointing. The long series, all so much alike, containing apparently proposals of marriage, but urging nothing in support of it except that the girl should pass the inheritance of her beauty on, so that it was quite difficult to decide whether it were even the poet she should marry, or somebody else. It seemed very cold and artificial. And then a plunge into complete irrelevance, addressed to a man, to the effect that Nature had intended him for a woman; an odd sort of compliment, she thought, though it was obviously intended to sound polite. Elsie began to skip. Some more to the woman, quite different, disillusioned and rather coarse; or perhaps it was another one, for surely the first had had golden hair. Her opinion of Shakespeare began, in spite of herself, to descend. He didn't seem even to like her, very much, or to think her beautiful, so what was it all about? She struggled on, however. 'Like an imperfect actor on the stage—' ah, here was something comprehensible. She read the sonnet twice, consoled and cheered to think that even Shakespeare, fresh perhaps from writing *Romeo and Juliet*, had been tongue-tied in the presence of the beloved object, even as herself. Perhaps that was what had made him write; perhaps she too would become a great poet, and Peter, wondering what had inspired her, would never know. (This would be to the fair lady, she supposed.)

She wandered about, skimming the parts that defeated her with word-play and conceits, lingering over the poems whose meaning was clear and in tune with her mood, those chiefly of unworthiness and the anticipation of death. But gradually she became bewildered and oppressed by the gathering darkness of a misery whose sources she did not understand, and turned the pages more rapidly, choosing at random here and there. From between two leaves a torn scrap of paper fell out, scribbled all over on one side with Leo's writing. She saw at once that it was not part of a letter, but a slip of old manuscript folded to mark a place, so gazed at it without qualms. There was something about Hank, about a bunk-house, about a Mexican saddle. She turned it over, chiefly to postpone the effort of turning to Shakespeare again. On the back was a pencil-scrawl, of the sort people write while thinking of something else:

Yet this I ne'er shall know, but live in doubt,
Till my bad angel fire my good one out.

Suddenly she felt as she had felt sometimes in the caves at home; that she did not want to go further on into the dark, that she must turn back now, while a glimmer of daylight still showed round the corner of the bend. As soon as one saw the sunlight, the feeling was gone, and one forgot what had made one turn. It was so now. She read 'When in disgrace with Fortune' over again, surrendering to its age-long alchemy of iron into gold. Then she put out the light, and, thinking of cypresses, of fountains, of moonlight and viols and nightingales, fell asleep.

CHAPTER NINETEEN

The ferry-boat was crossing laboriously, against the wind. As they waited for it on the river steps, Peter gazed at Norah with kindly approval. Bringing her here this evening had been an excellent idea. She had had an exacting week, poor child, before the death of her patient, and was looking quite washed out; the blow would do her good. It would be excellent, too, as he had just been telling her, if she and Elsie should get to know one another; her healthy common sense and normality were just what the girl needed, pitchforked as she had been from her impossible home into this rather eccentric *ménage*. Peter could not help feeling, now and again, a certain responsibility for this, together with a consciousness of not having, himself, got much forrarder with her lately. He had really had very little time. Contact with Norah would give her just the fresh impetus she must be needing. He had already talked of them to one another; at least, he had certainly discussed Elsie with Norah, and, he supposed, vice versa, though the precise occasion had slipped his memory.

Norah was wearing a simple cretonne frock, bare legs and sandals, a costume he approved. He disliked artificial-looking fashions, and had explained to her, convincingly, why they were psychologically wrong. (They had, of course, a superficial attraction when one was meeting a woman for the first time, but that was beside the point.) It had taken a certain amount of persuasion to induce her to come; her occasional diffidences were due, he supposed, to some unresolved inferiority complex. She had even asked whether they were expecting her, a suburbanism which he had gently but firmly laughed away. They were, in any case, expecting him, for he had met Elsie in Mawley during the morning and told her he was coming; she remained, he noticed, in spite of her efforts towards emancipation, painfully shy. It was not until an hour or two afterwards that the thought of bringing Norah had occurred to him. It had seemed an ideal arrangement, and still did.

Elsie occupied, indeed, a very convenient position in the fore-ground of all this reasoning. Somewhere further back was a less classifiable figure, presenting an issue not quite so clear. Quietly and by imperceptible degrees, whose progress he had not exactly graphed, the desire to give Leo's psyche a helping hand had turned into something not unlike an urge to put it in its place. Norah was very dependable; amusing, when she got over her initial reserve, always ready to cap one's anecdotes and to add the little extras which modesty forbade one to insert oneself, well supplied with entertaining London gossip which, because of the contacts she made in her job, was quite well-informed. She was, definlitely, an asset . . . Then there was Helen, a closed book so far, but very attractively bound . . . Still further back in the recesses of thought, only a shy faun in the brushwood, so to speak, was a kind of suspicion that Norah herself had been grow-ing a shade, a tiny shade too independent lately, nothing serious, but . . . in fine, Peter was sure that everyone would be very good for everyone else.

It was Helen who first saw the approach of the ferry-boat. She went up to tell Leo, who, because it was sunny and cool, was working on the roof, lying on her stomach with a cushion under her chest, a position not very favourable to writing but excellent for thought and for intervals of siesta.

'He seems to have someone with him.' Helen, standing, was visible from midstream, and returned as she spoke the cheerful salutation which Peter waved to her.

'Really?' Leo levered herself up a little on her elbows. She had an equally good view from between the bars of the balustrade, which, however, screened her effectively from sight. 'Well, what do you know?' she said inelegantly, 'He's brought a bird along with him. His regular, by the looks of it. How rich.' Shading her eyes against the light, she looked again. 'A bit on the sturdy side, but quite nice, don't you think?'

'Elsie didn't tell me,' said Helen thoughtfully, 'that he was bringing anyone. I wonder if she knew.'

'Oh, good God. Elsie.' The suddenness of Leo's movement dislodged a sheet of manuscript which she saved, just in time, from blowing overboard. 'No, but really, you know, this is the limit. Poor little devil. This isn't education, it's butchery.'

'I expect,' said Helen, 'he means it all for the best. She has to wake up sooner or later, you know.'

'But, damn it all. No, he ought to know better than this. It – it isn't civilized.' Leo's brows settled into a straight dark line. With sudden decision she said, 'I'm not taking it.'

'It looks,' said Helen mildly, 'as if none of us had much choice.'

'Does it? I wonder.' Leo propped her chin on her hands. Her eyes narrowed; a stranger might have thought her to be day-dreaming.

'Think again,' advised Helen. 'Think several times. And then don't do it.'

'Do what?' asked Leo absently.

'Anything you think of doing when you look like that. This is going to be embarrassing enough. without any sideshows from you.'

Leo emerged from her meditations.

'Have we got any of that face-pack left?'

'I think so. But surely you –'

'Well, go and spread some on Elsie and make her lie down with it for twenty minutes. Do you want to change?'

'No, why? Is anything the matter with me?'

'You were never lovelier. But if you don't, run along and be there when they arrive, because I do.'

'I don't fancy any of this. I don't like you when you behave badly.'

'Really I won't. I'll be almost imperceptible. Go and do your stuff. Please. There's a honey.'

Helen was unmoved by this, and by the smile which went with it. But the ferry-boat was nearly half-way across. She went, reluctantly.

'I'll show him,' said Leo under her breath.

Elsie had just finished her face when Helen arrived in the room. Absorbed in the task, she had not noticed the boat in midstream. She had drawn a cupid's bow which overlapped the line of her mouth in three places, and had attempted to rouge her cheeks with her lipstick, the result being not quite symmetrical either in shape or shade. Seeing that it would all have to come off in any case, Helen reflected that the pack would make a good pretext without hurting her feelings. Elsie accepted it readily. In its cloudy pink jar it looked and smelt exotic, and she found in herself a curious lack of objection to the delay. It was pleasant to lie with the glossy film on her face, feeling it tighten and crackle interestingly here and there, knowing that by now Peter was probably here, within twenty yards of her, but freed from the responsibility of having to do anything but think beautifully about him. Now and again she would anticipate the moment when, all preparations over, she would go downstairs, open the door, be face to face with him; and her heart felt mixed uncomfortably with her diaphragm, both of them throbbing like machinery.

A footstep outside made her open her eyes, the only part of her face at her disposal. Leo was passing the open door, and had paused for a moment to look inside. What a number of clothes she had, thought Elsie, sighing. Here were still more that she had never seen. Leo had on a plain cream shirt of dull heavy silk, beautifully cut, with the top button open; trousers of cambridge-blue linen with turn-ups and a knife-edge crease, a broad hogskin belt with two gilt buckles and sandals to match. She smiled encouragingly at Elsie, saying at the same time, 'Don't move your face, you'll crack it.' She looked quite dashing, thought Elsie (trying unsuccessfully to smile back without moving anything but her eyes) with that brown-gold make-up and russet lipstick. The whole outfit looked quite expensive; how odd to spend money on such things when one could have bought a really lovely frock. Leo waved to her, and went on downstairs.

Meanwhile, the ferry-boat had delivered its load. Peter effected introductions and apologies gracefully, but with that ghost of proprietorship which trickles through good manners, unaware, from the inward soul. Norah was evidently used to it. Helen felt for her, and took to her at once. She led them inside, and produced some beer.

'I've been telling Norah about your work,' said Peter, 'and she's very interested. We were hoping you'd show us some. Both the technical and the non-technical, of course.'

'I don't do any non-technical work now,' said Helen untruthfully. She was shy of her efforts, for her standard was high and self-critical, and she had a horror of appearing to pose as a serious artist; she had penetrated a few Bloomsbury backwaters in her day. Especially she did not intend to pose with the object of impressing Norah, who struck her as likeable and genuine. She brought out a file. 'These are for a book on eye surgery, by Bryn-Davies. It's coming out next month.'

'Bryn-Davies? Do you work for him?' Norah looked up, the last of her shyness gone. 'I've taken his cases in the theatre sometimes. He was a houseman when I was training.'

'You don't mean to tell me,' said Helen, delighted, 'that you trained at Hilary's? But this is marvellous. So did I.'

'Not really? When did you leave? But I was actually there that year . . . Not till October? . . . Oh, night duty, that accounts for it, of course . . . On Kingston? Then do tell me, what was the real truth about that Meredith business? I was too new a pro. to hear the inside story.'

Helen knew the inside story, and several others. Norah knew, and was delighted to relate, what had become of dear old Eliot and that bitch of a Sister Tutor. The drawings slipped to the floor, forgotten. Peter picked them up, and studied them with critical aloofness. The godfatherly benevolence he had felt at the start of the reunion was beginning to wear a little thin. He thought poorly of Hilary's, as a Jerome's man should, and Norah rarely mentioned it to him. This sort of thing, he felt, was well enought to set the ball rolling, but was outlasting its function. The number of people, of whom he had never heard, that Norah appeared to have known intimately before she met him, seemed unnecessary, even superfluous. He picked up another drawing, and scrutinized it austerely.

'The other way up,' said Helen, interrupting her narrative to turn it over for him. 'Well, after some weeks even Matron got to hear about it, so . . .'

'A friend of mine,' said Peter with determination, 'is thinking of writing a thesis on the psychopathy of matrons.' He developed the idea, rather amusingly. They ran it along politely for two or three minutes, and, rounding a corner, were back at Hilary's again.

Behind the screen of the portfolio, Peter glanced unobtrusively at the door. Elsie was most uncharacteristically late. And Leo; could she be out? He had, after all, said that he was coming, so it seemed hardly credible. But he had barely been here ten minutes, though it seemed longer. More probably – much more probably – she was getting herself up a bit. He was seldom wrong in guesses of this kind.

He had scarcely formed the thought when a long light step, definitely not Elsie's, sounded outside. Peter buried himself in the portfolio. After her behaviour last time, he felt that a little initial reserve would not be out of place. He looked up just in time to catch the tail-end of a cursory smile and nod. Leo's eyes were already travelling on. Lounging debonairly in the doorway, in a pose that made the most of very good tailoring, she remained fixed for a moment, returning, under dark half-dropped lashes, Norah's fascinated gaze. Her own stare conveyed a calculated reticence, like that of a poker player trying, without complete success, to suppress his feelings at the sight of a straight flush, or of a bibliophile who has spotted a priceless first edition in a twopenny junk-box. Then, like one awaking from a momentary trance, she turned on Peter a face which was the most formal of interrogation-marks.

Up to this moment, Helen had been making up her mind to disapprove of Leo altogether. It was all somewhat excessive and transpontine, and, besides, she felt she had been managing very adequately on her own. But the brittle *bonhomie* of Peter's intro-duction, stretched so tenuously over a sulk, was too much for her sense of humour. He had asked, she decided, for what was coming to him. On Norah's account her qualms had disappeared; Norah was quite well able to look after herself, and would be none the worse for a little encouragement to do so. And, looked at from another point of view, her neck was slightly, but reassuringly, too thick. Necks were a matter on which Leo was fastidious.

Taking one thing with another, Helen decided to stand from under. She got up to dispense more drinks, leaving the seat beside Norah vacant.

Leo sank into it, giving her trouser-knees a neat hitch to ease the crease. As she settled herself, she sent Norah a private little smile, as who should say, 'We managed that rather well, didn't we?'

Helen came to rest beside Peter, took up the drawings, and said with confiding charm, 'Do these really interest you? The best ones are a little further down. Now here's something that really was rather fascinating to watch, though you've often seen it I dare say . . .'

Peter, his field of vision thus circumscribed by good manners, went through motions of eager attention and shifted restlessly in his chair. His temper was not improved by a clink of glasses at the other side of the room, accompanied by Leo's voice saying, softly but audibly, 'To our better acquaintance.'

'. . . and these,' said Helen, 'I did for an American who came over here . . .' She described, in detail, the surgical procedure, contrasting English with American technique, and trustfully inviting Peter's opinion. Her deference would have been quite gratifying, at almost any different time.

Over in the other corner, things were going like a song. Not for nothing had Leo been meeting Helen's friends, in and out of hospital, for rather more than six years. The time being over-short for finesse, she led with the ace of trumps. 'You know,' she said, 'If I hadn't heard you and Helen talking as I came in, I'd never have guessed, in a thousand years, that you were a nurse.'

'Wouldn't you?' Norah's candid face warmed with pleasure. For reasons opaque to the lay mind, but crystal-clear to young women whose names appear on the State Register, she would have taken this as a compliment even if spoken in rebuke. As delivered by Leo, it was devastating. Peter himself had never paid her this tribute; though, as their acquaintance had ripened in the anaesthetic lobby of the theatre, the omission was reasonable.

'The great thing,' she explained, 'is to keep up some sort of a life of your own outside the job. When you take to sitting about in uniform in your free time, you may as well be dead. Your friend,' she added by way of a graceful return, 'isn't at all obvious, either.'

'That's why she's a friend of mine,' said Leo simply. (To him that hath shall be given was, she had long since discovered, a good rule of thumb.) 'I'm like you, I prefer untypical people. You and I are rampant individualists, I suppose. It's not fashionable, but it's a lot more fun. Don't you think so?'

Copying as far as possible Leo's air of negligence, Norah

agreed that it was. Helen had judged her correctly; she was well supplied with good sense. Tactics of pursuit would have alarmed her as effectively as they would have bored Leo, who, in any case, rated them abysmally low – not merely vulgar but amateurish, which was worse. In this case, two exclusive people had naturally drifted together. It worked like bird-lime. Norah had had more than two years of being improved; kindly, tactfully on the whole, amusingly sometimes, but unremittingly. Here was someone, clearly critical to a fault, who seemed not to think that any improvement was called for. It was immense.

'What are you laughing at?' she asked, further intrigued by a deep, *sotto voce* chuckle which Leo made no attempt to explain.

'Sorry. I was just thinking what an amusing time a person like you must have had in hospital. Subtly deflating these pompous sisters and so on. Though I suppose as a rule their hides are so thick you can't get through them without being depressingly crude. Still, you must have had quite a lot of quiet fun all to yourself.'

She had limned, with a few economical strokes, the secret self-portrait of four young nurses out of five. To Norah, such penetration on the part of an outsider seemed quite uncanny. She said, deprecatingly, 'Well, you certainly would blow your brains out if you didn't give your sense of humour an airing now and again.'

Shreds of this conversation drifted over to Helen, as she shuffled the drawings in search of another suited to exposition. She coughed convulsively into her handkerchief, got up, and made a solicitous fuss over the refilling of Peter's glass, which was only one third down.

'I don't know if orthopaedic surgery is at all in your line . . .' There were quite a number of orthopaedic drawings, illustrations to a monograph. Helen made the most of them. She had, at last, no reason to complain of an abstracted audience. Peter had become, suddenly, all eyes and ears. His head had come several inches nearer, and his comments were accompanied by intimate

little glances. They were received into a blanket of bland, innocent friendliness. Helen had had her share of admiration,
unforced to the point of occasional embarrassment; she could
well afford to be amused this time, and she was. A small convex
glass on the wall enabled her to see, without looking round, that
the effect was being sadly wasted in the proper quarter. She felt,
for a moment, quite sorry for him; her tender heart was apt to be
moved by the most temporary reverses. She even allowed him to
collect up her fingers accidentally, along with one of the papers,
and returned his pressure with a maternal little squeeze. Then
'Hullo,' she said over her shoulder. 'Where are you people off to?'

Peter, who had not the advantage of the wall-mirror, had been
preoccupied with the success of his outflanking move. He looked
up. The position at which it had been directed was no longer
there.

'Shan't be a minute,' said Leo airily. 'I'm just taking Norah to
have a look at the canoe.' They disappeared; Leo motioning
Norah, with a slight but gallant gesture, to precede her through
the door.

Peter gazed after them. There was a moment in which his jaw
actually dropped; an unfortunate moment, for it was an expression which sat so incongrously on his face that it brought Helen's
comic sense into play. She observed, with acute enjoyment, his
rapid recovery, his thoughtful reorientation, and his too obvious
resolve to make the best of a job which might turn out to be not
so bad after all. The sound of a shy, hesitant step on the ladder
cut short her entertainment; she had quite forgotten, for a while,
that the performance had been a benefit one.

Elsie's timing, though unconscious, had been perfect. She hit
the exact moment when Peter had re-concentrated all his charm
for the new *mise en scène*. As she appeared in the doorway, Helen
stooped to gather in her drawings, moving so briskly that Peter's
best smile passed clean over her head. He received it back
instead, from Elsie, in a pale tremulous reflection, like sunlight
on a pool.

'Well,' said Helen, getting up, 'I really must be getting something done about the supper. I hope those two on the river won't go too far; but I suppose we shall have to risk having it a bit overdone, shan't we?' She smiled at him with the most innocent sociability. 'Hullo, Elsie. You're just in time to look after the company while I'm gone.'

She moved smoothly off. Helen never bustled. She could accomplish more than most people without the appearance of effort.

Elsie had Peter quite to herself for more an half an hour. He acquitted himself with what, in the circumstances, amounted to credit, and was never once unkind. The talk was not, perhaps, exactly dynamic; but for this Elsie accepted, very readily, the whole responsibility. Like all shy people, she was used to conversations beginning to sag when she was called upon to support one end of them. Even with Peter it had happened sometimes before, though not for quite so long. She answered the questions he asked about her life and progress, and was saddened a little, but unsurprised, to find him not listening very attentively to the answers. She did not lose sight of the fact that in being thus *tête-à-tête* with him she was enjoying the highest felicity. But after ten minutes there was a strange intimation at the back of her mind that she had had it now, that she was already happy enough, that no more was necessary for the present. If, even, other people came in, and there were general conversation, it would not plunge her into despair. When, during a lengthy pause, Helen came to lay the table, she was conscious of something absurdly similar to relief, and jumped up to help in spite of Helen's assurance that there was really nothing to do. Here was the moment, she reaffirmed, on which her thoughts had been set for days; but now, in its very shadow, her mind had run ahead again, and she looked forward to she knew not what; to the next meeting or its anticipation; to sitting, this evening, and watching him quietly from a corner; even to looking back on it from the completed security of the past. For only precocity, or maturity, or unreconciled age are choked by biting off more than they can chew; to this, its natural exercise, youth is mercifully adapted, like childhood to green apples. Hunger is not so early awake; the taste and scent of love sustain, and, as with green apples, do it sometimes better than the substance. Cruelty and disillusion are the only untransmutable pains. For cruelty Elsie retained the instinct of a lingering childhood; against it her choice had guarded her safely enough. Disillusion had gone out of the door just four minutes before she entered it. Peter's first smile, as she arrived, she had somehow felt at once contained happiness enough to last the evening; and, ever since, an instinct wiser than herself had been advising her not to ask for more. Shakespeare, she remembered (trying to excuse and understand the feeling), had been shy too, like an imperfect actor on the stage. To-morrow, next week, there would be miracles. To-day it was enough to expect them; meanwhile she trotted in and out of the kitchen, busied herself with a dozen small distractions, and brought Helen into the conversation whenever she could.

'Where's Leo?' she asked, as she collected plates from the dresser.

'Out in the canoe,' said Helen, 'with Norah Haynes. (The cheese is on the top shelf.) Norah trained with me at Hilary's. She and Peter came along together. Have you laid a place for her, by the way?'

'Oh, no,' said Elsie cheerfully. 'I didn't.' She had just made good the deficiency when the canoe returned.

It was audible some minutes before it arrived, for just as it came within earshot, Norah had finished telling an amusing story, and Leo's delighted laugh, crackling like a boy's from deep to high, carried clearly across the water. Peter, whose perfunctory offer to help had been swept aside, got the full benefit of it through the open door, and felt an uncomfortable prickling at the back of his neck. The whole episode, he decided, was of the sort best ignored by an adult mind. One could only regret that a woman of Norah's native intelligence could, after two years' acquaintance with real values, be capable of such a lapse into the third-rate. He would intimate this to her in due course; she was, at least, capable of taking a hint. Meanwhile . . .

The canoe coasted in towards the bank, kissing it neatly under Leo's practised hand. They were humming, as they landed, a verse of 'Home on the Range,' which they had been harmonizing further up the river.

Where the graceful white swan goes gliding along
Like a maid in a heavenly dream . . .

Elsie thought the soft voices, in the gathering dusk, romantically sweet and sad.

'We must meet again,' said Leo, in the voice that means, You cannot step twice into the same river; better not try.

'Yes,' said Norah, assenting both to the spoken courtesy and the unspoken truth. She was trying, half-heartedly, to imagine what she would think about all this to-morrow morning. It had been so light, so gracefully unreal, like an indiscretion at a masked ball. She gazed at Leo curiously, over the tie-rope of the canoe. One had thought, as far as one had previously thought at all, of thick women in starched evening shirts, and intense, shy-making confidences . . . Norah found that, as after a moderate indulgence in champagne, little remained behind except a general impression that one had been unusually witty and charming, together with a feeling of light-hearted sophistication and no harm done. And indeed, anything that happens in a light canoe, even when moored, must needs be moderate enough.

Leo caught her eye and gave her a broad, outrageous, comprehensive wink.

'Come on in,' she said, 'and eat your supper like a good girl.'

They were both blinking a little in the electric light indoors. Peter ignored Norah's entrance with quiet unobtrusive dignity; so it was Leo who introduced her to Elsie, in a manner which did nothing to alter Elsie's belief that she had been a friend of the household for years. Supper went quite well; for a party of four women and one man, who moreover contributed very little, it had almost a swing. Norah was in excellent form; she was feeling, in fact, rather full of herself, and Peter's disapproval, of which she was quite well aware, she found to her own secret surprise had no effect whatever on her spirits. She was conscious of being one up on him, a most unusual feeling and quite astonishingly satisfactory. For Elsie, it was the best part of the day. When Peter did talk, he talked mostly to her; but these desultory moments, while they uplifted, called for no effort, and the general talk freed her from any responsibility for bridging the intervals between. She could sink into herself, look at him now and again; remind herself that it was she whom he had come to see, a truth evident now beyond mistake and sufficient in itself. Helen's personality at the head of the table was like a bland fluid holding everyone else's in smooth suspension. Only Leo, leading Norah on with concealed ingenuity from strength to strength, but already experiencing the sad ennui of victory, and Peter, who had even passed the stage of thinking what he would say to Norah on the way home, wanted the evening to end.

Its ending was, however, predetermined by the hour of Norah's last train home. Peter had indeed intended suggesting, on their way to it, that she should spend the night at his hotel instead. A kind of expectation of this kind had hung between them when they set out; fortunately, Peter thought, an unspoken one. He had decided, on reflection, to behave just as though nothing had happened, except that the invitation would not be made. That ought to answer sufficiently well. Of course, if it had been a man . . . An enlightened freedom from the least taint of jealousy was, he could claim without conceit (and often did) one of his specialities, to which it was almost a pleasure to give an occasional airing. Tolerance, generosity, detachment in a real situation; these satisfied the aesthetic sense, supported the ego, and incidentally, in practice, seldom failed to succeed. They flourished less handsomely in a soil salted with the ludicrous.

Peter was unaccustomed to having rises taken out of him, to the point of scarcely recognizing the operation when it was performed; he was, however, quite clearly aware of being not amused.

It was almost at the point of departure that his mercurial spirits began to recover. Suddenly it occurred to him that so theatrical an exhibition argued, after all, a certain interest in the audience. It might even be this odd creature's idea of an amatory challenge. At the moment of leave-taking, he decided, he would try this theory out. A quick thrust-and-parry of glances, a moment of tension, a flash of humour, the picking up of a gauntlet . . . it would be, anyway, a good exit-line. He began rehearsing it inwardly, but stopped because Elsie was looking at him oddly, and he suspected that his face was, perhaps, rehearsing too.

'I really shall have to go in a few minutes,' said Norah. 'What a shame.'

'*Must* you go back to town to-night?' Leo looked along under her lashes. 'What about a shakedown here, and a swim in the morning?'

Norah declined in unexceptionable terms; but Peter, who had seldom seen her blush, found the demonstration ill-timed. He rallied his forces, with more determination than ever, for the coming clash, and worked out a strategic plan by which his adieux to Leo would be slightly isolated, and left till the last.

'Why,' said Helen, turning in her chair, 'look who's here. Come in, Joe.'

'Hullo,' said Joe. He leaned in at the doorway, shabby, brown, unintrusive and placidly at home. 'I came for my line, but I've found it. Don't anyone move. Thanks for drying it, Leo. Good night.' He began to withdraw.

'Hey,' said Leo, 'hold on, you ass, what's the idea? There's still some beer.'

Peter stared at her. His eyes and ears seemed to be playing him false. Malice, innuendo, the whole fanfarronade had gone. A boy's smile, open and straight, a boy's unconsidered long-legged ease, transformed her as an actor is transformed when the coloured spotlight goes off and the house lights come on.

'Here you are,' she said. 'Best part of a pint. I'll get you a mug.'

'Well, thanks,' said Joe. 'I don't mind if I do. O.K., I know where the mugs are.' They met at the locker. Peter heard him say, amusedly, 'You've looking very natty to-night. Quite the dude.'

'Huh,' said Leo. It was an offhand aside of cheerful dismissal. She got out the mug and filled it; there were vague, casual introductions. Joe sat down, looking settled-in like part of the furnishings.

Peter looked at the clock. The process of deflation was complete. From incredulous refusal to admit it, rather than convention, he remained for another five minutes, during which he talked. He regretted it as soon as he had begun, but obstinately continued. As happens inevitably at such moments, he was resentfully aware of being slightly ostentatious and cocksure. Joe looked at him thoughtfully, with a reposeful interest which Peter's discomfort translated into smugness. His reaction communicated itself, as is the way of similar reactions, with little delay. Joe withdrew into a cool stolidity, and behaved with uncharacteristic correctness. The atmosphere acquired that unique stickiness which occurs in a room where two men are disliking one another politely in the presence of women.

It was Leo who, in the end, accompanied them to the garden gate. She started out with a casual and rather abstracted courtesy, and it was not until they were half-way down the path that a certain constraint descended on her, as if she had remembered something.

'Good-bye,' she said to Norah at the gate. 'I'm glad you came.' She smiled, and held Norah's hand a moment longer than was necessary. She was already bored by the episode and secretly ashamed of it; but she retained at such times (which had occurred before) the instincts of a gentleman. 'Good-bye Peter. Be seeing you, I dare say.' Their eyes met. In Leo's the swagger and defiance were still curiously absent, they had a half-smile, not exactly apologetic, but with a suggestion tentative and ready to be recalled, of appeal to see the joke and be friends. It was a moment Peter could have made use of ten minutes ago. The thought of Joe's face, tacit and unembarrassed, intervened.

'Thank you,' he said with an irony just decently clothed, 'for a delightful evening.'

The mocking slant came back into Leo's face. She said, to Norah, '*Auf Wiedersehen*, I hope,' whistled for the ferry with piercing efficiency, and went in.

They crossed to the other side in a silence beside which a transit of the Styx would have seemed frivolous.

'A bit after me regular time,' said Mr. Hicks, with a certain suggestive point, when they got over. 'Well, thank you, sir, I'm sure. Always a pleasure to oblige the *Lily Belle*. A couple of real nice, friendly young ladies.'

'Yes,' said Norah with animation, 'aren't they?'

Peter withheld his opinion.

CHAPTER TWENTY

Elsie decided that, before she met Leo, there would just be time for a Knickerbocker Glory. It was an extravagance, but a handsome one at the price – a gilt and marble palace, an orchestra in fancy dress, and a foot-high trumpet of baroque, exuberant colour and taste, all for one and sixpence. This was her fourth expedition to town; she had traversed, by herself, St. James's Street, the Mall, the Admiralty Arch and the Haymarket, and was feeling sufficiently metropolitan and *mondaine* even to enter the Corner House alone. She walked in, almost convincing herself that she had been doing it every day for years.

'A Knickerbocker Glory, please,' she told the waitress, and, while she waited for it, gazed about her, for Peter had once told her that much might be learned of human nature from studying the types in a London restaurant.

This was one of Elsie's good days; a maternal legacy of temperament, when accumulated pleasant trifles, or even the absence of unpleasant ones, were sufficient to fill the present with confidence and the future with promise. Her Viennese dress was freshly laundered; she was going, for the first time, to the ballet; she had been turned loose for a couple of hours while Leo saw a mysterious functionary called a literary agent somewhere off the Strand. More than all, Peter had met her in Mawley the evening before, had walked with her, discoursing brilliantly, for more than half a mile, and had not even bothered to go in and see Leo though Elsie had told him dutifully that she was at home. It was Elsie herself, he had told her, to whom he wanted to talk; he had had no chance lately, there was always a crowd. And he had talked indeed; ideally, from Elsie's point of view, for she had had hardly anything to do but listen; had told her the most amusing stories about odd and difficult people he had met and how he had dealt with them, and had assured her at the end that her company was refreshing and did him good. If, he had ended cryptically, she ever got tired of living in an orchid-house, he and she would slip off together for a blow of fresh air. It had almost been like the old days in Cornwall.

The conversation might have lasted even longer, she remembered with regret, if they had not just then run into Joe Flint, doing his domestic shopping (and, no doubt, part of Leo's as well) equipped as his custom was with an old string bag. He had grinned at Elsie, seemed to be about to stop, seen Peter, nodded, and passed on into the grocer's, leaving behind him an atmosphere suddenly and unaccountably chilled.

'Does he live in these parts?' Peter jerked his head at the grocer's closing door.

'Not all the time.' Elsie, anxious to restore the more personal and interesting *status quo*, had been brief. ' He lives in a sort of hut on an island, just up the river.'

'A solid type, I imagine,' Peter had said, raising his eyebrows.

'He is, rather.' An ill-defined feeling of guilt caused her to add, 'He's quite nice, really'; but the much more potent desire to please Peter made her voice tepid and neutral.

'What does he do? Or doesn't he?'

'He brews beer,' said Elsie, 'as his regular job.'

Peter merely nodded, as if this were just what he had expected.

Elsie would gladly have let it go at that, but she was a

conscientious girl. 'He writes a bit too,' she concluded, 'sometimes.'

'Amazing. What did you say his name was?'

'Flint.'

'Flint?' Peter seemed to find this entertaining. 'Well, I presume he doesn't use it to write under. It's been pretty heavily taken up already. If he does, I've certainly never heard of him.'

Elsie found this natural enough, since she herself, before meeting Joe, had never heard of him either. 'He is rather ordinary, I suppose. But he's quite good-hearted.' She had a feeling that *Remission* had Joe's correct name on the back, but it seemed unimportant, for a flash of intuition had visited her mind. She had mentioned meeting Joe in her letter; he had smiled at her just now; he had called last night. Could Peter suppose that she was becoming fickle? Hastening to reassure him, she said, 'Leo likes him. They've been friends for years, I believe. He's always in and out, coming to see her.'

'Indeed?' said Peter without warmth. 'Your sister's interests seem remarkably versatile.'

'Yes, Leo's interested in all sorts of queer things.' She would have been happy to elaborate, for Peter's impressions of Leo would, she was sure, be interesting, besides setting the conversation on its feet again; but Peter had remembered almost at once someone whom he ought to see. In order to keep her memories intact she had gone out of her way to avoid meeting Joe, who would, she knew, offer to take her back in the punt. Besides, there must be some reason for Peter's lack of enthusiasm. Joe would evidently have to be reconsidered.

At the moment, all these impressions were merged in a general sense that life was full of varied possibilities. Two women were talking French at the next table; the orchestra was playing, softly and lusciously, selections from romantic musical comedy. A young man at the next table had looked at her twice when he thought she was looking the other way. He was not exactly striking, but contributed to her feelings of sophistication and self-esteem. Elsie crossed her legs at the knee, wished she had a cigarette to smoke like the French ladies, and wondered what some of the girls at school would think if they could see her now.

She had played with this notion for a few seconds before she realized what had put it into her head. Her eye, in its review of surrounding humanity, had actually passed over a felt-hatted, wool-stockinged figure, sitting with two others a few tables away. Satchels and attaché-cases were piled beside their chairs. She looked again. The uniform was unfamiliar, but one of the faces was not. It belonged to Thelma Price, who had occupied the next desk to Elsie for a year; who had left, followed by waves of envy, to move with her parents to London and prepare for the University at one of the big public day-schools. Here she was, in uniform, drab and correct, without the least trace of make-up, school stamped all over her. And Elsie had coveted her lot, half a year ago! She had not looked round yet. With swift decision, Elsie went over to the cash desk.

'May I have a packet of cigarettes, please?'

How many, madam, and what brand would you like?'

'Ten, please. Er – those will do. Thank you.'

She went back to her table, crossed her legs more modishly than before, and lit up with the ease of no less than three previous experiments. A minute and a half later, drawn no doubt by the relentless compulsion of her will, Thelma looked round. Elsie gave her an easy, social smile. Thelma stared, stared again, said something to her friends and came over.

'Elsie Lane!' she cried, performing her part as if it had been written for her. '*Well!* Fancy! I couldn't believe it! When I saw you, I felt absolutely knocked flat.'

In a manner distantly copied from Leo, Elsie tapped the ash off her cigarette.

'Oh, hullo, Thelma. What fun meeting like this. How are you liking school? Do sit down for a minute and talk to me.' She added, casually, 'Have a fag.'

'Thanks frightfully all the same. I *do* smoke, of course, out of uniform. We mostly do, in the Lower Sixth. But you know what it is. Some stuffy parent, or someone, always notices the hat-band and reports it.'

'Oh, yes, of course,' said Elsie kindly. 'Bad luck.'

At this perfect moment the Knickerbocker Glory arrived, like a symbolic cornucopia. At Thelma's table, she had already observed, they had been having small coffees. Elsie turned to the waitress, her cigarette poised between two fingers. 'Will you bring another of these, please, for my friend?'

'No, really,' protested Thelma, with brightening eyes. 'I mean, thanks frightfully, but . . .'

'This is on me. Here, you have this one, and I'll wait. I'm just amusing myself in town for the day, so time doesn't matter to me.'

'No, truly, well, it's frightfully sweet of you.' Thelma dipped her spoon into the thick cream at the top, remarking with ill-concealed satisfaction, 'I really don't know what Joan and Phyllis will be thinking.'

'Oh, never mind. It's such an age since we met.' Elsie found that she was surprising even herself. It had taken this measuring-stick from the past to reveal to her her own progress. To prolong the sensation, she drew from Thelma her chronicle of the last year; the daily train journey from Golder's Green, the approaching Higher School Certificate, the family holiday at Weymouth. Thelma abandoned her efforts to give some of the high-lights a pale importance. Her mind was elsewhere, and the bulletin petered out. Elsie knew what was coming. She took out another cigarette, tapped the end of it, and lit it deftly. It was like waiting in the wings to come on and play lead

'You could have knocked me down with a feather,' Thelma said, 'seeing you here. Where did you . . . I mean, you've been away from home, haven't you? Are you – er – back with your people now?'

'It doesn't look like it, does it?' Thelma's hesitation in coming to the point added a final savour. She must think the worst, the very worst. 'I may as well tell you I took a bit of a chance, letting you see me. If it had been someone like Vera Piggott, I'd have made a dash for it without even waiting to finish my ice. Of course, I know I can trust you. But if you chose to walk out of that door and say you'd found me here, the police would probably give you a reward.' She waited a moment for this to take effect before adding, 'Not that I've *done* anything, of course. But they can fetch you back if you're under twenty-one.'

'I know. I heard the broadcast. It was most weird, hearing the name of someone I knew, just like a film. Just my luck, a thrill like this and having to keep it a secret. Wild horses wouldn't drag it out of me, of course. I don't suppose they'll ever catch you. You look so different and grown up, you can't be like any photos they've got. Your hair and everything. But aren't you scared, coming up to town like this, you might meet your people some day?'

'Well, it *might* happen.' Elsie was unwilling to dismiss any risk that could add to the glamour of the situation. 'It would be pretty awful. But you know, they only come up to London about once a year.'

'But my *dear*. Haven't you *heard*?' It was Thelma's turn; but glutton rather than epicurean, she rushed upon her moment, taking no time to revolve its flavour on the tongue. 'Your father and mother *live* in London now. They came about a fortnight ago. My mother met your mother shopping at Selfridge's, and she told her all about it. She was awfully upset, my mother said. They live in Hampstead. My mother's going there to tea.'

Elsie's ice arrived on the table before her. She did not even see it. Her face satisfied Thelma's richest expectation. 'But they can't have. We've always lived in Cornwall. They weren't even *thinking* of moving. Why, I've only been gone six or seven weeks.'

Thelma dropped her voice; a needless precaution, since the orchestra was playing *The Riff Song* fortissimo, but impressive.

'It was the scandal,' she said. 'I hope it isn't a *faux pas*, bringing this up, but didn't you have a sister who ran away too? This is only what my mother said, you know. She said your father threw up his practice, and he's taken a post with a firm that does housing estates or something like that.' Thelma's mother had also said that they would not be so well off, but that of course was unmentionable. 'Your mother said it's not living in London she minds, it's wondering what's happened to you. It must be rather awful for her, I expect.'

'I did write to her,' said Elsie. The whole content of life was shifting like a kaleidoscope. Linked by Thelma's presence to the laws of childhood, she felt her sense of sin grow terrifying and huge. Her parents felt closer than Leo and Helen, even Peter; the knowledge that an act of hers had shifted the course of their lives was appalling, unnatural. And Cornwall, the house, the garden, the familiar walk along the cliffs, struck away from all possible futures, dead at a blow . . . only then she realized that always, at the back of her mind, had been the thought that she would return.

Now, if she went back, it would be to a life as different from the old as her life of the present. Almost unconsciously, her mind began to probe at its possibilities. 'Does my father work at home now, or does he go to an office somewhere else?'

Thelma found this question a very natural one; she had been to tea with Elsie once or twice in Cornwall. Keeping, with careful attention to good form, all traces of comprehension from her voice, she said, 'He hadn't started, when my mother met yours. But I think she said he goes up to some place in the city, or out to where the building is, and doesn't get back till quite late in the day. I expect,' she added meaningly, 'your mother's often lonely.' She had been made a prefect lately, and felt it her duty to influence people for good. 'Don't think I'm prying,' she said earnestly; 'but I feel sure your mother would understand, and be all right about it . . . whatever you've done. She told my mother so, as a matter of fact.'

'I haven't done anything,' said Elsie desperately. 'I've been staying with – with friends.' Even at this moment, the slight shadow of anticlimax in Thelma's face did not escape her. Her

Knickerbocker Glory, scarcely touched, was beginning to settle and melt. It seemed symbolic; and most unfair. Her background would, she knew, have impressed Thelma profoundly if she could have described it without giving herself away. But there was one more asset, the best of all. Taking a deep breath, she said, 'I *have* been thinking, lately, of getting engaged. But of course, nothing's settled yet.'

'*Really?*' Suddenly Thelma's eager admiration, her envy, her respect, were like a disaster. It was as if one had bought some needless indulgence with an overdraft on the bank, which there was no hope of repaying. A flood of unwanted knowledge slid, as through a new-split fissure, into her conscious mind. She knew, and felt she had known always, that Peter only loved her a little, and occasionally; that, as she reckoned love, he didn't love her at all; that he was no more likely to marry her than he was Leo, Helen, anyone, even the chance-met girl who had arrived with him the other night. Confusedly she felt that she herself, mortgaging the future with an idle boast, had taken the virtue out of it, cut off its growth like a seedling that one kills with hot water. It seemed, almost at once, like a thought to which she had long grown accustomed; the news she had just had jostled it in her mind.

'Can I be your bridesmaid?' asked Thelma, who felt that this was due to her.

'Oh, it won't be for *years* yet. It's all in the air. I don't believe in getting married too young.' She was not trying to placate Nemesis, only to put the thing quickly away; and it was simply as a gesture of escape that she looked at her watch. It informed her that she had spent forty-five minutes where she had meant to spend fifteen. Thelma, consulted, said, 'If it's Sadler's Wells, you'd never possibly get there now before the queue goes in.'

'I shan't be very quick either, because I don't properly know the way.' She cared very little, unless Leo were annoyed. Reality seemed enough for the moment, without the assistance of art; besides, she regarded ballet, secretly, as something to talk about having seen rather than to see, and had been wishing all along that Leo had suggested a good straight play.

'I've got a free period,' said Thelma eagerly, 'till three o'clock.' She was reluctant to surrender Elsie so soon, with her half-told adventures and her probable capacity for being influenced further. 'Why don't you come for a walk with me instead, and we could talk some more – if you feel like it, of course, I mean. Your friend will have given you up by now, in any case.' The friend was probably, she reflected, an undesirable influence from whom it would be a kindness to separate her. The story of this afternoon would improve with keeping.

'Well, I don't know. really . . .' But she felt in herself an unwillingness to be alone with her news and her discoveries. With Thelma, she still felt dramatic and rather more than life-size, and the edges of reality were decently muffled. Already her mind was selecting a safely expurgated, but impressive saga. 'All right,' she said. 'We really might just as well': and leaned back in her chair, enjoying, against a background of chaotic thought, the sight of Thelma making her excuses to the intrigued, inquisitive Phyllis and Joan.

Leo watched the tail-end of the queue disappear into the theatre with feelings of exasperation sharpened by anxiety. She ought, she reflected, to have arranged to meet Elsie at Charing Cross and bring her here; she could be relied on to get into the wrong bus or otherwise lose her way. She ought by this time to recover it without undue alarm; still, the child would be flustered and disappointed, and Leo blamed herself. She strolled down to the box office; there might be a couple of returned seats, even separate ones would be better than nothing. There turned out to be only one, at the extreme end of the dress circle. She bought it, for Elsie if she appeared, or, if not, for herself.

In the end, she waited outside till the first interval. Was it possible, she wondered, that some observant constable had pounced on Elsie and identified her? So many people succeeded in disappearing every year that one had not taken the chance very seriously; still, it existed. At least, thought Leo, it would solve the problem which was becoming, as far as she was concerned, increasingly knotted. Leo was unused to responsibility, either material or moral, for other people; it sat on her heavily. The need to bowdlerize, for days on end, large tracts of her own personality in what had been the freedom and privacy of her own home, affected her less as a nuisance than as an insidious attack on her rather defiant intregrity. Now that she had managed to involve herself in bowdlerizing Peter as well, it had become, she felt at times, almost too much to deal with. In the intervals which these concerns allowed her, she thought often and unhappily about the household in Cornwall.

Beyond all this, the economics of Elsie's future, and even of her present, were beginning to nag. The budget of the *Lily Belle* was a fluctuant affair, based on haphazard give-and-take; to such systems of finance *à deux*, one-sided liabilities are disastrous. Leo for her own part had lived on Helen cheerfully for weeks on end, reversing the process when her royalties came in; their accounts, where any existed, had been scribbled on the backs of envelopes, correct, perhaps, to the nearest pound. This had now become, on Leo's side, unworkable. No mathematician, she had wasted hours of writing-time in inaccurate computation, whose results Helen tore up indignantly and threw away. The friction thus engendered, though no more than skin-deep, was trying to people used to no friction at all.

Leo found that her meditations had reached a point when the astute policeman had the hopeful promise of a *deus ex machina*; and became, at once, heartily ashamed of herself. She made another survey of the street, was rewarded by a trickle of audience emerging between ballets for a turn in the air, and decided to give it up. If nothing had happened, Elsie had her ticket home and knew how to get there; if anything had, there was nothing to be done. Leo went in, found her seat, and settled into it just in time for the rise of the curtain on *Façade*.

It happened to be an especial pet of hers. In particular, she never got tired of the Dago; he epitomized what seemed to her the more comic aspects of the heterosexual scene. The last self-satisfied wag of his tail as he accepted the coy invitation of the red handkerchief to come inside, rejoiced her this time as much as ever. She thought of Peter; thought how outraged by the thought Peter would be; and laughed again after everyone else had stopped.

When the curtain fell, she sat for a minute or two nursing her enjoyment, then got up to buy a programme because she had forgotten what the last ballet was to be. It was, she found, *Horoscope*, which was better than she had hoped. She read, with lingering anticipation, the familiar names, shifting in her seat from time to time to give more restless balletomanes passage to the street or the bar. When she looked up, a scattered lane of empty seats led her eye along till it was arrested, four or five rows forward, by the outline of a head she knew very well. It was Joe; preoccupied, at the moment, in reading his programme too. A little star of pleasure and happiness shot up within her, and hung for a moment like a rocket at the top of its trajectory, sharpening the edges of things with light. She rose in her seat, to make her way round to him; then stopped and sat down again, while the rocket turned earthward, diminished to a fading point, and went out. He had looked up from the programme in his hand, smiled and spoken; but not to her. He had not seen her, and she drew back in her seat, for she no longer wanted that he should.

The woman in the seat beside him was not, after all, in the least like the one in his book. In the first place, she was not so young; older perhaps by a few years than he. She might have given Leo as much as ten. It was hard to be sure, for she was of a type that matures early and ages late. She was not beautiful, or anywhere near it; but her face, a little too broad, and her firm quiet body, had the confidence of women who have never missed beauty, having had all they want from life without it. She wore a plain dark-red dress which was neither good nor bad; chosen, it seemed, with a thoughtless negative taste, assimilated to herself, and forgotten. She was almost wholly lacking in the paraphernalia of female competition; but its absence was like the absence of small change in the handbag of a queen. Hers was the rare, prideless assurance of the woman whose womanhood has not only succeeded, but has known what to take of success and what to leave aside. She was the kind of woman of whom other women say that they don't know what men see in her. But Leo knew.

She saw them talk together for a while, and then cease to talk. There was between them the accustomed ease of people for whom intimacy has long become a background, not a preoccupation. She knew, before she had watched them for three minutes, without hearing even the tone of their voices, that they were old lovers, grown, perhaps, a little careless in the security of years.

Well, she said to herself, turning her eyes away, this was nothing new. It had been a certainty familiar to her imagination since the first weeks when she had received Joe as a friend. She had not minded then. She had often believed since that she was glad of it. Why should it be different now?

For it was different; it hurt her bewilderingly, like a pain in some part of one's body that has always been healthy and strong. She looked at the woman again; her maturity, the sexual poise and confidence marked all over her, qualities Leo had seen and recognized with indifference elsewhere, were not indifferent now. They turned in the heart like a sword. There was no sense in it, she thought.

It was in her mind for a moment to leave the theatre, but the idea revolted her as soon as she had formed it; a female kind of resource, almost on a level with fainting or weeping or boned stays. It might even attract Joe's notice, for by this time all other outgoings were over. He might look embarrassed; he might smile, wave, introduce her. He might do all these things. She sat

looking before her, stubbornly confronting her own emotions as
one might try to outface an enemy by staring him in the eyes.
She had always, till now, got rid of unwanted things more readily by this means than by running away. But it was only like
thrusting oneself against something sharp, the pain increased as
one pressed it home. Perhaps, she said to herself, this only
seemed to matter because she had been in a mood, worried about
Elsie already. It might be better to consider that instead. Perhaps,
after another five minutes' waiting, Elsie would have turned up.
She would have been occupying this seat; noticing nothing,
probably, for she was unobservant, or remarking afterwards,
between earnest platitudes about the ballet, 'Joe was there. No, I
didn't speak to him. He was with a friend. Oh, just an ordinary
sort of woman.' ('Middle-aged,' Elsie would probably add.) 'She
looked quite nice. I think she may have been some sort of relat-
ion; they were rather like each other, in a way.'

Leo smiled; the bitter flavour of the joke was, for the moment,
restorative. She looked up, and was just in time to see that Joe
and the woman were talking again, before the returning tide
from the gangways silted up the space between.

The lights went down, the curtain parted, a blue dropcloth
displayed the signs of the Zodiac. The orchestra began. She sat
alone, not penetrated by the music; the warring measures of the
planets, disputing mortal destinies, had nothing to say to her, nor
the young lovers caught in their beams. With a passing irony she
recalled that she had been born in August, between the signs of
the Lion and the Virgin; a fancy of her mother's, born of this fact
and a chance-read magazine feature, had been responsible for her
name. The lion, she remembered, was fabled to humble himself
before the virgin. But this legendary reconciliation had, it
seemed, somehow failed to take place; perhaps something had
happened to spoil his temper.

She smiled into the dark auditorium, a hard fixed little smile,
and the delicate shifting lights and colours hurt her; beauty out
of the mind's reach, like water poured out before the thirsty. She

went out quickly at the end, while the audience was still relaxing its tension with the absurd, discordant noises of applause.

'I'm most awfully glad,' said Elsie, 'that you went in the end. I felt rather awful about it, but I knew you wouldn't think anything had happened to me, now I know London so well. I felt sure you'd understand; it's *so funny*, isn't it, meeting someone you know in quite different surroundings?'

'Yes,' said Leo. 'It is amusing.'

'I do hope you didn't miss the best part because of me.'

'No, that's all right. I didn't miss anything important.'

'I'm so glad . . . Thelma and I had the most awfully interesting talk.' The news was on the tip of her tongue; but, somehow, it got no further. She did not want to tell, to discuss, to be edged towards thought or decision by the definition of words. She did not want to know what Leo would have to say. Leo's thought was apt to have hard shapes and sharp edges, which came through any comfortable draperies in which one tried to wrap it. There was no need to begin thinking to-day; something might happen to-morrow, splendid, and significant, solving everything. She said, 'And I had the most marvellous Knickerbocker Glory; nearly a foot high, and covered in cream.'

'Darling,' said Helen, 'you're crazy, buying stockings like this when we've still got the milk to pay. Besides you'll be through them in five minutes; they're a size too small.'

'Try them against the red suit. They're for you.'

'You're crazier than I thought. Whatever for?'

'Can't imagine. I just walked into the shop and bought them. It suddenly struck me, for some reason, how much better I like you than anyone else.'

CHAPTER TWENTY-ONE

eter and Helen sat on a fallen log in the Great Avenue at Hampton Court. But for themselves, the stately vista was deserted; it was a weekday morning, and the few visitors had left for lunch. Peter and Helen had brought theirs with them, and were finishing it with the assistance of a large swan which, appearing with an apologetic waddle and a mien deceptively meek, had now reached the stage of snatching from their hands portions intended for themselves. As it gulped and swallowed, it fixed them with a yellow, malevolent eye.

They had come on the spur of the moment; Peter, killing time in Mawley, had met Helen emerging, trim and sleek, from the hairdresser's. It happened to be one of the days on which none of her surgeons had cases sufficiently curious to be worthy of record. She had accepted his suggestion that they should spend the day together as easily as if it had been the offer of a short drink, without going through any of the conventional motions of having other engagements. This had merely intrigued him; Helen had the looks, and the indefinable aura of success, which enable a woman to convey by acquiescence the idea that she is making no effort. Such a double-bluff would not, however, have occurred to her in a lifetime; it came quite naturally. Taking the lunch had been her idea. She had gone back to get it, without offering to bring him along with her, and had left him wondering. He was wondering still, but had every intention of finding out.

'There are still some tomato sandwiches,' she said. She fished one out for him; the swan, less preoccupied than Peter, forestalled him, missing her fingers by half a centimetre.

'This is ridiculous,' she said, in exasperation rather than alarm; she had met a number of swans. 'Give the disgusting creature the bag and let him take it away. Swans ought to stay on the water; it brings out their better natures.'

Without undue reluctance, Peter threw the bag as far as it would go. The swan made off, looking at him first like a boss gangster whose dignity has been upset. Helen, unruffled and cool in her candy-striped print, sat smiling after it. The sunlight glinted on her hair; she wore it down to-day, its bright curls just reaching her shoulders. Her slim hands, tipped with a delicate varnish of dusty rose, were locked round one knee. Peter shifted himself a little closer along the log.

'Swans ought to stay on the water.' He repeated the words with dreamy, mysterious significance. 'I agree with you, my dear.' He slipped his arm round her waist. Warm, slender and compliant, it yielded easily, but somehow non-committally, into his hold. She smelt like a clean little girl, of fresh-laundered cotton, dusting-powder, and sun-warmed hair and skin. He looked up; there was still no one about.

'What are you thinking of, with that solemn face?'

'Thinking?' she said in a kind of placid surprise. 'No, why should I be?'

'Why should you, indeed?' He worked his arm a little further round. It would have been quite easy, he reflected, to believe her stupid if one had not had evidence to the contrary. Perhaps, at this moment, she even was stupid; she had a faculty of disconnecting the more active part of her personality, as easily, it seemed, as turning off a switch. He tilted her face towards him, smiling into her eyes; she awaited, with contented passivity, the expected kiss, and accepted it as a lazy cat submits to being stroked. He had, as with a cat, the feeling that if her attention were distracted she would have forgotten all about it in a few seconds. Nevertheless she was pleasant to kiss; her superficial candour, her underlying indifference, made a teasing combination. He tried the effect of a little ardour; partly from inclination, partly with an eye to the situation which would be created by her refusal to respond. But the result was still inconclusive; she was sweet and yielding, but, behind it, he felt the smooth surface of her self-possession as undisturbed as a pool in the rock. There was nothing to take hold of, except what he held already; and, in a place which might become public at any moment, the possibilities of this were strictly limited. In any case, there was a cosy and amiable quality in her responses which made it impossible to develop anything in the nature of passion without feeling foolish. It was a pity she had shown so lukewarm an enthusiasm for the Maze.

Peter was not the man, in these circumstances, to neglect the interesting alternative of verbal attack.

'You're maddeningly elusive,' he said.

There was little in the material situation to justify this; but she received it without surprise. No, he thought, she wasn't stupid. She smiled at him, not archly, but comfortingly, as if to say, 'Never mind.' and rested her shining hair against his shoulder.

'Why?' he pursued, with deliberately brutal directness.

She sighed faintly. She might as well have told him, aloud, not to be tiresome. Peter was not thick-skinned; but determination, inquisitiveness, and boundless self-confidence produced an effective substitute.

'Don't you trust yourself with me?' he asked, dropping his voice. This, surely, ought to provoke something.

It did. She laughed; charmingly, not unkindly, with sunny amusement. When she had stopped laughing she kissed him of her own accord.

'Really,' she murmured, 'you are rather sweet.'

She kissed delightfully; but the pill tasted, in spite of the spoonful of jam. His determination became obstinacy.

'Then it's me whom you don't trust?'

She wrinkled her smooth brow; nothing could have conveyed more clearly that she considered the question meaningless. In the tightened pressure of his arm she nestled confidingly; it was as if she protected herself in an armour of down. But, more adaptable than the baffled crusader, Peter was quite ready to abandon the straight blade for the curved, silk-cutting scimitar.

'I think,' he said, 'in your heart you don't trust anyone. I wonder why.'

'I don't know,' she said simply, 'what you're talking about.'

'All men,' said Peter gravely, 'aren't alike, my dear. Does it seem odd that I'm not content simply to kiss you, satisfactory as that is; that I want you to trust me too?'

'I don't suppose it would seem odd,' she said in her soft kindly voice, 'if I knew what you meant by it. One doesn't simply trust people. One trusts different people for different things.'

'And you trust me – for what?'

'I haven't needed to think. Why, is it important?'

Her body was warm in his arm; she herself was like a gently smiling presence resting easily at a distance. He reached after it with words, seeking for something with which to touch it home.

'You trust Leo,' he said. 'With everything?'

'Of course not.' She seemed amused. 'I don't trust her to count the change in shops, or to remember to bring things back when she goes to town.' There was a pause, during which he felt her continuing the list in her own mind. 'I know what to expect of her; I suppose that's what you mean.'

'And she knows what to expect of you?' He raised his eyes meaningly to hers.

Unperturbed by his gaze, Helen said, 'She'd be pretty stupid if she didn't, after five years.'

'As long as that? Yours must be a very – unusual relationship.'

'I expect most relationships are unusual when one knows enough about them. We're pretty well used to ours; it seems quite ordinary to us.'

'It must demand great courage . . . from both of you.'

'What a queer thing to say. It takes less effort than any other relationship we've either of us tried. That's why we go on living together, naturally.'

She had drawn herself away from his arm; not in hostility but, just as he had imagined, like the stroked cat that sees a bird through the window. The positive current of her personality had been switched on. Its sudden vitality made her more interesting at the very moment when she became less accessible.

'You would sacrifice a great deal,' he hinted, 'rather than hurt her?'

She stared at him. 'You do have odd ideas. I don't need to sacrifice things not to hurt her. I keep telling you, we live together because we enjoy it. Anyone would think, to hear you talk, that we were a married couple.'

She delivered this staggering speech without as much as a shade of emphasis; merely with a gentle reasonableness. He was, for a moment, on the verge of abandoning all his principles by allowing himself to be shocked. Hastily he reassembled them.

'I suppose I shouldn't ask,' he said, 'what has happened to make you afraid of marriage?'

'You can ask if you like. But I'm not afraid of it, so there isn't much point.'

'You're young,' he said. 'You're very pretty; you're domesticated, I imagine, and, forgive my mentioning it, normally sexed. You may want to marry some day; what then?'

'Well if I wanted to, I should, I suppose.'

'You wouldn't find the decision hard to make?'

'What decision? The decision would have been made. You don't suppose Leo would want to keep me if she knew I wanted to be somewhere else?'

There seemed to be no penetrating her contentment. He became cruel, not in malice, but as, in the hospital, he might have applied increasingly painful tests to a patient who showed no signs of sensation.

'Perhaps,' he said, 'when it came to the point, you might be afraid to let her know.'

'*Let* her know?' She might have been repeating an incomprehensible phrase in a foreign language. She seemed to be about to say something, to think it not worth the effort and give it up. At last she remarked, 'I think you must have read a lot of novels, or something. People don't live that way.'

She could hardly have delivered, if she had thought it out for weeks, a more deadly insult to the *sanctum sanctorum* of Peter's self-esteem. He found it hard to believe, indeed, that the words had been uttered, or, if uttered, that they meant what they seemed to mean.

'You have,' said Helen serenely, 'such sensational ideas.'

He was speechless; but Helen, who had intended to go on talking in any case, did not notice it.

'Mind you,' she pursued with friendly toleration, 'I like men. They're perfectly all right in their way. I lived with one, once.'

'Really?' said Peter. Nothing else would emerge.

'Yes, for several months, while I was at the Slade. He was quite pleasant, but a bit of a cad.'

Peter had recovered, by this time, to the extent of caressing her gently and making a sympathetic noise.

'Not a cad as a lover, mind you. He did all that very well. He was just a cad to live with. Things like wanting all the space for his own work and not leaving me any room for mine. Or time. I don't think he liked, really, seeing me work at all. I was better at it than he was, that might have been one reason why. Between women, you see, an issue like that is bound to come out straightforwardly, but a man can cover it up for ages. And then, he thought I ought to like his friends but he needn't like mine. If I had a cold or a headache or wasn't feeling bright for the usual sort of reasons, he just used to go out; it never occurred to him to do anything else. Leo isn't any more domesticated than most men, but she isn't above filling you a hot-water bottle and fussing you up a bit. Well, anyway, he kept on assuring me he loved me, and I feel sure he believed it. When he asked me to marry him he was thunderstruck that I didn't fall into his arms with tears of gratitude. He kept on at me about it; he thought I was afraid of being a burden on him, I think. Finally he tried to make me have a baby so that I'd have to. He said it was for my good. I was tired of arguing by then so I just packed and went. I expect he's scratching his head about it still.'

'That's too bad.' Peter's soft voice, and the pressure of his hand, brought a smile and answering squeeze, but both were distrait; Helen had become interested in what she was saying.

'Shortly after that I took up nursing, and met a great many people, as one does. But instead of asking myself what they'd be like in some romantic situation, I always found myself imagining them shut up with me in a three-room flat. Only two people passed. One was an honorary surgeon who was fifty and happily married. Leo was the other. I've never regretted it.'

'And is that all?' asked Peter at length.

'Of course it isn't. You asked me why we were still living together at the end of five years. As far as I'm concerned, that's the reason.'

'And Leo? Is it as simple as that for her?'

'Leo can tell you about herself, if she wants to.'

He had come, he saw, to the blank wall of an impregnable loyalty. There was a generosity in him that acknowledged and was pleased by it. His vanity, on the other hand, impelled him to tap the wall here and there. It was sufficient to have found the flaw, he had no wish to exploit it.

'On your side,' he said, 'surely it entails a certain amount of – well, reticence?'

'How do you mean?'

'Do you tell Leo quite everything you do?'

'Nobody tells anyone everything. It wouldn't be interesting. I don't think whether I shall tell Leo things or not.'

'Will you tell her, for instance, about this afternoon?'

'Not if you don't want me to.' She spoke like someone who reassures a child.

'I was thinking,' said Peter, a little nettled, 'of her feelings, not of mine.'

'*Leo's* feelings? Whatever for? She'd laugh, of course.' Seeing his face and instantly contrite, she added, 'I'm so sorry. I thought that was what you meant.'

There was a pause during which Peter seemed to see, through Helen's sweet, gently concerned face, the outline of another. He was annoyed with the image and with himself; he had been enjoying, most of the afternoon, a pleasant pity for her. To recover this emotion, and the feeling of well-being that went with it, he said, 'Don't be sorry. I'm glad for Leo to laugh. There's too much loneliness in the world not to be glad of any human happiness one sees, however unorthodox – and precarious, perhaps. Believe me, I wouldn't do anything to make it less.'

As a pool is ruffled by a flicker of wind, Helen's blue eyes held, for a moment, the delighted appreciation of a joke, from which she seemed to withdraw into some private meditation. Next moment they were cloudy and soft with sympathy again.

'That's very sweet of you,' she said.

She rendered it so prettily that he was about to kiss her again, when he became aware of a sharp pain in his calf. It was produced by the swan, which had exhausted the remains of the sandwiches and, finding the bag itself unpalatable, had returned after the manner of the ancient Danes for a further subsidy. It pursued them, threatening and offensive, as far as the Lily Pond.

Peter took Helen home; as everyone did, even escorts who scorned convention or cultivated the remiss. In her presence such things became a reflex.

'Leo's out,' she said, discerning some occult sign from across the river. 'And Elsie's at the cinema. Never mind, you must come in and have an egg to your tea with me. I'll have to leave fairly soon, I'm going to the theatre. But I dare say someone will be in by then.' She added, presently, as they crossed the gang-plank,

'I'm not sure where Leo went to. Somewhere with Joe, I expect. We'd better leave them a couple of pints to come back to.'

She went into the galley to collect the meal. Peter wandered round the living-room; it was strewn, here and there, with traces of Leo's recent occupation. Her personality seemed still to be lounging casually about the place, as incomprehensible, now he had been discussing her half the afternoon, as ever. They had not, after all, he reflected, discussed her at all. On the table were some loose papers; one of them had a carefully drawn plan of a ranch with its corrals and out-buildings, annotated in a clear and somehow quietly authoritative hand; not Leo's scrawl, which he had seen before. An old, well-chewed pipe lay abandoned beside it. Peter found the set-up irritating; since Helen would be wanting to lay the table, he swept the collection up and dumped it on one of the lockers in a heap.

She must, he decided, for all her arrogance, be fundamentally lonely. (It was not Helen, making pleasant domestic sounds within earshot, of whom he was thinking.) This Joe person was probably a symptom of it. A simple doglike creature, Peter guessed, who would put up with anything or be too dumb to notice it. What she needed was a really constructive relationship. Perhaps she realized it and, when it offered, became defiant, as the subject who has most need of psycho-analysis is loudest in condemning it. Helen's placid kindness, the dim harmless neighbour with whom she pottered about the river – well, they did little enough damage, no doubt, but where were they getting her? Eccentricity in women always boiled down to the same thing. She wanted a man.

Helen was coming, with the fruit of her labours on a tray. Her cooking, he found, was on a level with her looks. What after all, was she doing here? No doubt she hadn't told him everything; well, that would come. He hoped that Elsie's session at the cinema was beginning rather than ending; one did not want to shirk anything one could do, but she was, undoubtedly, heavy going. If Helen left first he could leave with her; in fact, it might be better not to wait. He was preparing his excuses when Helen went out to fill the kettle again.

It was a still day, on which small craft could approach without a warning ripple. Peter heard none, till the hull he sat in was softly jarred by the impact of a punt. Elsie, he thought; oh damn. Then from the floating deck outside he heard Leo's voice, easy and clear.

'Come in and see if there's some tea left.'

'Well, I . . . No, thanks, maybe not to-day. I think I might get something done this evening. The canoe looks pretty good, now it's dry.'

'Bill Brooks says we made quite a job of it . . . It's time I put in a spell myself, now you mention it. I've got to get this pie-eyed heroine rescued. I can't think why on earth he should want to bother, in the middle of the round-up too.'

'Don't forget his horse will be pretty blown if he's been cutting out cattle for long.'

'It gets shot quite soon. Thanks for working out all that stuff, it'll keep me going for days . . . Here, wait a minute, this looks like a bit of yours. Yes, that's the lot, I think.

'Bye, Joe.'

'Bye, Leo.'

There was a moment's pause; Peter could hear an armful of oddments being dumped outside. Then Leo strolled into the room. Her hands were in her corduroy pockets, her head was up. For a few seconds she did not see him; the sun, outside, had been in her eyes. She took out a cigarette and lit it. Her face had a kind of watchful happiness; she looked like someone who has been lately in peril, and who holds, in the moment of safety, to a vigilance it may yet be too soon to relax. She threw the match from her cigarette quickly away; she seemed to be throwing a thought away with it too.

'Helen,' she said.

'Well, Leo,' said Peter, getting up from his chair.

She did not start with surprise; she seemed to withdraw into herself for a moment, before she came forward to meet him.

'Well, Peter,' she said. 'Did you and Helen have a good day?'

She was smiling; it might have been in mockery, he could not tell. Suddenly it mattered very little.

'Yes,' he said. 'Most successful, thanks.' He was smiling too. The challenge, thrown and accepted, made them lose the thread of their irrelevant words.

Helen came back and said, 'The tea won't be a minute. Is Joe coming in?'

'No, he's gone home to work. I'd better go and clean up before I eat. Shan't be long.'

She was, however, a little longer than usual. When she came down again, she had changed into the scarlet dress.

CHAPTER TWENTY-TWO

With half-disapproving appreciation (for his tastes were conservative), Foxy Hicks looked at Helen's silver-grey dress, gathered up round her to diminish contact with the grubby seat of the ferry-boat, and her little velvet jacket frogged with silver lace. Pretty, but no warmth in the things, he thought. 'Going out enjoying yourself, Miss Vaughan?'

'Yes,' said Helen. 'I'm going to the theatre.'

The girls nowadays, thought Mr. Hicks, get too much gadding around; they lose the fun of it. Outings meant something when I was a lad.

'Miss Lane will be crossing you back, I reckon,' he said, 'in that canoe.' He disapproved on principle of canoes, which had a high nuisance-value in the hands of trippers who couldn't steer them.

'I'll be coming back by car, so we shall cross at one of the bridges lower down.'

'Ah,' said Foxy, with a rufous wink, 'home with the milk, as they say?'

'Not as bad as that.' She smiled at him, pleasant and agreeable-like as usual; but she looked, he thought, a bit middling to-night. As if in answer to this reflection, or to one of her own, she said, 'It's rather a bore, really. I didn't feel like turning out. But it was too late to put it off.'

'You young ladies, you get so much gaiety you get blasé.' He pronounced it rather like 'blowsy.'

'Yes,' said Helen, replying absently to the general sense, 'I expect it's that.'

It was beginning to be twilight. Between the willows on the island, a yellow patch of lamplight appeared. Foxy remarked, conversationally, 'Mr. Flint sitting at that writing of his again. Funny thing to me what he finds to write about, living by himself in a hole-and-corner place like that.'

'He likes not being disturbed, I suppose.' I wish to God she thought, he'd come in with Leo to-night. She never runs into trouble when Joe's about. For Brutus, as you know, was Caesar's angel . . . Why, when one's mind is upset, should it throw up ridiculous tags? Inappropriate too. She turned to look over her shoulder at the *Lily Belle*. No lights on, she thought, only the fire. Well, it's early yet . . . I suppose after all, she could hardly have done better than she's done this time. Neither of them has any capacity for hurting the other; she can only hurt herself. But I wish it were over.

Lights were beginning to spring up, here and there, on the opposite bank, with the soft gay promise of an early summer evening. Helen let her mind blow clear of thought; she began to slip, almost unconsciously, into the mood she would need for the young man she was meeting, who had shown, last time, the first almost imperceptible signs of becoming difficult.

'Want a cigarette?' said Leo, sitting up.

'No. And neither do you. What a restless thing you are. Come back here and be quiet.'

'Quiet?' She laughed, and went over to the box on the table. Peter, from the couch, watched her movements with interested attention. She lit her cigarette at the electric fire, and settled beside him again.

'You can finish it now,' he told her. 'I don't make love to any woman while she's smoking.'

'Thanks, I will.' She sat upright, blowing shadowy rings into the glow of the fire. Its red light, shining on her red dress, made it luminous like a signal at night. 'I'm sorry, I'm afraid I'm often very bad form. You think I'm the sort of person who'd bring out a packet of crisps in the middle of Beethoven's Fifth, don't you?'

'No,' said Peter, 'I think you're nervous, if you want to know.'

'Nonsense. Why should I be? Seeing this room is for all practical purposes the front hall and anyone might come in at any moment, that would be too ridiculous, wouldn't it?'

'You know perfectly well there's nobody in the place but ourselves. Put that thing out and relax.'

'Elsie will be in before long. And Helen isn't away for the night either.'

'I wish they both were,' said Peter softly, 'don't you?'

'I think it's probably all for the best myself.'

'Isn't that another way of saying yes?'

'I'm sure it must be, if you say so.'

'Why are you so defensive,' he murmured. 'You weren't a few minutes ago.' She was silent – tensely silent, he thought. When he craned round to see her face, he discovered that she was laughing.

'I'm sorry,' she said. 'But I suddenly thought of the Victorian villain who twirls his moustache and says, "Why do you fear me, little one?" I wonder if the things we say will sound just as funny, fifty years from now.'

'Well,' said Peter unexpectedly, 'why do you, if it comes to that?'

'As a matter of fact, I don't believe I do, much. I can't think why.' She had discovered with other men that there was almost no limit to the amount of truth with which she could get away in the guise of irony; she was becoming reckless about it.

'Let me tell you that your sense of security is very ill-founded.' It had only been a random thrust, after all. Her bluff had succeeded again; its success was necessary but monotonous, like the success of a card-trick one did for a living. Why did we begin

talking, she thought wearily; oh, yes, I remember why. Her cigarette was smoked three-quarters down; she put it out.

'About time, too,' said Peter, slipping his arm under her shoulders.

Helen's right, thought Leo, he's really very sweet. I wonder
how they got on this afternoon. He's probably nicer with Helen;
everyone is. She can afford to be honest and kind. Her reserves
are just decencies; there's nothing behind them she daren't have
found. He's better in himself than ever he'll have the chance to
be with me. I can know that and not mind, because we didn't
start as friends; thank God, I haven't broken anything this time.

'That's better,' said Peter, taking breath. 'Why were you so
jumpy before?'

'I don't behave like this at home. I never have, till this
evening.' It's a relief to be able to say something to him that's
true, as far as it goes. He's so generous. He asks nothing better
than that I should tell him how to do me good. Or more probably, by now, he thinks he knows. Here he is, so near, and here am
I quite safe with myself. Thought's secrecy must be one of the
most wonderful of the works of God. Everything else is
explorable, or violable, or reacts to chemistry, or can be laid
open with a knife. But thought can only be given. That's the ulti-
mate dignity of man.

'You're not happy,' said Peter. 'Are you?'

'If I were, I should consider it a smack at Providence to say so.'
He only wants to know how to be kind to me. Why not; why do
I feel I'd sooner have my throat cut? Properly considered, it seems
very unreasonable. I think I see why. It's because he *knows* it's
more blessed to give than to receive. Perhaps the blessing is one
of those things that goes if you think about it – like Joe's Arizona
drawl . . .

'What's the matter?' asked Peter.

'Matter? Nothing, why?'

'You started away then like an overbred horse.'

'I thought I heard someone at the gate, but it wasn't.'

'I think I know,' said Peter gently, 'what's in your mind.'

'Do you?' said Leo. Her eyes had narrowed, dangerously.

'You're afraid of upsetting Helen, aren't you?'

There was a pause; filled for Peter, as it lengthened, with an established conviction of truth.

Leo loosened her shoulders comfortably in his arm. 'Yes,' she said, smiling at him with renewed confidence; 'Helen would put powdered glass in my food if she saw us. Or drown herself, perhaps. Didn't she strike you like that?'

'Of course not.' He spoke with indulgent reproof. 'But you have a guilt-complex towards her. Isn't that true?'

'I expect you're absolutely right. I ought to try and get rid of it, oughtn't I? What do you think would be the best way?'

Peter spoke to her about it, seriously, and with scrupulous fairness to all concerned. Helen herself, he assured her, would be the first, if she understood, to agree with him.

'It's very nice of you,' said Leo, 'to take all this trouble with me when I behave so badly. Thank you. I feel much better now.'

She leaned back her head, and dropped her lashes. Peter concluded his theory with a short demonstration. It was quite satisfactory.

A chain of barges came down the river, long shadows in the surface mist on the water. The leader of the string had a matting fender across the bow, like a grinning mouth, under two staring hawser-holes, giving it a face like a dolphin's. Its siren bellowed, and one could fancy the thick lips curled backward to let out the sound.

'Elsie will be coming in,' said Leo. 'It's nearly ten.' She pushed Peter away, and sat up. 'Do something about your tie, for heaven's sake, before you forget.'

'If you're not careful,' said Peter, 'you'll be repeating the mistakes of your parents over that child. She isn't too young at seventeen to know what people look like who've been kissing. She ought to be starting herself in another year.'

Leo sat back and looked at him, her hand, which had been

pushing the hair back from her eyes, arrested in the midst of its movement. It isn't credible, she thought. But it is, of course, there was the other day. He'll do it again, or something worse, if I say nothing now. And I shall feel an accessory. I must make myself tell him somehow, it seems the least I can do for her. She sat silent, confronting the image not of Elsie but of her own pride. Her will was paralysed as if it were murder that had been demanded of her; it seemed, by her own rule of living, scarcely less. The still-unspoken words in her head gave her the horror she would have felt at being herself betrayed. She could not utter them.

'I see I've upset you,' said Peter, looking at her with kindly penetration, 'by that rather abrupt reference to your parents. I'm sorry; I do understand. But you know, it's much better really, to let the air in on these things.'

Mechanically, Leo finished her interrupted gesture and let fall her hand. She looked at it for a moment, then smiled at him. 'You're always so sensible. I think you'd better go, though, now. Do you mind?'

'Of course not, my dear,' he said sympathetically. She was emotionally disturbed, he thought, and didn't want her sister to see it; women were like that.

A cool eddy of breeze, fresh with green scents and water, drifted in through the glass doors. It struck pleasantly on Leo's forehead; she realized that the room was hot, and full of cigarette smoke.

'I'll come to the gate with you,' she said.

Night was already taking away the colours of things; but every bush and tree had its faint shadow, and the light a strangeness, for the moon was up already and its white patterns were beginning just to be visible through the pallor of dusk. Dew had fallen, and was cool about their ankles. Across the bridge, the empty tow-path was visible on either side. They stopped at the gate.

'Good night, Peter.'

'Well, Leo.' He enfolded and considered her, pleased with the evening. 'This is where I say "Thank you for having me," isn't it? But I shall save that, I think, till another time. Just in case.'

Leo laughed. 'That's really rather good,' she said. 'I must remember it. You have some very nice lines, Peter.'

There was an interlude. Leo thought idly, This must look most picturesque, if there were anyone to see. Moonlight and roses, and young love.

'The only drawback,' Peter remarked presently, 'to this charming spot, is that when it isn't overrun with people it's always just about to be. But when you come up to town to see me, all that's going to be different. You are coming, aren't you?'

'I might,' said Leo. 'I think perhaps I will.'

'I'm glad about that.' He submitted her face to a last searching tender scrutiny and a kiss, and left.

He went down the towpath at an easy swinging pace, pleased with himself, with the air which the contrast with London was still fresh enough to sweeten, with the lights which came out from moment to moment at intervals along the bank, like irregular beads on a loose string. Elsie too, as she walked homewards from the cinema, with the sound of steel guitars and Hawaiian ululations in her ears, loitered happily, repeating to herself what she could remember of the 'In such a night' speeches from *The Merchant of Venice*.

When the sweet wind did gently kiss the trees,
And they did make no noise – in such a night
Troilus methinks mounted the Troyan walls . . .

When she got in, she thought, she would go up on the roof for a little while, and think about Peter.

    In such a night
Stood Dido with a willow in her hand
Upon the wild sea-banks . . .

She had almost collided with him before she saw him.

Her feet, the breath in her throat, the blood in her body, seemed all to stop together. It was too much. She could not even speak to him.

'Hullo, Elsie. Are you going to cut me dead?' The general affection he was feeling for the universe reflected itself in his voice.

'No,' said Elsie with a little gasp. 'I didn't see you. I – I was just coming back from the pictures.' All day she had been wondering whether Peter would look in. (Helen, when she came home for the sandwiches, had not said where she was going, which was nothing unusual.) Now he had come and she had missed him.

'See a good film?' he asked absently.

'Yes. Awfully good. It was called *Flower of the Lagoon*.'

'Oh, you ought to have gone to the French one at that little flea-pit round the corner. They seem to get quite good stuff there; old, of course. Taking a walk?'

'Well, sort of.' Could it be possible that he meant to come with her? 'It seemed too nice to hurry in.'

He said, with paternal kindness, 'Leo's expecting you, I think.'

'Oh, is she?' There was a note in his voice which she perceived, but did not, or perhaps would not, understand. 'Have you been over there?' She said to herself, trying to believe it, that he had gone looking for her.

'Yes. I've been there all the evening. Leo and I have been having a little talk.' A kind of warm expansiveness, of mixed origin, made itself felt in him: the urge to instruct, to receive well-earned appreciation, to distribute around him a little of his general sense of well-being 'I expect you've noticed for yourself,' he said, 'that this sister of yours is a – a rather unreconciled and lonely person. I felt that as soon as I saw her. But I think she and I are going to understand each other much better now.'

Elsie heard. The words themselves by-passed her intelligence altogether; she scarcely knew what they had been. But somewhere, under veil after folded veil of illusion, a woman recognized the unmistakable overtone of male possessiveness and self-congratulation. It was, for the first second, knowledge and nothing else, just as a deep bullet-wound may feel at the impact only like a jolt or a dull external blow.

'Are you?' she said; and was not even surprised to find that she had spoken exactly as if he had said that Leo would take tea with him to-morrow afternoon.

'I think we are. I shouldn't say anything when you go in; people as reserved as she is don't always like to be noticed, you know . . . Well, as you say, it seems too good an evening to stop indoors. I'll walk along with you part of the way.'

'I'll have to hurry,' said Elsie. She spoke quite naturally, almost briskly. 'I'm rather late as it is. Please don't bother. I'll have to run.' He stood looking after her, his eyebrows raised in a faint incurious surprise, while the sound of her footsteps, the irregular thudding sound of an overgrown child, faded along the gravel at the water's edge. She ran on and on, looking ahead of her into the gathering dark, passing, without a glance, the garden hedge and the gate. Her throat and chest began to hurt her, but she still ran, feeling the long beams of reality wheeling and steadying, converging on the line of her course, like a fugitive pilot who knows that in a moment the searchlights will meet in a single, inevitable point of light.

Left alone by the click of the closing gate, Leo threw up her head, like someone receiving a challenge. The shadows were growing stronger; in the deepening moonlight the leaves of the roses shone like fine dark metal, and near her the flowers had a pale cold scent. All the clearness was like bright cutting edges, searching the mind. The night breeze was rising; it lifted back her hair, and was cold in the neck of her dress. Something was unfastened, which was not astonishing. She set about fixing it, humming softly and defiantly to herself a swift little running tune.

A stranger steps up and he says, 'I suppose
You're a bronc-ridin' man by the looks of your clothes?'
Says I 'Guess you're right, there's none I cain't tame,
Ridin' tough ponies is my middle name.'

At this point, something seemed to amuse her a little.

There was a faint movement on the far side of the garden
towards the river. But the night was full of slight stirrings and of
sounds. Most of her attention was on a tiny, elusive little hook,
just under her collar.

. . . They say there's a cayuse that's never been rode
And the guy that gets on him is bound to get throwed . . .

The little hook slid into its eye. She turned to go in, took a
single step, and stopped in her tracks, as motionless, for a
moment, as the path of the moonlight. A shock like a cold wave
broke over her heart. She stood still: the wave grew hot drench-
ing her body. There was no time to consider it. There was no
time for anything, but to smile and to step forward; to say to herself, in the instant that was left, that everything would be well, as
it had always been.

CHAPTER TWENTY-THREE

J oe tied his punt to a stump in the garden, and strolled leisurely round towards the bridge, enjoying the evening, and the scent of the tobacco-flowers which, in the deepening dusk, were spreading their moth-like whiteness for the creatures of the night. He had settled down to work before he missed his pipe or remembered where he had left it; and had found, as usual, that cigarettes were not the same. Scarcely detaching his mind from that of the character on whom he was working, he had pushed off in the punt to get it, thinking as he went, and comfortable in the certainty that Leo would do nothing to interrupt or detain him; she took other people's work more seriously, if anything, than her own. He wandered absently over the grass, in no hurry, preserving by instinct the quiet that suited his mood, his feet falling softly in their rope-soled shoes. It was a pity, he thought, that a light was necessary to write by; his imagination was always more fertile in the dark. He might, in his preoccupation, have collided with the two standing shadowed under the climbing roses by the gate, if Leo had not laughed. At the sound he stopped, backing sharply against the stump of the apple-tree, and stood there for a moment to collect his thoughts. Three parts of his brain had been turned inwards, and what he saw seemed at first less real than its images. Almost at once he

gathered himself together, prepared to move silently away; but it
seemed now that any movement he made must produce some
revealing noise. He hesitated, conscious at first only of an acute
embarrassment, while the seconds lengthened. When he did
move, a leaf rustled under his feet, and he hesitated again. His
eyes were accommodating themselves to the darkness, or the
moon was brightening; he recognized for the first time the man
who had been at first glance only a formless encircling blur.

Well, he thought, I can't stop here: I must get away somehow,
and quickly too. But he found it suddenly difficult to move. A
person of some discernment about human emotion, he was not
slow to recognize the nature of his own; he thought it, not particularly shocking or surprising, but a pity, and a thing to be got
over, by oneself, as soon as possible. He prepared again to depart;
but Leo had seemed for a moment about to turn his way, and
again he lingered. Perhaps, he thought, he might have mistaken
the man; and he looked in the hope of finding, after all, a
stranger whom he had never seen and, with luck, would never
see again. The sky lightened more as a cloud thinned; yes, it was
Peter sure enough. In any case, it was no concern of his.

So he had been wrong after all, it seemed, that afternoon in
the punt. It was merely that Peter would do, but he would not.
This thought was followed by a brief and shadowy perception of
some fragment of the truth, which anger swept almost immediately away.

I'll get out of this, he thought, go back to work and get shut of
it. Her amusements are her own affair. He remembered the concentration of mind which had been so sharply broken; of all
things to be avoided were emotional tie-ups in the place where
one was working. His choice of the island had been a kind of
extreme expression of this. And the sooner I get back there the
better. He tried to remember what he had come for in the first
place, and failed.

It was interesting, he thought, the reality of these transitory
feelings while they lasted, like the reality, larger than life, of

dreams. A hundred casual recollections of her added themselves to the half-seen shape that leaned back in Peter's arms filling in the outlines clearly. He noticed for the first time, because Peter made it evident, that her dress was unfastened a little way at the throat. He had been swimming with her unnumbered times (he remembered her old shrunk swimsuit, a gesture to convention rather than a garment) without even the surface of his emotions being disturbed; and now, for no logical reason, this. To-morrow morning, he thought, I shall see her probably, diving off the boat for a swim, and wonder what it was all about. It hadn't occurred to me that I needed a woman to-night; and it wouldn't now, if I were working. One uses it up.

Just then she lifted her head, looking almost towards him. He saw her face, smiling, unhappy and perverse. He shut his teeth, and stared hard at the ground. This is plumb crazy, he thought, not recognizing the idiom of his boyhood; this won't get me any place. This is senseless destruction. A good evening's work; a good friend, too, as straight as a man. As it is I shan't get down to anything more now, to-night . . . There's something destructive too in her. He doesn't see it; he looks eminently pleased with his efforts, damn him. Has he . . . No. I think not.

She'll see me, he thought, if I move now. It was a miracle, indeed, that she had not seen him already; and, when Peter's head bent over hers, he moved out from the tree's shadow again, to go. To-night's obsession, he thought, would not, thank God, survive five minutes' normal conversation with her. They had been good and useful company together for nearly three years. He had, as a rule, no difficulty in seeing his own moods objectively, and had no doubt of being able to do it to-night, once he could get away. He would remember, for an hour or two, her defiant and reckless face; his imagination, in which it had disturbed a kindred recklessness, would keep him awake perhaps till the dark before dawn; and what would it matter? He would sleep till eleven instead of eight next morning, and that would be the end of it.

She's put me in my place once already; no, twice, if you count that damned silly couple of minutes on the Chelsea Embankment. He paused, remembering it, with his hand on the rough bark of the apple-tree. And here she is with someone who presumably suits her. So what gives me this idea that I could have her to-night? He paused over the thought, found it hot and unprofitable, and pushed it aside. And supposing I could, what afterwards? Afterwards we should want things back as they were before. Against the thought of their day-to-day companionship, what he felt seemed, even in the moment of its force, unreal. He was not twenty, to see romance in wrecking something sane and good for the sake of a disastrous impulse. The conclusion of all this was obvious, and he translated it, at last, into action. He had got half-way across the garden; already it was all falling into the past, and he was, in anticipation, alone on the river, setting straight his mind and holding it at arms' length for analysis, when he heard the click of the gate.

Peter too was leaving. He waved his hand to Leo; a filter of moonlight, full on his face, revealed an expression of grave, self-satisfied benevolence which Joe found ultimately insufferable. It could take only a moment or two to catch him up and knock him into the river; and, during the moment of his disappearance, Leo, standing between, scarcely existed for Joe except as the most evident obstacle to this. Then, suddenly Peter was gone, and there was only Leo to see.

She was humming 'The Strawberry Roan' between her teeth (he remembered teaching it to her, one evening on the island), and prosaically buttoning her dress at the neck. As soon as she turned to go in – which was almost at once without a glance at the receding figure on the towpath – she saw him.

For a moment neither of them moved. Everything else in the garden, the swaying willows, a bird-rustling among the tangled roses, a grasshopper, the lap of the water's edge, seemed full of whispers because they were so still.

'Why, Joe, is that you?' She came to him over the long grass, which made a soft whishing noise about her feet, smiling. The colourless light bleached her face and clothes, showing only the darkness of her hair; but he knew that she was blushing by her eyes, which were too bright. 'I never heard you.'

'I'm sorry,' he said, not looking at her. 'I ought to have made more noise.'

'Oh, that's all right.' Her voice had the slightly altered timbre of people who, however trivially, have been making love. He could hear that she was still a little out of breath. 'I'm very glad to see you, as a matter of fact.'

'Well, thanks.'

She was quite close now, and looked up at him quickly. It will be all right, she was thinking; we only need to behave quite ordinarily for a minute or two. 'Come on in, if you've time. We've got some sherry.'

No doubt, thought Joe savagely. 'Sorry, I can't stop. I only came –' he remembered, as he spoke, the reason '– to collect my pipe.' Indoors there would be a light. He tried to pretend to himself that she had noticed nothing, that their thoughts were entirely secret from one another. All I need is to go home and sleep this off; it will be all right in the morning.

It will never do, Leo was thinking, to let him go like this; we shall be strained and different in the morning. We must have a drink and laugh it off. The afternoon in the punt had come back to her, with the sharpness of a thought which one knows to be shared. That his pride could be hurt now seemed, indeed, a kind of cruel joke. She took his arm and squeezed it. 'Oh, don't be a lemon, Joe. Come in and talk to me sensibly about something. I've been exasperating myself.'

He stepped back, taking his arm away. This in itself shocked her as if he had slapped her face.

'It's no business of mine,' he said slowly. 'But what a waste.'

There was no human creature less given to censure. For the first time she began to be afraid, and reacted with anger.

'Waste of just what, do you imagine?'

He did not answer. Her anger left her. The moon was at his back; he stood there, silent, compact and dark. There came over her, like a kind of sickness, the consciousness of being a woman, detached for a moment from all accompanying thought. She could feel it, even before she spoke, invading her voice, and the way she stood. To feel this with Joe was terrible, and must stop. She struggled against it, and tried to exorcize it with a laugh.

'I was just getting the moonlight out of my system. It didn't take long; it never does. Don't behave as if it were hydrophobia.'

He said, 'I don't think I'm being very intelligent to-night. Forget I was here. I'll look in to-morrow.' He was going to add 'Good night,' and walk away. The syllables sounded in his head, but did not come, and he stood where he was. The clouds had blown away now altogether from the moon. Their faces were clear to one another.

No, her mind cried out to her; oh, no. But it was lonely and afraid, and its cry was thin. They were standing a couple of feet away from one another; she seemed to see him, not with her eyes but with a sense of touch. Her mind grew stunned and silent, leaving her to the decisions which had already accumulated in the past. She moved towards him, without knowing why; because of the long habit of trust between them, because Peter had left her ready to reach after any certain reality, even this ruinous one; because there had always been rest here and freedom, and it seemed even now that she only had to ask. He took her by the shoulders, and held her a little away.

'Don't be angry.' She had not known that she had words ready to say; they came now like late and foolish guests, whom everyone has forgotten. 'Nothing happened, you know.'

He seemed not to hear. He stood still, holding her shoulders as if he were listening to something within himself. She went on talking; it was as if the words had taken charge of themselves.

'You see, it's easier when it isn't important. It sounds silly. I don't know why it is. Don't worry about it. It doesn't signify. It didn't mean a thing.'

He drew her towards him, without haste. He moved like someone who, reluctantly, is obeying an order.

'Let's see whether this will,' he said.

While he looked at her in the garden, he had thought of kissing her like this, and it was as if the thought had come to life in his arms, her first moment of stillness and slow unfaltering response; they seemed nothing to wonder at because in desire he had known them already. Her strong slim body wakened in his embrace, and, as he held her, he did not remember that she might have resisted, for this was a fulfilment of his thought. The violence of his own mood cut him off from everything but the moment, and she too seemed detached from the past and future, having the suddenness of dreams; he forced the pace to a breathless crescendo and did not consider what she might think or feel, for she answered him like imagination. But at last, when he pulled back her head meaning to kiss her throat, he saw her face, lost and desolate staring past him into the dark.

'Leo,' he said. They looked at one another. Anger and bitterness were struck away from him; only the passion they had stirred remained, deepened strangely with remorse and compassion and that sense of the tragedy of things which lay always not far below the tranquil surface of his spirit, and found its way often into his written, but rarely into his spoken words.

'Leo. Before God, I'm sorry. I meant this not to happen, too.'

She said, slowly and with difficulty, 'Have you wanted it to, then?'

'No, I swear it. Never till now. I saw you, over there, and . . . that's all.'

'Is that the truth?' she whispered. 'How funny.' She laughed, painfully and soundlessly; he could feel the rise and fall of her breast.

'Don't. I'm sorry. You don't believe me, do you? I was going away.'

'Oh, yes,' she said. 'I believe you.'

'We were good together, weren't we?' he said, and stroked her hair. 'And now there's nothing, I suppose. That's what you meant, isn't it, that's why you kept me off. Nothing but this, now, to-night.'

'Yes,' she said. 'That's all.'

For all men kill the thing they love: the bitter rhyme stirred in his mind, and he covered her face with his own, feeling her pain quicken desire in him, and his own pity helpless except to drown them deeper. He thrust her head backward and pressed open her mouth, longing for the easy forgetful sensuality which their natures denied them, and knowing that she too was trying to lose herself in vain. Her breath caught in her throat; her hands strained against him, slackened and fell. The coward does it with a kiss, he thought (bringing the verse and the kiss together to their unsparing conclusions) the brave man with a sword.

He lifted his head. It was full night; the last rusty streak of sunset had faded, the river reflected the luminous sky, empty, like dark, rippled glass. Clouds had covered the moon again, and diffused its light so that it seemed to come from everywhere, the water, the earth, the sky. A grasshopper burred somewhere at their feet.

'Nearly three years,' he said. 'And now . . .'

'As long as that?' There was so little of her voice left that the effort with which she kept it level hurt him. He loosed her a little to look at her face.

'They were good years, too,' he said. 'Don't think I've forgotten because of this.'

In spite of everything she was aware of his perception like an unsteady but still sensitive hand, reaching towards the inner doors of her thought and brushing lightly, uncertainly, against the locks. She drew away a little and stood straight on her feet, making a last desperate recovery of herself.

'Never mind, Joe.' She tried to speak as they had been used to speaking together, when something they had taken trouble over making refused to work, or their plans had been wrecked by the weather. 'We just had a run of bad luck, that's all.'

Confusing the effect with the intention, she did not know how far the one came short of the other; and what she saw in his face when she had spoken, she did not understand. He was moved beyond all that had passed before; by her forlorn and breaking courage, which tore at his emotions; by something unconquerable in her, which, below the levels of consciousness, his instincts received as a kind of defiance. The two forces met in him, opposed and united; he pulled her back to him with an abruptness like anger, and began to kiss her again in a kind of blind deliberation, confused between the desire to console and subdue her; using as if by calculation all the experience he had, and, because he had passed the point of self-understanding, quite unaware of it. He was aware only of her, of the difficult abandonment of her last defences, the slightness of her body when its proud self-sufficiency was gone, and the bewilderment in her face turned to his as if she were searching it for her own lost identity. His instincts approved; and, this part of their purpose achieved, made room for the tenderness which all along he believed he had been feeling.

'How could we know?' he said, finding his own voice altered; he was shaken beyond what he had believed was possible any more. 'You've never let me touch you, all these three years.'

Memories streamed through her, like images distorted in flood-water; of the times when he had hauled her from the river into the punt when he had met her swimming; of rock-scrambles when he had heaved her up bodily to a hold that was above her reach; of the day when, during a brief phase of experiment with jiujitsu, she had been locked in his grip, on the floor, for five minutes at a stretch. They passed, like illusions, and vanished, and the floods covered them.

'You wanted things as they were,' he said slowly. 'I know that. Perhaps I did too; I can't remember. Maybe it'll come back again. But there's only one thing we can know to-night.'

She did not answer. His words were a sound, and a caress among many caresses; her mind, still struggling to find itself again, took no hold of them.

He held her closer. 'Let's do this well,' he said softly. 'Let's make it a damned good bonfire. We'll have that, anyway.'

She had become a stillness in his arms. In the distance, slowly nearing and coming clear across the water, a party of trippers in a rowboat were singing 'Show me the way to go home.' She moved her head a little away, as if she were listening to the sound.

'Well?' he said.

With a quick movement she turned towards him, looked him in the face and said, 'Yes. All right.' The conclusion had been foregone to him, and, he supposed, to her also; so that something which was almost amusement stirred in a corner of his mind, she had spoken so much as if, for instance, he had bet her she couldn't punt a canoe for twenty yards.

The boatload of trippers was getting nearer. They had started the chorus again; they had evidently become attached to it. 'I'm tired,' they intoned in a slurred andante, 'and I want to go to bed.'

He laughed under his breath, kissed her hard again, and felt her shiver.

'What is it? Did I hurt you?'

'No'

'God, I could. What is it, then – cold?'

'No, I . . . Yes.'

'What? Here . . . cold now?'

'I'm all right.'

He had, suddenly, a feeling of something that had happened before. Then he remembered the morning on Scawfell Pikes, when the rock he had belayed to had given way. He had thrown himself, with a split second to spare, at a doubtful hold which by miracle proved sound, and braced himself to take her weight; but the pull had not come. She had managed somehow for herself. 'O.K.' he had called, 'I've got you.' She had been below out of sight; her voice, when she answered, had sounded just like this.

'I could say a lot of things' – he looked past her at the water – 'but what's the use?'

'Don't worry now.'

'There's one thing. If you're afraid of my trying to drag this on, don't be. That shall be just as you want. I give you my word.'

'Thanks, Joe.'

'. . . and it's gone right to my head,' sang the rowboat, drawing abreast of them.

'Do you want to go in,' he said, 'and get a coat or anything?'

'No. Let's get away.'

'We'll go to the island. Just wait till that lot goes by.'

They went down to the water's edge, and stood under the willows beside the punt. He put his arm round her shoulders.

'You won't be cold soon. I promise you that.'

'I'm not now, really.'

'I wonder how this never happened before.'

'Joe.'

'Yes?'

'Don't see me again very soon after this, will you?'

'Anything you say. Must it make a difference? Just now I don't see very far ahead.'

'You don't have to, if you remember.'

'I'll remember. For God's sake let's get away from here.'

He cast off the tie-rope as she stepped in, and lifted the pole out of its slings. She saw him about to recede into a black silhouette against the gunmetal surface of the water, leaving her alone. It was important not to be alone; it was the only thing, now, that mattered. 'Can't we paddle?' It seemed, as soon as she had begun, a foolish thing to say, and she brought it out indifferently.

'Not now,' he said. 'It's quicker to use the pole.'

He thrust it down into the water; she could see nothing of him except a dark shadow stooping and straightening, hear nothing except the quickening slap of the ripples as he drove forward. He was going very fast. She dipped her hand over the side and the water dragged at her fingers. A fish jumped with a plop and splash, and a blundering moth made a soft flurry against her face.

The pale half-lit clouds shifted in the sly, moving under a light wind the way of the stream. She felt as if she were drifting, quite alone, through outer space. A strand of willow stroked across her hair. The punt glided through a half-turn, and stopped. She saw him, outlined against the water, brace the pole against the side of the punt, and drive it down into the river-bed. He stepped over from the tail of the punt, and knelt beside her.

'Would you like to stay here?' He was short of breath from the speed he had made; it roughened his voice a little. It was dark under the willows; she could barely see his face. He put out his hand, reaching for her in the shadows, and touched her breast.

She had forgotten that in summer, when the nights were fine, this was the place where he slept. Twenty-odd years of civilization had not cured him of preferring the sky over his head. They were here; she had thought there would be a few minutes longer, while they went over to the hut.

'Yes,' she said. She felt herself shivering, and tried to control it by clenching her hand on the edge of one of the floor-slats.

'I'll go in,' he said, 'and get a rug. It gets chilly later on.'

She said nothing; he got to his feet again, and stepped ashore. She heard his quick footsteps on grass, and then on gravel.

Leo sat up in the punt, and stared about her, at the black dangling lace of the willows, the water, and the sky. She had known that this would happen, if he left her alone; but she had not been able to say anything. She had never been able to tell people that she was afraid; she had only been able to revenge herself on them.

It will happen again, she thought; it will be too strong for me. One forgets everything. I shall turn on him like the others. Not many people know enough to hurt Joe. I do. And afterwards I shan't be able to kill myself, even, because of what it would do to him. He must be there by now. He'll be coming back.

She heard, clear in the stillness, the creak of the wooden door. No footsteps followed; he must have gone in. Everything in the place was easy and ready to hand; he would not be long.

It was a very small island; there was nowhere at all to hide. The punt was there, under her feet, but she never thought of it. One did not take other people's craft without asking; on an island it was unthinkable to take them at all. Rules like this were so settled a part of life that it never crossed her mind.

Beyond the arch of the willows, the smooth pale sheet of the river slanted away upstream. Two warm red splashes of light shivered on its surface; she had left the electric fire burning in the *Lily Belle*. It was only a couple of hundred yards away. She and Helen had often swum to the island and back again.

Getting to her feet, she jerked open her dress and stepped out of it, and loosed her shoes. Her one-piece slip was short enough to swim in, but one of the straps slipped down over her shoulder without the dress to hold it in place. She pulled that off too, feeling it tear in her haste, and lowered herself soundlessly over the side. The day had been fresh, and the chill of the water forced a gasp from her which she stifled between clenched teeth. For a few moments she had hardly breath enough to swim with, but she struck out with long strokes, out from the shadow of the trees into the pale wide water. The sense of freedom regained, of power over her own body and the element it moved in, the effort warming her blood edged with the panic that had launched her, gave her a feeling of desperate exhilaration. She struck out faster, her arm flashing out over her head.

Footsteps sounded on the bank she had left. She would not look round. She floated for a moment, listening, but he did not call, and she swam on, fixing her eyes on the red rippling light ahead, shutting off her mind from everything but that and her own speed.

There was a clean-cut splash behind her, a moment of silence, a quick breathless laugh. A mallard, drowsing on the water, squawked shrilly and took to its wings, clumsy with sleep, beating over her head. The silence of her stealth was shivered to bits like a broken shield. She forgot her science, and the economy of effort that makes for pace, and felt her stroke shortening as the sound of his hard steady thrust began to overtake her. She could hear him breathing, now, between the strokes.

Flight had always been shocking to her, and pursued flight a nightmare. There were dreams she had, which she had learned to break by turning and facing what came behind. There was no waking now. Her heart pounded in her throat. She looked over her shoulder; he was only a couple of yards away, panting and smiling, lifting his head sideways from the water to shake it, as a dog does, out of his eyes and hair. His arm shot out again, and his hand closed round her ankle. He let it go before she could sink, laughed, overhauled her, and gripped her waist.

'Give in, Amphitrite.'

She twisted, quick as a fish, in his arm; but he held on, turned in the water, and pulled her to him. A stifling blackness broke over her mind. She joined her hands round his throat to thrust him away: the dark water, cold and blinding, covered her eyes and crept up through her hair. She sank, dragging him with her. His grip held for a few seconds; then through the hammering in her ears she felt him pull at her arms and throw back his head. But he still felt strong and confident, and her fear, blotting out thought, clenched her grip, only knowing to make him powerless. They went down and down. He seemed, now, scarcely to be resisting. A trailer of weed curled against her ankle, softly, like the exploring feeler of some creature lying in wait.

Something struck her teeth violently together; her head seemed to burst in a great white star. It was a cracking blow, square on the point of her chin. For the necessary moment, it wiped out everything. Then she felt the water coming into her mouth, and knew, for the first time, the terror of drowning and nothing else. She fought her way to the surface, choking, with blank eyes, unaware of his supporting hands.

'Easy now. Let yourself go. I've got you.'

Dazed and passive, she let him turn her face upward, and felt, presently, the pull of his hands at her armpits. There was water in her throat; she choked it away and heard her own voice, hoarse and changed, saying 'Let me go; I can swim all right.'

'Hold still,' he said sharply. 'I don't want to hand you another one.'

She ceased to struggle, and lay watching the sky over her head until the willow-trees shut it away. He steadied her to her feet in the breast-high water.

'Sorry I had to do that.' He was still breathing hard; it took the expression out of his voice. 'It's the only thing. I hit harder than I meant, though. Did you bite your tongue?'

'No.' She pulled herself towards the bank; her arms, lifted from the water, felt like lead. 'I'm sorry. I – I don't know what happened. I lost my head.'

'My fault. It's a silly game, catching at people out of their depth.'

He clambered up the bank and pulled her up after him by the hands, then let her go. A faint outline in the gloom, he stood silent for a moment, not touching her. Without his support her own weight felt limp and heavy, almost too much for her feet to bear. She gave a laugh, which she did not recognize as her own.

'It's pretty poor, isn't it, holding a person's neck who's trying to life-save you.'

'Oh, that. Nothing to it. Strong swimmers are always the worst; it's a well-known fact.'

He moved away. She stood, swaying on her feet, her hands pressed to her eyes.

'Here.' His voice came from behind her; the rough wool of the sleeping-rug went round her shoulders. 'Go on up to the hut, and have a rub down. My dressing-gown's behind the door. I'll come in a minute.'

She went up through the trees, on to the open grass, hearing no movement behind her.

The door of the hut stood open; she went in, feeling in the dark the shapes of familiar things, for she knew it as if it were a room in her own home. There was an electric torch in the pocket of his dressing-gown. She found the matches and lit the lamp, watching the known shadows, estranged like enchantment, flicker on the wooden walls, the typewriter on the big deal table, the manuscript strewn beside it, a paragraph crossed out with long decisive strokes; the folding bed in disorder where he had pulled the rug away. From a ledge on the wall a carving, in some smooth dark wood, of a negro's head, seemed to watch her as the shadows moved over its deepcut eyes. She went for the towel and saw, in the Woolworth mirror he used for shaving, her own face, white and set, with dark dilated eyes and dripping hair. Suddenly she felt bitterly cold, and, taking up the rough towel, rubbed herself till her skin hurt, but still without getting warm. She combed back her hair (she knew where everything was, he had lent her most of it some time or another), and corded the dressing-gown round her, rough and heavy against her sides.

'Can I come in?'

At the sound of his voice, even and friendly, just as she had heard it a thousand times, the light seemed to alter and settle, the shadows grew familiar again. She could see, on a shelf in the corner, the mouth-organ which he still called a harmonica, a dented thing with the plating rubbed away; it had been given him by one of the ranch-hands and had been old when he was a boy. He kept it for luck, he said. She remembered how he had shown her how to play it, somewhere about midnight, on the last night she had spent here. 'O, bury me not in the lone prairee . . .' She had picked it up, in the end, quite well.

'Sure,' she called, her voice sounding her own again. 'Come on in.'

He opened the door, in his old flannels and leather belt, smiling at her, his shoulders in the lamplight still shiny with water. Her dress and slip were over his arm; he threw them, casually, on the back of a chair.

'Br-rr,' he said, giving himself a little shake. 'Let's have the stove on.' It was an oilstove with a red glass chimney; the light of it made the room seem warmer, even before the heat struck through. He dipped into the can of drinking-water, filled a saucepan and stood it on the top. 'Coffee in a minute. Can you remember if I had a shirt on when I started out?'

'Yes, I think so. Some sort of flannel one.' As she spoke she remembered, suddenly and vividly, the feel of its texture in her arms, and looked away.

'I thought I did. It'll keep wherever it is. Have you got the towel anywhere?'

She tossed it over to him, and watched him scrub it over his rough curly hair. The room was growing warm; everything seemed drawing together about her into an encircling security and comfort.

'Have a cigarette' – he dried his hands to light it for her – while I make the coffee. Put your feet up and get your breath.' She curled herself up on the bed, wrapping the dressing-gown round her bare ankles; there was plenty of it to spare. He spooned out coffee and condensed milk into the saucepan; one could never believe, watching Joe make coffee, that the finished product would be drinkable, but it always was.

'I wish,' he said, strolling over to the table, 'that you'd take a look at this sometime and tell me how it strikes you.' He tossed a new novel into her lap. 'I think it falls pretty heavily between two stools myself, but I'd like to be wrong because I met the man once and rather took to him. I've got to review it for the *Mercury*.'

She turned the book over, tasting it here and there, trying to pick up a thread in it and focus her mind. Joe had gone over to the table again and was sorting out his manuscript, clipping a chapter together and putting the cover on the typewriter. Her eyes left the book in front of her, and rested on his bent head and the line of the lamplight on his shoulder. Presently he turned and came back to the saucepan; she picked up the book again.

'He writes rather well,' she said.

'Very well. That's the pity.'

She turned the pages; whenever she ceased to read, her mind was wiped as blank as a slate. Joe strained the coffee into a jug, poured it out into two thick china mugs and brought one over to her.

'There's something in this,' she said, tasting it.

'Only a spot of rum. Not much. Good for the circulation.'

She smiled back at him, for the first time. 'I saw a film of the circulation once. Like a lot of hoops bowling along. A frog's foot, they did it with. The coffee part's good, too.'

'M-m. I've made better. Throw it down while it's still too hot to taste.' He sat down beside her, nursing his mug between his knees. 'I saw a damned funny thing once. A couple of hearties had a slight misunderstanding and tried to life-save each other. In Parson's Pleasure it was, while I was up at Oxford. One of them tried this slugging trick, and the other, who'd only been turning somersaults in the water, didn't think a lot of it and slugged him back. They churned up the river like a couple of alligators. Then the vice-president of the Union came out of the huts; having missed the preliminaries he thought they were both drowning and didn't feel equal to the double event; so forgetting he was stripped to the buff he went haring round the screens and started waving his arms at the first punt he saw, which was full of Somerville women. They thought he was an exhibitionist gone berserk and tried to make off, but they only liked to look one way, so by the time I'd found my pants and got there they were going round and round in the water, and the chap was just about to leap in and swim out to them so as not to waste time.'

Leo choked over her coffee, and put it down on the floor to laugh. Once she began, she found it hard to stop. She caught her breath and said, 'You never told me that one before.'

'Oh, surely. Look, your cigarette's gone out. Have another.' He bent over her to light it. 'You're going to have a hell of a bruise there in the morning.' He took her chin in his hand, turning her face towards him. She smiled up at him; his face, shadowed with the light at his back, smiled back. The yellow lamplight, the rough primitive room like a room in the backwoods, were suddenly beautiful. 'I caught you a crack with the punt-pole, if you remember. Slipped out of my hand.'

'Clumsy devil. You ought to have paddled, like I said.'

'Yes.' He looked down at her, no longer smiling. 'I know that.'

There was a silence. A launch went by, swift and purposeful in the night. They were still while its sound lasted. Then he collected the empty coffee-mugs, and took them over to the table.

'That lamp keeps smoking,' he said idly. He bent over it, his shoulders making a great shadow over half the room. 'Maybe it wants trimming.' He touched the key, the flame leaped, then dwindled; the light became a little pool on the table, and went out. She could see, after a few seconds of blankness, the pale glimmer from the uncurtained windows and his outline against it, his face still turned to the dead lamp. 'That's torn it,' he said evenly. 'The wick's gone in. I'll have to fix it when it cools.'

Her cigarette burned in front of her, a point of light making the darkness emphatic. He must have turned off the stove when the coffee was finished; she had not noticed because she was no longer cold. His shadow moved across the window towards her. She felt a contraction at her heart, and drew back a little, feeling behind her the planks of the wall.

'I was going to have a cigarette,' his voice said, close beside her, 'but Lord knows where the matches are.'

'Take a light from mine.' She held it out, leaning forward, her eyes on its red spark. He rested his knee on the edge of the bed beside her, and took her wrist to guide her hand. But both their hands were still.

The cigarette was drawn gently from between her fingers. She watched it move away and downwards, and disappear on to the floor. His weight settled beside her, and a board in the wall creaked as his back came to rest against it. He took her hand in both of his, and held it against his knee. The pulse that had been beating in her head quieted. His hands were steady, hard and warm. She moved back a little, relaxing against the wall, and found herself resting on his shoulder. He moved his cheek softly against her hair.

The memory of the river flooded over her, realized and fully understood for the first time. She was filled with a horror of herself; and she must have moved her hand, for his grip tightened. She clung to his fingers, as people cling to ease a moment of physical pain.

'Joe,' she whispered. 'You know I . . . You know I tried . . .'

He said gently, into her hair, 'It's hell, getting cramp in the water.'

She turned and flung her arm round his neck, hiding her face against him. He gathered her on to his knees, holding her as one holds a child.

'Let it go. Let it go, my dear. It's over now.'

'It's never over. Sometimes I think I'd be better dead.'

'Let it go.'

'It isn't that I . . . You see, it's only . . .' She could not go on.

He finished for her, easily, it seemed without emotion, 'Something went wrong the first time.'

She shut her eyes. She was trembling again.

He moved his head a little away. As if it had been light enough to see him, she knew that he was looking past her, at the pale blur of the window.

'Do you remember,' he said at last, 'that morning on Scawfell Pikes? I suppose you might say it was a pretty close call.'

'Yes,' she said, wondering, 'I suppose you might.'

'Did it strike you at all that most people wouldn't have led straight on up that chimney, afterwards, without asking you first how you felt about turning back?'

'I shouldn't have liked it if you had.'

'No, I suppose not. That wasn't the reason, though. I couldn't have made the descent from where we were then.'

'Don't talk such rubbish,' she said, almost forgetting what had gone before. 'Why, that part was as easy as climbing a tree. I could have done it on my own.'

'Yes, you rather enjoy a vertical view, don't you? I used to wonder how soon you'd spot my lukewarm enthusiasm for what

the manuals call "a sensational prospect". You were always pointing them out to me, I remember. The fact is when I'm climbing
at any height, I can't look straight down for more than a split
second; I get vertigo if I do.'

'Joe. Why didn't you say?'

'Why didn't you?'

The tautness of her arm round his neck relaxed, and she shut
her eyes again, but not in fear.

'It doesn't really matter,' he said, ' if you know what you're up
to and have someone you can trust at the other end of the rope.
There's nothing to it. Except that there are always some people
who need to go on.'

She turned her face upward, trying to see him. He bent his
own, and kissed her, slowly and deliberately, holding her like a
woman now and not like a frightened child. She felt his gentleness
and carefully controlled skill, and a confidence that was imposed
on himself for her support, not fully felt: and remembered his first
kisses in the garden. Something seemed to break in her, and a
great fountain of tenderness and loyalty washed through her, as if
her body and mind were being filled with light. She became no
longer of importance to herself. Whatever happens, she thought,
everything must and shall be well for him; and she turned to confront her fear for his sake; but it was like facing one's death and
finding that one has died already and the spirit is free.

As his kiss ended, she put her hand behind his head and drew
it down again.

'It doesn't matter any more.'

He scarcely returned her kiss, but caught her to him and held
her still; a sheltering, almost a tragic gesture, like that of a
woman. They were quiet, with his face against her hair, while
there passed between them a force of emotion so strong that the
physical was swept away in it, and she felt, without knowing
why, her eyes fill with tears.

'Leo,' he said at last, under his breath, 'if you'd rather, now I'll
take you home.'

She said, quite simply and with an open mind, 'Is that what you want to do?'

'No.' He moved his hand over her head. 'But we can do that, or anything, now.'

'Yes,' she said. 'I know.'

The wide gown, loosened already, was slipping from her shoulders. She pulled the girdle-cord, and let it fall away. He took her back to him, stooped with her and laid her on the pillow. She felt his lips move against her eyelids.

'You'll be all right,' he said. 'I'll look after you.'

In the *Lily Belle*, in the little buff and green room they called Helen's, a light went on. To Elsie, the soft glow seemed, after hours of lying face downward in the darkness, a white glare, scorching her eyes. She got up from the bed and, blind at first as if in sudden darkness, felt her way to the water on the dressing-chest, for she was thirsty from lying so long awake. Standing there to drink it, she saw taking shape out of the dazzle, in the glass before her, her own face, its plainness underlined by weeping and strain, her limp hair, her awkward schoolgirl's body. For the first time they were real; she believed in them; they were not a disguise in which a lovely future hid, ready to break forth like winged creatures in the spring; they were herself, and would always be, for now he had accepted them. Her life would be lived within their boundaries.

She had cried her eyes dry; as if her mind too had been emptied, it received for a little, as from without itself, an alien clearness. She thought, I could have loved him from a long way off, and never wanted anything, and been happy. It would have been like Monica Hathaway at school, but better. People say it's a bad thing. But it makes poetry live for you, and music, and the sky at night, and after it's over, some of it goes into them and lasts the rest of your life. You forget the silly parts quite soon, and you're left, in the end, with something you're not ashamed to remember. Not like this.

As long as I live, I shall be a person whom someone made love to because he was sorry for her. But I know, now, that it wasn't even really making love. Just being sorry: nothing else.

Leo was sorry for me too. It must have been difficult to keep me from knowing how they felt about each other. It happened at first sight, I suppose. I can see it all now. The night he came to supper here, and she went on the river with that friend of Helen's; he could hardly talk to me, waiting for her to come back. Everything's been easy for Leo. She's always believed in herself; she's never been afraid.

I thought I hated her, but I don't. To hate people you have to feel they've robbed you, that they've kept you down. I was down from the beginning. If he hadn't loved Leo, he would have loved someone else. He'd never have loved me. How could he? I shall never be able to make anyone love me now. You have to believe, first, that you're a person who can be loved.

She put out the light, and went over to the window. Everything was dark, even the island in midstream where the lamp had burned, on other nights, later than all the rest, blinking when the wind swung a willow-bough across it. Her mind turned, in its unhappy drifting, to the afternoon Joe had spent teaching her to punt. I didn't know it at the time, she thought; I didn't think about it, but I was quite peaceful and contented then. He's such an ordinary sort of person; but he seemed, somehow, to make ordinariness fun. I wasn't ashamed of anything, or believing in anything that wasn't real. I wonder if he's lonely too, sometimes. I don't suppose anyone would fall in love with him either. He's so awfully unromantic. It's a pity; I expect he could make some rather dull sort of woman very happy. If she'd never met anyone like Peter. Peter. I wish I'd died when I was ill at home, I wish I'd been dead before he came.

It's a punishment to me, she thought, leaning her head against the window-frame, for running away. Mother loved me, and I made her unhappy. Leo said you paid for making other people suffer. (But Leo never seems to pay.) I was never meant to get away with things; even at school I was always caught when other people weren't, and had to go back to detention on Wednesday afternoon. I must go back to Mother and Father now, and make it up to them. Nobody else wants me, anyway.

At least, she thought, I won't be mean about it. It isn't Leo's fault. She and Peter are affinities, I expect. They couldn't help themselves. I must write her a letter before I go, and tell her I understand. She did her best about me. Like Peter. Everyone meant to be kind. I suppose it must be simply me.

She put on the light again, and looked in the dressing-chest for something to write on. Her diary was there: she tore a leaf from it, the leaf for to-morrow. She would not be needing it now.

Helen moved across the garden, down to the water-side. The dull moonlight shimmered on her fair hair and her dressing-coat of pale green satin; she looked ethereal, like a water-spirit seeking its element again. But she had gone to see if the canoe was there.

It rode at its painter, neat and toylike, its fresh varnish shining slickly. The cushions, which she had taken out that evening for the night, had not been replaced in it. The dinghy was beside it, the oars dry. Leo and Peter must have gone to town.

She went back again to the room on the upper deck, lit a cigarette, and looked out of the wide window. The river was still; away downstream the island rode like a black barge. She had hoped to see a light on it; it would have been company of a kind.

She can be certain of me, because I'm free. I've gone where I chose, and had what I fancied, and I'm here because this is better. I can never be sure of her. It's like keeping a wild bird that loves you because it's got a broken wing. If the wing knits up, then you know; one way or another. That would be something real, one could bear that. But to watch this trying and falling down again, each time it's as bad as before, it hurts both ways.

It's been too long, now. I shall never really know, I suppose.

That may be better, for me. Perhaps it won't be so bad this time, for her; not so far to fall. But, in a way, that's the worst; to see her getting practical about it. I wonder what Joe would say, if one could ask him. Give her rope, or something, I suppose. He's easy-going, is old Joe. Sometimes I've thought . . . But that's another thing that's gone on too long.

I'd better get to bed. She won't feel like talking when she comes in. If Elsie weren't here she could have slept in that room, if she wanted, and been quiet by herself. It must be restful to be Elsie, not touching reality at any point of the compass. I wonder how it feels.

She put out her cigarette and lay down; but for a long time her eyes were open, looking at the river and the changing clouds.

In Mawley, in the best bedroom of the Red Castle Hotel, Peter, with his mouth slightly but not ungracefully open, was sleeping the sleep of the just.

The square of the window sharpened, and, enclosed in its dark frame, the trees defined themselves greyly. Over the water hung and turned, in infinitely slow spirals, the drifting wreaths of the mist. A bird cheeped, found that it was too early, and sank into the fluffed warmth of its feathers again.

Leo came out of a sleep so deep that, for a moment, she could not remember where she was. Her thoughts held only a shapeless colour and light, such as one brings back from a dream when the horn gate has closed already upon its story. She held them about her, feeling only that they were better than anything the day could give. But at the first touch of her will, they condensed into consciousness.

She knew where she was, and why; her mind was like water holding a still reflection, her body, heavy with peace, gave back dim echoes of pain and delight, too quiet to stir it from tranquillity. She lay as she had fallen asleep, still in his arm with her own flung across his breast, her head on his shoulder. If she moved a little she could see his face; but she did not move, lest it should wake him.

It was easy to be still, for only her mind was waking, as if sleep were a pool from which she had raised her head, while her limbs still drifted under its smooth surface. It was better, after all, to be awake and remember.

So many kinds of contentment were mixed together in her; the contentment of the adventurer after peril, of the captive after release, of the woman after love. They were falling already into the stuff of her life, and she had almost ceased to wonder at them. She thought instead about what she had learned of him, and how like it was to what she had already known. She knew now that his love affairs had been like his books, few and good and deeply felt, passionate in impulse, patiently complete in execution; she knew that hack-work had never coarsened his style. She knew too something she had not known before, that some trouble in his life, solved or reconciled long ago, had left hidden in him an instinct of compassion so strong that he was ashamed of it as if it had been a kind of violence. For a time she had released it; and after its cause was gone, when he himself had half forgotten it, some of its power over him had passed to her. She knew that she had possessed his imagination, suddenly and unawares. She thought of all this as she lay watching the night thin away in her half-shut eyes. She did not think that she loved him finally and irrevocably, because it was a fact too certain for thought, and, besides, it had become an old story.

He lay half-turned towards her, companionable and warm. He was used to sharing a bed – she knew that too – and to sharing it kindly, with someone he was prepared to find there in the morning. He was sleeping very quietly; she could feel his breathing, shallow and soundless, not like the breathing of a sleeping man. Then she knew, without moving or opening her eyes, that he was awake, and had been awake already for a long time.

Through all those moments of clouded, dreamy well-being, he had been lying with open eyes, looking out above her head at the creeping light, solitary in his own thoughts; facing, with the straightness he could not have escaped if he had wanted, the implications of what had happened, and what would happen if it went on. He had been thinking – she was sure, as if he had turned to her and told her – of his half-written book, needing a steady mood, solitude and time; remembering the mistress who had been easy to him, who had accepted for years, without destructive suffering, the part of himself which in the end, would still be all that he would have to give. His thoughts seemed to flow to her, dearly and inescapably; they might so easily, at another time and place, have been her own She felt them with the mind of a friend who could share and approve them; it was only to the woman in his arm, naked and newly born, that they were desolation and loss.

Her first choice had been true, she thought; they were only possible to one another, ultimately, in the relationship of man to man. They had been allies, acknowledging one another's codes of living, and making the same reservation of themselves. The ghost of their old companionship seemed to be lying here beside them, with a face of its own like the face of a dead boy struck down quickly in a smile. He was smiling now, with a boy's cheerful unpitying scorn, at the woman holding the man who looked out beyond her, the silly fool in love, for whom nothing would be enough.

Go ahead, said the ghost, smiling at her. Hang round his neck, the way you did last night in the river. He'll take it for a bit. He won't expect the same guts from you that he did from me.

He won't let you drown him. He's got horse-sense; it's one of the things I always like him for. It won't be a lot of fun for him, handing you off; you'll leave a bruise on him that will last longer than the one he's put on your face now. But what do you care? Women are all the same.

'You're awake,' said Joe's soft voice against her ear. He tilted up her face and kissed her. 'Come over on my other side, darling, my arm's gone to sleep. How long have you been foxing there?'

'Only a second.'

She smiled at him; but something in her face made him look from her to the growing light in the window, and say quickly, 'It's early yet.'

She turned into his arms, and felt him relax, she had broken the circle of his thoughts, and, loosing himself from them in relief, he was becoming sleepy again. It was still no more than twilight. But presently a brightening greyness forced itself under her eyelids.

'I must go soon,' she said.

'Not yet.' He roused himself a little to add, 'We've been out so often before breakfast, no one will think anything of it. They might wonder if they saw you now.'

'I'd like to be back before Helen's awake. She'll begin to think something's happened to me.'

'Hasn't it? It has to me.'

She laid her cheek against his. It would begin or end from now; and in this moment it seemed to have begun before her own life, and that she could as easily destroy the morning.

'Leo.'

'Yes?'

'You know, don't you, this can't end here.'

'My dear,' she said, 'it's to-morrow now. It has ended.'

'We said that. But not now.'

'Now more than ever. You know that's true.'

'It would tear up our lives,' he said slowly. 'I've thought of all that. But it might be worth it.'

'It might be. But it never is.'

As she brought out the words she was herself incredulous of their bleakness. Was this all she could say to him, for everything? He was silent now, and she had time to remember. He had looked after her, as he had promised, with a generosity so self-concealing that only instinct had made her aware of it, till she had been able to release both of them from the separate consideration of You and I. She had not known that there would be a moment when her fear would overtake her again, but he had known; or that she would want the comfort of speech, but he had given it. Now for all this she could not offer as much as a gesture, a kiss or a tightened arm; he was too quick to understand.

'I suppose,' he said presently, 'I knew this. I've never known you say a thing and not stick to it.'

'Or you,' she said.

'I won't go back on it, if it's what you want.'

She said, smiling, 'It was a damned good bonfire, wasn't it? In spite of so much water.'

'What do you want, Leo? Do you think you can get back into your sweater and corduroys and disappear as if they were the cloak of darkness?' He leaned on his elbow, looking at her. 'There's nothing you'll be able to hide in them now from me.' She felt her body clean and beautiful, as the sun makes it.

'There's nothing I'll want to hide from you.' she said.

'Leo. Do you mean –'

'So we'd better just not meet at all. There's a lot of room on the river.'

He said nothing. It seemed to her that she had been speaking for a part of his own mind. Over her head, on the joists of the ceiling, there were racks fixed to hold rods and tackle; she remembered the day they had put them up together.

He turned to her out of this thoughts, with sudden fresh insistence.

'Leo. Darling, look here. I can work any place where there's a door that shuts, and so can you. I'd been thinking anyway that when this book was done I'd take a trip to Arizona. We'll go now. We'd be in time to see a bit of the fall round-up. Wouldn't you like to know how you look in a Stetson, Tex?'

He pulled round her face, smiling at her. She turned it away, out of sight. When she could bear to speak again, she opened her mouth to say gently, 'Don't be fantastic, my dear, these are your people, how could you take a woman there?' But she was still with the words unspoken, realizing what it was that, as yet half-unconsciously perhaps, he had implied.

'We'd have to go on a cargo-boat,' he said. 'At the moment I don't think I could run to a liner. It takes longer but it's more fun.'

She looked up at the roof, counting, carefully, the brass hooks in one of the joists. In the end, she found she could bring it out quite easily. 'Thank you, Joe dear. But I don't suppose I'd ever write another line if I saw the real thing. Imagine how safe and modern it must all be now.'

His voice altered. 'I don't know how much you know about me,' he said slowly. 'I've taken you for granted so long, it seems incredible when I think of it. But, on my side, nobody's going to be really hurt by this. I'm as sure of that as anyone reasonably can be. I don't suppose you want to know anything more.'

'No,' she said. 'Thank you for telling me.' She paused for a moment, and went on, 'On my side, there's Helen. I don't suppose you want to know any more about that, either.'

'I don't think I need to,' he said quietly. 'I'm very fond of her. But Helen will never be without resources.'

With sudden recollection, she said, 'Elsie would. Entirely without . . . You see, my dear, it's everything. 'Too like the lightning . . .' Look, the sun's beginning to rise.'

They turned their eyes, together, to the first bright slant of green along the willows. Somewhere among them a bird began to sing, on a low clear note, agonizingly joyful.

He lifted himself to look at her. Her life seemed for a moment to stop still; for she had seen in his eyes, at last, a question in answer to which she knew she could not lie. But there was too little vanity in him: he did not ask it.

'Shut your eyes.'

She closed them, and he covered them with his hand.

'You see,' he said, 'It isn't morning.'

There was already in their kisses the salt taste of farewell.

She turned more closely into his arms. He had been awake,

she remembered, longer than she. She could, perhaps, make it a little easier for him to leave her.

Smiling and apart, the dead boy's ghost looked upward, approving the neat varnished rack across the joists, and a workmanlike mend in the roof.

CHAPTER TWENTY-FOUR

A bar of sunlight fell across Helen's eyes. Even before she opened them, she knew that it must be late. All was well; she had not to leave for town before noon, and her wrist-watch, when sleepily she reached for it, showed ten-fifteen. Yet all was not well, for some reason she could not at once remember. It must be the oddness of Leo's having overslept too; she woke by habit, about eight, at whatever time she had gone to bed. Reflecting no further, Helen turned with a hand outstretched to rouse her, and found herself alone.

Her memory cleared. For a moment her mind made the heavy protest of the sleeper awakened to trouble before the brain or the body are ready. She repeated to herself last night's reassurances. But, before she had got to the end of them, she had thrown back the covers, caught up her dressing-gown as she went, and run barefoot down the ladder. There was no sound anywhere. The dinghy and canoe were in their places; the galley was as it had been left the night before. If Leo had gone out this morning, it was without a meal, without having waked either of the others or laid the table; and it was after ten.

This time it had been so light, so trivial, so – Helen accepted the word that till now she had avoided – so calculated; foolproof, safety-first. Well, then; perhaps it had justified itself. What if it were the first time Leo had stayed away all night without warning? Helen implored herself not to be an old maid; but without effect. With reluctance, even with shame, she knew that she was afraid.

She turned from the galley into the living-room, and stood still. So great was her relief that she felt, as people do at such moments, a little cross at the waste of mental strain. Leo was there, with the old rug they kept for sun-bathing thrown over her, lying on the couch asleep. It seemed immediately obvious that, late as she must have come in, she should have done this, and that she should have closed the curtains to shut out the early sun which would, by then, almost have risen. Helen went cheerfully across to fling doors and curtains open. Neither the noise nor the light made Leo stir.

'After ten,' Helen began to say. But at that moment, coming near, she saw the face on the cushions by daylight. She was silent, before the dead blank abandonment of weariness, the dark transparent eyelids, the outlines of the face dulled as if by deep anaesthesia. For the first time she saw that Leo was fully dressed. From under the edge of the rug a fold of her red skirt hung crumpled like a rag. A smell of river-damp came from her tumbled hair. Helen leaned nearer, looking at what had seemed at first to be a shadow on the edge of her jaw. The light, falling full on it, showed a dull, darkening bruise.

Helen's first and characteristic reaction was to go out into the galley and make tea. The electric kettle made it a quick business, nearly as swift as Helen's accompanying thoughts.

She's been tight; because she'd made up her mind to go through with it this time – I knew that – and it was the only way, I suppose. That bruise; she must have fallen, walked into a wall or something. Let her sleep. Another hour, all day if she only can. But then she'll wake after I've gone, with Elsie staring at her I expect, and asking her if anything's the matter . . . Oh, God, thought Helen, what a waste, what a damned shame.

There was a kind of finality in sleep like this; as if the mind had come to a blank wall and only sleep was left; it was like a death in little. Helen, who had seen sleep and death in many shapes, found her mind travelling back eight years. 'The ward's fairly quiet to-night. Try and get some gauze folded for the drums. But keep a good watch on that peritonitis in the corner; she isn't going to do. Might hang on for a week, but you never know. No, no relatives to send for; she wouldn't admit to having any. Something queer there. Half-hourly pulse chart. Mr. Harper says it's no good calling him; he can't do anything more.' Looking back, it seemed to Helen that at the first moment when she had gone behind the cretonne screens with the watch in her hand, and seen the sleeping face on the high pillows, her sense of protest had been as personal as it was now.

She put down the cup and saucer, noisily, on the table. 'Wake up, Leo,' she said lightly. 'It's after ten. Here's some tea.' (Try and drink a little of this, Miss Lane.)

Leo's eyelids flickered. She lifted them, slowly. (I was dreaming. I'd forgotten I was here. You're new to-night, aren't you?) She contracted her eyes against the sunlight (Helen thought of an incautious flicker of the night sister's torch), then turned over quickly, and hid her face.

Helen began to move about the room, busily. As she moved, she talked, keeping her eyes on what she was doing. 'I'm only just awake myself. Did you have a lousy evening? Mine was deadly. Roy suddenly reached the stage of explaining how he's so complex no one else understands him. The worst of it is, I know he's going to die on me like an operatic tenor, always popping up for another aria. I wish I were more good at getting rid of people.'

Leo sat up, and pushing aside the rug, looked down at the crumpled scarlet of her dress. 'I got in late,' she said. 'I didn't want to wake you.'

Shaking cereal out of a packet, Helen said, 'I guessed you'd be here. Elsie's not down either. I'll call her presently, when you've changed.'

Leo stood up. 'Thanks for the tea,' she said. 'I'll have it when I come down.'

With her hair brushed, dressed in her serge slacks and dark-blue jersey, Leo looked whiter than before, and the bruise showed up more strongly. 'Thanks for the tea,' she said again.

'Have another cup, that will be cold.'

'I'll have this first.' She drank it thirstily, straight down like a glass of water, and sat looking at the empty cup in her hand. Helen took it from her, and refilled it. Once again she saw the cretonne screens with roses and birds on them, the draped light over the head of the bed, and remembered thinking, 'If she would talk. The effort might finish her. But if she doesn't . . .'

She put the filled cup back on the table.

'Did you go through with it? '

'Yes.'

'Don't worry, my dear. You needn't ever see him again.'

Leo took the tea and began to drink it, a little more slowly because it was hot. Her face had the impenetrability which only the extreme of unhappiness can set between people who know each other well.

'I never shall,' she said.

Helen looked at the clock, measuring the time that was left before she must leave to catch her train.

'How tight did you have to get?'

Leo looked up. Her face, for the first time, expressed something. Helen thought, if she was sober, it's worse. I wonder how much worse. She laughed, convincingly, and patted Leo's shoulder. 'Well, you never get to the end of human nature. If the Archangel Gabriel had told me Peter would clip a woman on the jaw, under any provocation whatever . . . Cheer up, darling. After all, it does leave you square.'

'Peter?' The pain in Leo's face had changed to a wondering blankness. She might have been trying to recall where she had heard the name. A kind of dim recollection came into her eyes; she put her hand in her pocket and felt, mechanically, for a cigarette. Turning away to light it, she said, 'It was an accident. Joe dropped the punt-pole. It slipped out of his hand.'

'Dropped the . . .' Helen's voice trailed to a standstill. She stood with the butter-dish, which she happened to be holding, still in her hand, staring at Leo's back. 'Joe dropped . . .' Her face altered. She put down the dish on the table, moved forward a step or two, and stayed where she was. 'Oh, Leo,' she said. 'My dear.'

Without turning round, Leo said, 'Don't now. I don't think I . . . Look here, I don't seem to be doing anything about breakfast. You'll be late if you do it all. Go up and dress, and I'll finish while you've gone.' After a moment she added, 'Don't get Elsie down yet, do you mind?'

Helen paused for a moment; but Leo did not move.

'All right. I'll get on. I ought to start in just over half an hour . . . I'll see if Elsie's about anywhere. If she is, I'll give her the pumping.'

'You can if you like,' said Leo. 'But I did it this morning, before I turned in.'

Helen went upstairs. It was then that she saw the outer door of Elsie's room, swinging slowly, open, in the slight wind. She went inside.

Leo, she found, had not been impatient of her delay. She had breakfast finished. She was staring, distantly, at the table, as if she might be wondering how it had got there. Helen looked at the clock, counting desperately the minutes to her train. She sat down, and began to pour out tea. Fifteen minutes at the latest. Without interrupting the flow from the teapot, she said, 'I suppose you didn't notice anything out of the way about Elsie, did you, last night?'

Leo took her third cup of tea, and started on it as if it were the first. 'I didn't see her. I went out before she came back.'

'She didn't say anything about going anywhere, earlier on?'

'Going anywhere? I don't remember. I think she said she was going somewhere . . . She went out, anyway. Yes, she went to the cinema.'

'I know. I just wondered if you'd know of any reason . . . Don't worry about it now – I suppose she just felt like it – but she seems to have packed her things and left.'

'Has she?' Leo picked up her tea and finished it: she seemed to gather herself together, as people do when someone is making conversation to which they know they ought to attend. 'Why did she do that? She wasn't here. She hadn't come in.'

'When I got back, she was in bed. Or, anyway, in her room. The light was on.' Helen took the cup which Leo was holding to be filled again. When this was done she said, 'She left a note for you. You don't want it now, do you? Don't bother this morning. I'll read it, shall I, in case there's anything we ought to do about it. Don't worry now. Here's your tea.'

'Thanks,' said Leo. 'If you don't mind. I'll read it presently. I'm sorry I'm so dim this morning. I didn't sleep very long.'

Helen took the letter out of her pocket and opened it. Looking straight in front of her, Leo went on drinking her tea. But presently her face sharpened and grew aware. She turned and looked at Helen, who had almost finished reading.

'What does she say?'

Helen folded the letter together.

'She says she's gone home. She thinks it's time she did.'

'I'd better see it,' Leo said.

'You don't need to. There's nothing in it. Look, my dear, I'll have to go in a minute. Go back to bed, why don't you, and get some more sleep. There's some medinal in my drawer, take . . . No; I know where it is; I'll put some out for you.'

'I'll read it now. I'd rather.'

Helen handed the letter over. She looked at the clock again, and got up from her chair; but at the door she stayed, though she had not meant to stay.

Leo read to the end of the letter, stolidly, without the least change of expression. When she had finished, she turned it over and read it again. Then she put it down on the table, and made as if to rise; sat down again, and began to laugh. She laughed quietly, almost silently; the gasping indrawn breaths that supplied her laughter, though they shook her body, were silent too. Helen came over quickly, and took her by the shoulders; but Leo laughed on, her elbows on the table, her face in her hands.

'Leo,' said Helen crisply, 'be quiet.' The sound of her own voice made her feel a curious vague consciousness of her clothes. It was some years since she had worn the ones to which the voice belonged. Leo's shoulders grew still. She took her hands from her face, dazedly, as if she had been sleeping.

'Sorry,' she said, and reached in her pocket for a cigarette.

Helen said, 'It had to happen. It's better this way. It's better than if she knew how things really were.'

Leo got up, putting the letter in her pocket. 'A sharp instrument, I suppose,' she said; and began carrying the breakfast things through into the kitchen. Over her shoulder she remarked, 'The family will be calling, when they know where she's been. It will be just like old times. You always said you'd have liked to meet them.'

Helen looked at the clock. Five minutes. She had brought her hat and gloves down with her when she had dressed. If she caught the next train, and was lucky with a taxi . . . if the case started a little late . . . There was something one used to say when one's own resources were dry. Joe knows most things. Ask Joe what he'd do. For Brutus, as you know, was Caesar's angel . . . She picked up her hat.

Leo moved about the room, folding the rug that lay on the couch, straightening things here and there. In her vague progress she came to the pile of papers on the locker. Mechanically she gathered them together. The plan of the ranch lay on the top; under it the pipe, hidden till her movement slid it out. She picked it up, and turned it over, distantly, in her hand.

'He'll want this,' she said. 'I must get it to him somehow or other.' She spoke as if everything else were simple, and this one difficulty absorbed her thoughts.

Fixing her hat at the wall-mirror, Helen said, 'He'll be along for it, I dare say.'

'No,' said Leo. She opened one of the lockers, the one for oddments, and put the pipe away.

'Don't think about it. Go and get some more sleep . . . Joe's sensible. He's not like the others. He'll come back again and be just the same.'

Leo said, as if to herself, 'Even that might happen, I suppose.' She looked at the clock. 'You'd better hurry; you'll miss your train.'

'Yes. The next one wouldn't get me there . . . Look, Leo I don't think I'll go to-day. I don't think I can be bothered. I don't feel like it. I'll write and say I wasn't well, I can afford it once, I've never done it before.' She began to take off her hat again.

'Whose day is it?'

'Morgan Greaves.'

With sudden concentration, Leo said, 'Don't be silly. You can't cut Morgan Greaves. You got everything else through him. Don't take any notice of this, it's nothing, only a hangover. I'll be all right when I settle down and do some work. Don't worry, Helen. I swear there's nothing for you to worry about.'

'I ought to go.' said Helen slowly. 'He's trying a new approach that's never been done before.' She came over to Leo, and looked into her face. 'If I do go – will you promise –' She stopped, faced with words for what even her thoughts had not openly formed.

'Yes,' said Leo. 'Of course, my dear.' In the commonplace and slightly apologetic voice of one who fears to stress the obvious, she added, 'How could I? He'd think it might be his fault in some way. One couldn't do that, to anybody. Even if he were no one in particular, even if I didn't love him.' She began to move away, and turned back again. 'It all blows over. We'll be all right, darling. Good-bye.' She kissed Helen, and went out quickly into the galley.

Helen went with her graceful brisk walk towards the ferry. She looked capable, *soignée*, on terms with life. She was thinking,

She'll have peace and quiet, at least, with Elsie not there. (Our little Trojan filly; she looked so harmless and forlorn, standing outside the gates on the windy plain, but she brought her Ulysses sure enough . . . Oh, well.) So now I know. But, of course, I've known for years. Two years, I think, as near as I can remember. That's a long time to go on telling oneself the same lie . . . I got all this over before we met each other; if not, I might have been the one. It's luck, it's a shape that makes sense, it's perfectly fair. Whatever happens, that's the thing to remember. To see things straight, not to arrange them round oneself; if one keeps that, one keeps everything in the end.

She had reached the ferry-steps, and called in her warm clear voice across the water. Foxy waved to her from midstream. He had a little job on hand; but it would wait for Miss Vaughan. He bared his brown teeth in a pleased, welcoming smile.

In the centre of Oxford Circus, the policeman stood, a large man, surrounded by his almost visible island of phlegmatic calm. The signal-lights changed, and the dam which had held the current of Regent Street was opened; at his sides, against Oxford Street, the sluice-gates closed. He surveyed the moving and the arrested streams, observing, and fixing with a minatory eye, a car trying to edge in on the outside of the line, a street bookmaker's tout, a dithering woman making up her mind to cross at the moment when the Oxford Street traffic was about to proceed. Under his gaze, the car and the woman desisted, the tout looked purposeful and hastened on. The signals blinked again. Regent Street froze, Oxford Street melted and flowed. He looked at his watch. Half an hour to go. The road felt hot under his feet, his blue tunic was making him sweat; but his fatigue and irritability concealed themselves, without effort, under the impassive stolidity of his training. A telegraph-boy on a bicycle was trickling dangerously up the traffic-line. A girl with a suitcase was standing outside Swan and Edgar's, eyeing him. In a few moments, choosing the moment when he needed all his attention for something else, she would plunge across, anxious to know the quickest way to West Dulwich, or whether he had seen a lady pass in a black hat. Why in Christ's name, he thought, they can't ask a man on a beat . . .

Elsie considered him; his size, his sternness, his hieratic impersonality. They satisfied her; she saw that she had reached the end of her quest. She lingered for a moment; it was the last moment she would spend, to-day, alone with herself, and she wanted its emotional content to be worthy. But now, at the instant of her gesture, it seemed that already her life had moved on beyond it. Hers was not a spirit equipped to endure nakedness for long. It had begun to gather round it the garments in which it would protect itself during the coming years. She was going to live in London now. There would be cinemas, shop-windows, perhaps a secretarial training now that it could be had near at hand; a twopenny library not miles away on the bus but in the next street. She was conscious of these thoughts diluting the high instant of tragedy. For one breathless draught she had taken its stinging waters neat; but they would be diluted now for the rest of her life. I shall never forget him, she thought; but already within her, truth was losing its sharpness, she was passing from the failure that has courage to know itself, into the deeper failure that disguises and evades. All those slight refusals of reality, which, separately, had represented choices within her power to make, made up a cumulative sum whose weight was beyond her will and her strength, not only to move but to understand. With Peter, with Leo, with Joe, with herself, there had been moments when the life of her spirit had stirred and spoken, calling softly for the difficult relinquishment of an idea, a step from safe ground into the dark, a movement of daring and danger in the mind. She had let them go by; and now she could no longer remember them. In this last pause of hesitation she turned again from the knowledge of her own confusion, to the gesture she had planned. Its drama and pathos comforted her. She stepped out into the road, crossing on the amber light to the exasperation of a London General omnibus and several cars.

The policeman turned to her, solemn and attentive, not inter-rupting his more urgent preoccupations, but concentrating them in the tail of his eye. To Elsie it seemed that the axle-tree of London stood still, with herself at its centre. She drew herself erect.

'I have come,' she said clearly, 'to give myself up.'

Leo had washed the breakfast things, made the beds, dusted. There was nothing else to do. This was the time of day when she settled down to work.

She went upstairs, and opened her desk. The manuscript ended in mid-sentence: 'The lightning movement of his hand to his gun was masked by –' She had been writing it yesterday after-noon, when Joe had called her name under the window. The rest of the sentence had been so obvious that she had gone down-stairs at once, not troubling to finish it. She sat staring at the paper, wondering why it mattered so much that the phrase had gone; for sometime, to-morrow or in a day or two, she would know and perhaps even care what it had been about, and would think of another. The movement of his hand towards his gun . . . the movement . . . It was not for these, but for other lost words that her mind was seeking. In the moment before they slept, when already she had been beginning to dream and perhaps he also, he had said something, peacefully and sleepily, nothing of importance, nothing new. She had heard the sound; to the words she had not attended, there had been no need, for all possible words had been contained between them. She remembered the tone and the rhythm, the slight movement of his throat against her forehead; a short sentence, four or five words, not more. It was strange not to have foreseen that their loss would be like the loss of a year of life.

She shut the desk, got up and went to the window. It looked up-river; it was Elsie's room that faced towards the island. She tried to think about Elsie, to feel the sense of failure and remorse, to care what she was doing now and what she would become; but it was like trying to grasp something with crushed fingers. She was only glad to be alone. It would come, she supposed, to-morrow or the day after, like the movement of his hand toward his gun which was masked by . . . She passed her hand over her face, and felt a dull soreness from the bruise on her jaw. Last time she had been aware of it, it had not been her hand that had touched it. She shut her eyes, remembering the look in his when the growing light, and an incautious movement of her head, had first showed it him in the morning.

It was only one o'clock. More than half the day was still ahead; and then to-night, to-morrow, day after day. She looked down at the river, remembering its coldness closing over her head. It had been easy; one had been thinking of something else; it was not till he had struck her that the sense of life had come back with its saving fear. The water went by, smooth and still, tempting her with its silences. She turned quickly back from the window into the room. There must be something to do, some mind-dulling activity in which to hide.

The impulse to kill thought, when she recognized it, sickened her; escape would punish itself, she had learned that lesson now for good and all. There was nothing to do with pain but to forge and temper it and make it true. He had done it once (she would never know, now, when or why) and she could do it also, as she had followed him up the chimney on Scawfell Pikes; her mind, like Elsie's, clung to its habits. She went to the bookcase and took out a volume of Plato, much worn and handled; a transla-tion, for she knew no Greek. As she turned the pages back and forth, her eye came to rest in the middle of the *Lysis*.

For these things are called friends for the sake of a friend, but our true friend seems to be of a nature exactly the reverse of this; for it was found to be our friend for the sake of an enemy; but, if the enemy were removed, no longer, it seems, do we possess a friend.

Apparently not, said he, according at least to our present position.

*But tell me this, said I. If evil be extinguished, will it be no
longer possible to feel hunger or thirst, or any similar desire . . .*

She sat staring at the words, unable to read further, for even
those she had read already she could no longer see.

The doorbell had rung twice before she heard it. She had
promised Helen that if the butcher were late again she would say
something. Her face in the glass looked, she found, much as
usual. She went down.

'Afternoon, Miss Lane,' said Foxy Hicks. He winked. This
implied nothing in particular; it was Foxy's habitual greeting to
her, founded on a joke so ancient that she, at least, had forgotten
what it was. By a kind of reflex, she returned the grin which was
its correct response.

'Afternoon, Foxy. Want the pliers again?'

'Nah,' said Foxy knowingly. 'Not to-day. Too hot for work to-
day. Just had forty winks in the bottom of me boat, that's me this
afternoon. Might of made it eighty, only I woke up and remembered this little job. Promised Mr. Flint I'd let you have it
sometime to-day.' He groped in his pocket, remarking as he did
so, 'Shan't be seeing no more of him for a bit, seems like. Give
me his punt to lay up. Use it, he says, if it's any good to you; I
dunno when I'll be wanting it again. Not me, I says, I ain't never
learned, silly lopsided way of getting along if you ask me. Ah,
here we have it, slipped down the lining.' He fished out a crumpled envelope, grubby and dog-eared. 'Looks a bit worse for the
heat, don't it? Must have laid on it when I was having my nap.'

'Oh, thanks,' said Leo. She put the letter, without looking at
it, into her pocket. 'Have a cigarette to take along.'

'Well,' Foxy acknowledged, 'it never comes amiss, as they say.'
He stuck it behind his ear, winked, and departed about his affairs.

Leo went up to her room, and took the envelope out of her
pocket, mechanically straightening out the creases and bends.
The 'Miss Lane' in the middle of its blank surface looked cold
and strange. They had never written to one another, except for

a few utilitarian lines to fix a meeting. She put the letter down unopened; lit a cigarette; extinguished it; and slit the paper, with a quick jerk.

The letter began, without preliminaries or any opening form of address:

After all, there wasn't enough room on the river. By the time you get this, I shall be in London; and, next week, on the way to Arizona, which will be neither as I remember it nor as you have convinced me that it ought to be, but which used to have, and probably has still as much room as anywhere.

I can only suppose that this must have been going on for some time with me. I wanted not to see it, for various reasons; and you had your own – better ones, it seems to me now – for singing me to sleep again whenever, in spite of myself, I was on the point of waking up. You developed the knack so well that you used it once or twice, I think without knowing. But didn't you know that this morning would be once too often, and too late? When these things come to the surface, they take their revenge.

Perhaps you were right; perhaps we couldn't have made it. You have the citadel of freedom in you without which, to me, people are only so much breathing flesh. I salute it and I would invade it at the first chance you offered me. Men are so constructed, God knows why. Some women surrender it, to their loss and ours, and are shocked by our unthankfulness; some just sit in it and smile, for as long as we like to go on making fools of ourselves. Some fight. You would. Perhaps I've wanted that; it would take too long, now, to tell you why. None the less we should hurt one another and ourselves; and that's the least of it.

There are two people in you. One of them I have known much longer than the other. I am missing him, already, as much as I ever missed a friend. I should like him back –

sometimes. But you know, now, how much he counted for when he came between my woman and me. I sacrificed him; I even made use of him. When occasion arose, I should do it again; sometimes, no doubt, with polite expressions of regret, sometimes without, sometimes not even knowing what I did. At last, we might wake up one morning to find that I had killed him. I tell you this, not because I approve or defend it, but because it's true and you ought to know. I think you do.

I can't tell how much he means to you. Perhaps, ultimately, he is you, and has the immortal part of you in his keeping. Only you can know, and even you may not be sure. It is the fashion to find in such things a casual product of cells and environment, or a disorder to be cured. I think their roots may go as deep as the soul. To the friend and companion I had, if his integrity comes first of all, I am worse than useless now, I am an enemy. Yet in spite of myself, I think I have written the whole of this letter, so far, to him.

I had something else to say to the woman who came to me out of the water . . .

The rest of the paragraph was direct, naked and unashamed. It swept her like a physical embrace; she knew he had intended it so. Now, in the moment of separation and loneliness, the memories it evoked were scarcely endurable; and perhaps he had intended this also.

I shall be at this address for the next three days. If you come to me now, we can go on into this thing with our eyes open. I dare not, and will not, take you any other way.

I promised everything should be finished if you chose it. Did you trust me, and believe that this was only to say good-bye? Already, you see, the word I gave to my friend is worth no more than the letter. If chance brought us

together now, it would be worth nothing at all. There's a lot
of room on the river, but not enough.

I leave you with the burden of decision, a meanness I
have despised in other men. But there are decisions no one
has the right to make for another human soul. Don't come
to me in doubt, or in any belief that we shall talk like
friends, and weigh for and against, and help one another to
a reasonable choice. I can warn you of this now, and that is
all. When one wants a thing too much, one loses sight
equally of truth, obeying or denying desire. The last counsel that, as a friend, I have to give you, is not to trust this
letter either. It's as honest as I can make it, which means
that it's rotten with tricks. Even while I write it, I have
been possessing you in my thoughts.

If I have left out, all this while, the thing with which it
is customary to begin, you will know why. Love is a word,
like God, which can be used to beg every kind of question.
We made our own word, and I'll stand by that. Come, if you
can see it that way, and what we have we will give one
another. I know you too well not to trust you, whichever
you choose.

She thought this was all; but an odd scrap of paper came away
from behind it.

I enclose this because, if we don't meet again, the rest is
about nothing; it belongs to you, and is the only token I
have. It's a good many years since I gave up the unequal
struggle with verse; but I woke this morning with the
beginning of it in my head, and you were sleeping, so I finished it.

She read on down the sheet; but thought and feeling were
overburdened in her. It was a shape of words on paper, she
could not give it meaning or form. After a time she did not

measure, she found herself leaning from the window that looked up-river. Noise, and the shaking of the house-boat, had roused her. A steamer was passing, sardine-packed with trippers. Someone was playing an accordion amidships. As they drew level, those who found their exuberance too good to keep to themselves shouted to her, and waved caps and bottles over the rail. She smiled at them, and waved back, as she always did; and found that she was waving with the half-sheet of notepaper that was still in her hand. As the noise faded, and the rocking of the floor under her began to settle, she turned from the window, finding it strange, when she knew her own thoughts again, that so much should have passed within her in what had seemed an absence of herself; stranger still to find that she remembered clearly the lines which, flagging for a moment's respite, she had seemed to read with the eye alone. She turned the leaf over, for she had stopped before, with the end of the page.

> . . . this instant breath,
> Children forgetting birth, and spirits death.
>
> Fire-pillared night with cloudy noon confound,
> Folded in twilight of the unpromised land.
> Beyond this bound
> No prophet points us. Here in your empty hand
> Sleep the stone laws, the serpent and the rod,
> The wilderness, the god.
>
> Suns in our souls have fallen, moons been hurled
> From their grieved ocean-beds to make this world
> Which now so still
> Keeps sabbath, cradled in our resting will.
>
> Seek not the end. It lies with the beginning,
> As you lie now with me,

The night with cock-crow, lust with the light unsinning,
Death with our ecstasy.

The past and the future closed together in her, a weight and a
meaning too strong for the tiny bridge of the present to bear; as
if they would crack it with their force and leave her, blank and
nothing, in the gap between. There was a moment when she
wanted the bridge to break, and let her escape from both of
them. But the bridge held; and, in the very interval of refusal and
fear, she found that she had crossed it, not now, but already,
while the trippers cheered and played their accordion, and she
waved from the rocking window.

Scarcely knowing what she did, but moving as if with purpose
over a task she had come prepared to do, she began to go about
the room, making a pile on the bed of things chosen, with
dreamlike certainty, in the order of their importance to her; her
manuscript, her portable typewriter, an armful of essential books,
the objects of habitual necessity like brush and comb; then,
working more slowly as the need for choice began to arrest and
confuse her, clothes. The thought of their occasions and purposes
woke her; she stared at the swathe she held, a suit, an afternoon
frock still on its hanger, her corduroy slacks. From the middle of
the pile came a warm, fragile scent. She let the rest fall to the
floor, looking at the green dress from which it came, the dress
which was not hers.

Suddenly she flung her other arm across her eyes, and, standing as she was in the middle of the room, began to cry; hard sobs
with struggling pauses between, painful and ashamed and
resisted, like the crying of a beaten boy.

There were footsteps on the bridge below, and someone
knocked a cheerful little tattoo on the outer door. She heard
nothing; she was retasting, with the intolerable sharpness of
finality, five years of happiness, contentment which, to the part
of herself that it satisfied, had been complete.

Then, in the blankness of pain, when the physical sensation of tears – the first she had ever shed in this place – was making a kind of sheltering dullness in her mind, an inconsequent presence, an unbidden image, appeared in it; the grubby little acquaintance of the railway platform, with his mouse-coloured hair and his thirst for knowledge about retractable undercarriages. She wanted to ask him what he was doing here, wandering out of limbo into this moment of time, and why he had changed his face so that it confused itself with Joe's face when he was explaining something which interested him and which he was anxious to share. He stood and looked at her, the uninvited guest, quietly and unapologetically at home, as Joe had always been; like someone whose presence does not need an explanation.

Slowly, Leo put back the green dress on its hanger, taking care, as she had always taken care with Helen's things, not to crush it or involve it in the disorder of her own. She hung it in the wardrobe again; and, moving blindly forward, flung herself on the bed beside the pile of books and papers. Her tears had changed; their flow and rhythm were different, release without humiliation, the tears of a woman.

While she lay there, the doorbell rang. Quickly, without thought, she jumped up and locked the door of her room, then lay down again, covering her face. The bell rang once more, a couple of minutes later; but the pillow, and the sound of her own weeping, shut it out.

Peter strolled away, back over the bridge and through the garden. It was too bad that no one was at home; he had called to say good-bye, because his holiday would be over to-morrow. Never mind, he would write or look in another day. His disinterested plans would keep. The book on elementary psychology and the significance of dreams, which he had brought to lend to Elsie, would do next time he saw her. It would tidy up some of the loose ends with which, he feared, her mind was still too generally fringed. And perhaps he would invite her to town one day, some time when Norah was free, and they would all go together to see a really good French or Russian film. *Flower of the Lagoon*, indeed. Ah, well, there was plenty of time. Considering that he had started her from scratch, he did not feel dissatisfied with progress on the whole.

It would be a pity – and it should not be necessary – to let Helen drop. She was the prettiest girl he had seen in a long time, and easy company. Besides, he would be taking up a certain amount of Leo's time in the immediate future, and one must set about such things tactfully, not let her feel excluded or left on one side. It should not be difficult; she was fond of Leo, and when he had succeeded in ironing out some of the maladjustments there, would like him the better in the end.

As for Leo, things were going so well that already he was looking ahead. It should take very little, now, to edge her out of those corners of escapism, those retreats from life into the *Boys' Own Paper*. He had dipped into one of her efforts: the writing showed average competence; with a little emotional and mental stimulus, she might be stirred to attempt serious work and even, in time, make something out of it. His own usefulness to her would, of course, be temporary, and before long he intended to introduce her to a friend of his who liked women of her type and whose psychological layout, as observed by Peter, ought to link on to hers very nicely: so it would all continue to be interesting for quite a while yet.

A bank of cloud, which had been hiding the sun, slid away from it; the light, swept from the edge of silver along which it passed, struck keen and lively on the willows and the water, sharpening leaves and wavelets and giving a sparkle to the fresh breeze. Peter whistled a little tune under his breath. It wasn't much one could do, he thought, but one helped, one eased things along, one left something constructive behind. To-morrow there would be work again, bringing its solid irreplacable satisfaction; and, along with it, new people, new personalities behind the façade of trauma and disease, new opportunities for a word in season and a guiding hand. Life stretched before him, like an immensely amusing amateur theatre, in which sometimes one played the lead, sometimes effaced oneself with the lighting or the costumes and added one's unseen quota to the effect just for the love of the game. Even now, at twenty-eight, he had not succeeded in making up his mind which was the better fun. Perhaps he had not tried. Why choose, when one could have both?

He loitered in the sunshine, looking contentedly at the willow-trees rippling in the sun and wind on the deserted island, and beginning to think about his tea.

AFTERWORD

On re-reading this forty-year-old novel for the first time in about twenty years, what struck me most was the silliness of the ending.

Leo and Joe have both been credited with reasonably good intelligence. He at least, the brighter of the two, would surely have had sense enough, in the sober light of the morning after, to steer them clear of such inevitable disaster. Sexual harmony apart, one cannot contemplate without a shudder their domestic life, hitherto so well arranged. Of course, more doomed and irresponsible unions happen in real life every day; but it is naïve to present them as happy endings.

Tempting as it may be, with such a distant book, to start reviewing it as if it were by someone else – as in effect it is – one had better go on to recall what caused it to be written.

In 1938, I was staying with a friend in the small hotel of a French fishing village, somewhere near Hardelot. I think it was in Boulogne that we picked up a copy of *The Well of Loneliness*, then still banned in England. It was a thick, pale brown paperback, a collector's edition I expect today, but too bulky to have a chance at customs, so we left it behind. Every morning, before getting up and starting out for the beach, we used to read it with the coffee and croissants, accompanied by what now strikes me as

rather heartless laughter. It is a fact however that we both found
it irresistibly funny. It had been out ten years, which is a long
time in terms of the conventions; but it does, I still think, carry
an impermissible allowance of self-pity, and its earnest humour-
lessness invites irreverence. Solemn, dead-pan descriptions of
Mary knitting stockings for Stephen – and when there was real
silk! – and mending her 'masculine underwear' (what can it have
been? It was long before briefs; perhaps Wolsey combinations)
are passages I can still not read with entire gravity.

I was working just then on my second book; it came out in the
week of Dunkirk, sinking without trace. *The Friendly Young
Ladies*, my third, was written in the pauses of full-time hospital
nursing. I had given it up when my first novel brought me in
enough to live on; now, I was seeing again terribly ill and dying
and bereaved people, and this time, as well, young men suddenly
disabled for months or years, often for life, facing their future
without complaint. (Years later, when the dust had settled, I
wrote about them in *The Charioteer*.) Looking around at the lot
of these fellow creatures, I thought it becoming in people whose
only problem was a slight deviation of the sex urge – not neces-
sarily an unmixed tribulation – to refrain from needless
bellyaching and fuss.

If at this time there was a book to whose excellence I looked
with envy, it must have been Compton Mackenzie's *Extraordinary
Women*. Set in an idyllic, pre-tourist Capri, it is a masterpiece of
gentle satire, wit, style and pervading unbitchiness; better on
the whole than *Vestal Fires*, in which he explores the male side of
that human comedy. Only now, looking it up in a reference book,
I learn to my surprise that it preceded, not followed, Radclyffe
Hall's book. I had always taken it for, so to speak, his *Cold
Comfort Farm*. It is all there: poor Rory, with her French bulldogs
and *boxeuses*, her monocle which in moments of emotion falls
into her drink, her Villa Leucadia, her sad pursuit of dandified
caddish Rosalba, her uncomfortable boiled shirts. But no, she
must have been done from life. There are magnificent social

disasters, in the grand English tradition later upheld by Anthony Powell: the concert cut short with crashing chords when Cleo, the pianist, observes Rosalba flirting with someone else; the appalling party where people make scenes and lock themselves in rooms, and the sole, awful male guest feels it his mission to cheer the poor girls up; the debacle of the white peacocks; Rosalba's impulsive offering of Rory's piano, borne on the shoulders of staggering porters, to an unimpressed visiting celebrity; it is all done with benign good humour and with moments of high seriousness. Not all the extraordinary women are absurd; some are civilised, philosophical, and make their lives without fuss. It continues to amaze me that, only a year after the first edition of this delicious and durable book appeared, Radclyffe Hall, enjoying all the freedoms conferred by independent means, could bring herself to sound so woebegone a note.

Would she, had the word been then in vogue, have described her protagonists as 'gay'? I shouldn't wonder. This splendid Old French word, once trailing clouds of glory, resounding with the trumpets of the lists and the songs of troubadors, has become a casualty as deplorable as 'disinterested' which likewise has no real synonym. Whether the subject is politics, sociology or sex, nothing is so damaging as euphemism; like air-freshener, it proclaims a bad smell below. 'Poor' has remained an honourable term, while 'underprivileged' has drawn to itself associations with bed-bugs.

Conventions change; but defensive stridency is not, on the whole, much more attractive than self-pity. Congregated homosexuals waving banners are really not conducive to a goodnatured 'Vive la différence!' Certainly they will not bring back the tolerant individualism of Macedon or Athens, where they would have attracted as much amazement as demonstrations of persons willing to drink wine. Distinguished homosexuals like Solon, Epaminondas or Plato would have withdrawn the hem of their garments; Alexander and his friends would have dined out on the joke. Greeks asked what a man was good for; and the

Greeks were right. People who do not consider themselves to be, primarily, human beings among their fellow-humans, deserve to be discriminated against, and ought not to make a meal of it.

That is what I would describe as an explicit statement. Unfortunately, that adjective too has become a cut-down word. In this truncated sense, I have sometimes been asked whether I would have written this book more explicitly in a more permissive decade. No; I have always been as explicit as I wanted to be, and have not been much more so in recent books. If characters have come to life, one should know how they will make love; if not it doesn't matter. Inch-by-inch physical descriptions are the ketchup of the literary cuisine, only required by the insipid dish or by the diner without a palate.

There is much in *The Friendly Young Ladies* which I would now write differently, supposing I could be bothered to write it at all. To one passage at least I can still respond wholeheartedly: Joe's opinion on p. 176 of the demand that writers should be ready to cook their books for good causes. One can only reflect that in 1937, the approximate date in which the story is set, Joe didn't know he was born.

Mary Renault, Cape Town, South Africa, 1983

THE ODD WOMAN

Gail Godwin

Jane Clifford is in her early thirties, smart, attractive, and seemingly kitted out for life with a job as a popular teacher at a midwestern college, and an affair with a married man. But Jane knows better. And she wants more. She knows what she wants – passion, romance, 'an age of bustles and rustling silk, fine manners and literary soirées' – and what she doesn't want – to hand her life over to a man. And after a lifetime of looking to books for the answers to life's conundrums, she seems to be finding only more questions . . .

'Could be compared, in sensitivity and brilliance, to Doris Lessing and Margaret Drabble . . . Godwin's best and most ambitious book' *New York Times*

'Godwin is brilliant' Joyce Carol Oates

CONFESSIONS OF A FAILED SOUTHERN LADY

Florence King

With a new introduction by Sandi Toksvig

'Granny worked so hard at my rearing. She was a frustrated ladysmith and I was her last chance . . . This is the story of my years on her anvil. Whether she succeeded in making a lady out of me is for you to decide, but I will say one thing in my own favour before we begin. No matter which sex I went to bed with, I never smoked on the street.'

When Florence King was born, her Granny, a would-be Virginia grande dame, moved in. 'Anybody could have a family,' writes Miss King. 'She wanted a race all to herself.' Granny's dream of raising the perfect Southern belle failed dismally with her own daughter, a chain-smoking, baseball-playing tomboy given to wild expletives. Florence is Granny's last hope . . .

'The only way you can fail to enjoy this book is if you have contracted bubonic plague' Rita Mae Brown

'I beg anyone with a bone of humour in their body to rush out and purchase it' Gerald Durrell

LOLLY WILLOWES
Sylvia Townsend Warner

Lolly Willowes has endured twenty years of self-effacement as a maiden aunt when she decides to escape her extended family and move to a small Bedfordshire village. Here, happy and unfettered, she revels in a new existence, nagged only by the sense of a secret she has yet to discover. With her cat and the Devil, Lolly Willowes discovers that secret – witchcraft – and is finally free.

Deliciously wry and magical, *Lolly Willowes* is Sylvia Townsend Warner's piquant plea that single women should find liberty and civility, a theme later explored by Virginia Woolf in *A Room of One's Own*.

'She had a talent amounting to genius' Rosamond Lehmann

'Witty, eerie, tender' John Updike

**You can order other Virago titles through our website: *www.virago.co.uk*
or by using the order form below**

☐ The Odd Woman	Gail Godwin	£7.99
☐ Confessions of a Failed Southern Lady	Florence King	£7.99
☐ Lolly Willowes	Sylvia Townsend Warner	£7.99
☐ Cassandra at the Wedding	Dorothy Baker	£7.99

The prices shown above are correct at time of going to press. However, the publishers reserve the right to increase prices on covers from those previously advertised, without further notice.

Virago

Please allow for postage and packing: **Free UK delivery.**
Europe: add 25% of retail price; Rest of World: 45% of retail price.

To order any of the above or any other Virago titles, please call our credit card orderline or fill in this coupon and send/fax it to:

Virago, PO Box 121, Kettering, Northants NN14 4ZQ
Fax: 01832 733076   Tel: 01832 737526
Email: aspenhouse@FSBDial.co.uk

☐ I enclose a UK bank cheque made payable to Virago for £. . . . .
☐ Please charge £ . . . . . . to my Visa/Access/Mastercard/Eurocard

Expiry Date ☐☐ · ☐☐   Switch Issue No. ☐☐

NAME (BLOCK LETTERS please) . . . .

ADDRESS . . . .

. . . .

. . . .

Postcode . . . . Telephone . . . .

Signature . . . .

Please allow 28 days for delivery within the UK. Offer subject to price and availability.

Please do not send any further mailings from companies carefully selected by Virago ☐